THE BACCHAE

A MYTH RETOLD

CHRISTY POTTER

Top Down Publishing
P.O. Box 61
Stockertown, PA 18083

http://www.ChristyTheWriter.com

Ordering Information:Quantity sales. Special discounts are available on quantity purchases by corporations, associations, and others. For details, contact the publisher at the address above.

Published in the United States of America

ISBN 978-0989165167 Main category —Ficton - General. Author Potter, Christy. The Bacchae - A Myth Retold

Print Edition

For John Updike, Saul Bellow, and Jonathan Franzen,
with a heart full of gratitude

Acknowledgments

There are a few people without whose help this book would not have been possible. My heartfelt thanks to Dr. Daniel Agatino, for the legal advice; Deanna Butters, for the information on dementia; Mark Rudd, for his first-hand accounting of the 1968 student riots at Columbia University; Chery Pauls, for explaining to me what a pregnant woman's doctor checkups were like when she was hauling me around in 1968; my many former newspaper colleagues for all the great years in the newsroom; and finally, to Euripides, for giving me one hell of a great play to modernize.

Damsels, the lion walketh to the net!
He finds his Bacchœ now, and sees and dies,
And pays for all his sin!—O Dionyse,
This is thine hour and thou not far away.
Grant us our vengeance!—First, O Master, stay
The course of reason in him, and instil
A foam of madness. Let his seeing will,
Which ne'er had stooped to put thy vesture on,
Be darkened, till the deed is lightly done.
Grant likewise that he find through all his streets
Loud scorn, this man of wrath and bitter threats
That made Thebes tremble, led in woman's guise.
I go to fold that robe of sacrifice
On Penthet's, that shall deck him to the dark,
His mother's gift!—So shall he learn and mark
God's true Son, Dionyse, in fulness God,
Most fearful, yet to man most soft of mood.

From The Bacchae, by Euripides,
which premiered in 405 BC at Theatre of Dionysus in Athens

Introduction

Dax Benton looked at his reflection in the bathroom mirror through a bleary squint. He generally tried to avoid seeing himself after a party like this one, but he'd lost a contact lens somewhere and the other one seemed to have melded itself completely against the maddeningly spongy surface of his right eye.

The previous night had been wild, even by Dax's standards. He dropped the freed lens into its tiny plastic cage of solution and splashed his face with cold water, which made his mascara run. He'd expected last night to be a party, as only a New York party can be, but last night was a frenzy of wine and dancing and sex and drugs far beyond what he'd anticipated. He vaguely remembered the Plaza's manager tapping on the door of his suite, suggesting that he keep it down, then with a wink leaving Dax to enjoy all the abundance his successful journalism career and influential family name had afforded him – half of it in twinkling bottles on the mirrored cabinet, the other half naked and doing lines of coke off his coffee table and each other. Some of the women he didn't even recognize as he'd picked his way past the tangle of bodies strewn between him and the bathroom.

He swallowed three aspirin dry and turned on the shower, stepping immediately into the spray. He closed his eyes and clenched his teeth as his warm skin staged a protest against the stinging cold. His breath caught, his muscles stiffened. These constant assaults on his physical body, on all his senses, were what kept him going. Without them, he had no doubt he'd die. No one understood the wretched excess that fueled his existence. The women who sought him out, begging to worship on their knees before him, came close to understanding. They ached, without questioning why, to pull some of his undefinable magic into themselves and knowing no other way to do it than to suck it in through their hungry mouths and eager bodies.

The only other person who could even come close to understanding the headiness true power wielded, Dax knew, was his father. Once a power-ful man himself in the New York newspaper world, Zachary Benton was long retired, but his legacy would outlive them all. Although at home Zachary had done his best to be a regular dad, the boy knew his father's reputation and idolized him. He'd learned early on that he could ask his father as many questions as he wanted about the newspaper business and current events, but he was ill-advised to speak to Hanna, his father's wife, about anything. Of course, that just made Dax more determined to needle her, knowing there was little if anything she could ever do to him. But over the years her icy personality and controlling behavior kept Zachary out of the house and Dax out looking for excitement on the streets of New York.

The bits of news and gossip about his famous, powerful father that trickled down to Dax's impressionable ears would have scarred any other boy but to Dax, it was manna from heaven, fuel for his own burning fire. He knew from a very early age he was meant for more than the mundane life his classmates and friends seemed to not only accept but thrive on. He was meant for more, and he'd found more.

He stepped out of the shower, rubbing himself with a stiff hotel towel before slipping into the white bathrobe hanging on the back of the door. He smiled at his reflection in the mirror. He had come home to make them pay – the bill was due.

He walked back into the main room of the suite and surveyed the carnage. The body on the enormous bed was most definitely dead, and it was more spectacular than Dax had even dared hoped it would be. Tattered bits of skirt were blood-glued to the helpless legs that draped over the edge of the mattress, halted in their last-ditch effort to flee. The smeared lipstick, a garish pin-up girl pink, made the face look cartoonishly hilarious. The open eyes contained the invisible snapshot of those last grisly moments, the gaping wounds like wax in the now-cold flesh, and the blood, in violent slashes across the sheets that had spread, widening slowly, like the bed itself was opening its mouth to scream. Dax had never realized women could be so violent.

On the rest of the bed, on the floor, and in the armchairs and sofas scattered around the palatial suite, the women had begun to awaken, if in fact they'd ever slept. Bodies writhed in early-morning passion, tidy white lines repeatedly disappeared from sticky, smudged mirrors. Two of the women on the bed were painting each other with champagne, and Dax, growing hard again, watched his aunt Aggie uncork another bottle of wine and tip it up into her mouth while her free hand, dried crimson with her son's blood, explored the younger woman stretched out beside her.

Dax leaned over the body on the bed, staring right into the expressionless, ashen face before pulling the tangled blonde wig off his cousin's head and dropping it to the floor.

"You got what you deserved, Philip," he said. "You shouldn't have gotten in my way."

Book One
Zachary

Chapter 1

Zachary Benton once told a radio interviewer early in his career that he'd known he was going to be a newspaperman since the day he stopped growing. It had been a throwaway comment at the time, but journalists know a great sound bite when they hear it, and the line had been repeated so often Zachary started to wish he'd never said it at all. The day one of the magazines ran a political cartoon showing Zachary, about two feet tall, declaring himself a newspaperman since he "didn't need to be a big man for that," was the day he swore off interviews for good.

In truth, Zachary meant what he'd said. The problem with so many who called themselves journalists was that they weren't smart enough to distinguish between the figurative and the literal. Zachary had merely meant that the day he reached his full maturity, he'd looked at himself in the mirror, and the Zachary he saw there was standing behind a desk at a metro newspaper, gazing out across the newsroom. Seeing that image of himself, he experienced one of those moments that only happen to a lucky few: he knew where he belonged.

When he told his parents he was going to be a journalist, they had not been pleased. His father was a prominent New York attorney, and Zachary knew they wanted him to follow the same path. But he had a fascination with not only news, but the news behind the news. Reporting a story was one thing, and seeing one's name in a byline brought its own heady rush, but to Zachary, the real beauty was in the events that led up to a story, digging deeper into understanding the people behind what was reported, finding out what motivated them, how they got to the point where the story went from a routine moment in someone's life to a front-page headline. And in post-World War II New York, Zachary found there was no shortage of such moments.

As a child, Zachary had been a relentless and unapologetic people-watcher. In high school, the girls called him Creepy Benton because they'd frequently catch him gazing at them for longer than they were comfortable with – much longer. Trying to tell them that he wasn't fantasizing about touching their breasts or smelling their hair had only gotten him into more trouble. But he knew that if he'd said he was just trying to imagine what they did when they were home alone and no one was watching, things would have just gone from bad to worse.

But it was true. Zachary was convinced that not one person alive was all that they seemed to be. Everyone has a side they keep hidden, even unintentionally, and if you were able to catch a peek of a person who didn't know they were being observed, you could see it. He developed an intense fascination with catching people off guard, whether it was glimpsing someone through the crack of a door or observing them walking down the street alone and lost in their own thoughts. The person you are when you're alone, Zachary believed, is the person you really are.

It was that kind of curiosity that made journalism such a natural fit for him. As a young reporter at the New York Beacon, he was able to get the details that other reporters couldn't, and his copy rose through the pages until nearly every day it dominated the front page. War-weary Americans were eager for any news that might bring them joy, or hope, or at least the reassurance that they weren't alone. Zachary's stories were in-depth, and colored with detail that made people want to keep reading, even be willing to stop mid-sentence and turn to the jump they had to flip through several pages to find. When a reader finished a Zachary Benton story, they didn't just feel they were informed on the day's news, they'd lived it.

While his stories split New York City wide open for the public's prying eye, Zachary kept himself safely closed off. No one really knew him, much less understood him, and as his success as a journalist grew, he found he preferred it that way, even though he had nothing to hide. At least not at first.

He had been at the Beacon for five years when he set his sights on buying it. The paper could be so much more than it was, and Zachary often found himself making notes on areas that could be improved, better ways the Beacon could compete with the New York Times, even ideas for organizing the staff more efficiently.

Zachary continued to grow as a journalist, his reputation in New York getting stronger with every story he broke. He lived in a tiny apartment on the Lower East Side and walked to work instead of taking a cab, putting every penny he saved into the bank. While his friends were spending whole paychecks to take their dates to Rao's and dancing at the Rainbow Room, Zachary kept his focus on his career, reminding himself that while his friends were rocketing toward middle age with burnout and bankruptcy on their tails, he was already getting ahead. There would be time enough for lavish dining and dancing when he was the best known and most respected newspaperman in New York.

It was on August 14, 1955, when Zachary had been a reporter at the Beacon for exactly six years, four months, two weeks and three days, that the publisher announced to the staff that he was retiring and the paper would be put up for sale. Before the day was out, Zachary had made an offer. Two weeks later, the deal was inked.

"It was a harebrained moved, boy," his father thundered when Zachary told his parents. "All it will take is a jump in ink prices or a printers' strike and you'll lose your shirt."

"As always, I deeply appreciate your support, Dad," Zachary responded drily. Some fathers would have clapped their sons on the back, maybe shared a celebratory cigar, but Cornelius Benton spent all of his children's lives making sure they knew he didn't want to be a father. With Zachary in particular, Cornelius was jealously competitive. When the boy came home with a report card full of As and one B, Cornelius criticized him for not achieving straight As. When Zachary got straight As the next semester, Cornelius told him he obviously was taking only easy courses. Whatever Zachary did, Cornelius set out to prove that he could do it better, or that it was a fluke Zachary could do it at all. As he grew, Zachary learned to steel himself against these assaults with constant silent reminders that the problems were not his – they sat squarely on Cornelius.

At his apartment that night, Zachary broke out a bottle of single malt scotch he'd been saving and drank a solitary, silent toast. Before long, he wouldn't be drinking alone. People would be clamoring to raise a glass with him.

Now to show the world what Zachary Benton could really do.

Chapter 2

"Zachary Benton, this is Hanna Whitcomb."

Zachary took the limply proffered hand of the parchment-skinned woman in a pale blue silk dress that mapped out her every hill and valley and said he was very pleased to meet her, although he wasn't at all sure that he was. Her green eyes were cool, like a jungle cat, and she moved with the same fluid grace. For all her beauty and practiced charm, there was something about Hanna Whitcomb that made Zachary uneasy, and at the same time drew him to her with a maddening intensity.

"What do you do, Mr. Benton?" she asked when he'd dutifully gotten her a martini from the bar. Her voice was odd. It wasn't as throaty and gravelly as one would expect from the bombshell look of her, but neither was it high-pitched. It was light, slippery. He almost wasn't sure she'd spoken at first.

"Please, call me Zachary. And I'm a newspaperman."

"Oh my, how exciting," she murmured, her eyes flicking over his shoulder in case anyone else was nearby who would prove more worthy of her attentions.

"It is," Zachary said. "It really is."

"Mmm," she said, sucking on the olive from her drink, her eyes still not on him. Suddenly Zachary was furious. Who was she to ignore him? She was obviously just some society-driven spoiled rich bitch. She ran her tongue along the olive before closing glossy red lips over the pick and pulling it, olive-less, back out. He longed to kiss that mouth, and then jab the pick into her neck.

"I'm the publisher of the New York Beacon," he blurted. He was embarrassed at this display of pubescent awkwardness, and angry with her for reducing him to it, but to his relief, her eyes widened a bit. He was in.

"Really? That's wonderful. I had no idea you were so successful."

10

It was almost a purr.

"Well, I've only been the publisher for a couple of years, but I was a reporter there for a long time. I'm surprised you've never heard of me."

"I don't follow the news very often, darling. I find it so upsetting to read about the wars and crime and problems in the world. I have a very sensitive soul."

Zachary laughed. She looked up sharply.

"I'm sure you do," he said hastily, apologetically. "I was just laughing because… well, because you're right, of course. It is terribly upsetting, the state of the world today. But you can't blame the press for that. We only report what's happening."

Hanna shrugged one white shoulder and finished her martini.

"Would you like another?" Zachary asked. Part of him wanted nothing more than to get away from this woman and never have to think about her again. The other part of him wanted to keep her by his side for as long as he could.

"That would be lovely, thank you."

He hurried to the bar and back again before anyone else could swoop in on her. What a horrible woman. He loathed her but couldn't fight the intrigue he felt.

"So tell me about you," he said, taking a deep pull on his scotch, the ice crowding up against his lips and teeth.

"What about me?" she responded.

"Everything. Where are you from, did you go to school, what do you do?"

"I'm from New York. I grew up in Chelsea. I graduated from Vassar and I'm a legal secretary at a firm in Midtown."

"Vassar. Impressive."

The condescending shrug again, but this time it launched a dismissive wave of her manicured hand.

"It was an education. My father insisted I had to have one. I know he was right, of course, but I could have landed this job with the brains I had before I set foot onto the campus. They taught me nothing but that with a Vassar diploma on the wall, people take you slightly more seriously."

Zachary couldn't take his eyes off her. He'd never met a woman like her anywhere. The only thing more staggering than her beauty was her arrogance.

"So how do you like working as a legal secretary? They must pay you well." The second sentence tumbled out of Zachary before he could grab it. He knew it sounded prodding and invasive, but he'd only meant that most secretaries would not be able to afford to dress the way she was. The diamond bracelet on her wrist had to have cost more than the salary Zachary made in his entire first year at the Beacon.

"They pay me fine," she said coolly. "And it's a job. Nothing I hope to do for the rest of my life, but I am learning a lot about the legal system."

"Well, it sounds very interesting," Zachary said lamely. He was losing her attention – the green eyes were gliding around the room again.

"Listen, can I call you sometime?" he was mortified to hear himself asking. *What are you doing? She's a cold, conceited bitch!*

"You can try." She extracted a card from her shiny clutch purse and handed it to him. "Well, I must be getting back to the party. It was a pleasure meeting you, Zachary."

She slithered off, evaporating into the crowd so completely he didn't get so much as a glimpse of her the rest of the evening.

He waited three days before he called her, figuring that was long enough to keep from appearing too desperate but not so long she would have forgotten him.

"Oh, hello Zachary," she said. He couldn't tell from her tone if she was glad to hear from him or not.

"I was wondering if you're free for dinner Friday night," he said. "I thought we could go to the Algonquin." It was more than he could have afforded just a few short years ago, and now he was eager to take his place in New York society. Dining at the Algonquin with a woman like Hanna

Whitcomb on his arm was the best way he could think of to do that.

She accepted his invitation, and he picked her up that night in a Lincoln he'd borrowed from a friend. She looked beautiful, in a dark pink silk dress that was not quite as revealing as the one she'd worn when he met her, but still showed her perfect figure to advantage. Zachary was inordinately pleased to catch a whiff of Joy perfume as she slid into the car. She'd taken some trouble to get ready for their date. That had to be a good sign.

Dinner went well, and by the time Zachary took her home, he was awash in elation and despair in equal measure to realize he was falling in love with her. She offered him a cool, smooth cheek to kiss when he walked her to her door, but made no comment about wanting to see him again and somehow he dared not ask. He leaned against her building for an hour after she went upstairs, smoking and replaying every detail of the evening in his mind. He had done everything perfectly, he was sure of it. How could she still be so unmoved?

Upstairs, Hanna had changed into a silk dressing gown and settled into her bed before reaching for the telephone to call her best friend.

"I've just had dinner with the man I'm going to marry," she said.

Three months later, Zachary Benton and Hanna Whitcomb were married in a lavish ceremony at St. Patrick's Cathedral, followed by an enormous reception at the Waldorf-Astoria. Hanna's father paid for everything without as much as a whimper. Zachary's own father swaggered around the reception, a fat cigar clenched between his teeth, but not so tightly he couldn't brag about his boy, the big shot newspaper publisher who was going to put the New York Times right out of business, which of course, as his doting and supportive father, he had always expected of Zachary. Hanna's father, who Zachary now knew was one of the top stockbrokers on Wall Street, wasn't much better.

Seated at the head table, Zachary took his new bride's hand and gave it a squeeze. She smiled at him but gently withdrew her hand and picked up her drink. Zachary was too happy to care. Society page photographers were swarming around the reception, flashes exploding like little fireworks. Prominent New Yorkers were everywhere, shaking hands and kissing cheeks. Mayor Wagner stopped at the head table to shake Zachary's hand.

"Well done, my boy, well done!" the mayor enthused. "First you take over the Beacon, then you snag Jeremy Whitcomb's little girl! Well done."

"Hanna," the bride said, smiling tightly.

"Beg pardon?" The mayor turned to her.

"My name is Hanna Whitcomb-Benton. I'm not Jeremy Whitcomb's little girl. And I got married, not snagged."

"So sorry, I didn't mean to offend." The mayor, face flushed and tie loosened, kissed Hanna's hand in an elaborate, exaggerated gesture. "You are indeed Hanna Whitcomb-Benton, and you are a fine and upstanding member of New York society."

Hanna withdrew her hand from him too, Zachary noticed with no small degree of satisfaction.

When Zachary took Hanna into his arms later for their first dance as man and wife to Vic Damone's "An Affair to Remember," he suddenly realized he had never felt this good, this happy, this grounded, in his entire life.

Chapter 3

It didn't last. Zachary knew from watching his own parents that married love is a mutable, volatile entity, yet it still surprised him when he realized his marriage to Hanna had suffered the same fate. He was never sure when it happened, because in his honest moments, he admitted they'd never been one of those fiery couples who laugh and fight and fall into bed at every opportunity. Theirs was more of a partnership, a mutual support, a cool but solid friendship. Zachary liked having Hanna on his arm at New York society events, and Hanna enjoyed being Mrs. Zachary Benton, especially as his reputation grew.

He often pondered their lack of passion, especially in the early years of their marriage, but he couldn't for the life of him picture Hanna in the throes of lust, her hair wild, her skin glistening. No matter how many fantasies he tried to concoct with her in them, he always ended up seeing her face as she'd looked the day she'd stopped at the paper to talk to him and gotten printer's ink on her white Burberry coat.

They had sex, of course, as she assured him she wanted a child as badly as he did. She wasn't altogether convincing when she said it, but Zachary had no reason to doubt her until the day he was looking for a new razor in the bathroom cabinet and found a diaphragm in a small pouch. He stared at it in disbelief for a moment before slowly putting it back where he'd found it.

That night, he leaned over and kissed the side of her neck.

"Isn't it about time for you to be ovulating?" he asked. "Because I'm really in the mood to make a baby."

"I didn't know you were so in tune with my cycle," Hanna responded calmly, putting her magazine aside. "But yes, now that you mention it, tonight is a very good time for us to try. Let me just go freshen up."

Zachary was so angry he could barely perform, finally faking a climax just so he could get away from her. He lay awake long into the night, glaring at the darkness and wondering what would drive his wife to lie to him about wanting a baby. Zachary had always imagined having kids, and now that he was married and in a good position career-wise, it was incomprehensible to him that his wife wouldn't want the same thing. Even worse, that she would say she did and then go to such great pains to make sure it wouldn't happen.

The next morning, he was up and out of the house early. Throwing himself into work was the only way Zachary knew to ignore the gnawing pain in his gut. He started spending more time at the paper, the Beacon's readership growing steadily under his focused leadership. Everyone said he had the brass balls of Hearst and the clout of Pulitzer, but with a finesse and charm that was all his own. Most people didn't know whether they loved Zachary Benton or hated him, but they all respected the hell out of him. Everyone, that is, except his wife. While his career flourished, his marriage stagnated. He knew what was happening, he could see it slowly unraveling, but what he didn't know was how to fix it. Or if he even wanted to.

Chapter 4

Zachary loved New York. He felt at one with its spirit, its bluntness, the way it seemed scuffed and shiny at the same time, old and new, rich and poor, top and bottom, with that coating of something indefinable that seals it off, separating it from all the other great cities of the world. On days when the newsroom became too oppressive, he would slip out, exhaling with the same relief when his feet found the pavement that others felt when they went indoors. He'd walk for hours, holding the city's hand, not watching the people as much as feeling them, sharing their existence without making eye contact. Crowds of people, speaking different languages, going different places, wearing different clothing styles, different music running through their heads, stressing about different things, yet all with that feeling of oneness that only New Yorkers can understand. There were millions of them, but they all shared that 13-mile long sliver of Manhattan. It was every man for himself but they were all in it together. Even the street people, camped in doorways and sitting on curbs, only their shabby coats and the hulking sides of the municipal garbage cans shielding them from the wind… refuge, refuse… even they understood that there's no place else they would be because there's no place else to be.

Zachary was rarely recognized, out on these walks. His sunglasses and expensive suit would not give him away, not when half of the men surging up Fifth Avenue were dressed the same way, and Zachary wasn't the sort of man usually known by sight. Even after he'd been the publisher of the Beacon for many years, he was known by name, by reputation, summoned when a high-flying politician got caught with his hand in the till or the girl, and cursed out when he wouldn't agree to keep it out of the paper. Above all, Zachary Benton was recognized as a good man, a fair man, and a damned great newspaperman. To cover up a story as a political favor may have gained him powerful allies at city hall and in Albany, but it would have cost him far too much in integrity. What Hearst and Pulitzer had done, Zachary was determined to undo. He wanted to wash the yellow back out of journalism, to restore it to what it used to be: a haven for citizens to find out the facts and make up their own minds. It made him some enemies, but when those in power who failed to buy him off saw that their rivals had also crashed into the immovable wall of Zachary, they relaxed a bit.

Zachary knew he was respected and feared as the most powerful journalist in New York, but he rarely thought about it. It was just a fact, like knowing he could get on the D train and be in Coney Island for a Nathan's hotdog in an hour. He didn't dwell on it. He didn't have to. The other newspaper people in New York dwelled on it enough for all of them. Zachary's focus was journalism, and only journalism. Often, after a long day, he'd get into his Mercedes, turn the key, and sit in the damp darkness of the parking garage, trying to remember where he was going. Eventually he'd light a cigarette and drive home, the silence of his car still echoing with the sounds of typewriters and the deep throbbing of the press.

Tonight, however, he couldn't face going home to Hanna, and he was too exhausted to spend another moment at the paper. He found a parking spot a couple of blocks from his favorite bar and headed over, wanting nothing more than to lose himself, lose everything, for about four drinks' worth of awhile.

As he sat nursing a scotch, he looked around the bar. A woman in a corner booth was fixing her makeup in the mirror of her compact and bared her teeth to check for errant bits of lipstick. She was alone but, Zachary was sure, only momentarily. She had that look of having just had someone else nearby. Longer-term alone looks different. An older couple came into the bar, arms around each other, smiling ahead into what was going to be an amazing evening. An exhausted looking man in a suit and untied tie sat at the end of the bar, staring down into his whisky and soda without blinking. He felt Zachary's eyes on his and glanced up. Zachary lifted his glass in a little salute and the man lifted his own.

"Top you up, Mr. B?" the jovial bartender gave the bottle of scotch a little shimmy.

"Yes, thanks." Zachary wished he'd have gone to a bar where the bartenders didn't know him. He didn't want to be Zachary Benton right now. Zachary Benton had problems at work and problems at home, and while everyone has both kinds of problems at one time or another, that was cold comfort when the someone was you. Zachary needed time to think, to clear his head, although he was well aware that trying to clear his head with scotch was like trying to clean a window with honey.

"How about one for your drinking partner?" a female voice beside him caught him off guard. She hadn't even been there a moment ago.

"I don't have a drinking partner." He squinted at her though the smoke from his cigarette.

"You will if you buy me a drink."

What the hell, he was too tired to argue with another one of these damned creatures. He signaled the bartender.

"One for the lady, please, Darren."

She picked up her glass and lifted it in a little toast.

"To you… Mister…"

"Zithmar."

"Zithmar?"

"It's Armenian. I'm not from around here." He was pulling every bit of this straight out of his ass, but he had a feeling the buxom brunette didn't really care. Or understand.

"You don't have much of an accent."

"Thank you. I'll let my voice coach know you said so. He'll be pleased."

"I'm Francesca."

"Pleasure."

Zachary lit another cigarette and offered her one. She accepted and cupped her hands around his for a light, as though they were outside in a wind storm.

"So what do you do, Mr. Zithmar?"

"Please, call me Abe."

She exhaled a dainty stream of smoke twined in a laugh.

"Okay…what do you do, Abe?"

"I'm in shipping."

"Oh, that must be interesting."

He studied her.

"Not really," he said. "Look, Francesca, we're both adults here. You've been silently asking me something since the moment you sat down here, and the answer is yes. I'm only in town for a short time, so it has to be tonight. Here's where I'm staying." He reached for a cocktail napkin and wrote the name and address of a hotel on the Upper West Side. "If you're there in an hour, great. If not, it's been nice talking to you."

He dropped a twenty on the bar, went out the door, and got into a cab. Within half an hour, he'd checked into a room at the hotel. Ten minutes later, Francesca tapped on the door.

Chapter 5

Zachary began to pour so much of himself into the Beacon that he felt it was taking on his personality, sometimes his soul. When he'd see someone reading it on the street, he'd feel momentarily exposed, as though he had awakened to find himself standing in Times Square in his jockey shorts. Every letter to the editor may as well have been personally addressed to him.

It took its toll on Zachary, but the Beacon had never been stronger. Not one issue went to press until Zachary had checked every page. He worked late into the night, every night, on the following day's issue, and went over that day's issue with a fine-toothed pen when he got home. He was constantly watching the New York Times to see what they were covering, any formatting changes they made, what their staff turnover was like. He was focused, he was driven, and he was making his staff crazy.

"Mr. Benton, is everything all right?" Stan Logan, the Beacon's managing editor, asked one day, knocking tentatively on Zachary's office door. Zachary looked up from the dummy sheet on his desk.

"Yes, why do you ask?"

"Well, for starters, you're dummying the paper. And that's my job."

"I'm not dummying any pages for this issue. I'm just playing with some ideas for a new format."

"A new format? Why do we need a new format?"

"We don't necessarily need one, I'm just experimenting with possible layouts if we did change our print format."

"Like what? Tabloid?"

"Maybe. I don't know. Look, nothing is definite, Stan, I'm just messing with it."

Stan took the hint and left.

"He keeps making unilateral decisions and he's driving me nuts," he muttered to Jason, the sports editor.

"I know, he's a mental case," Jason sympathized under his breath. "But he's the best in the business."

Zachary soon discovered that he could work hard at the paper all day and late into the evening, stop for a drink, and on the way home find no shortage of women willing to let him pound out his tired frustrations on their bodies. By the time he got home to Hanna, he was relaxed and spent, and they passed most evenings in a state of, if not contentment, at least peace. It wasn't how Zachary had envisioned his life, but he found it worked for him. In fact, it worked pretty damned well.

Chapter 6

Sarah Thomas knew she was going to be a journalist from the day she published her first newspaper. It was a small publication, aimed at a specific demographic – namely her family – and printed painstakingly on gray construction paper with black crayon. She had meticulously stacked the six pages together, made holes in them with the punch she'd borrowed from her father's desk, and inserted brads into each one. It had been a work of art, a true labor of journalistic love, and had her parents possessed the ability to award her the Pulitzer Prize for Journalists Under the Age of Ten, they would have.

Sarah dreamed of living in working in New York City like her father did, and imagined herself out on important stories, notebook and pen in hand. But from her family's suburban home in Connecticut, Manhattan may as well have been on Mars. The Saturday her father told her he needed to take the train into the city on some business and asked her if she wanted to go along was reported in Sarah's diary as The Most Important Day Of My Whole Entire Life. To her seven-year-old mind, there was no place more glamorous, more packed with excitement, than New York City and her trip in with her father did nothing to disabuse her of that notion.

As they stepped off the train and walked out onto the streets of Midtown, Sarah clung to her father's hand and stared up at the upward-sprawling city with unabashed wonder, feeling as though she'd been transported to a magical wonderland, a beautiful sparkling place in which nothing bad could ever happen to her.

"Hey, watch it!" a man shouted at a passing bicycle messenger, who turned and spat on the ground near Sarah's feet before whizzing away. Sarah stepped over the bubbly splat and continued to gaze upward, dreamily. Her father smiled to himself and shook his head. For weeks afterward, Sarah's diary was filled with page after page of the wonders of the city, all that she'd seen and done during the trip with her father, followed by more pages of her plans to move to New York and be a Real Journalist, one who would be respected and recognized and read.

Unlike some little girls, who change their minds about their aspirations a thousand times before puberty, Sarah's dreams never wavered. As the fiercely focused editor of her high school newspaper, she declared it her "destiny" so often that when the yearbook came out, it included a candid photo of her working, busily and importantly, in the j-room, her dark red hair in a careless bun, a pencil behind her ear, glasses slipping down her nose, blue felt-tipped pen in her hand. The caption didn't even include her name, just the words "Journalism is my destiny."

Sarah dreamed of a job at the New York Beacon, but never dared to hope she could ever actually pull it off. She had gone to Columbia, worked as a stringer for any publication in the city she could, and by the time she graduated in 1965 magna cum laude, had a portfolio that some who had been in the business for years would have envied. Still, when she sent her resume to the Beacon, she knew it was a long shot. The longest shot. Over the fence. Going, going, gone. If she'd been better at sports, she would have realized that's a home run.

Deep inside, Sarah knew what she really wanted was to work with Zachary Benton. She had followed his career for years, feeling a thrill she couldn't quite pinpoint when he'd taken over as publisher of the Beacon. Zachary, she knew, felt the same fire she did. Her father would bring home a paper every night, and she'd take it to her room after dinner and read it cover to cover. It wasn't long before she found out that any story with a Zachary Benton byline would not only be good, it would be breathtaking. He didn't just tell her what was going on in New York, he showered her with it, letting her hear the sounds, smell the smells, feel the emotions. His descriptions of scenes, his details about the people he talked with stayed with Sarah for days after she'd read the article. She had never encountered another journalist like Zachary Benton.

"Mr. Benton, this is Sarah Thomas. She's the Columbia grad we talked about." Stan had just begun interviewing Sarah when Zachary came striding into the newsroom.

"Hello, Miss Thomas. I'm very glad to meet you." Zachary, with his shock of black hair and dark skin that always made him look as though he'd just been polished, towered over Sarah, offering his hand.

"Yes," she said stupidly. Zachary Benton. *Zachary Fucking Benton*. This was like meeting the pope for her. She couldn't get her words to line up. "I mean, yes, it's also good to meet you too, Mr. Benton."

"Zachary," he said, smiling. His hand was surprisingly soft, considering how big it was. "I saw your resume and clips. Very impressive. I hope you'll be joining our team."

"Wow," Stan whispered as Zachary strode away again. "He's never told anyone to call him Zachary. You start Monday."

Chapter 7

Sarah learned quickly that working in a metro newspaper newsroom was a huge leap from a university newspaper, even Columbia. For the first few months, she found herself relegated to the cop shop beat, and writing up bland articles about the goings-on in city schools that were buried so far inside it sometimes took her an hour to find them. She always got the feeling she was quietly being hazed, but rather than upset her, it secretly thrilled her. She was one of them now, even if she was standing on the very bottom rung of the ladder looking up.

The senior reporters, who called her "Cubby" when they deigned to speak to her at all and never invited her to their after-work happy hours at any number of upscale Midtown bars, didn't bother Sarah. Neither did she particularly admire them. Their work was pedestrian at best, save for the occasional scoop – particularly tasty when the scooped paper was the New York Times. They just didn't seem to have the fire in their bellies she'd always believed was crucial to keeping a great reporter going.

Zachary, on the other hand, she worshipped. He was a journalist of his own caliber, bold and unafraid, and Sarah always smiled to herself when she'd see him go striding out of the newsroom, tucking his slim reporter's notebook into the inside pocket of his jacket. He couldn't stay away from reporting no matter how hard he tried, although now he always said it was "research."

Sarah's fanatical devotion to Zachary only grew stronger the longer she was in his employ. She tried not to let the other reporters see it, but that wasn't all that difficult since none of them really spoke to her. The bigger question was whether Zachary could see it. She didn't know.

Everything changed the day she broke the story that the Court of Appeals in Albany had given the nod to the Port Authority to go ahead with its plans for a World Trade Center on Manhattan's lower west side. She'd banged out a short piece for that day's paper, but did a longer, in-depth follow up for Sunday's edition. She interviewed David Rockefeller, president of Chase Manhattan Bank, whose brainchild the World Trade Center was; Oscar Nadel, chairman of the Downtown West Businessman's

Association, who was not in favor of the project; Austin Tobin, executive director of the Port Authority, who very much was; and several lower Manhattan business owners who went on the record as saying the Port Authority didn't belong in the real estate business. She even got the architect, Minoru Yamasaki, to disclose some of his ideas for the design. Her story was a huge sensation, and made the front page of the April 7 edition, the first since the end of the printers' strike and a 700-plus page whopper that people talked about for months. Sarah's reputation as a serious journalist was cemented. Her colleagues treated her with a new respect, but she felt she was on top of Olympus looking down when Zachary called her into his office.

"Well, Sarah, I don't think I have to tell you what a great job you did on that World Trade Center piece," he said, when she was seated across from him.

"You don't have to, but coming from you that would be mighty nice," she smiled.

Mighty nice? She was disgusted. *Who are you, Daisy Mae?*

But Zachary just laughed.

"You showed real journalistic drive on that piece," he said. "Thanks to you always having your ear to the ground and fast instincts, we were able to break that story. That's a huge coup for us. And your follow-up piece was outstanding."

To her chagrin, Sarah felt the color start creeping into her face.

"Thank you," she murmured.

"I've discussed it with Stan, and we'd like to put you on the city hall beat. I know it's a big jump from what you've been doing before, but I think you've proved yourself."

Sarah was stunned. Covering city hall for the Beacon was something she'd dreamed of since her Columbia days. She was elated. And terrified. And elated. And terrified.

"Wow," she said, finding her voice. "I'm just... I don't know what to say. Thank you, Mr. Benton."

"Zachary."

"Thank you… Zachary." She moved the name around on her tongue and decided she liked the flavor. "Zachary. Thank you, Zachary."

She stopped when she realized she sounded like an idiot again, but Zachary seemed delighted with anything she said and did. Might as well ride that wave before it crested.

Sarah flourished on the city hall beat and made solid connections, even with Mayor Lindsay, who may not have liked her any better than he liked any press people, but respected her and knew she would always be balanced in her coverage. People began to recognize her, and associate her name with the Beacon. When the 1967 Pulitzers were announced and several went to the Beacon, no one was surprised that one had Sarah's name on it. The other reporters began asking her to come with them to the bars after work. She was over the moon until the day she was outside Zachary's office and heard him on the phone.

"She's a hell of a reporter, I know. Thank God I had the foresight to put her at city hall. No one there can resist a good-looking girl. And this one has a hot body and a great mind. She could have brought down Tammany Hall if she'd wanted to."

Sarah had turned and gone the other way to avoid crossing in front of Zachary's open office door. Her face was in flames. All this time she'd thought he respected her professionally, but all he'd really put at city hall were her breasts. She was devastated, and she was mad as hell. Buried in her anger was the tiny grain of knowledge that Zachary had said she had a great mind and was a hell of a reporter, but that had been secondary in his comments.

She seethed at home all that night, and all the next day at work. Before she left for the evening, she walked up to Stan's desk and calmly placed a sealed envelope in front of him.

"What's this?" Stan asked, looking up at her.

"It's my resignation, effective immediately. Please tell Mr. Benton he'll have to find another pair of tits to send to city hall."

And she turned and walked out, her heart roaring in her ears, aware of

Stan's stunned silence trailing behind her all the way to the door. She'd left the paper and gone straight to her favorite dive bar a few blocks away.

"Hey, Scoop," the bartender said when she walked in. "You look like hell."

"Thanks, Brian," she said wearily, dropping onto a barstool. "It's been a hell of a day."

"What's your poison tonight?"

"Jack Daniels. Straight up. Make it a double. In fact, just leave the damned bottle."

"Wow," Brian said, obediently brandishing the bottle. "You aren't kidding around."

Sarah knocked the whisky back in one shot and motioned for another.

"What's going on?" The bartender's curiosity finally got the better of him. He was used to helping people drown their sorrows and barely listened to their incessant whining, but Sarah had been coming here for ages and wasn't usually a big drinker. Or whiner.

"I quit my job," Sarah said. "I decided I wasn't going to sit there and be treated with disrespect." She threw back her shot. "You know the kind of disrespect I mean? The kind the suffragettes fought to rid us of, Brian. And furthermore I wasn't going to spend one more day being taken for granted by a paper that is run by a man who thinks so little of women that he is willing to lose the one who has worked the hardest to make his stupid paper as respected in this city as it is."

"Oh shit," the bartender breathed, his eyes behind her, his voice barely audible over the other sounds of a bar at happy hour.

"Come on, Brian, I know that was a great speech and all, but I didn't know you'd take it that hard," Sarah said, but he was already heading toward the other end of the bar.

"Hey!" she called, irritated. "Where are you going? What about my whisky?"

"What about your job?" A familiar voice at her elbow made her jump. Zachary stood there, comically out of place in the run-down bar. Sarah glanced up at him, then turned away.

"I don't have a job," she said. "I quit when I found out my boss thinks I'm just a piece of ass."

He pulled out the barstool next to her and sat down.

"In the old days, a gentleman asked a lady if it would be all right for him to sit down."

"In the old days, ladies didn't drink whisky and use expressions like 'piece of ass,'" Zachary countered, raising his hand to catch the bartender's attention.

"Whatever the lady is drinking, she'll have another. And the same for me."

"A double," Sarah said.

"All right, a double," Zachary said.

"Honor to have you in my bar, Mr. Benton," Brian said, pouring more whisky.

"Thank you, it's nice to be here," Zachary said, lifting his glass in a little salute.

Sarah couldn't help thinking what a stupid conversation this was.

"Look, why are you here? I would think the kind of bar where a broad like me would hang out would be beneath you."

"You certainly are fired up," Zachary observed.

Sarah slammed her glass down on the bar.

"Fired up? FIRED UP? I'm absolutely livid. How dare you tell... whoever... that the only reason you put me on the city hall beat was because I'm attractive?"

"I see you were eavesdropping outside my office."

"I beg your pardon, Mr. Benton. I was about to pass your office and I overheard what you said. I was in the wrong place at the right time. If you want privacy when you share your outdated, misogynistic views, I'd suggest you close your office door."

"I think you should come back to work."

30

"I think you should fuck off."

Zachary laughed. He couldn't help it. Sarah turned to stare at him.

"I'm sorry," he said. "It's just that you're absolutely right. And if the situation had somehow been reversed, I'd have told my boss to fuck off. And probably stormed off to drink whisky."

Sarah wasn't laughing.

"I'll ask you one more time. Why are you here?" The liquor, simmering in her belly along with the knowledge that she had nothing more to lose, was making her bold.

Zachary grew serious. He swirled the drink in his glass, watching it as if the answers would float to the top like a Magic 8 Ball.

"To apologize," he said finally. "But more than that, to make it right."

"I don't think you can make it right," Sarah said. "I have been working for you for two years, and I thought you respected me as a journalist."

"I do. Just between us, I'd be happy if I were half the journalist you are."

"Thanks for that," she said drily. "But you'll have to forgive me if I don't believe you."

"If you heard what I said on the phone, you know I said you're a hell of a reporter. Because you are."

"Yeah, I heard. But that part kind of got lost in the other stuff about my hot body."

Zachary kept his eyes on his drink, unable to look at her.

"Well, the truth is, you are attractive. And if it's sexist of me to say this, then so be it, but attractive female reporters often get better stories than males. Sources instinctively trust women reporters more than they do men. It's just how it is. And the fact that female reporters – real reporters, good ones – are in the minority, well, that just makes them all the more intriguing."

Sarah didn't respond.

"I can still feel the doubt waves emanating from you," Zachary said.

31

"Those aren't doubt waves. Those are fuck-you waves."

"Fine, fuck me. But in some part of that stubborn brain of yours, you know what I'm saying is true. And incidentally, it's not just male sources who find female reporters easier to trust. Women would rather deal with a female reporter too. And it's a scientific fact that people like other people more when they're attractive."

Sarah laughed without smiling.

"Now you're quoting science," she said. "That's rich. You're too much. Let me tell you something, Mr. Benton. I'm the best reporter you've got on that staff and you know it. The fact that I'm a woman is incidental. At least it should be. Journalism has no gender. You fought your way to the top, just like I'm doing. That story you did on the homeless in New York? The one where you slept outside with them for a week? That was the most brilliant piece of journalism I've ever read. How would you like it if someone categorically diminished something you'd put your heart and soul into just because you were born with a penis? Because guess what, Zachary? I had no say in my gender. But I do have a say in my career. And I will not spend it working for a man who thinks all I have to offer are my tits."

Zachary was staring at her.

"My homeless story? That was probably 15 years ago."

"Yeah? So?"

"You read that?"

Sarah was suddenly self-conscious. She looked away, her anger dissolving fast under the warm intensity of Zachary's gaze.

"I've read all your stuff," she said. "I used to get the Beacon back home in Connecticut. I've followed your career for as long as I can remember. You were like Elvis to me." She knocked back the rest of her drink and looked at him seriously. "But before you get even more big-headed than you already are, you should know you made one lousy locker pin-up."

Zachary tried to laugh but the lump in his throat wouldn't budge. He took a sip of whisky. Several long moments went by before either of them spoke.

32

"Look, Sarah, you're right to be angry," Zachary said finally, softly. "I diminished you and your work with my thoughtless comments and I want you to know that even if you don't come back to work for me, I'm very sorry. I won't make such a mistake again."

Sarah motioned to the bartender for another drink.

"So you're not going to beg me to come back?"

"Would it work?"

"Yeah. Yeah, I think it would."

"Then I'm begging."

An hour later, they were in Sarah's bed.

Chapter 8

It would have been easier on everyone if it had been a whisky-soaked one-night stand, but as Zachary lay in the dark, Sarah asleep in his arms and New York serenading them with nighttime street sounds, he realized this would not be an affair he could brush off. Long before this night, he had known in the deepest part of his soul that Sarah was becoming all to him. He cursed himself for the momentary macho display on the phone that had nearly cost him everything. A piece of ass? She should only know that from the moment he first met her, he felt a connection to her unlike anything he had ever experienced, and over the next three years, it had just gotten stronger. Only Sarah understood how important his career was to him. Hanna, although she appreciated the prestige it brought her, resented the time Zachary devoted to the Beacon.

From that night on, they existed only for each other. In Zachary, Sarah found what had been missing from her soul. Seeing herself through his eyes, she became aware of her every gift, and her every flaw. He never criticized her, that wasn't Zachary's style, but every interaction with him taught her more about herself. Since her earliest days as a dreamy, creative child, Sarah had lived in her own head, observing the world around her as though watching through a window, seeing but not thinking of being seen. It was a habit that had followed her into adulthood, and as a journalist, it served her well. But with Zachary, Sarah slowly came to realize she wasn't gazing out a window anymore but looking into a mirror. In him, she saw who she really was, and who she really wanted to be.

She felt guilty, of course, because she was fully aware that Zachary was married. She knew Hanna's name but beyond that, the woman was as indistinct as fog in the distance. To keep herself from feeling like a complete tramp, Sarah did her best not to think of Hanna at all. Sometimes at the paper, she'd look up from her typing and see Zachary at his desk, his head bent over something spread out in front of him, and she'd feel a deep sense of balance and peace, knowing that as long as he was there, the world made sense.

At night in her bed, he belonged to her. His life elsewhere was not important in those moments. All that mattered was that he was beside her, warm against her, breathing new life into her.

"Do you think anyone at the paper suspects us?" she asked him one night as they sat on her sofa sipping wine he'd brought. Her feet were on his lap and he was rubbing her arches with his knuckles.

"No," he said thoughtfully. "I don't. We're never anything but professional when we're at work. Why, did someone say something to you?"

"No. Oh God, no. I would have told you instantly if they had. But I just sometimes wonder if anyone suspects. I wouldn't want your wife to find out."

She was testing him. He stopped mid-rub, his gaze trained on her foot. Neither of them had ever mentioned Hanna.

"I don't know if I want her to find out or not," he said.

"Zachary!"

"Well, I'm sorry, Sarah, but I don't. We have not been happily married for a very long time. Maybe ever."

He suddenly looked exhausted and very old. He took off his glasses and rubbed his eyes. He didn't want Sarah to know about the other women he'd bedded in frustration and anger at Hanna, not because he wanted to keep anything from her, but because he was afraid she would think less of him. Since the first night they'd made love, there had been no one else. Looking at her now, he knew there never would be. The emotions were stacking up in Zachary, threatening to spill over. He resumed rubbing her feet.

"I didn't want to cheat on her. I know all of this sounds like the usual bullshit married men say to their girlfriends, all that 'my wife doesn't understand me' stuff, but the truth is, I didn't set out to find someone else, to be unfaithful to Hanna, and certainly not to seduce you. But once it happened, then what?"

"Then what?" Sarah echoed. She was beginning to be sorry she'd brought it up.

"Then this," Zachary said, squeezing her foot. "Then this." He gestured around Sarah's small apartment. "Then us. I've never felt more at home, more myself, with anyone than I do with you. I've always been so focused on my career that I never took the time to get close to people, not really. And as a journalist, it's better that way, you know that. But when I met you, I suddenly felt like I could see myself clearly. And I realized that for all my bravado, all my ladder-climbing and success and ambition, I had never really seen myself before. I'd seen myself for what I am, but never for who I am. You make me feel open. I don't know how to put it any better than that. You make me feel open and … real. What I have with you is a true sense of identity. Of hope. Hope for tomorrow, hope for forever. I will live and die for you in this life and spend all eternity with you in the next." He touched her hair, her cheek, trying to make her feel what he couldn't get his mouth to say properly. "Sarah, my Sarah. I love you."

They were crying.

"Oh Zachary." She could barely get the words out. Swinging her feet to the floor, she leaned over and kissed him.

"I love you," she said. "I love you more than I ever dreamed I could love another person."

His arms closed around her. Her heart was pounding against his chest so hard he couldn't feel his own. He buried his face in her hair, breathing her in. He knew at some point he would have to decide what to do, but in this moment, nothing else mattered.

Chapter 9

The phone rang during dinner, as it often did. The housekeeper slipped into the dining room and, avoiding Hanna's white-hot stare, quietly told Zachary he had a phone call from the newspaper.

"Thank you, Ilsa. Excuse me, please," Zachary said to his wife, stepping out to the phone in the small alcove under the stairs. Hanna, watching him go, tried to get the wine she'd just sipped down through the constriction in her throat. She knew who was calling her husband, and even if it was official newspaper business just the idea of the young woman's voice invading her home made Hanna furious. She had no concrete evidence that her husband was having an affair with his reporter, but she knew it. She felt it, with that certainty only a cheated-on woman has, the one that makes her temples pound and the back of her mouth taste like iron. She poured herself more wine and pushed away her untouched dinner plate. In a few minutes, Zachary was back.

"I apologize for the interruption," he said, taking his place again and picking up his fork.

"I wish you'd tell your staff not to call you at home during dinner," Hanna said stiffly. "Some of them in particular," she added quietly. Zachary ignored that.

"The newsroom has gotten a tip about a protest being planned at Columbia University tomorrow. They have to keep me informed. You know this."

"Oh, they certainly keep you informed all right," she responded, trying to make sure she wasn't slurring her words. The wine was making her fuzzy and she wondered vaguely if it was too late to slow it with food. Probably. She refilled her glass and looked defiantly at Zachary, her chin lifted slightly in that look he knew so well. He had once found her strength and outspokenness appealing, such a refreshing contrast to the placating housewives his mother and her friends had been. "The Cookie Baking Crone Club," Hanna had called them once, and Zachary had laughed. Now he often caught himself wishing his wife was a bit more reticent and respectful of him. He may as well have wished for the moon to turn cartwheels across the sky.

"If it happens, this protest could be a big story," Zachary said, refusing to take the bait.

"It's just another stupid protest," Hanna said. "The whole country has been rife with them for the past two years."

"Well, this one is in our backyard, and you know as well as I do that when Ivy League students decide to mobilize, it's a whole different story than when high school dropouts get high and take to the streets in Haight-Ashbury," Zachary said. "We have our best reporter ready to go out there in the morning."

"Ah, let me guess. The lovely Sarah. Yes, she's a regular Nellie Bly. The next Barbara Walters."

"Sarah is the best reporter we have and you know it."

"Best at lots of things," Hanna muttered, some of her wine sloshing out from her brimming glass. She stared at the spreading crimson dot. It looked like a gunshot wound, then a Rorschach test. She saw her husband and his attractive young reporter in a passionate clench.

"Hanna, I will not listen to this. If you have something you'd like to say to me, say it. Be an adult. If you do not, then please stop behaving like a petulant teenager and let us finish dinner in peace."

Hanna slammed her open palm down on the table, making the dishes clatter.

"Hanna." The warning in Zachary's voice was now unmistakable. She got to her feet, swaying slightly.

"You finish it," she said. She turned and walked out.

Zachary took off his glasses and rubbed his eyes. The housekeeper startled him when she opened the side door a second time.

"Mr. Benton, I'm so sorry but it's the paper again. She says it's urgent."

He hadn't even heard the phone.

"Thank you, Isla. I'll take it in my office. Please clear away Mrs. Benton's place and bring me a scotch on the rocks."

He went down the hall to his office and closed the door before picking up the receiver.

"Zachary, I'm sorry to call again but I can't reach Stan." Sarah's voice was harried.

"Please don't be sorry," he said. "What's wrong?"

"I just had a call from a Columbia student who said this protest tomorrow could, and probably will, turn into more of a race thing than anyone realizes."

"I thought the whole idea of them building a segregated gym was what started this in the first place."

"It is, but that's students versus the university. The student who just called me said the black students are starting to want to split from the white students because the white students don't really understand the problem."

"I'm not sure I do either," Zachary said.

"Actually, I think I do. I talked to this kid for quite awhile. The white students want to rally the whole student body. The black students think they're not focused on what really matters right now, which is stopping construction of the gym."

"Oh, I see. Well, that will make it more interesting, student versus student on an issue that until now they've been united on."

"I think I can get interviews with the students tomorrow. The kid who called said they specifically discussed calling me before all this went down. I'm one of them, I guess, so they seem to trust me. As much as they trust anybody."

"Excellent."

"That's it, really. I just wanted to let you know," Sarah said.

"I appreciate that," Zachary responded, then lowered his voice a bit. Sarah could feel his smile. "And it gave me another excuse to hear your beautiful voice one more time."

Upstairs, Hanna quietly replaced the receiver with shaking hands.

Chapter 10

April in New York is full of promise. The city emerges from winter with a big ta-da, as though it had secretly been changing into its dogwoods and daffodils behind a curtain of snow, preparing to dazzle everyone. All that came before was rendered unimportant – the bottomless hollow mood of winter, disappointment, lost chances and wasted time, even death momentarily held no sway in the face of that first breath of springtime.

The promise that morning wasn't so beautiful, but exciting nonetheless. At least it was to Sarah, whose every journalistic instinct told her today was going to be huge. She sat in her car, engine idling, across the street from where the previous night's caller had told her the students would be meeting. She glanced at her watch, even though she knew it wasn't time yet. She'd been restless all night, awake early, feeling unwell. She pushed it aside with ginger ale and aspirin, refusing to give in to illness and miss what could be the biggest story of her career so far. She was always fighting off whatever bug other people carried into the newsroom on the shoulders of their misguided belief that they were just too damned important to call in sick.

Her thoughts wandered to Zachary, as they did about a thousand times a day, and how much she wanted, even just once, to blow the lid off a really huge story, as much for him as for herself. He had believed in her when no one else had, taken a chance on a young Columbia grad with more ego than experience, and she was constantly aware that she could never repay a debt like that.

Even now, in the months since they'd become lovers, Sarah could tell Zachary respected her as a journalist, and she thrived under his mentoring. Although Stan was in charge of the day to day editing of the news and ran the assignment desk, Zachary was a very hands-on publisher, always in the newsroom, talking to people, offering his help, and keeping things light with an occasional joke, which were invariably terrible but everyone laughed anyway because it was Zachary and while he was amazing, he was also vaguely terrifying. Sarah often wondered if anyone on staff suspected what her relationship with Zachary had morphed into, but she doubted it. They were excruciatingly careful.

She was shaken from her reverie by a sharp knock on her car window. A young black man motioned for her to roll her window down.

"You're the lady from the Beacon, right? Sarah?"

"Yes, that's me."

"I'm Jordan Williams, with the Student Afro Society."

Sarah grabbed her bag and notebook and got out of the car.

"It's good to meet you, Jordan," she said, shaking his hand. "Are you the one who called me?"

"No, that was a friend of mine. He said he heard you're a Columbia grad and pretty groovy, for a reporter."

Sarah laughed.

"Well, thanks. I think."

"We're starting to get together in Low Library right now to get organized. But this is starting to be about more than the gym."

"Race, your friend said on the phone. He said it was about race."

"Well, the whole thing is about race. I mean, you know they want to have segregated entrances to the gym, with the back door – the one that faces Harlem – for black students. That's what got all of us pissed off for starters. The students call it Gym Crow."

"Hang on, I have to get that down." Sarah dug in her purse for a pen and began scribbling notes. "But your friend said the race thing is also starting to divide the students."

"The SAS wants to keep our protests focused on stopping construction of the gym. But the white students, the SDS, want to rally the whole student body to protest the gym, Vietnam, everything. They're really losing the focus. And if we can't find some common ground here, the SAS is going to break off from the SDS."

"What's SDS?"

"Students for a Democratic Society."

"Can we go down to the library? Can I sit in?"

"That's why we called you. We want someone to take the students' side on this."

"Jordan, come on. You know I can't take sides."

He grinned at her.

"I know," he said. "Come on."

They headed into Low Library where students were already assembling. The air was thick with young enthusiasm and righteous indignation. Anger was carving the first lines onto the young faces, but beneath the anger, Sarah felt something else. Hope, maybe bordering on naiveté, that they could make a difference. It hadn't been that long ago that she'd walked this campus, cocooned in her own world, wrapped in her friends, her studies, and the careful future she was planning around journalism. How much had she missed, she wondered now, by staring so fiercely ahead that she couldn't see what was happening just on the other side of her blinkers? The Cuban Missile Crisis, the Kennedy Assassination – as an aspiring journalist she'd watched them unfold in the news, even practiced covering them for some of her classes, but she never wondered how she should get involved, mostly because her limited journalism training had already taught her to report the facts while keeping herself out of the fray. But as she looked around the room now, she knew it was going to take all her skill to stay neutral this time.

In the newsroom later, Sarah sat at her typewriter, lost in thought. How could she possibly put into words all that she'd witnessed that day? The students' passion, their belief in equality, their anger at the government and their school that had been stirred together and brought to the boiling point, only to spill over onto each other?

She rested her head on her open palm and tried to think of an opening paragraph. Leads were usually one of Sarah's strengths, but right now all she could think about was how exhausted she was. She knew she was going to have to give up and admit she was getting the flu, but she had to put this story out first. They were holding the front page for her. She stared out the window without seeing the night, seeing only the faces of the students, angry, yelling, marching. They wanted to affect change and were trying to do that the only way they knew how. Students loved to stomp their feet and shout that they had a voice, that they had rights, but the truth was, they didn't. Not really. No one but the politically powerful in New York had a voice. Zachary had been half joking when he said Sarah could have taken down Tammany Hall, but he had no idea how much she'd love to have done that. She wanted to blow the doors off every corrupt office in the state, in the whole country. It infuriated her that policy makers could so easily be bought by special interest groups, by lobbyists and spin doctors she always pictured scurrying through city halls, through Capitol Hill, dodging in and out of the shadows, all whispered promises and filthy secrets, money going from hand to hand to hand, stuffing the machine, bloating it grotesquely, until it got all the way to the top and the whole mess exploded and rained shit all over the little people.

The mental image she'd conjured made her stomach turn and she bolted for the ladies' room where she threw up. *Get a grip, Sarah*, she thought, leaning her head on her arm. She drew a shaky hand across her mouth and waited to make sure she wasn't going to throw up again. She needed to finish that story and fast. She obviously had no choice about getting sick, but she'd never missed a deadline and wasn't going to start now.

She washed her hands and splashed her face with water. Taking several deep, slow breaths, she headed back to the newsroom, stopping at the water fountain for a drink on the way. Settling back down at her typewriter, she began to write.

"Tensions reach the exploding point this afternoon at Columbia University where student protesters have taken the dean and another administrator hostage until their demands are met.

The Columbia faction of Students for a Democratic Society (SDS), the largest radical student organization in the country, took Acting Dean Henry Coleman and Proctor William Kahn hostage in Hamilton Hall. The group has a list of demands they want met before they will release the hostages, who inside sources say have not been harmed.

The Beacon has received a copy of the list of demands. Among them: That construction of the gymnasium in Morningside Park be stopped, that the university cut all connections to IDA, that the ban on indoor demonstrations be rescinded, and that criminal charges arising out of protests at the gym site be dropped.

Coleman told student leaders that he would not give in to any demands 'under a situation such as this.'

The roots of the unrest can be traced back to last year, when students Bob Feldman and Michael Klare found what they say is a reference to Columbia's membership in IDA, a little-known consortium of 12 universities that functions as a Pentagon think tank. University officials have denied any institutional connection with the IDA.

Student protests began to boil in earnest last week, when the Columbia administration attempted to suppress anti-IDA student protest on campus. Additionally, students are protesting the university's plans for the Morningside Park gymnasium, long a bone of contention between the university and residents of Harlem, who see the school's use of the park as little more than an elitist land-grab.

With this week's assassination of Dr. Martin Luther King Jr. causing the issue of race to peer out the windows of even the ivory towers of Columbia University, both SDS and SAS activists have become outraged by rumors that the Harlem-facing entrance is to be for blacks only. The university, however, says the position of the doorway is due to the eleven-story gym's physical location on the park's steeply inclined slope. Harlem is at the bottom, Morningside Heights is at the top.

Morningside Heights and West Harlem residents have been fighting construction of the gym for years. Mayor John Lindsay also opposes the project, and the first days of construction already have been marked with violence and protests. Police arrested 26 people from the university and the community during the first two weeks of construction of what's now known on campus as 'Gym Crow.'

Taking the administrators hostage appeared to be an impulse by the students, who are occupying Hamilton Hall. Still less planned were the invisible lines the students drew down the middle of their own factions, separating them by race.

An already complicated issue became even more so as black students, members of the Student Afro Society (SAS) told the SDS they wanted to occupy Hamilton Hall alone, and while some black students shouted at the departing whites that they were still in solidarity, the mood among the white students wasn't so positive as they moved their protest out of Hamilton, leaving half of their power base, and their hostages, behind.

The Beacon is continuing to follow this story as it unfolds."

By the time she'd filed her story, Sarah was so tired she could only faintly remember getting into a taxi and asking the driver to take her home. "I just need to sleep," she mumbled to herself as she crawled into bed. "I will kick this flu by tomorrow and be back at Columbia in the morning."

But when she woke, she was throwing up again. She called her friend Cindy and asked her to bring over matzo ball soup. She didn't have many female friends in New York, but she and Cindy had met at Columbia and stayed fairly close.

"You're sick? Call the deli and have them deliver. I don't want your nasty flu bug."

"You're a nurse!"

"That doesn't mean I want the flu."

"You know, your bedside manner sucks," Sarah muttered. "Come on, I never ask you for favors."

"You always ask me for favors," Cindy corrected her. "And you never did return my suede jacket."

"I'm not making the connection, but if you bring me soup, you can take the jacket back with you."

"Oh, fine. I'll be by in a couple of hours. I think I can sneak out of here for lunch today."

By the time Cindy arrived bearing a carefully balanced brown paper bag, Sarah was up and dressed.

"What the hell?" Cindy said. "You don't look sick."

"The funny thing is, I feel fine. I've been fighting off this flu for the past few days. It kind of comes and goes."

"It comes and goes? The flu doesn't come and go. What are you talking about?"

"I felt like shit last night at work, for one thing. But I feel worst in the mornings. For the past few mornings, I've woken up sick, but then I start feeling better. So then I assume I'm not sick, but then in the morning I'm sick ... again..." Her voice trailed off and she and Cindy stared at each other.

"Holy shit," Cindy said. "Sounds like you're pregnant."

"I'm... what? Shut up. I'm not pregnant. Shut your mouth, that's ridiculous."

"Sarah! Listen to yourself. You're sick in the mornings? Then you're fine? When was your last period?"

"It was just... uh, let me think. I can't remember." She reached for her purse and pulled out her pocket calendar. She counted up the days and slowly looked up at Cindy. "Eight and a half weeks ago."

"Eight and a half weeks? You haven't had a period in eight and a half weeks and you're just now figuring this out? And they said you were the smart one."

"I can't be pregnant."

"Why can't you? Have you not had any sex?"

"I've... what kind of a stupid question is that?"

"That's how you get pregnant," Cindy said drily. "Trust me, I'm a nurse."

Sarah was staring at the calendar in her hand, praying she'd somehow miscalculated. But no matter how many times she stabbed her finger feverishly at the little squares, the answer came back the same.

"You need to call your doctor," Cindy said, resting a hand on Sarah's shoulder. "Better you find out so you can deal with it."

Sarah sat on the couch for a long time after Cindy left, trying to untangle her thoughts. She would call her doctor, but she already knew the answer. She laid a slender hand on her still-flat belly. Although she knew it was impossible, she would have sworn she felt a tiny movement deep inside.

Chapter 11

Pregnancy agreed with her, Sarah decided, studying her face in the bathroom mirror as she brushed her hair. She'd always regarded her willow-thin body as a bit too skinny, but she wasn't one of those women who spent a lot of time obsessing about her looks. She had more important things to obsess about. But now she couldn't help but notice how great her skin looked, and how thick and shiny her hair had gotten, how much fuller her breasts looked. Once the body-slamming nausea had finally subsided, she found she actually enjoyed being pregnant.

The problem was that she was starting to show. She'd managed to keep it hidden under loose tunics and flowy skirts, but she knew it was time to tell Zachary. She wondered how he'd react. She wondered a lot of things, like what this meant for her future with him, if she'd have to quit her job, and how long before crazy-ass Hanna tried to run her down in the middle of Lexington Avenue.

Motherhood was a sub-dream of Sarah's, one she'd always found herself idly thinking about, but knowing that if she had to choose between squeezing out kids and being a journalist, she'd die childless. Still, in her early days of covering school board meetings, she'd watch young mothers from the PTA come before the board to discuss the school carnival or parent-teacher night, and she'd envy their devotion to their children, their involvement in the schools so thorough they were on a first-name basis with the principal and knew without looking at their calendars when it was their turn to be playground monitor. She would picture them at home, taking off their aprons and hanging them up before leaning over their kids at the kitchen table, checking homework, breathing in that shampoo-and-puppy smell children have, then later tucking them into bed, listening to prayers, and a flurry of goodnight kisses to round out another successful day as Mom. It made Sarah ache a little to remember her own happy childhood in the suburbs of Danbury, boisterous family dinners, school plays, report cards, family vacations and squabbles with her siblings that had seemed catastrophic at the time. As she'd grown older and more invested in her career, she often found herself wondering if she'd cheated herself by not opting for marriage and a family.

Now she wouldn't have to wonder anymore about the road not taken. She'd left tread marks down both roads. And although having a child by another woman's husband – and her boss, no less – wasn't exactly what Sarah would have chosen, she couldn't contain her joy. The child inside her was a gift, a precious gift she'd been given at a time in her life when she was most able to appreciate it.

While she wasn't one to hide things from Zachary, she found she actually enjoyed this secret. She kept it close to her, hugging it throughout the day and all during the long nights she lay awake, thinking of Zachary at home with his wife. During the early days of their affair, those thoughts had plagued and tormented her, doing their danse macabre all around her head, first hinting, then whispering, and finally shouting that she was a fool not to accept that Zachary was married, and that as Sarah lay alone in the vast coldness of her bed, Zachary was most likely thrusting himself into his wife's body, smug and secure in the fact that he had the best of both worlds. And who was Sarah, in the grand scheme of things, to make any demands on him? She was still just a reporter, and Zachary was one of the most powerful men in New York. If he wanted to spend an energetic couple of hours at her apartment during the day and go back to his lovely wife and perfect home at night, Sarah knew there was nothing she could do but open her arms and her legs, and spend the interminably long nights trying to squash down the ache inside.

But from the day Zachary had told her he loved her, the ache had dissipated. Now her nights were spent with her hands cupped around her belly, smiling her secret into the familiar darkness of her bedroom.
A part of Zachary was growing inside her. It bound them inextricably together, and there was nothing Hanna could do, nothing anyone could do, to take this baby away from her.

She put down her hairbrush and looked into her own eyes, feeling herself being drawn into her mind, something she had done since she was a child. It was during these intense moments of introspection, the times she spent wandering the far reaches of her own thoughts, that Sarah had become comfortable in her skin. All her worries, all her insecurities, all her doubts were like dusty boxes in the corners of her mind, and when she stumbled over one, she'd pull it out, open the lid, and sort through it. She never found anything she was truly afraid of, and anything uncomfortable she dragged out into the light. Nothing is as frightening in the light. When she was twelve, a girl at school had teased her about her big nose, and in bed that night, Sarah had dragged that thought out. It was the Thomas nose, one the family had always joked about, their badge of distinction, on the medium side of big and slightly bulbous. Sarah felt the sharp sting of her classmate's assertion that her nose made her a freak, an oddball, a standout. But she thought it over and by the next morning, she'd decided her nose was the best thing that could have happened to her. She pulled her hair back from her face with a rainbow headband and went to school that day with her chin up and her nose leading the way. If it made her stand out from the others, all the better. She was born to stand out.

This was no different. She wasn't ashamed of her unmarried status, of having a baby with a man who was legally bound to someone else. Most of the time now, Hanna was barely a dot on Sarah's radar. She just didn't matter. Zachary belonged to Sarah, and he always would. She moved her hands down until they rested comfortably on either side of her belly and closed her eyes, a slight smile on her lips. Her instincts told her the baby was a boy, and she knew he would be a great man. His energy burned within her, making her feel alive and vibrant at a point when most pregnant women were feeling sick and exhausted.

She had to be at the paper early in the morning but she couldn't sleep. She longed to call Zachary, to hear his dark liquid voice on the other end of the phone, yet she knew she dared not risk it. The next day at work would have to be soon enough.

After a restless night, Sarah was the first one in the newsroom, and she relished the rare silence as she made herself a cup of the chicory root tea she kept in her desk drawer. It was already promising to be a warm day, but in the quiet newsroom, Sarah shivered. She knew Zachary would not be angry with her about the baby, and she knew she wanted to carry the pregnancy to term. Still, a faint but persistent feeling of dread hung about her like a stalker she kept catching peering in the windows of her mind.

She wandered into Zachary's dark office. It always felt like a living, breathing space to her, warm with his presence and pulsing with his energy even when he wasn't there. She was safe here, where she could feel close to Zachary and still look out onto her beloved newsroom. She ran her hands along the various objets d' Zachary that neatly lined his desk. A hand-stamped leather pencil cup, a blown-glass paperweight, an odd and small sculpture of what appeared to be a contortionist clown, his note pad, his Rolodex, a coffee mug. She traced the rim of the mug with one long, white finger, lost in disconnected, abstract thoughts.

"Sarah!" Zachary's voice from the doorway made her jump. "I'm sorry, I didn't mean to startle you." He came in and, although there was no one else in the newsroom yet, closed the door behind him. "What are you doing here so early? Are you all right?" He took her cold hands into his warm ones. His face was gentle, kind, and wreathed in such love it made her breath lodge in her throat.

"Zachary, sweetheart," she began, then faltered. Everything she had been about to say suddenly sounded stupid in advance and her tongue felt thick and uncooperative. She frowned.

"What is it, my love?" He was starting to look alarmed. "Something is wrong. Tell me, please."

"I'm pregnant." Sarah's voice, usually strong and throaty, was now barely audible, a thin strand of sound. She raised her eyes to meet Zachary's.

"Pregnant," he said. His face was neutral, still, his voice sounding like it was coming from somewhere else. Sarah's heart had just started to sink under the weight of her mistake when his laugh rang out, a deep, free, joyous sound. "Pregnant! Oh my love, that's wonderful!" He pulled her into his arms, laughing and turning about in a wild, loose dance of elation. Sarah's feet dangled like a rag doll as she rested her head against Zachary's strong chest, weak with relief.

"I knew you wouldn't be angry, my love," she said, her voice muffled by his suit coat. He stopped dancing and set her down so he could look into her face.

"Angry? I could never be angry, my Sarah, this is our baby, our love made flesh."

"But Hanna..." her voice trailed off. She didn't even know how to finish that sentence. Even when neither of them was specifically thinking of her, the reality of Hanna hung between them like a vapor. Sarah watched his face now, seeing the muscle in his jaw clench, his face clouded over by an expression she could not read.

"You have nothing to worry about," he said quietly. "Hanna is my problem, not yours. And not ours." His face cleared and he smiled down into her eyes, once again alive and alight with love.

"How are you feeling? What are you drinking? Is that coffee? Is that good for the baby?"

Sarah laughed.

"It's chicory tea, like always," she said. "You're becoming a protective father very early."

"A father," Zachary said, as if hearing the word for the first time. "A father. Oh dear God. I'm going to be a father." His eyes moved behind Sarah, pulled by something she couldn't see. He was gone from her, for a long moment, before suddenly he laughed again and clapped his hands. "I have always imagined what it would be like, and thanks to you, my love, I'm going to find out. I suppose I will need to buy sneakers."

"Sneakers?"

"For playing catch," he explained.

Now it was Sarah's laugh that filled the room.

"Oh Zachary, you are a perfectly lovely, wonderful man," she said, touching his cheek with her fingertips. "But sweetheart, I really don't think you're the catch type."

"No," he said thoughtfully. "No, I don't suppose I am. Well, maybe I can... I don't know. Bring him to the paper with me?"

"The paper," Sarah said decisively, "is the perfect place for him to grow up."

Chapter 12

Sarah had never known the height and width and depth of happiness she felt during the early months of her pregnancy. She had always been happy, content with her life and her place in the world, but this ran deeper, enveloping her so tightly that sometimes it threatened to spill out and she would laugh and hug herself just to get some relief from the way it squeezed her from the inside.

Her relationship with Zachary grew and flourished alongside the life inside of her. He spent as much time as possible with her, often having dinner with her at her apartment, rubbing her feet while they watched television, running to the market whenever a new craving hit, and every once in a glorious while when Hanna was away, spending an entire long, warm night in her bed, waking her at dawn with his hands and his mouth. They never spoke of his wife, and although Sarah often wondered what, if anything, he was planning to tell her, she found herself unwilling to ask, lest the spoken words shatter their perfect crystal happiness.

Zachary, however, carried the secret like a lead weight inside. His options were limited, he knew. He could keep spending as much time as possible with Sarah, even after the baby was born, walking the perilously thin line that divided his two lives. That plan had its dangers, he knew. The instant the rival papers got a whiff of the baby, it would be all over the news. But the other option, coming clean with Hanna, was unthinkable. If he told her the whole story, she'd ruin him. He also couldn't tell her he was unhappy and wanted out of the marriage. She was far too shrewd for that. She'd dig until she found out the truth, then she'd ruin him. Before he could lose himself in noble fantasies of abdicating his throne and, like the Duke of Windsor, dropping into the arms of the woman he loved, Zachary realized that more than himself, he feared for Sarah. If Hanna launched the kind of hate campaign in New York he knew full well she was capable of, Sarah would be finished in the city as a journalist, maybe altogether.

Zachary didn't love Hanna, he knew now he never had, but he respected her. And the knowledge of what she could do to him had turned the respect into fear. He knew that if he ever crossed her, he would be finished as well. So his only two options, he finally realized, were no options at all. At night, while Hanna slept in their palatial, satin-canopied bed, he would pace back and forth on the patio, chain smoking and tossing up fevered questions to the cold, silent moon. He lost weight.

He drank too much. The only respite from the heavy reality of his life was in Sarah's arms. He'd escape to her apartment whenever he could, staying as long as he dared, and revel in the feeling of family. The house he shared with Hanna was a spacious brownstone with every luxury and convenience money could buy, but home was Sarah's small apartment.

He sat dutifully beside Hanna in church every Sunday morning, but his spirit only stirred when he walked through Sarah's front door.

"Zachary, my love," Sarah said one evening, handing him a glass of scotch before settling beside him on the sofa and tucking her feet under herself. Her belly pushed her soft floral dress out in such an endearing way Zachary couldn't resist leaning over to kiss it. She laughed and touched his head. "This is important."

He sat up again and smiled into her earnest face. "What is it, my sweet baby?"

She fiddled with the fringe on the throw pillow next to her.

"I am not sure how much longer I'm going to be able to hide my pregnancy at the paper. I've already seen a couple of the women eyeing my belly. I don't have that many loose clothes."

"I've been wondering about that myself," Zachary said thoughtfully.

"I just want to say that if it's better I quit, then, well," she took a shuddering breath. "I'll quit."

"Like hell you will," Zachary said. "There's not another reporter at that paper who is fit to carry your AP Stylebook and you know it."

"Thank you, my love, but the problem remains. People will either think I'm a promiscuous slut who doesn't know who the father is, or else they'll connect the dots somehow and figure out that it's you. I'm still not sure we haven't been seen leaving the office together."

"So we leave the office together, big deal. You're a reporter, I own the paper. We work together. Newspaper people are known for hanging out in their own little cliques."

"You're missing my point. I'm showing, Zachary, and about to be showing a lot. My Olive Oyl body is making it pretty obvious pretty fast."

"Olive Oyl. Please. Well, maybe you could take a leave of absence."

"A leave?"

"It's just a thought, but maybe you could take leave from the Beacon and just rest. You know, hang out, sleep in, watch television, go to museums, eat too much, whatever it is pregnant ladies do."

Sarah considered that.

"I might die of boredom."

"I'm pretty sure that's medically impossible."

"I'm exhausted enough lately that the idea of some time off does appeal to me," she admitted.

"Well then we'll get the paperwork filled out tomorrow," Zachary said. "And don't worry about the gossip pipeline at the paper. I'll take care of that. No one wants to mess with me."

The idea of being separated from Zachary during the day was horrible, but she could see the sense in what he was saying. She was suddenly so tired she could barely keep her eyes open. Zachary gently helped her undress and tucked her into bed, like a child.

"Goodnight, my sweetest love," he whispered, but she was already snoring.

Hanna was sitting on the window seat when Zachary came in.

"Hello, darling," she said, her eyes cool and unreadable over the top of her wine glass. Zachary could sense danger – the air was thick with it.

"Hello, darling," he echoed, crossing the room to kiss her smooth cheek.

"How was your day?" he asked, moving to the bar to pour himself a drink and to try to act normal. The feeling of unrest was palpable. It felt like a movie, with a bad guy in a black stocking cap about to jump out and bludgeon him with a baseball bat so Hanna could call the police, sobbing "Intruder!" before cashing the life insurance check and running off to Barbados with the pool boy. Good thing they didn't have a pool. He sat down on the sofa.

"So." Hanna glided across the room and sat down beside him. "When's the baby due?"

Zachary felt his heart skip. She couldn't know. She couldn't possibly know.

"What baby is that?" Zachary asked, forcing himself to sip his drink calmly. He knew Hanna could destroy him, even with something she only suspected. But her eyes were calculating, brimming with malice. She knew. For the first time in his life, Zachary Benton was afraid.

"Sarah's baby. Your baby, darling. Your little bundle of bastard."

Zachary didn't respond.

"Oh come on, Zachary. Did you think I wouldn't find out? I have eyes and ears all over this city, darling. And my friends, bless them, would do anything to protect me from a philandering husband."

Zachary met his wife's gaze levelly.

"What would you like me to say here, Hanna?"

"I don't want you to say anything. There is nothing for you to say. But I will say this, Zachary. I will not be made a fool of. And I will not lose my status as Mrs. Zachary Benton." Her eyes were winter. "At least not through a divorce."

Her meaning sliced through Zachary's muddled mind like a shard of glass and he realized his earlier fears of Hanna trying to destroy his reputation didn't even scratch the surface of what she was capable of.

My God. She's going to try and have me killed.

His blood ran cold as the end of that thought caught up with the rest of it.

Or Sarah.

Zachary stayed in his home office that night with the door locked, lying on the Corinthian leather sofa, staring out the window but seeing nothing. He wanted to call Sarah but he knew he didn't dare, not with an extension in the master bedroom. Hanna may have even had the phones tapped. He didn't know what she was capable of, but he would put nothing past her. All he knew for certain was that he couldn't put Sarah and the baby in danger.

Would Hanna actually try to have him killed? He'd heard rumblings over the years of her father's dubious business connections, and he knew his wife was cold, but was she capable of murder? As he stared out across the night sky, he remembered the look in her eyes when she'd accused him and he realized how horribly he'd underestimated Hanna all these years. She was capable of anything.

His mind went back to her father, trying to remember if he'd heard he actually had mob connections or if it had just been innuendo. If he did, Zachary had no doubt Hanna wouldn't hesitate to avail herself of their services.

He took off his glasses and pinched the bridge of his nose. He was being paranoid. It was the middle of the night and he was just being paranoid. He'd been caught in an adulterous affair. It happened all the time, to lots of people. Why did he automatically assume Hanna would have him rubbed out? It didn't make sense.

And yet it did. He could still see the look on her face. *At least not through a divorce.*

It was his selfishness that had stirred up this hornet's nest. As he'd told Sarah, he hadn't intended to cheat on Hanna at all. She had always been aloof, but part of Zachary wondered for a long time if he had made her even more that way, with all the late nights at the paper, the business calls during dinner, the work he'd bring home on the weekends. He may have never loved her, and he was equally sure that she'd never loved him, but he was in awe of her, and there was something about her he'd always rather liked. She was the right kind of wife for a newspaperman of his stature in a city like New York. She looked good beside him and was gracious and well-mannered, while remaining cool and standoffish. He never had to worry about her drinking too much gin during bridge games with her girlfriends and spilling newspaper secrets. They'd been a good match, but somewhere along the way he became less of a husband to her and more of a status symbol, and eventually he wasn't a husband at all.

Still, Zachary refused to take all of the blame. Hanna wasn't exactly warm to come home to, she never had been. She never complained about his long work hours, but instead grew increasingly distant, punishing him with long silences, closed doors, and the roadblock of her turned back when they were in bed.

The day Sarah had turned in her resignation after overhearing Zachary's stupid remark on the phone was the day he finally knew his marriage was over. Walking into the newsroom and seeing her empty desk and the look on Stan's face as he sat there with her letter of resignation in his hand was like a jolt of electricity to Zachary's heart. He hadn't felt it beating in years, and now it was racing, overcoming all his senses, shocking him with the realization that if he lost Sarah, he'd lost everything. He knew her favorite bar and he went there, never even thinking who might see him going in. He didn't care. He just had to get to her. And when they'd left together… Zachary cursed silently. It wasn't the first time he'd led with his emotions, but it was the first time in many years. This was why he'd stopped feeling and only let himself think. The brain was nowhere near as dangerous as the heart.

When he was sure Hanna must be asleep, Zachary slipped out of the brownstone and walked two blocks to a pay phone. He dialed the home number of James Brandt, the head librarian of the New York Public Library. He lit a cigarette as he listened to the interminable ringing. He was about to hang up when a groggy voice answered.

"James? It's Zachary. I need a favor."

"Zachary? What the hell? What time is it?"

"I have no idea. But I need a favor."

James, awakened from a deep sleep, rubbed a hand over his face. Finally he sat up and reached for his glasses.

"Okay, you need a favor. I know I've called in a couple to you over the years. What can I do?"

"I need to get into the library."

"What do you mean?"

"Now."

"NOW?" he glanced at the clock beside his bed. "It's two in the morning."

"It can't wait. Please, James. You know I wouldn't ask if it wasn't urgent. I need access to your microfilm."

"Son of a bitch. You can't keep normal hours."

"I can't keep normal anything."

"Fine. I'll meet you there in half an hour. Go around to the side entrance."

Zachary was already there and waiting when James came striding up.

"I don't know what's going on, Zachary, but there is literally no one except maybe the mayor I'd do this for."

Zachary clapped him on the shoulder.

"I appreciate that, old buddy. You know I wouldn't ask if it wasn't important."

James unlocked the door and locked it behind them.

"You know where everything is," he said. "I'll be in my office. Let me know when you're done."

Zachary thanked him and made his way to the row of microfilm readers. He wasn't even sure what he was looking for, which made it more difficult to find. He finally just pulled out a reel and loaded it into the machine. Six reels later, he stopped in his tracks, his eyes fixed on an archived article in the back pages of the New York Times from 20 years earlier that said Jeremy Whitcomb had been charged with racketeering.

"Money laundering, bribery, obstruction of justice…" Zachary read under his breath. He scanned the next paragraph and stopped cold. All charges had been dropped. There was no mention of why. And although he searched another dozen reels, he could find no further mention of Jeremy Whitcomb at all. Zachary slowly got to his feet, put all the reels back and shut off the lights. His hands were ice cold.

He was the first one to arrive at the newspaper office the next morning. He sat at his desk, smoking a cigarette and thinking. He'd decided during the night what they had to do, for Sarah's sake and the baby's. Now he just had to convince her.

By the time she came in, several other reporters were already at their desks. He waited for her to get settled, then picked up the phone and buzzed her extension.

"Morning, Zachary," she said. She sounded cheerful and wonderful and Zachary suddenly couldn't breathe.

"Good morning. May I see you in my office, please?"

"Uh oh. Am I in trouble?"

"Just please come now."

His terse tone was reflected in her face by the time Sarah appeared in his doorway. He motioned for her to close the door.

"We need to talk about that leave of absence you requested," he said.

"Leave of… oh right. My leave of absence."

"Sarah, listen to me. I am only going to say this once and I desperately do not want to be overheard so I'm not going to speak very loudly. Hanna knows about the baby. She confronted me last night."

"Oh my God. What happened? What did she say?"

"That's the chilling part. She wasn't angry or shouting or anything. She just sat down and calmly asked me when the baby is due. I tried to play dumb, but she called my bluff. I don't know how she knows, but she knows."

"Well, good then. You can move in with me."

"I don't think so, my love. It's too risky."

"Too risky? But Zachary, now that the secret is out, we can finally be together. There's no shame in building a life with someone you love."

Sarah was suddenly, horribly aware that she was about to cry. Damned hormones.

"No, my love, there isn't, and we will be together. But for right now, I need to make sure you are someplace safe. Hanna is, well, unstable. She said some things last night that left me convinced she may try to hurt me."

"Hurt you?" Sarah stared at him, uncomprehending, before the truth slowly dawned. "Oh my God, you mean she might try to kill you?"

"No, she would never do it herself. Too much manual labor involved."

"That isn't funny, Zachary. This isn't a joke."

"Look, I don't think she will poison my drink or suffocate me in my sleep, if that's what you're worried about. She would never do anything that could easily be tied to her. She's crazy, but she's not stupid. If anything happens to me, it'll be done by someone else, under her direction. I cannot take the chance that she'd arrange for something to happen to you and the baby as well."

Tears, fat and silent, were sliding down Sarah's face. Zachary handed her a tissue.

"Please, my love, listen to me. I was up all night thinking about it. I have a friend, an old and trusted friend, Alan Bernhardt, who will help us. I spoke to him early this morning and told him what's going on. He lives in a small town in the Midwest now, barely a dot on the map."

"The Midwest?" His point was pushing its way past Sarah's anguish.

"Oklahoma. About an hour outside Tulsa."

"You're sending me there, aren't you? You're banishing me to the middle of nowhere. Me and my baby."

Zachary could feel her anger beginning to crowd in on him.

"You're sending me away like some knocked-up teenager who has to go live with 'an aunt' until the crisis is past. Why don't you say what this is really about, Zachary? It's about me making the great Zachary Benton look bad!"

"It's not about appearances," Zachary began, but she cut him off, her anger now bubbling over.

"Yeah, bullshit. You are hoping that – what? That I'll meet some nice corn farmer and settle down and have babies and make blue ribbon-winning pies for the county fair?"

"My love, you're not listening."

"No, you're not listening. If I embarrass you that much, I can disappear on my own. I don't need-"

"Goddammit, Sarah! Listen to me!"

His outburst startled her into silence. He had never raised his voice to her. He glanced into the newsroom and saw a couple of people looking in their direction. He dropped back to a whisper.

"This isn't some kind of soap opera we're living here, some after-school special. This is real. This is real life and it's serious. Hanna is dangerous. I never would have thought it of her, but after last night, I believe – everything in me believes – that she's going to try and have me killed. She'll make it look like an accident so she can play the bereaved widow and get away with all the money, everything. I cannot run the risk of her hurting you as well."

"But I don't want anything happening to you either."

"I know, but I will be better able to catch her at this, to stop her, to bring this whole thing to a sane, rational conclusion and be free of her if I don't have the added worry of your safety. Please, my love. My friend Alan will meet you at the airport. He has a small rental house that's empty, and you can live there for now, where you'll be safe. I'll join you as soon as I can. You can rest, maybe even write that book you always talk about."

Sarah was crying. She didn't answer. Her head ached. She suddenly felt as though she were watching a movie she wasn't enjoying, about some pitiful woman who had given up everything she'd ever dreamed of to have an affair, and a baby, with someone else's husband. And now she was being exiled, sent away in disgrace, cut off from the only person who mattered to her. Something moved in her belly, as though stirred by her thoughts. She put her hand over the bump and felt a new strength slowly building inside her. Zachary wasn't the only one who mattered to her. Not anymore. She raised her head and met his pleading, distraught gaze.

"I'm going home to pack," she said quietly.

That evening, when her bags were zipped and waiting by the front door of her apartment, Sarah stood at the window, looking down on the streets of New York. She was filled with the heavy, wet feeling that comes after a bad breakup. Finally, restless, she grabbed her jacket and hurried out of the building, the urgency increasing with every step as she realized she had to say goodbye to her city. The feeling that she was never going to see any of it again wouldn't be shaken.

She walked for blocks, for miles, maybe a hundred years, she didn't know. New York at night is a completely different city than New York during the day. In the sunlight, it was postcard New York. It belonged to everyone. At night, the feeling was different, exclusive. If you were on the streets at night, you were either a very confident local or a tourist who paid too much for theater tickets. Sarah walked, breathing it in, memorizing every lamppost, every brownstone, every bad parking job. She ran her fingertips along railings, the tops of garbage cans, the ragged fluttery notices stapled to utility poles.

She realized simultaneously that she was exhausted and also insanely far from her apartment. In her last goodbye to her beloved city, she descended into the nearest subway station. She had always loved the subway, much to the chagrin of her Connecticut friends, who were constantly expecting to hear that she'd been mugged by a thug or flashed by a pervert or both.

She found it interesting, the way the subway worked. Not the electricity of it, nor the detailed system of underground tunnels that spread out under the city like some kind of rat-filled, vibrating bedrock, not even how fast it moved. Those were engineering details that held no particular fascination for her. What she found interesting were the details inside the subway cars. Everyone at any given time who was riding the subway had one thing in common: they were going someplace else.

But didn't that hold true of anyone she saw out and about, riding on a crosstown bus or in the back of a taxi? No, that was different. There was a freedom in getting around above ground, an openness. You could wave to people outside as the sunshine gathered extra warmth from the window glass before settling on your arms and your face. Hi guys! Look at me! On the bus! To walk down the steps into the rank-breathed mouth of the subway was to surrender to the underworld of the transportation industry. It was dark, dank, and moody, like the graduate student she once dated who smoked clove cigarettes and wore turtlenecks and a beret relentlessly. To ride the subway was to make the conscious decision to step down, to where the only ones who could see you were the others who had made the same decision.

Yet she rode the subway every day. From the first day she'd moved to the city, she knew that her overpriced and undersized address in Greenwich Village would only get her so far. If she wanted to be a real New Yorker, she had no choice but to step down. Taxis and buses were for tourists and locals who lacked imagination. The subway was for hard-core New Yorkers, who got on and off the trains with a bored expression, if they even looked up from their book at all, and never trailed a finger over the colored lines on the map or strained to hear what the conductor said. They just knew. They always knew. Ask any New Yorker on the street what subway to take to Times Square, or Battery Park, or Junior's Cheesecake, and they'd rattle it all off, including any place where you'd have to change trains, without hesitation.

Instead of finding this intimidating when she'd first moved to the city, she'd been intrigued. She wanted to learn this language, to crack their code. For awhile, it didn't seem she ever would, but one day she found herself getting on the train and getting off four stops later without thinking about it. She'd become fluent when she wasn't paying attention.

Riding the subway was hardcore. It was about getting from one place to another without seeing anything along the way apart from aged tiles flashing past in the cracked yellow light. Sometimes the cars were virtually empty, but during rush hour people were pressed against each other, feet dovetailing together, bodies bumping, hands jockeying for pole space, armpits swaying closer to faces than faces would be comfortable with in any other setting. But on the subway, it was just a fact of life. Even the times the train would abruptly stop and go dark, everyone mentally shrugged and waited it out.

Coming up from the subway always made her feel like a mole, surfacing, blinking, trying to get her bearings and familiarize herself again with everything she'd left behind just moments before. She'd jumped on a blind bullet that transported her to another part of the city and anyone who didn't find that fascinating was, as far as she was concerned, missing a vital point New York was always trying to make about what it really is, underneath.

With a final glance around, Sarah said her silent goodbye and went back into her apartment to wait for Zachary.

Chapter 13

They spent their last night together in Sarah's bed, making desperate, anguished love. Zachary wept like a child as she held him. Not for the last time, he cursed his weakness at getting all of them into this situation. How could the most powerful, most respected newspaperman in the country be so stupid as to let his prick make the decisions?

But as he looked down into Sarah's lovely, open face, resting in the crook of his arm, he knew it had never been physical. Not really. Making love to her had, from the first time, been about far more than sex. He hadn't even wanted to touch her, that first night, for fear of shattering the gossamer veil of perfection his heart had wrapped her in. She was more than a woman to him, more than an employee, more than someone whose work he respected. She had started out as all of those things, but somewhere along the way, she had slipped into another level of his being, touching him in places he hadn't known existed – tiny, dim corners of his soul where he had long ago stored the bits of him that mattered, a few key pieces of his puzzle that he kept hidden, saving himself for who or what, he was never sure. But Sarah had found them, dusted them off, finished the puzzle before Zachary even knew what had happened. It wasn't that she made him feel young – it was far more than that. She made him feel possible again. Facing himself now, whole and complete, he knew he would never be able to repay all she had given back to him.

"This is more than love," he whispered into her hair. "This is everything."

The wheels of the plane moved up and locked into place. Sarah leaned back and closed her eyes, trying to keep the tears tucked safely away. She knew she was doing the best thing for herself, for her baby, and for Zachary. He had helped her into a cab early that morning, while it was still dark, minimizing the risk of anyone seeing her. It seemed to Sarah an unnecessary precaution as her taking a cab from her own apartment wasn't likely to raise any suspicions, but she had never seen Zachary so fraught with fear and worry.

"Come with me," she begged as they waited for the cab in the dim light of her apartment.

"I will come as soon as I can," he promised, holding her hand as though it were the last vestige of hope he had in the world. "I am going to talk to my lawyer about what to do about this situation with Hanna, and as soon as it's all settled and I feel it's safe, I will fly out to you. I'll be there before the baby is born and we can start our life, start our family."

"You cry more than I do lately," Sarah teased gently, handing him a tissue, though her own eyes were wet.

"I know," he said, wiping his face and putting his glasses back on. "Thanks for all these feelings. Very convenient."

She smiled faintly to herself now, remembering. In an odd way, she was looking forward to this new chapter. The idea of them raising their baby far from the steely, impersonal gaze of New York City appealed to her in a way she found more than a little surprising. Maybe she would learn to bake pies. And sew. Images of farm-grown apples and little baby overalls lulled her to sleep. The stewardess, approaching with the beverage cart, noticed the bump of Sarah's belly pushing against the seatbelt and, smiling, let her sleep.

Chapter 14

"Sarah?" A voice found her through the noise of the crowded airport. She glanced around and saw a sandy-haired man with a kind, worn face smiling at her. He held out his hand.

"Hi, I'm Alan Bernhardt."

"Oh! Alan! Yes, hi. I'm sorry, I was just… I don't know. Looking for someone with a sign, I think, like a limo driver. "

"I didn't need it," he said with a smile. "Zachary described you perfectly, even if I hadn't seen your picture in the papers when you won the Pulitzer."

Sarah laughed, flattered.

"Oh, well in that case, uh, thanks."

"Zachary told me he's shipping your things to you, so I assume this is your only bag?"

"Yes, just my carry-on. He's shipping everything else out to me today."

They crossed the parking lot to Alan's waiting truck. It was muggy in Tulsa, and for a moment, the heat from the pavement and the city rising around them like a painted backdrop made Sarah's heart ache for New York.

"We've got a pretty good ride out to your new place," he said. "So just let me know if you need to stop or anything." He couldn't help glancing down at her belly. When he realized what he'd done, he looked away, embarrassed. Sarah smiled.

"Don't worry, it's okay," she said, settling back into the seat.

Alan kept up a lighthearted chatter on the drive out of the city, and Sarah was grateful. She didn't feel much like talking, but he didn't seem to mind her truncated, quiet answers, although she did her best to be affable.

"Zachary told you our story," she said at one point, dropping the sentence somewhere between a statement and a question. "He said he trusts you."

"He did, and he can. So can you. Zachary and I have been friends since college. I'd kill for him, and he'd do the same for me."

"You seem so different from each other."

Alan laughed comfortably.

"Zachary's all hard New York glitz. I'm a country boy now, but I haven't always been. I was born and raised in Los Angeles, and I lived for awhile in New York. I came out here one Christmas to meet my girlfriend's parents, and before I knew it, she'd put a ring on my finger and had me sitting on a tractor in the middle of a corn field."

Sarah smiled and shook her head.

"Love catches you off guard sometimes," she agreed.

"That it does."

Dolly Parton sang quietly from the truck's radio. Sarah leaned back and looked out the window at the rolling fields and shimmering flat stretches of highway. It was easy, on the insulated island of New York, to forget what the rest of the world looked like, or that there even was a rest of the world. The prairie slipped past, endless, with only dirt roads and irrigation systems to break up the monotony of the fields. They were mesmerizing in their sameness, perfectly even rows of crops smoothing away the rough edges of Sarah's psyche caused by the slow erosion from within of the belief that people were basically good and that everything was going to turn out fine. Somewhere in her career, she'd begun to see only the bad, the deceptive, the shards of negativity and anger and selfishness that lurk just behind everyone's eyes, no matter how normal and kind they seem on the surface. The danger is always there. Anyone is capable of anything.

Only when she fell in love with Zachary did Sarah begin to rediscover her primal belief in goodness. There was an openness, a purity about Zachary, a gentle strength that reminded her of a giant redwood, mighty, strong, unyielding, unending. She saw something in the depths of Zachary's eyes she'd never seen in another, yet always felt she'd been seeking. She had stumbled upon a secret garden, untrodden, unspoiled, planted so many years ago with the intention of being shared yet remaining hidden, undiscovered, until she opened the gate. Some mistook his ethics and fairness for weakness, but nobody ever made that mistake twice. Zachary Benton was nobody's doormat. Sarah got a particularly heady joy from watching him at work, powerful newspaper-man Zachary, then a matter of hours later, seeing gentle, tender Zachary as she lay in his arms. He was an inexhaustible delight to Sarah, and the missing him was suddenly so intense that for a moment she couldn't hear what Alan was saying.

"I'm sorry, what?"

"Here's your new hometown."

He gestured out the windshield of the truck at a sign that said "Welcome to Greenview! Home of the Warriors!"

Dear God, Sarah thought as loudly as she dared. The town was right out of a Faulkner novel, all tidy lawns and pretty houses, neighbors chatting over fences, ice cream parlors and locally owned hardware stores. Even the traffic lights seemed to blink calmly: Reckon y'all can go ahead and cross if you'd like.

Alan turned down a lovely street lined with mature oak and cottonwood trees, then pulled the truck to a stop in front of a small house. It was tidy and white, with a small lawn and a neatly edged sidewalk. A quaintly weathered rocking chair on the porch and a window box exploding with pink and white flowers completed the picture.

It was ghastly. Sarah had a sudden impulse to turn and run all the way back to New York, pie recipes and gingham dress patterns in her wake. Alan was watching her, an expectant smile on his face.

"It's lovely," she managed, just as the front door opened and a smiling woman in blue shorts and an American flag t-shirt came out, waving.

"Oh, there's Maggie," Alan said. "That's my wife. She's been in there cleaning and getting it ready for you."

Sarah opened the door and stepped out of the truck and into the hot Oklahoma summer. New York had been hot, but this was beyond hot.

This was trying to kill her, she was certain of it. The heat radiated up from the ground and swallowed her whole. Her cotton shirt and bohemian skirt were already sticking to her skin, and she could feel the sweat pooling in her bra. Her feet felt enormous in her sandals. The direct sun slowly and deliberately touched her head, as though trying to decide whether or not to go ahead and set it on fire. A random blast of prairie wind whipped her skirts around, stinging her legs with little bits of grit.

"Welcome to Oklahoma!" Maggie said with a laugh, shielding her eyes. "Come on inside and we can talk."

Sarah followed her in while Alan pulled her bag out of the truck. She felt better the moment she stepped under one of the huge, shady trees, and better still once she was in the cool, clean little house.

"It's great to finally meet you, Sarah," Maggie said, hugging her as though they were old friends. "It's so exciting, having a celebrity living in our little rental here."

Sarah laughed awkwardly.

"I'm nowhere near a celebrity," she said. "But thank you."

"Well, I don't recollect we've ever had any Pulitzer Prize winners from Greenview," Maggie said. "So that's close enough to celebrity for me."

"This house is really adorable," Sarah said, partly to change the subject and partly because she really was beginning to like it a bit now that she was inside.

"Oh, thanks," Maggie said. "We bought it a few years ago. Alan fixes it up between renters, but we've been real lucky. No one has trashed it yet."

"So I'll be the first," Sarah joked.

Maggie looked startled.

"I'm kidding," Sarah said. "I'm too tired to even think lately, much less trash anything."

"Yes, I heard you're expecting," Maggie voice dropped to a whisper on the last word, as though they were sharing an exciting secret.

"Yes, I am," Sarah whispered back, patting her belly.

"That's wonderful. Children are a real blessing. Now let me show you around right quick and then we can have some iced tea."

The tour took all of about two minutes as the house was truly tiny, but Sarah had to admit it was very cute. Still, she felt as though she'd landed in a galaxy light years from New York. Maggie showed her the bedroom, with lacy white curtains and a surprisingly big bed covered with a white chenille spread. The bathroom had a clawfoot bathtub with a shower, and the kitchen was small but fully furnished with a stove, refrigerator, and dishwasher, all in modern harvest gold. A percolator stood near a gleaming toaster, and Sarah wondered for a moment if they'd bought all these things new just for her. A lump crawled up her throat and she cleared it as she reached for Maggie's hand and gave it a squeeze. She was suddenly grateful for these people, for the way they wanted to help her, to shelter her, to take care of her. Maggie, seeming to understand, squeezed back.

"Now why don't you go sit in the living room where it's cool and I'll get us some tea," she said. "I made it this morning. It's sun tea. Is that all right with you?"

"Yes, that sounds great," Sarah said, sinking back into the sofa and wondering what sun tea was. A small air conditioner hummed busily in the window and she kicked off her sandals and felt herself starting to relax. Maggie came in with two glasses of iced tea and handed one to Sarah before sitting down in the other end of the sofa.

"So how was your flight?"

"Good. It was good. I'm afraid I slept for most of it."

"Is it easy to sleep on a plane? I've always wondered."

"You've never flown?" Sarah wasn't sure she understood.

"Nope, never. Whenever we'd go on vacation with the kids, we'd always go camping, or drive down to Six Flags Over Texas, a couple of times we went out to Wyoming to stay with some of my cousins who have a ranch there, but no, we've never flown anywhere."

Sarah felt as thought she'd gone through a wormhole.

"Of course, you probably fly a lot, with your job and all," Maggie said.

"Actually, no. Not really. All I cover for the paper is New York City, so now that I think about it, I don't really fly that much at all. We did when we were younger, though. My parents liked San Francisco so we flew out there a fair amount, wine country and all that. And to Disney, of course." Her voice trailed off as she realized she was probably sounding like a privileged snob. But Maggie just looked delighted.

"Wow, that's really something," she said. "Maybe one of these days, I'll talk Alan into taking the grandkids to Disney."

"Who's going to Disney?" Alan asked, coming in the door with Sarah's bag. Setting it on the floor, he pushed his baseball cap back from his forehead and, taking a big blue handkerchief out of his back pocket, wiped his face with it before stuffing it back into his pocket and settling the cap back firmly on his head. It was almost a choreographed movement, fluid and smooth. Sarah was mesmerized. It was hard to imagine him ever living in New York, or Los Angeles for that matter. He seemed to belong here, to have always belonged here.

"I was just telling Sarah maybe one of these days we'd take the grandkids to Disney," Maggie said. "Where've you been?"

"Oh, I was talking to Harold," Alan said. "He was showing me his new riding lawnmower."

"What on earth does he need a riding lawnmower for? His lawn's the size of a postage stamp."

"I know it. Not to mention his fat ass could use a good waddle around the yard now and then."

"Alan, what a thing to say," Maggie said, glancing at Sarah.

"Oh yes, I'm deeply offended. No one ever says unkind things about anyone else in New York," Sarah said.

They both laughed, and Maggie went to get Alan some tea.

"Now," Alan said, settling into the armchair. "There's just a couple of things we want to make sure you know."

Sarah nodded, unsure of what to expect.

"First of all, you're safe here. This town is quiet, sheltered, friendly, and the only crime is that danged riding lawn mower of Harold's. He lives next door, by the way, and is a real nice guy. That's the other thing I want to tell you. Nobody here knows your name, where you're from, or who you are. Just Maggie and me, and we haven't told a soul. We figured you could tell people as much or as little as you want, but given that Zachary is a little concerned about you being located, I might suggest you not give your real name. Just keep Maggie and me in the loop about what you tell people, so we can make sure our stories match if anyone asks us anything."

Sarah again had the odd sense she was watching a movie about someone else's life. She was a Pulitzer Prize winning journalist, a New York City girl, a tough cookie. What was she doing sitting on a sofa in Greenview, Oklahoma, barefoot and pregnant, drinking some kind of tea she didn't understand and trying to decide on an alias?

"You can keep to yourself as much as you like, but this town doesn't get a lot of new people," Maggie said. "So I'm sure word is already getting around that there's someone new here. Oh, also Alan put a bicycle in the back for you to use. It's a decent bike, it belonged to our daughter before she went away to college and insisted she needed four wheels instead of two. But you can use it to get around wherever you want to go, although you could also walk anywhere. It's a pretty small town. There's a grocery store, a drug store, and a dry cleaners right on Main Street – you just go out your front door here and make a left and it's at the end of this street."

"We came in on Main Street," Alan added.

"Oh, right, sure you did," Maggie said. "That's good then, you've already seen it. The library is about four blocks that way," she pointed. "And there are three pretty big churches not too far away either, if you're a church person."

She didn't wait for an answer, to Sarah's relief.

"Also, if there's anything you find around here that needs doing, just give me a holler," Alan said. "I own a little construction company, and if I can't get over here and you need something quick, one of my boys will take care of it."

"Now," Maggie said, with the air of really getting down to the important business. "The women in town are kind of nosy."

"Yeah, kind of," Alan said with a snort.

"Oh, shush. I just want her to know. Now when people notice your condition," she patted her own belly, "you might hear some gossip about nobody ever seeing your husband around. You handle that however you want. This isn't the 50's anymore. It's 1968 and people need to get with the times. You don't owe anybody an explanation but, like Alan said, whatever you tell people, just let us know so we can back you up."

They were both looking at her with wide, smooth faces, lined by the prairie sun but uncreased by guilt or guile. They were so nice, and she realized in a rush that she felt safe for the first time in a long time. She felt tears prickle at her eyes and she cleared her throat.

"I don't know how to thank you," she said. "I'm just so grateful."

She started to cry and Maggie leaned over and put her arms around her.

"It's all right, honey," she said. "We're your friends now. You'll always have us in your corner."

Chapter 15

Zachary lay on Sarah's bed long after she left, holding her pillow tight against his face. He knew it wouldn't be long before they could be together for good, but he couldn't help feeling a deep, aching sense of loss, and of dread. Part of it, he knew, was the ordeal he was about to face with Hanna, but the emptiness, the feeling that everything inside him had ceased to exist, was all Sarah. He finally got up before he cried himself to sleep like a brokenhearted teenager. He showered and dressed, then rang her doorman with instructions for shipping her boxes to her Oklahoma address and a request for a taxi. When the doorman buzzed to say the cab had arrived, Zachary gave him an obscenely large tip with his thanks for the man's discretion, then slipped out the door and into the cab with a practiced fluidity. He knew it was risky, leaving Sarah's apartment building in broad daylight, but he wasn't sure Hanna would have been able to arrange for surveillance so quickly. Or maybe she could. He was really beyond giving a damn at this point.

When he arrived at the paper, he shut himself up in his office so he could think. The first thing to do would be to call a staff meeting to explain Sarah's departure. No, a staff meeting was making too big a deal out of it. He'd be better off telling a couple of people and letting the word get around. No, that was dangerous. For a group of professional communicators, this bunch had an insane knack for turning office gossip into a birthday party game of Telephone. A staff meeting was really the only way. Okay, a staff meeting it would be. He'd call it for right after deadline, and he'd tell them … what? That Sarah was ill. That she'd been feeling unwell and went to stay with relatives until she … got better? The doctor had ordered her to a warmer climate to cure her … tuberculosis? God, everything that came to mind made her sound like a Dickens orphan. He'd have to tell them she quit. She quit and moved away to deal with a family issue. They could speculate all they wanted – they would anyway – but if he said it was a private issue with Sarah's family, they wouldn't press him for details.

He picked up the phone on his desk and buzzed Stan.

"Please notify the news staff I want to meet with everyone as soon as the paper has been put to bed," Zachary said. "It will only take a few minutes."

He could hear the curiosity in Stan's voice, but the editor didn't ask for details and Zachary didn't offer them. No one ever really panicked unless they got called into his office alone. A staff meeting offered the safety of numbers. After he spoke to Stan, he called his lawyer.

"Frank, it's Zachary Benton. Start your meter, buddy, I'm about to make you filthy fucking rich."

"Do you want to come in and see me?"

"Eventually yes. But right now it needs to be over the phone. I have a staff meeting soon. I just need to get you working on this."

He spilled out the whole story, relieved to be free of the burden and under the safety net of attorney-client privilege.

"My God," Frank said. Zachary could hear him take a cigarette out of the case he kept on his desk and light it. "My God."

"So I need your advice. I need to know what I can do to protect myself, both physically and financially, from Hanna. It's a mess, I know it is. We're still living in the same house. We're still married. Maybe I should move out."

"Don't move out," Frank said. "Honestly, stay where you are. Since you're asking my advice, the best thing you could do right this moment is go home, apologize to her, tell her the whole thing's off with Sarah. Tell her Sarah skipped town, you don't know where she went, tell her whatever you want, but tell her it's over with Sarah and that you want to work it out with her."

"I'm not sure she'll believe me."

"Stop thinking like an honest newsman and be an actor, for shit's sake. You have to make her believe you're on the straight and narrow, then pray to God she doesn't try to have you bumped off. Right now, the best thing you can do to protect Sarah and yourself is to ooze remorse from every pore."

Zachary lit a cigarette of his own and rubbed his eyes.

"Ultimately, I want to get a divorce, and a restraining order if I need it. Then I want to go to Sarah and be with her when the baby is born. It doesn't give us much time, she's already almost into her second trimester."

"It gives us enough time, but just. You need to start this making amends thing tonight. Do you hear me? Tonight."

"Okay," Zachary said. "Okay, yeah. I'll do it. I'll do it tonight."

"After things die down a little, come in and see me and we'll figure out the next steps."

"Just a couple of quick things and I'll let you get back to work," Zachary said, surveying the small sea of faces around the conference room table. "First of all, that the New York Press Association awards are coming up, so anything you want entered needs to be to Stan by the end of the month. Second, the janitor has asked me to remind you all yet again to stop throwing half full paper cups of coffee into your trash cans. Seriously, people, that's disgusting. Don't let me get that complaint anymore or I'll make you drink it. Those of you who float your cigarette butts in your old coffee are in for a real treat. And lastly, Sarah Thomas has asked me to tell you all goodbye for her as she had to leave us rather suddenly to attend to some family matters."

A rumble went around the room.

"I know, I know," Zachary said, holding up one hand. "I told her she will always have a job here and she said she'd let us know when and if she is able to come back. But for now, that's the status. Stan will be talking with a couple of you later today about taking over what she was working on."

When the meeting was over and his mumbling staff had shuffled back to the newsroom, Zachary sank down into a conference room chair and scrubbed his hands over his face.

"Mr. Benton, who do you want me to put on the city hall beat?"

He hadn't even realized Stan was still in the room.

"Oh, Stan. Right. Uh… let me think. I don't know. I don't honestly know. Who would you recommend?"

"Well, just off the top of my head I was thinking Rick."

"Rick it is," Zachary said, lightly slapping his hands on the top of the table to try and disguise the fact that he wasn't sure who Rick was. Good God, how out of touch had he gotten with his own paper? "An excellent choice. I can't believe I didn't think of Rick myself right off the bat."

"She hadn't started any new features yet, so I think we're good on everything else," Stan said, consulting the notebook in his hand. "I was really only concerned about city hall."

Zachary wished city hall was his only concern. He glanced at his watch and decided to try and write an editorial before the day was out. He needed to focus. He needed to start paying attention to his paper again. He needed to maintain his status as the most respected newspaperman in New York. He needed to find out who the hell Rick was.

When he pulled his car into a parking spot near his brownstone that night, Zachary sat for a moment, thinking. A bottle of champagne and a dozen long-stemmed red roses, fresh from the florist, lay on the seat beside him. He hated everything he was about to do, hated it with every part of his soul that had the capability of feeling hate, yet he knew he had no choice. He'd painted himself into a corner and now all he could do was wait for things to dry so he could make his escape. The worst part was that he not only felt trapped and angry, he felt guilty. Horribly, heavily, overwhelmingly guilty. The Zachary Benton everyone found morally infallible had cheated on his wife with a woman he worked with and got caught. It was a cliché of the worst kind, and he'd done it. He was in for the fight of his life to keep the story from spreading around New York, and right now he wasn't even sure he had the strength to face his wife.

Chapter 16

Headlights on the dark wall defied the expensive drapes and played a silent, plotless movie for Hanna as she lay awake beside Zachary, sleeping with his back to her. She didn't need to turn to look at him, she knew what she'd see: the curve of his arm, the odd little bump he had right where his arm met his shoulder, his head resting on the indent in his pillow. Even his breathing was familiar to her. She knew just how asleep he was by how deeply he was breathing, and the precise moment when a snore was imminent.

She'd felt empty since the day she had found out about Sarah's pregnancy, as though her spirit had quietly departed, leaving her to contend with the shell. The shell that had to be washed and dressed and fed no matter how little she felt like it. Food in particular had become a daily ordeal. She ate very little but drank a lot of wine. So much wine, but somehow it was never enough to render her as numb as she wanted. She'd considered switching to vodka but she instinctively knew it wouldn't get the job done either. She'd lost weight and scarcely slept, lying awake for long stretches every night, wondering how Zachary could have betrayed her as he had. She never would have dreamed that the upright, ethically celebrated Zachary Benton would ever cheat on her like this. She knew she'd never really loved him, but she'd liked him. Even more than that, she'd trusted him. She enjoyed being Mrs. Benton, going to the press club and all the city's most prestigious events and always getting the best table at restaurants while others stood in line outside. Although she didn't know for certain, she suspected he'd had bar room encounters with other women, as most of her friends' husbands had, but they were nameless and faceless, and she knew in her gut that if he had, he'd been discreet and never seen the same woman twice. Until Sarah. Until perfect, lovely Sarah, who connected with Zachary in a way that Hanna never could, Sarah who not only understood his drive but shared it, Sarah who was the only real threat to Hanna and the perfect world she'd built around herself.

Since Sarah had gone away to God knew where and Zachary had assured her it was all over, he had been attempting to make amends, bringing her gifts, coming home early some nights, even trying, in a fumbling and oddly pubescent way, to make love to her. That one she'd nipped in the bud – the thought of his hands on that reporter made Hanna's skin crawl – but the rest of the time she accepted his overtures if not exactly warmly at least decently and with grace. She needed him to stay, at least until she figured out what to do.

She had been completely serious when she told Zachary she would never agree to a divorce. Her status as the unofficial First Lady of New York gave her an inordinate amount of satisfaction and the fact that Zachary was a respected journalist gave her, she privately felt, a considerable edge over her political counterparts. Their husbands were always getting caught in financial schemes and sex scandals, but Zachary was seen as being above the fray, holding himself to a higher standard.

Hanna turned her gaze toward her sleeping husband and finally admitted to herself that she could actually kill him for this.

Book Two
Sarah

Chapter 17

The prairie wind whipped grit against Sarah's legs as though trying to get her attention as she walked downtown to her doctor's appointment. Maggie had recommended Dr. Weatherby, who had delivered her own four kids.

"He's getting a little long in the tooth, but he's still a heck of a good doctor," she had assured Sarah. "And he'll keep everything quiet. Nobody in town's gonna know your business."

Of course, that would be seriously unethical, Sarah thought, *and I'm pretty sure Dr. Weatherby knows that.* But she'd just smiled and thanked Maggie for her help, not wanting to shatter the obvious pride she took in her good old doc.

Sarah had worked out her story shortly after her arrival in Oklahoma a few weeks earlier, although she'd kept to herself so much she rarely had to use it. She told anyone she needed to that her name was Sarah Adams and that her family and Maggie's were old friends from way back, she had no family, her husband was on active military duty, and she was staying in the Bernhardts' rental home so she could have some privacy but not be totally alone. It was a simple story, direct and with enough of that down-home feel about it that Sarah was pretty sure no one would question it. Alan and Maggie agreed when she told them. She had considered using a different first name for added security, but she was afraid she wouldn't remember to respond when someone addressed her, and she knew her acting skills weren't good enough to pull off a hard of hearing act.

"Please have a seat and fill these out," the receptionist said when Sarah approached the desk to give her name. She handed her some papers clamped onto a battered clip board. Sarah took a pen from the cup and sat down in the dark-paneled waiting room.

Name. Address. Date of birth. Only her birthday looked familiar to Sarah as her pen moved down the form. Pregnant Sarah Adams lived at 126 Apple Blossom Street in Greenview, Oklahoma. Sarah Thomas lived in a New York City high-rise and wrote for the Beacon.

Sarah suddenly missed Zachary so much she couldn't breathe. Alan had let Zachary know she had arrived safely and had given him the phone number at Sarah's house. He had called a few times, his low furtive voice making him feel even further away. Yet he had assured her repeatedly of his love and that he'd be flying out to join her as soon as possible. His fear of Hanna finding her had begun to seep into the usually fearless Sarah. She felt oddly exposed anywhere she went, even here in Greenview, as though at any moment Hanna could pop out from behind a bush and take her down. She knew the biggest slice of fear she felt was a mirror of Zachary's own, because in quiet moments in her house, she felt sheltered, as though she'd found a dry cave in the middle of a monsoon. After she'd been in Oklahoma for a few weeks, she'd come into her house, close and lock the door behind her, and immediately feel wrapped in a feeling of safety. No one knew where she was. No one could find her. She was safe, here with her baby, the little boy she had already named Dax.

"Sarah Adams?" The nurse's crisp voice called. "Dr. Weatherby will see you now."

Sarah hoisted herself out of her chair, in that way she'd always hated seeing pregnant women hoist themselves, as though getting out of a chair was the single most taxing thing in the world, like they were qualifying for the Olympic hoisting team. And now here she was. Hoisting.

The nurse showed Sarah into a smaller room. She climbed up on the exam table to wait, wondering why she always felt like a child again at the doctor's office. A mix of fear, anxiety and excitement always started percolating inside her the minute she got up on the crinkly-papered exam table. When she was a child, she used to think that maybe the doctor would find something horribly, exotically wrong with her. Maybe he'd tell her that she had acute rheumaflipadipahemotitis, or worse. On the other hand, he might tell her that she was the single most perfect specimen of humanity he had ever seen, and if she didn't mind waiting, he wanted to call all of his doctor friends to come take a look at her. Sarah smiled to herself and stroked her belly.

"I don't know what he'll say about me, Dax, but I know he'll say that you are perfect."

She felt the baby stir, as she often did when she spoke to him. She closed her eyes and leaned back, stroking her belly and humming softly.

"That's a nice tune." Dr. Weatherby's voice from the doorway made her jump. She laughed and blushed a little.

"Somewhere along the line, I started singing to him," she admitted. "He's really active in there, and it seems to calm him down."

Dr. Weatherby's kindly old face crinkled into a smile.

"So you think it's a boy?"

"I just kind of feel like it is, yeah. I've named him Dax."

"Dax? That's unique."

"It means 'leader.' Of course now that I'm attached to his name, I'll be wrong and it will be a girl."

"A lot of mothers have a strong intuition about their baby's gender, and more often than not, they're right," he said, opening her file. "So let's assume you are too and find out more about you and your little dude." He clicked his pen. "How far along are you?"

"A little over twelve weeks, I think."

"Have you been sick?"

"A little at first. Not as much now. Sometimes I'm tired, but other times I have these weird surges of energy. The heat really gets to me, though."

"Ah, welcome to summer in Oklahoma. Just wait til tornado season. Then we'll have us some fun."

After he had checked all her vitals and seemed satisfied, he sat down again, made a few notes in her file, then clapped his hands and rubbed them together.

"Well, everything seems normal. What do you say we take a listen to the heartbeat?"

Sarah smiled faintly, her mind running madly in a circle. She'd always imagined her husband with her at this moment, her hand in his while they waited, expectantly, excitedly, breath-holdingly. But she was alone. And she knew, deep in her heart, that she was going to be alone for awhile. The baby moved, as if sensing her thoughts.

She looked up, meeting Dr. Weatherby's kindly gaze.

"Yes," she said, forcing a smile. "Let's hear that heartbeat."

Sarah lay back on the exam table while the doctor put his stethoscope into his ears. He lifted her shirt and pressed the cold metal sensor against her belly, moving it around a bit until he stopped, his face intent.

"There it is." Dr. Weatherby's face was as delighted as if it were the first time he was hearing this miracle. "Listen to that little ticker go!"

Sarah blinked away tears, watching the doctor's face as though it were a direct link to her baby, bringing her the message that everything was all right, that everything was perfect.

"I can't be positive, of course, but I'd say your instinct is right," Dr. Weatherby said, moving the stethoscope a bit. "The heartbeat is a bit slower, which usually means it's a boy. Female hearts tend to beat faster." He straightened and smiled at her, draping the stethoscope back around his neck.

"Well, I'd say everything is shipshape for you and your little one," he said, writing something in her chart. "Come back in a month and we'll check up on you again." He laid a comforting, warm hand on Sarah's belly. Sarah felt Dax react with a jerk and a kick.

"Wow, you don't often feel a baby move that much this soon," he said. "He's a lively one. I'd say you're going to have your hands mighty full with him."

Zachary sat at his desk, his head in his hands. He had a staff meeting in twenty minutes and he could barely function. Sleep was something he'd forgotten how to do since Sarah left. He couldn't stop thinking about her, wondering how she was feeling, aching with the knowledge that their baby was growing every day and he wasn't there to see it. He glanced at his watch and picked up the phone. Her voice on the other end was sleepy. He always forgot the time difference.

"Good morning, my sweet love."

"Zachary!" Her voice was instantly awake. "Oh my God, my love, I miss you so much!" She laughed and then started to cry. Her tumultuous rush of emotions brought tears to Zachary's own eyes.

"It's good to hear your voice, my love," he said, trying to keep his own voice steady. "I don't want to stay on the phone long since a big long distance call to Oklahoma will cause questions in accounting, but I had to touch you in any way I could. I miss you too, my Sarah."

"I'm so glad you called. Every day there is so much – so many things I want to tell you, to share with you..." her voice trailed off.

"How are you feeling?"

"Not too bad. I have a lot of energy during the day, although the heat gets to me sometimes. At night I'm exhausted. This is one big kid you gave me to haul around. But I'm not sick anymore, so things are okay. The doctor says we are both healthy and fine."

Zachary brushed away tears with an impatient hand. The last thing he needed was to walk into a staff meeting looking like he'd been crying. He listened to her chatter about her new life for as long as he could, resenting the hell out of his watch and how fast it suddenly seemed to be turning.

"I've got to run, my love. I will call again in a couple of days. I love you, my Sarah."

"I love you, my forever," she answered softly. "Across every mile."

Zachary hung up, feeling better for having heard her voice, and worse for missing her. He reached into his desk drawer for aspirin, swallowed three with a sip of tepid coffee and, taking a deep breath, strode into the conference room. Most of the staff was already seated around the conference table, drinking coffee and talking. A couple of the usual latecomers slid in behind him.

"Okay, gang, I want to keep this brief today as I know we've all got a lot going on," Zachary said. "Who's working on what? Scott?"

"Following up on a couple of cop shop stories and trying to get ahold of that coach out in Staten Island, the one that girl says fondled her."

"Good luck with that," Stan said. "He won't talk. Not if he's smart."

"What part of 'coach from Staten Island' don't you understand?" Scott asked to a rumble of laughter around the table.

"What else?" Zachary said. "Denise?"

"I'm working on two big features, one for Sunday on the new curriculum at Southside Junior High. It's been pretty controversial."

"Good. And the other?"

"Going on a ride-along with a cop who's assigned to keep an eye on protestors."

Zachary turned to Stan.

"That should be your Sunday feature."

"Assuming anything happens," Stan answered.

"Listen, I can't walk to the corner for a goddamned cup of coffee anymore without running into some kind of protest," Zachary shot back. "I think it's safe to say she'll get something. Could be a hell of a feature. Nice job. What else? Jason? What have you got cooking in sports?"

"Giants pre-season stuff. I got a couple of stringers shaking the bushes for some high school stuff. 'Bout it."

"Great. City hall? Rick?"

"I've got an interview lined up with Mayor Lindsay on the teachers' strike. He hasn't been willing to go on the record until now but his office said he's ready to talk and wants us to have it first."

"Excellent. Great work. This all sounds good, gang. Anyone have any questions or need anything before we wrap this up?"

Murmurs to the negative bubbled through the room before Zachary heard Rick's voice again.

"Mr. Benton, when is Sarah coming back? Any word?"

It was a left-hook question that caught Zachary completely off guard. He felt the back of his neck get hot as he realized he had already hesitated a fraction too long.

"I haven't heard from her," he said. "But when I do, I'll find out what her plans are and keep you all informed."

Back at his desk a few minutes later, Rick glanced around before picking up his phone and dialing quickly.

"It's me," he said in a low voice. "He has definitely been in touch with her."

Chapter 18

She couldn't believe she had ever considered August in New York to be hot, Sarah thought as she walked through Greenview's small downtown. New York's got nothing on Oklahoma. At this point she was starting to think the surface of the sun had nothing on Oklahoma. Yet another gust of hot prairie wind whipped around her illustratively. She missed walking through Midtown, the cool bursts of air rushing out to meet her every time someone exited a building.

More every day, Sarah felt as if she were in a perpetual state of suspended animation, wedged into the narrow gap between who she used to be and who she was still to be. Part of her was starting to really like Oklahoma and her quiet, sheltered life in Greenview. Her friendship with Maggie had grown into a genuine love, and she felt protected and cared for by her and Alan. She'd gotten to know most of her neighbors, and despite her initial reservations, now found herself wearing hand-me-down maternity outfits from the woman next door, and six extra pounds' worth of Midwestern cooking courtesy of one across the street and three down the block. When they had all gotten together and decided Sarah wasn't feeding herself properly she wasn't sure, but apparently they had as casseroles, zucchini breads, Crock Pots leaden with the weight of soup and chicken and baked beans, glass bowls full of bean dip, and vinegar-drenched three-bean salad kept finding their way into Sarah's tiny kitchen. She had never eaten so many beans in her life and she was farty enough without them. Still, it was easier than cooking for herself, especially at night when she was exhausted. Her energy level during the day was uncanny, even Dr. Weatherby called it "stranger than a three-legged pole cat," but at night she was so tired she could barely move.

The heat, of course, was the worst part. She felt it so extremely sometimes she didn't want to leave the house, just pull the shades and spend the day lying under the air conditioner watching soaps and The Price is Right, but at the same time that odd energy made her itchy to keep moving. So here she was, wandering around downtown yet again. She turned down a side street she'd never visited and, about half a block in front of her, saw a beautiful stone church with steps that were invitingly shady. She hurried ahead and sank down with a sigh onto the top step. Pulling a handkerchief out of her bag, she dabbed at the back of her neck. Her voluminous red hair made her head and neck perpetually sweaty, even when she had it up like today.

"Are you all right?" A voice from the doorway startled her. She turned to see a young man with a neatly trimmed beard smiling down at her. He wore a white shirt, sleeves rolled up, dress pants, and the impression that he'd had a tie on at one point, although it was nowhere to be seen.

"Yes, thanks. I'm fine. Just needed to sit for a moment."

He sat down beside her, stretching out long legs and rather big feet in a pair of slightly scuffed wingtips. From this level, Sarah could see he wasn't quite as young as she'd originally thought – probably about her age.

"It's brutal out today," he agreed. "I'm Von, by the way."

"Sarah," she answered, just as her eyes found the church sign over his shoulder. "You wouldn't happen to be Revered Von Humboldt, would you?"

"I might be," he answered, giving her a cartoonishly cryptic look out of the side of his eye. "Who wants to know?"

Sarah laughed.

"Figures I'd decide to cop a squat at a church and immediately run into the minister."

"Well, I do work here, so…" He shrugged. Sarah laughed again, then shifted a bit as Dax kicked her in the ribs. Von noticed her discomfort.

"Do you want to come inside for a few minutes? It's air conditioned and I have cold bottles of water in the refrigerator."

"Holy water?" It was out before Sarah could stop it.

"Nah, we're just Presbyterian. It's Perrier."

"Oh, fancy." Sarah got to her feet.

"It's my guilty pleasure," he said, pulling open the heavy front door. "I always have some around. I've never been that fond of tap water. I'm a bubble guy."

In the dim light of the vestibule Sarah blinked, trying to adjust her eyes before following Von through the empty sanctuary. The walls, painted a warm, golden yellow, suffused the room with a baked, comforting look. Dark beams of rough-hewn wood ran up the walls every few feet, and two of them met in the middle of the ceiling, tied neatly together with a massive light fixture that screamed 1940.

"Horrible, isn't it?" Von said, following her eyes.

"I actually kind of like it," Sarah said. "Vintage."

They passed row after row of dark wooden pews, their tops worn smooth by years of grasping hands and resting hymnals and fingers that trailed along them for no other reason than the mute joy that smooth wood brought to fingertips. The seats were covered with long cushions covered in deep burgundy. Two blue hymnals were stacked neatly at the end of each row. The air smelled still, heavy with candle wax and old books and a hundred years of prayers, both habitual and fervent.

"My office is back through those doors," Von gestured.

"If you were anything other than a minister, this would be really creepy," Sarah said.

"I'm aware." He unlocked a slightly battered door that had been half-heartedly painted white somewhere along the way. "And I never actually said I was the minister. Bwa-hahahaha!"

"I'm too tired to even care," Sarah said, sinking uninvited into a deliciously plush armchair. Von laughed and handed her a bottle of cold Perrier from a tiny refrigerator in the corner. She took it gratefully and drank half in deep, long swallows.

"So," he said, leaning against his desk. "You're pretty pregnant."

"Thanks for noticing."

"And very blunt. My finely honed sense of geography and impeccable linguistic gifts tell me you're not from Oklahoma. Wait… wait, don't tell me." He held up one hand and closed his eyes for a moment before opening one to peer at her. "Boston?"

"Ohhh, close. So close."

"New York."

"Wrong direction."

"Chicago."

"Ding ding ding. I moved here a couple of months ago."

Von got up and handed her another bottle of water, taking the empty one from her hand and dropping it into the trash can.

"Ignoring for the moment that Boston is actually not anywhere close to Chicago, tell me your story. You left Chicago and came to Greenview, Oklahoma for… the vast cultural opportunities? The weather? Tourist season?"

"All of the above," Sarah said. "Actually, I came here…" she faltered. It felt odd, lying to this man. He'd been nothing but kind to her. And lying to a minister had to break some kind of commandment somewhere. Or at the very least, a strong suggestion. Still, it was a small town. She couldn't risk it. Von was looking at her expectantly.

"Sorry," she said, moving a hand to her belly. "The baby kicked. It distracts me. Anyway, I came here because my husband is in the service, in Vietnam, and I have friends in town, old family friends, who wanted me to stay here until the baby is born, maybe longer, so I don't have to be alone."

"That's very nice of them," Von said. His smile was genuine. Sarah thought she might cry. "Who are your friends?"

"Alan and Maggie Bernhardt."

"I know them," he said. "They don't attend here, but you know how it is in a small town like this. Everybody knows everybody. And everybody's business."

"Well, you didn't know anything about me," Sarah said. "So it seems to be the old Greenview grapevine is falling down on the job."

"That may be, but more than likely it's because I've been out of town for the past two months, working with a church in Denver that needed some help getting settled. Our associate pastor has been filling in, although I will have to speak to him about these holes in his report to me."

"I didn't think ministers were supposed to gossip."

"Gossip? My dear Sarah, gossip is for old ladies chattering over the backyard fence while they're hanging the clothes out to dry. Ministers do not gossip. We share relevant parish news."

"Oh I see," Sarah said. "I stand corrected." She finished the second bottle of water and unexpectedly belched.

"Oh man, excuse me. I am so sorry."

"I've been around pregnant women before, you know. No need to apologize. You can burp in my office anytime."

"So kind. Anyway, what about you? I don't hear a Midwestern drawl in you."

"Not yet, but they assure me it's only a matter of time. I'm from a little town just outside of Seattle."

"Wow. So how did you end up here?"

He gave her a funny look.

"I was called," he said. "Minister. You know."

"Oh, right. Yeah. Duh."

"I've been here about ten years. Actually, it will be ten years in November. I got here just in time for Advent."

Sarah's mind flashed back to Christmases in Danbury, the Advent calendar her mother would hang in the kitchen, the eagerness of waiting for it to be her turn to open one of the tiny paper windows, the family lighting the candles every Sunday night, then joining hands to pray, and Sarah, while wanting very much to be reverent, was unable to stop her eyes from darting to the presents glittering invitingly under the tree.

"Advent," she said aloud. "I haven't thought about that in a really long time."

"Seems a long way off when it's this hot, but you're welcome to join us this year."

Sarah blinked back tears yet again.

"That's very sweet of you," she said. "I'd like that."

"Can I get you more water?"

"No, but thank you. In fact, I really have to get going. I need to get to the library before it closes."

"Ah, the library. A fellow bookworm, then. Tell Dorothy I said hello."

"Dorothy?"

"Librarian," he said, pulling another bottle of water out of the refrigerator. "Here, take a bottle for the road. It really is brutal out there."

After a quick but awkward goodbye in which Sarah just managed to suppress the urge to hug him – she really needed to get back to New York, and fast – she settled on a two-handed handshake before making her escape.

Halfway to the library, she realized she had no desire to go there after all and instead went home and sat on the porch swing, holding the bottle of water and watching the summer day slowly go out.

Chapter 19

Zachary was finding that little but work held his attention these days, and as a result he was putting in more hours than ever. Being at the paper for such long stretches benefited him in two ways: he was much more hands-on than he'd been in ages and was getting a better feel for where he should make the changes that needed to be made to stay competitive with the Times, and Hanna could easily verify where he was if she chose to. He still made a point to not stay at the paper too late, and tried to keep up the contrite husband act.

His wife was a bigger puzzle to Zachary than ever. She seemed to have forgotten all about Sarah, which is precisely what worried him to the point of sleeplessness nearly every night. He didn't believe for a moment she'd put the whole thing out of her head. Hanna didn't work like that. But she didn't call to check up on him during the day, and at home, she was her usual cordial, cool self. Everything was fine, exactly as it always was. And it spooked the living hell out of him.

"I don't know what she's up to," he said to Frank in a late phone call from his office one night. He spoke quietly, even though he knew the staff had gone home hours before. He had become completely paranoid. "She hasn't mentioned Sarah at all."

"And you want her to?"

"No, of course not. But doesn't that seem odd to you? Any other victimized wife would still be shouting and threatening divorce, or actually filing for divorce, using the old silent treatment, guilt, something. Anything but acting like everything is normal when it clearly isn't."

"Well, but you said you haven't given her any reason to think things aren't normal. You've been at work every day, visibly and verifiably at work, and you've been at home every night like a good boy. You've been acting like everything is normal, so why shouldn't she?"

"Because Hanna isn't a forgive-and-forget type of woman, Frank. She hasn't gotten past this. I'm telling you, she's starting to really scare me."

"What do you think she's going to do? Lull you into a false sense of security and then wham you in the head with a frying pan some night when you walk in the front door?"

"No. That's not how Hanna operates. If she's planning something, it will be much more subtle than that. And she's never touched a frying pan in her life."

When they hung up, Zachary sat in his office for a long time, thinking. The sun had set around him but he didn't bother with the lights, and only the soft orange glow of his cigarette would have given away to anyone who happened past that there was someone sitting there.

The more he thought about what he'd said to Frank, the more convinced he was that he was right. If Hanna was going to exact her revenge, it would be clean, neat, and in a way that couldn't be tied to her. Staring unseeingly out into the dark newsroom, he wondered if he really had anything to worry about or if it was just the toxic combination of stress and insomnia playing with his mind. If Hanna was going to do something, wouldn't she have done it by now? Zachary was too tired to think.

A sound from the other side of the newsroom made him start. It had been nothing more than a click, very soft, but in the silence of the room it echoed like a gunshot. He knew all the sounds the building made at night – the custodian leaving, the random sounds the press made as it cooled down, the building's ancient ventilation system. This was a sound he'd never heard before.

You're losing it, Benton. Go home and get some sleep.

Home. No place in New York had felt like home since the moment Sarah's plane lifted her off the ground. He stopped on his way back and picked up a bottle of Hanna's favorite wine. If she wanted to pretend everything was normal, he'd beat her by a point and pretend he was wooing her. No flowers this time, no jewelry, that would be too obvious. Just a nice bottle of wine she liked. Simple and nice, which was basically how she reacted when he handed it to her.

"Thank you, darling, how nice."

"It's been a long week and I thought we deserved a little treat," Zachary said, taking off his suit jacket and tie.

"You have been working a lot of hours," Hanna said, taking two glasses from the hanging rack by the liquor cabinet. "Is everything all right at the paper?"

"Yes, it's fine. I'm just trying to figure out what we need to do to compete better with the Times. Seems like every ten seconds, those bastards are throwing something against the wall and the masses are stampeding over to see what it is."

He uncorked the wine and poured them both a glass.

"Mmm, well I'm sure you'll figure out how to give them a run for their money, darling. You are Zachary Benton, after all," Hanna said, looking at him steadily. Her green eyes still reminded Zachary of a cat's – cool, calculated, issuing an unspoken challenge. Try me. He looked down into his wine glass, giving it a swirl.

"I wonder sometimes if I'm too old to play the game anymore."

"Don't talk silly," Hanna said. "Of course you aren't. You built the Beacon to what it is now. After Howard closed the World, no one thought there would ever be a newspaper that could rival the Times at all, let alone the poor old Beacon. The Beacon is a force to be reckoned with, because Zachary Benton is a force to be reckoned with."

It's just too bad he's no match for Hanna Benton, she added silently, giving her husband a glassy smile over her wine.

Zachary wasn't sure how to respond to that, but fortunately at that moment Ilsa summoned them to dinner and he was spared.

Chapter 20

Another long day, trailed by an even longer night. Insomnia had always been rare for Zachary, but when it decided to pay a visit, it stayed awhile. Once his brain was used to waking up at a certain nonsensical and pointless hour, it kept at it night after night. It was persistent and annoying and there was nothing he could do but grit his teeth and wait for it to stop, like a kid kicking the back of his seat on a crowded airplane.

With the gentle movements of one trying not to disturb a sleeping tiger, Zachary maneuvered himself out from beside Hanna and wrapped himself in his robe. The house was dark but for patches of anemic yellow from the streetlights below, and he wandered into the living room and sank into a chair. Leaning his head back, he closed his eyes. Gradually the tension that had gathered in his back and shoulders from worrying – about the paper, about not sleeping, and about Sarah – began to ebb away, and he melted into the city's night song.

Night sounds are nothing like day sounds. Common noises are magnified, out of context. The sound of tires on wet pavement cut through the velvet silence at odd intervals. Others are out early, or maybe late, everyone at this hour a little private satellite of existence, everything focused inward with no one else around to help diffuse the crowding thoughts that press in, jockeying for space, trying to prioritize themselves but doing it badly.

Daylight joins people, a blanket of consciousness that's thrown over everyone, making them aware of others whether they want to be or not. Stop for pedestrians in the crosswalk, wave to an acquaintance, hold the door, hand your money to the cashier, smile vacantly at a stranger, not sure what message you're supposed to convey with that but feeling it's your duty just the same. Maybe it's nothing more than an acknowledgement that you see them. That they exist. That they are momentarily in the middle of your consciousness and so they matter. Awake in the middle of the night, no one feels they matter.

Outside the window, Zachary could hear a worker, maybe two, unloading boxes from a truck and taking them into a nearby store. A morning delivery, so that shelves will be stocked and neat when customers arrive and they'll never have to wonder how everything got there, about the night sounds that carried it all in, past Zachary sitting by his window in the dark. He could hear that the cardboard in the truck smelled wet, the earthy cold odor of grocery store stock rooms and discarded pizza boxes.

He heard the lift gate buzz and clang shut, and the truck drove away. Voices bubbled up from the street. A man laughed. A streak of orange and pink was beginning to seep through the curtains, and Zachary realized he wasn't ready to let go of the night yet. He got up quietly and went back to bed, the city whispering to life behind him.

Chapter 21

Sarah woke late, much later than usual, and lay awake, looking out the window at nothing, her hand on her belly, taking comfort in Dax's slight movements. He wasn't a morning person, that much she knew already, but like his mother, he was perpetually restless. She was fascinated with the process of pregnancy, but in a way that was as journalistic as it was maternal.

Sitting up, she reached for the notebook and pen she always had nearby and started to write.

"GREENVIEW, Okla. – Once famed, now fat journalist Sarah Thomas is awake early, pondering what the day will hold and how much worse one could possibly need to pee than she does right now, and how much more she could hate the idea of having to get up to do it. Ms. Thomas is, by her doctor's estimation, six months along. The child, whom she's convinced is a boy, she has named Dax. Ms. Thomas further believes that Dax is his mother's child in many ways, a belief buoyed by the following facts:

Mother and Child are both late-risers and do not find the early morning hours particularly palatable.

Mother and Child are both exceptionally high-strung and short on patience.

Mother and Child both have a demonstrated fondness for the grape although Mother's penchant for red wine has been tempered by both her pregnancy and the fact that Child regularly sends up intense and demanding cravings for grape juice. Mother suspects this is because Child is not yet aware of the gift of nature that is wine.

However, Ms. Thomas does concede that Dax is also his father's child, citing the following irrefutable points:

Mother is sure Child is devastatingly handsome, despite never having seen him. Never mind how she knows, a mother just knows.

Mother has frequently experienced Child's kicks to her kidneys, and more frequently, bladder. While Father has never kicked Mother in the bladder, or kidneys for that matter, Father does fearlessly go his own way and do his own thing – kicking convention in the bladder, if you will."

Sarah read back over what she'd written, then laughed, shook her head, and tossed the notebook aside. Enough of that nonsense. If she was going to write, she really should just go ahead and get started on that book she was always talking about yet never actually starting.

After breakfast, she decided to take a walk, maybe try again to make it to the library. It was a gorgeous fall day in Greenview, and the autumn breeze, timid at first before blowing bolder, had finally chased off the stubbornly hot last days of summer.

She walked slowly in the direction of her destination but in no real rush. With the kids back in school, Greenview felt like a subdued version of its summer self, as though it were quietly mourning the end of warm days, missing the laughing kids toting small plastic inner tubes emblazoned with Spiderman or Underdog heading for the town pool, the smell of backyard barbecues hanging low and comforting in the air, families walking downtown to the ice cream parlor at dusk.

Sarah found it a little hard to believe she'd been in Greenview for three months already. Somewhere along the way, it had begun to seem like home. She felt as though she'd stepped into an alternate universe the day she got off the plane, and for awhile she'd fought it, chewing at invisible restraints, so homesick for New York some days she thought she'd go crazy. When the boxes of her things that Zachary had shipped arrived in the mail, she'd left them stacked by the front door for weeks, telling herself she was going to have to ship them back soon as she wasn't staying long. Even as she grew accustomed to her new surroundings, made a few friends, and finally unpacked the boxes, she kept warning herself not to get too comfortable or she'd never get out again. Then she crossed some invisible emotional threshold and one day realized she'd come to love Greenview. While she still missed Zachary with something akin to a physical ache, she'd begun to think of making their home here, away from the noise and crime of the city. She imagined herself in jeans, sitting beside Zachary at Dax's soccer game, cheering enthusiastically. And the next day she'd get stuck behind some meandering Sunday driver, and it was Tuesday, or she'd overhear some tattered bit of small-town gossip in the grocery store and her heart would take violent flight back to New York, where thing may have still been insane, but in a broad, impersonal, much safer way.

The library had the look of having been built sometime in the 50s, but still had that old library smell about it. She was browsing through the new fiction and an odd assortment of large print mysteries when she heard a man's voice say her name. She turned to see the affable minister and Perrier pusher heading toward her.

"Hello, Rev. Humboldt," Sarah said.

"You are going to have to stop calling me that, uh, let's see." he glanced at his watch. "Right now."

"Von, then. Hello, Von."

"It sounds better when you say it. You almost sound like you're from back east, kind of a Yankee accent going on there."

Sarah smiled and slipped the book she'd been holding back into its spot.

"That's funny. I've never heard that before."

"So what's new?" Von asked. "How are you feeling? Better now that the days are cooling off?"

"Yeah, much. The summer was just hellishly hot. Is it always like that here?"

"Pretty much. Autumn is beautiful, though. You'll love it."

"I love it already."

"Hey, any chance you're free for lunch? I was about to head over to that new salad place. My treat?"

"Sure, sounds great," Sarah said. "I didn't have any plans and a salad would hit the spot." The Midwestern cuisine was making her feel like a hippo, although to be honest, she'd never turned any of it down either.

They chatted like old friends over lunch. Sarah found herself more re-laxed around Von than she did with anyone else in town, except Maggie and Alan. There was an easy openness about him that dissolved all her ideas about clergymen being stiff and stern. He was so kind and warm that she felt guilty all over again for lying to him about who she really was, about her past.

"Von, do you think there's anything God can't forgive?" she asked him impulsively as they sat over coffee.

"Well, the generally accepted answer to that is that the only sin God can't forgive is unbelief."

"Mmm. So anything bad you do is forgivable?"

"If you seek forgiveness. God doesn't just go around tossing forgiveness at people who screw up. There has to be repentance."

"Yeah, I understand that. I was just wondering if there's ever a time when what a person does is just so horrible that God says 'Wow, see, now that I can't help you with. Get out of here.' Like a really pissed-off dad. Oh, sorry. A really angry dad."

"Gee, I've never heard swearing before," Von said drily. "But to answer your question, I don't believe there's anything that God will not forgive a sinner for as long as the sinner repents and seeks forgiveness."

"So if Hitler or Mussolini asked for forgiveness on their deathbed, God would forgive them?"

"I think that's pushing the assumption pretty far," Von said. "We have no idea what Hitler or Mussolini were thinking on their deathbeds. Given what we know of their characters, it seems to me highly unlikely they felt remorse at any point. But that said, I don't presume to know how God deals with people in their final moments."

Sarah toyed with her spoon silently.

"Is there something on your mind?" Von said gently. "Somehow I don't think you're really all that worried about Mussolini's afterlife."

What a relief it would be to unburden herself to this man, to pour out her whole story, to let him reassure her that Sarah Thomas, who went to Sunday School every week in Danbury and loved reading Bible stories at night with her parents was still a good girl, that sleeping with someone else's husband had been something she'd never intended. But then, she imagined him asking her, what did you intend, when you were half-drunk and arguing with him heatedly in a bar? When you went back to your place with him? She looked down at her swollen belly and knew she would have no answers.

"No," she said, softly. "There's nothing on my mind. Just making conversation."

Chapter 22

Autumn always made Zachary feel it was a crime against nature to stay inside, especially in New York, where the cool breeze winding in and out among the skyscrapers made the city look different somehow, even before the leaves confirmed it.

This was one of those days, and he had taken a rare morning break from work and was strolling up Broadway with no particular destination in mind besides just out. He needed to clear his head, and everything at the paper reminded him of Sarah. Now that he was out, he realized that her imprint wasn't on the paper, it was on him.

He passed a small children's boutique and, after pausing to look in the window, went in and bought three picture books: Corduroy, The Snowy Day, and The Best Word Book Ever. Zachary had no doubts that the child he and Sarah had created would be a genius, and he wanted to instill a love for reading as early as possible. As he walked out carrying the small bag, he was suddenly awash in a feeling of happiness and peace. Buying something for the baby made the whole thing seem more real and brought his little family closer to him.

He felt so good he went into Zabar's and bought half a pound of mixed olives, a big bag of bagels, and a container of whitefish spread.

"Lunch is in the conference room!" he announced when he came whistling back into the newsroom. "Zabar's. To you from me, just because I'm a hell of a guy."

"What's gotten into him?" Denise asked Stan when Zachary had gone back into his office.

"Beats me," Stan answered. "And if there's whitefish in there, I officially don't care."

Zachary closed his office door, picked up the phone and called Sarah.

"Hello, my love," he said. The surprised and unmistakably happy sound she made brought the first genuine smile to his face in ages.

"I was about to leave and then I'd have missed you! Oh my God, I'm so glad

I didn't leave!" She sounded like she was about to cry.

"Are you all right, my love?" he asked. "How are you? How are you feeling?"

"Except for these damned hormones that make me feel like I'm about to burst into tears basically all the time, I feel pretty good. No problems, no complaints, nothing worth writing a letter to the editor about." It was one of their running jokes. "Are you calling from the paper?"

"Yeah, I put bagels and spreads from Zabar's in the conference room. All the wildebeests stampeded over there already."

Sarah laughed.

"I hope you got extra whitefish. Three people almost quit last time we had Zabar's because Stan put it all on one bagel." Talking about Zabar's, the paper, and Stan made Sarah so homesick she had to swallow hard several times to keep the tears down. Zachary's voice was a balm to her sore soul, and she held the receiver tight against her ear as though it would bring him closer.

"I did. Couldn't make that mistake twice. I also bought something for the baby. Three somethings."

"Oh, Zachary! You are a sweet, adorable man. What did you get?"

"Promise you won't tell him, otherwise it won't be a surprise."

"I won't," Sarah dropped her voice to a whisper.

"Books. Three books. Kid books."

"Oh, kid books. Good. For a second I thought you were going to say Lolita and War and Peace."

"First of all, that's only two books. And second of all, I'm getting him those for his first birthday."

"Interesting you're saying 'him.' I've had the very strong feeling lately that it's going to be a boy."

"I didn't even realize I used the masculine," Zachary said. "I wonder why I did that. What makes you think it's going to be a boy?"

"Absolutely nothing but a hunch. Mother's intuition. Although

Dr. Weatherby thinks so too. And can I tell you something? I've been calling him Dax."

"Dax. Dax Benton. I like it."

"I haven't even seen the kid but somehow I know it suits him."

"So do you truly hope it is a boy, or are you trying to brace yourself because you secretly really want a girl?"

"The funny thing is I don't honestly care either way. I've been thinking about it, and I really and truly don't. I'm just so excited for us to start our little family."

"So am I," Zachary admitted. "I felt happy for the first time in ages today when I bought those books."

"I don't want you to be unhappy, my love," Sarah said. "I know our situation right now isn't ideal, but we have everything ahead of us."

"I know," he said. "You're right."

The sadness in his voice belied his words. He'd been so happy just a short time ago, thinking about her, but now that he was hearing her voice on the phone, he remembered just how far away she actually was.

"Oh Zachary, my sweetest love, my handsome prince, please listen to me. We have come so far. We have grown so much, as individuals and as a couple. We are so close to having all of our dreams come true. Please just relax into our today and dream with me about our tomorrow. I love you. I love you more than I even have words for. You are all to me. Everything."

A single, fat tear slid down Zachary's face and he wiped it away.

"I love you too, my Sarah. You are the very breath in my body."

He heard the sounds of the newsroom filling up again with sated reporters.

"Sounds like the brutes have been fed. I'd better go," he said. "I'll call again soon."

When they hung up, they each sat, looking at the phone in their hands, their thoughts tangled in each other.

Chapter 23

Autumn was having the opposite effect on Sarah that it was on Zachary. She welcomed the cooler temperatures, especially this year, but she always felt the same toward the end of summer – somewhere between melancholy and resigned. She knew she had to accept that it was over, but she didn't have to be happy about it.

She tried, various years, to pretend autumn wasn't coming, insisting it was still early August until well past the 20th, until people started to argue with her. It didn't matter anyway, how much she tried to deny summer's end. Even if she stopped looking at the calendar altogether, she felt it in her spirit – the slight shift of energy, that vague sense of impending change, the feeling of veiled urgency in those around her who were trying, as she was, to wring every bit of summer out of what was left. They crowded onto the beach, into the farmers' market, the pool, the museum, forced jollity thick in the air as everyone tried not to glance over their shoulder at what was coming.

As a child in Connecticut, she had enjoyed summer, like any kid, swimming and going to camp and chasing fireflies and savoring the faintly naughty feeling of staying up well past her school-year bedtime. Summer used to feel like parole to Sarah. She'd loved school overall, but that last day in June was interminable, the weather already hot and waiting like an impatient playmate just outside the building's double doors. She and her classmates had watched the clock that definitely must be broken, fidgeting, not making any attempt to concentrate, and the teacher, used to this, expecting this, had planned nothing more for that last afternoon than popcorn and a movie, and even those rare treats couldn't keep the kids focused. Sarah had always found the last minutes to be the longest, stretching out agonizingly while she sat, every muscle on taut alert like a sprinter waiting for the crack of the starter pistol, so that by the time the dismissal bell rang, she almost screamed, grabbing her backpack and bolting out the door of the classroom and streaming down the hall with the other kids in a flood of eager, sweaty little bodies, until they burst through the doors and sucked in great, hot breaths of sweet, sweet freedom.

Summer had always carried with it a bit of mystery to Sarah. She would sometimes see kids from school at the pool, or at the townwide Fourth of July fireworks and watermelon festival, but for the most part they splintered apart during the summer, going off to camp or on family vacations, living their own little private lives for those few months, and when fall came and they all went back to school they were familiar stranger to each other, weighed down by stiff new jeans and backpacks full of school supplies that had traitorously appeared in the stores in early August. Bodies had grown a little taller, faces had slimmed down, sun-darkened freckles and lightened hair bore reassuring testament to themselves and each other that it really had been summer, and that probably it would be again, but not for so long it was best not to think about it too much. But summer memories were soon crowded out by the excitement of school and friends, autumn activities and Halloween. Fall was a beginning.

But now… well, now Sarah was crowding up on middle age, and autumn was just different. What had once felt like a beginning now was tinged with sadness, finality. She knew, in the part of her brain where she kept her rational thoughts, that the year was a circle, a cycle, and she'd get summer back again in a few months. But like Brussels sprouts standing in the way of ice cream, it wasn't easy to swallow.

She'd tried, last year, to cheer herself up by buying school supplies. At a tiny, ancient store in Greenwich Village, she'd found a cigar box and filled it with glittery pencils and a rubber eraser and a pen that wrote in pink ink and smelled like bubble gum, and in the very back of the store she discovered, with a little cry of happiness, a Big Chief tablet. Her feeling of elation lasted until she got home. Then she looked at her school supplies, remembered that she was old, opened a bottle of wine, and spent the evening writing depressing poems and bubble gum-scented expletives in the Big Chief tablet.

She could easily identify when she'd fallen out of love with autumn. She was just never quite sure why. Maybe it was the reminder that she was getting older, that her own seasons were changing. Watching the color-shifting leaves now just made her miss Zachary and dwell on her own mortality, on missed chances and wasted time, on spilled milk and spilled tears, on what had been and what never would be.

Chapter 24

"Honey, I'm a little worried about Sarah," Maggie said to Alan as they were getting ready for bed. She was putting on her nightgown as her husband brushed his teeth in the bathroom. Through the open door she could hear him moving around and picture everything he was doing. His routine never varied. She began to brush her hair.

"Worried about what?"

"Oh, she's just kind of... I don't know how to describe it. Mopey, I guess is the best word."

"Well, she's pregnant and far from home," Alan said with annoying male-minded simplicity.

"I know, but this seems like more than that. There are times I'm talking to her and it seems like she's not even really listening."

"And you have me for that."

Maggie gave a thin smile.

"Yes, I have you for that. But I'm being serious. I am worried she's getting depressed or something."

Alan kissed her on top of the head as he passed her on his way to the bed.

"I think it's sweet the way you're always such a mother hen," he said. "You and Sarah are close enough now that you can talk to her about it, I'm sure, if you're that worried."

Maggie fiddled with the brush, not really seeing it, lost in thought.

"Yeah," she said finally, turning toward the bed. "Yeah, I think I will."

"Tell you what," Alan said as his wife slid beneath the covers. "If you think there's anything to worry about after you talk to her, I'll call Zachary. How's that?"

"That would be great, honey. Thanks."

He kissed her and shut off the light. In four seconds, he was snoring, but Maggie lay awake for a long time. She had these feelings sometimes, a kind of intuition, and she was usually right. For the past few days, she'd felt strongly that something wasn't right with Sarah, but she had no way of knowing what it was, how to fix it, or if it was still looming, how to prevent it.

"Sarah, sweetheart, are you all right?" Maggie asked the next day as they were going out for coffee.

It was a simple enough question, and obviously asked with the best of intent, but for some reason it irritated Sarah. She was homesick for New York, she missed Zachary, and she couldn't stop watching the news. Every day it felt more and more like the world was moving on without her, things she should be reporting on, news she should be sending out to New Yorkers, and she was stuck out here in Hooterville, waddling and hoisting and farting.

"I'm fine, Maggie, but thank you for being concerned," she said. "I appreciate your friendship more than I'm sure you even know." Maggie waited while Sarah pulled her front door shut. "It's funny but just this week I realized I've stopped locking my front door. It wasn't even a conscious decision."

"I didn't know you ever did lock it," Maggie said. "In fact, I'm not even sure I knew there was a lock on it."

They walked down the sidewalk in the direction of downtown. They'd begun going for coffee every few days at a Ginny's, a little cafe that Sarah had immediately fallen in love with. With the exception of the distinctly Midwestern décor – gingham tablecloths, stalks of wheat in milk bottles on the tables – it could have been one of the many little cafes that always cropped up along New York's side streets. The owner, a petite and smiling blonde woman named Ginny, was fascinated by Sarah and even ordered chicory root tea to keep in stock just for her.

"At least the weather has cooled a little," Sarah said conversationally as they crossed Main Street.

"Excuse me," a man called from the bay of the gas station on the corner. They stopped and he held out a map.

"Can you tell me how to get back on the highway?" he said. "We stopped for gas and now I think I'm a little turned around."

Maggie gave him directions, peppered with her usually chattering and irrelevant commentary.

"Thanks," he said. "The people in the Midwest are as nice as I'd heard."

"Why thank you, kind sir," Sarah said, giving an elaborate curtsy. The man looked confused but Maggie burst out laughing.

"She's just being a wisenheimer," she said. "She's not even from here. She's from back east."

"No kidding," the man said. "Not sure how you ended up here, but you look like you fit right in."

Sarah didn't know how to take that.

"I'm Walter," he said, then gestured toward the van still sitting at the gas pump. Sarah could see an attractive young woman in the passenger seat. "That's Lalitha."

"I'm Sarah," she said, lifting a hand toward the woman in the van, who waved back. "This is Maggie."

"Nice meeting you both," Walter said. "We'd better get back on the road. Thanks for the directions."

"I always think it's interesting," Maggie said as they settled into their usual table by the window in Ginny's, "How many people blow through Greenview and seem surprised by it."

"Surprised how?"

"You know, surprised that it's so rural, so small, so ..."

"Flat?"

Maggie laughed.

"Well, yeah, flat too, but it's almost like they get their feet on Midwestern soil and look around with the same kind of awe I imagine people from here get when they visit New York or LA."

"Like, damn! It really does exist!"

"Yes!" Maggie said. "Exactly. And it's really interesting how people here react to outsiders who pass through." She lowered her voice. "It's like the way Ginny is around you. People who pass through from other parts of the country bring this breath of outside with them, showing people here – people who have never felt the need to leave the prairie for any reason – a little peek of what life is like in other places. It's hard to explain, but you can definitely feel it."

"I met the Presbyterian minister the other day," Sarah said. "He told me he's from Seattle."

"Oh did you? Pastor Von's a nice guy. And actually, yeah, he's kind of a good example of what I mean. When he first got here, people were all like 'Seattle! Wow! What's that like? Rain all the time?' It's like they don't care enough to travel and see for themselves, but if someone can bring the experience to them, they're all for it."

Ginny brought Maggie a cup of coffee and Sarah two bags of chicory tea and a tiny silver pot of hot water.

"You ladies want anything else?"

"I'm starving," Sarah said. "Do you have any of that apple pie you had the last time we were here?"

"I do!" Ginny beamed. "I just baked it this morning."

"Great, bring me the whole thing and a big fork," Sarah said. The other women laughed.

"I'll have what she's having," Maggie said, and Ginny hurried behind the counter.

"It's funny you should ask me if everything's all right," Sarah said a few minutes later as she dug her fork into the flaky, buttery crust of Ginny's apple pie. A thick slice of cheddar cheese rested on top.

"Why is that?" Maggie felt her heart give a little jump of anxiety. "Is everything all right?"

"Yeah. Overall, yeah. I just keep missing newspaper work."

"Oh!" Maggie was a little taken aback. She was sure it was something more than that, but she figured it was better to let Sarah tell her whenever she was ready, if ever she was. "The work in general? Or the ... Beacon, is it?"

"The Beacon," Sarah nodded. "And it's mostly the Beacon, but I miss news reporting in general."

"Well, I heard the local paper here is looking for a reporter to help out with covering the town council and the school board. I can give you the editor's name if you want to go talk to him."

Sarah smiled wistfully at her pie, thinking of press conferences with Mayor Lindsay, the riots at Columbia, the new World Trade Center, Vietnam. *She could have taken down Tammany Hall.* Her Columbia diploma and Pulitzer Prize flashed through her mind. Now she was sitting in a coffee shop in Greenview, Oklahoma, wearing a bandana skirt, eating pie and thinking about asking if she could cover the school board meetings.

"Maybe," she said quietly. "I don't know that it's such a good idea, though."

"Why not?" Maggie asked, sipping coffee.

"I'm pretty sure I write in a big, New Yorky style. I think I'd stick out. And the last thing Zachary would want me doing is sticking out, especially in print. He's so nervous about Hanna finding me."

"Mmm," Maggie mused, staring out the window over the rim of her cup. "Well, I can't imagine that Hanna subscribes to the Greenview Daily Bugle. And you are using a different last name. And besides, who says Zachary has to know? You're not supposed to tell a man everything."

This nugget of folk wisdom made Sarah laugh.

"You don't tell Alan everything?"

"Oh honey," Maggie said, lightly smacking Sarah's hand. "If I told Alan half the stuff I do, he'd have divorced my butt years ago. Do you think he knows his morning coffee is half decaf? Or that I keep a bottle of brandy all the way in the back of the cereal cupboard?"

Sarah smiled and wished she had more pie.

"But those things aren't dangerous," she said. "I think Zachary would consider it dangerous if I were to write for the paper here. He wants me to keep my profile so low I'm invisible."

"Well, I see your point. I just don't like to think of you miserable here. And even less do I like the thought of you high-tailing it back to New York because you're homesick."

"It takes me twenty minutes just to get out of my chair," Sarah said. "So I'm not too likely to do any high-tailing for awhile. Hey, Ginny! How about some more pie?"

Chapter 25

Later a cocktail of heartburn and anxiety kept Sarah pacing around her small house, thinking about what Maggie had said. There's no way that Sarah Adams, small town reporter in the middle of Oklahoma that had a readership roughly the size of one square block in New York, would be found out by Hanna Benton, much less anyone else. She just missed reporting, missed the buzz of the newsroom, missed watching and listening and then turning what she collected into news.

The next morning, she called Maggie and got the name of the editor, Fred Thompson. By that afternoon, she was on the phone with him.

"Sure, I'd love to meet with you, Sarah," Fred said. He sounded older, affable and so relaxed Sarah wondered how he ever decided to get into the news business. "Come by anytime. I'm here all afternoon, if you want to come today."

Sarah agreed, before she had a chance to talk herself out of it. When she arrived at the paper's office, on a street she'd not been down yet, her heart sank. Somewhere in the back of her mind, she knew she shouldn't be picturing the Beacon's building, yet what she saw was so diametrically different from what she was used to that she was pretty sure she made her disappointment audible. The Bugle was in a small, ramshackle building with cracked sidewalks pushed up at all angles by a giant, ragged elm tree in the middle of the grass. Broken venetian blinds haphazardly covered Depression-era windows. She would have turned and fled but her dismay was outvoted by her curiosity. How did such a flytrap put out a paper? She'd seen the Bugle in newsstands around town. It wasn't the Beacon or the Times, but it was a decent little paper.

She opened the door and stepped into the office and, apparently, 1945. A dehydrated-looking old woman sat at a battered wooden desk, typing methodically. There was no one else even in the building, as far as Sarah could see, although there was a bigger room behind the woman with three empty desks in it. Phone books, ashtrays, pencils, notebooks and cameras were slung everywhere. From somewhere deep in the back, she could hear the familiar low rumble of a press.

"May I help you, dear?" The woman said.

"Uh, yes. I'm Sarah Adams. I have an appointment to see Mr. Thompson."

"Oh yes, Miss Sarah Adams. He is expecting you. I'll let him know you're here."

The woman made no attempt to keep from staring at Sarah's belly, and she instinctively put her hands over it.

"Sarah! So good to meet you!" A large, jolly man with a horseshoe bald head and horn rimmed glasses came up from the back. He extended his hand and shook Sarah's enthusiastically. "Come on back to my office."

As she sat down in the chair across from his desk, she could see him making a better attempt at not looking at her stomach but still failing.

"I had a big lunch."

He looked startled for a moment, then laughed.

"I didn't mean to stare," he said. "I was just surprised."

"Not as surprised as I was."

"Is that right?" He leaned back in his chair, beaming at her. She told him the story she'd gotten so used to rolling out for people that by now she half believed it herself.

"So you have some newspaper experience, I gather?"

"Oh, some," she said. "I have a degree in journalism but lately I've been a homemaker, getting ready for the baby. I can write, though, so you don't have to worry about that."

She prayed he wouldn't ask for a resume or references. A writing sample she could provide, but much more than that and she was screwed.

"Well, we actually could use a reporter here, if you'd like to help fill in. It's temporary, at least that's what we're expecting. Megan, one of our full-timers, is on leave, helping her grandparents up at their farm in Nebraska. Her grandmother had a stroke."

"Oh dear," Sarah murmured, feeling a response was expected. She was running some mental calculations: if the reporter was out for, say, three months, that would pretty much bring her back to work around the same time Sarah was due. It could actually work out really well.

"Yeah, sad situation," Fred was saying. "She'll be back, though, just not for awhile. We have two other reporters, one full time and one part time, but believe it or not, it's a pretty big workload for two people."

"Oh, I believe it," Sarah said, not believing it.

"The other full-time reporter, Max, is out on a story right now. The part-timer, that's Brad. I actually don't know where he is right now. He comes in and out at weird times. Ellen, that's the woman at the front desk, keeps better track of them than I do."

"And what does Ellen do?"

"Pretty much everything else," Fred said. "Classifieds, circulation, types up weddings and Ann Landers, keeps us in doughnuts. Oh, we do have one ad guy. Donald. He's very good. If it weren't for him, we'd have gone belly up a long time ago."

"What's your circulation?"

"Oh, 'bout 1,400, give or take."

"Wow, that's pretty good. More than I expected."

"Well, we're the county seat," Fred explained. "The other little towns around here all take the Bugle because we cover their towns too, and we're the only paper in this area. The only other real paper anywhere even close is Tulsa, and they don't bother with Greenview."

"And sports?"

"Max and Brad kind of split that up. We cover Greenview High, of course, they have a hell of a football team, and some other minor sports. Track and such."

"And the reporters take their own photos?"

"Yeah, but they're not very good, between you and me. We have a couple of decent cameras, pretty nice Leicas, but they're not photojournalists and don't really like taking pictures."

"Have you thought about hiring photographers?"

"Well, that'd be nice, but we don't have the budget. Maybe someday.

Maybe when you help us win the Pulitzer."

Sarah glanced up sharply but he was chuckling and shaking a cigarette out of the packet on his desk, oblivious to the impact his joke had.

"Mind if I smoke? Want to see the rest of the place?"

"No and yes," Sarah answered. He walked her through the newsroom, the small production area behind it where the waxer gave off a warm, familiar smell and tooling lines and pica poles hung from a pegboard.

"The press is in the basement," he said. Sarah could feel the low rumble beneath her feet.

"I'm surprised you print on site," she said. "I know some smaller papers send theirs out to be printed."

"Yeah, we looked into that, but it was too expensive and too time-consuming to send it out since, as I said, the biggest paper around here is in Tulsa. Two hours just on the road made it too hard to get the paper printed and back here in time for the carriers to pick up their stacks. So we decided, oh let's see, some 20 years ago, just to print it here. Got us a good little printing press and a young fellow from town who is pretty darned good at running it."

"That's great," Sarah murmured, honestly impressed and more than a little touched at the work this tiny paper put into itself.

"So?" Fred said when they'd returned to his office. "What do you think? Want to write for us?"

"Yes," Sarah said, the words surprising her a little. "Yes, I'd love to."

Chapter 26

"Are you positive?" Hanna said. "I need you to be absolutely certain or it's no good to me."

She listened intently to the caller's response.

"I see. All right. Thank you very much for the information."

She hung up and sat on the sofa, thinking. Her anger with Zachary had long since passed and she was now utterly calm as she considered her options. Staying with him was out of the question. She would be the laughingstock of New York soon, one of those pathetic women who stayed with her philandering husband out of some misguided sense of obligation or worse, forgiveness. To forgive was weakness to Hanna, and to have forgiven him would have merely invited him to do it again. And, as it turned out, she was right. Her informant had just let her know he'd seen Zachary several times coming out of various children's shops in the city. She knew Sarah was definitely no longer in New York, but wherever she was, Zachary was obviously not only still in touch with her, but planning a future with her. And Hanna would not be made to look like a fool.

She picked up the phone again and dialed a number in New Jersey.

"This is Hanna Benton," she said. "I'd like to arrange for a problem to be taken care of."

"That's a pretty tall order, Mrs. Benton," the gruff voice on the other end said when Hanna had explained what she wanted. "Doing a hit like that in the middle of Midtown is risky. If you leave it to me, I'll work out a less visible place to do it."

"No. It happens at the Beacon or it doesn't happen at all. That's where he met the whore, that's where it ends."

"But you don't even know when you want this done."

"I'll get back to you with the specifics. You just do what you need to do in the meantime to get ready. It has to be done exactly as I specify, and it has to be flawless. Do you understand me? No wounds, no missed shots. Dead. Do you hear me? Dead."

"Yes, Mrs. Benton, I hear you. I'll take care of it."

Chapter 27

Zachary was walking to his car in the parking garage when he heard it again, the same click he'd heard in the newsroom a few days prior. His was one of the few cars in the garage, and the soft sound was amplified. He had begun to feel more and more lately as though he were being followed, and although the feeling of being followed in a dark parking garage was so Hollywood it was laughable, Zachary wasn't laughing. His heart pounding, he unlocked his car door, got in, and locked the door with shaking fingers. He closed his eyes for a moment and tried to get his breath under control, but they snapped open again and he whirled around to look in the backseat. Empty. Maybe he really was losing his marbles. What was a click anyway? It could have been anything. But the feeling that it was the same click he'd heard that night in the newsroom wouldn't leave him. He drove home in silence, his shoulders and back tensed against an onslaught that wasn't coming.

When he walked into the brownstone, he could immediately tell Hanna wasn't home. He found a note from her on the kitchen table that said she'd forgotten to tell him tonight was her bridge night and she wouldn't be home until late. Relief flooded through Zachary and he changed his clothes and poured himself a stiff drink before settling down on the sofa with a book he'd been wanting time to read. He didn't get far before his exhausted mind and body overruled him and he fell asleep, the book open in his hands. He woke with a start. That click – he'd heard it again. He was sure of it. But no, how could he have heard it? He'd been sound asleep. He was so agitated lately the click had begun to infiltrate his dreams. He sat up, rubbed his eyes, looked at his watch. It was nearly midnight. He wondered if Hanna had come in, but upstairs their bed was still made, smooth and tight. He undressed and crawled between the sheets, but couldn't fall asleep again.

While her husband was getting into their bed, Hanna was lying in a different bed, in a tiny studio apartment in SoHo, smoking a cigarette.

"There are too many things that could go wrong, Hanna," Rick said. "I just don't think it's a good idea."

She turned her head on the pillow to look at him. With one long, elegant finger, she stroked his cheek.

"I know you don't, darling, but I do. And you know all the benefits you get for staying in my good graces. You just had one of them."

She hooked one bare leg over his and gave the sexy, silken laugh that always turned him on. Hanna was like Lauren Bacall to Rick. Sexy, smoldering, mysterious. He kissed her beautiful mouth.

"Promise me I won't lose my job."

"Darling, Zachary was so hung up on his mistress and his whole secret little life that he didn't even know when you were hired. And now he's completely distracted by me acting like everything is fine. You are far below his radar right now."

"He'd fire me if he knew any of what's going on here."

"That's a big if, lover, and we both know it. Now listen to me very carefully as I don't think you've fully comprehended what I'm asking of you. You're not to follow Zachary. I have someone else doing that. All I'm asking of you is that you find out where Sarah is. Look how easily you found out that he's still in touch with her. That was a stroke of genius, darling. Investigative journalism at its finest."

Her flattery was shallow and insipid and shouldn't have worked, but somehow it did.

"In case you don't know it, there are 49 other states in the union, and that's assuming she hasn't left the country," Rick said. "I'm not sure tracking her down is going to be as easy as getting Zachary to let it slip that he's been in touch with her."

"You'll figure it out, darling," she said, putting out her cigarette and pulling him close. "You're such a clever journalist. One of these days there'll be a Pulitzer on your desk. In fact, I guarantee it."

Chapter 28

"You took the job?" Maggie said the next day when Sarah broke her news. "That's wonderful!"

"It's just temporary, and like you said, I'm pretty sure what qualifies as headline-worthy in Greenview isn't going to make it into the New York Times, so I'm sure I'm okay. I just needed to do something – I'm going stir crazy."

"I know, and I'm really glad for you," Maggie said. "Are you going to tell Zachary?"

"I think I will. Knowing Zachary he'll find out anyway, and I'd rather he hear it from me so I can reassure him I'm being careful. Honestly, Mags, he's so paranoid about Hanna it's almost weird. I mean, she's a bitch, don't get me wrong. But he seems to think she's actually dangerous. I didn't see it at first, but now he's got me paranoid about her too."

"I've never met her," Maggie said, handing Sarah a glass of iced chamomile tea. "I only know what Alan has told me, and he just met her once, I think."

"The thing is, I honestly do feel bad. I wish I didn't, in fact I wish I could hate her, but for some reason I just can't. I don't love her, mind you. I think she's a cold person and that Zachary deserves better. Hmm, I guess on second thought, I do hate her."

Maggie smiled.

"Nah, you don't have it any you to hate anybody," she said. "But she does sound like a real peach."

"Mmm. But the thing is, I didn't set out to try and steal Zachary away. I don't want to be a homewrecker – who wants a label like that slapped on them? I feel like Hester Prynne."

"Seems to me you're taking all the blame onto yourself," Maggie said. "Did you hogtie Zachary? Did you force him into bed at gunpoint? Did you tell him to fall in love with you or you'd blow his head off?"

Sarah laughed.

"Yeah, okay, I get your point. Still, I keep finding myself wrestling with all these stupid feelings of guilt about Hanna."

"Well, I'd say that ship has sailed," Maggie said pragmatically. "I think all you can do now is let Zachary take care of what's going on in New York while you focus on yourself, your baby, and the future. I'm sure even Dr. Weatherby would tell you to go easy on the stress."

"Please. If Dr. Weatherby could see a side-by-side snapshot of my life here versus my life in New York, he'd have a whole new definition of stress. Compared to what my life was like six months ago, I'm practically comatose now."

"Well, I'm glad you came to Greenview, in that case," Maggie said, giving Sarah's hand a squeeze. "You're all safe and sound here."

"You can take Megan's desk," Fred said when Sarah reported for duty the next morning. "She's pretty organized so I'm sure it's not a mess and she should have pens, a stylebook, typewriter paper, all that stuff. If you need anything, just let Ellen know. All right now, you ready to get to work?"

"Ready, Chief."

"Great. I want to do a feature on the new law enforcement center they just built right outside of town. We need to get on it – they're already open. Think you can tackle it?"

"Sure," Sarah said. He gave her the police chief's phone number and a file folder with some background information on the project. She sat down at her new desk and looked around. She was alone in the newsroom. Fred had said Max would be in later and he didn't know about Brad. Near the front door, she could see Ellen pecking away on her Smith-Corona. The newsroom had a stale smell of old paper and ink, dust and typewriter ribbons.

And there's the name for my memoirs, Sarah thought glumly. *Dust and*

Typewriter Ribbons: The Arrested Development of a Reporter.

The dim quiet of the Bugle's newsroom was making her so homesick for the bright, busy newsroom of the Beacon that New York felt a million miles away. She stopped that thought before it could fully develop. No sense in being maudlin. In the front office, Ellen got up to greet a man who had come to the front counter. Sarah glanced at the phone on her desk, glanced back up to make sure Ellen was still occupied, and before giving herself a chance to think the better of it, made a collect call to Zachary at the newspaper.

"Sarah? Are you all right?"

"I'm fine," she said, feeling suddenly guilty for taking the risk of calling. "I'm calling from my new job."

"Your new… job? What kind of a job? Why do you need a job?"

"Why do you think I need a job? I'm bored and restless and I miss covering the news."

"What kind of a job?" he repeated, just before the realization caught up with him. "Oh my God, you're working at a paper, aren't you?"

"Yeah," she said. "The little paper here in town."

Zachary was silent so long she thought the connection had been broken.

"Zachary?"

"I'm here," he said. "Well, you know I'd be happier if you were hidden away in a cave somewhere, but I also know how you are, once you set your mind to something. Just please tell me you're not using your real name in your byline."

"Of course not," Sarah said. "I'm Sarah Adams across the board here. The only ones who know me as anything different are Maggie and Alan, and I don't think even they remember my real name anymore."

"I'm proud of you, you know," Zachary said. "You're a hell of a reporter and an amazing person. That paper is lucky to have you."

She felt tears starting to sting the back of her throat.

"Thank you, my love. It's just temporary, actually. I'm filling in for a reporter who is on leave. I'll be done a little before my due date."

Zachary felt a secret rush of relief.

"I'd actually like us to talk a little more about that when we have time," he said. "I'll have things wrapped up here by then and will be out there with you well before the birth, but we need to talk about dates and make some concrete plans."

The thought of seeing Zachary again made Sarah's heart skip a beat, and at the same time the image of polished New York-bred Zachary strolling through downtown Greenview in cowboy boots and a big belt buckle was hilarious. And kind of a turn-on.

"I have to go, my love," Sarah said, seeing Ellen returning to her desk. "I hope we can talk again soon. I miss you so much I can't take it."

"I miss you too," Zachary said. "From the inside out, I miss you. But my love, just remember that there is coming a time when we don't have to prepare for our tomorrows because we'll be living them."

When she hung up the phone, Sarah turned on the gooseneck lamp on her desk and opened the file Fred had given her. The law enforcement center, located on the outskirts of the eastern side of Greenview, had opened about two weeks prior. The paper had done some spotty coverage of its construction over the past year, but nothing too in depth.

"Hey Fred," she said as he walked past her on the way to the coffee pot. "Do we know anything about the bidding process on this law enforcement center?"

"What do you mean?"

"Did they do a request for bids, do you know how the winning bidder was chosen?"

"I assume so but I can't say for sure."

"Mmm." Sarah studied the paper in front of her. "Was there a referendum?"

"Yes, that there was," Fred said. "We covered that with the regular election stories. The morgue is on the other side of that half wall by my office.

Want me to help?"

"Thanks, but I'll find it. I'd like a chance to poke around there anyway."

"Self your help!" he said and, laughing at his own joke, got a cup of coffee and went whistling back to his office.

In the morgue, Sarah decided to go back through most of the year to see what, if anything, she could find for background. She pulled out several months' worth of papers and piled them on a low counter. Blessedly, there was an old barstool nearby and she sat down to thumb through the pages. The familiar smell of newsprint felt like a hug from an old friend. She turned page after page, becoming slowly, thoroughly absorbed in stories about this small Midwestern town, so vastly different from what the big New York papers covered. No sex scandals, no murders, no violence in the streets here. There was coverage of Vietnam, of course, metallic, staccato wire stories that devoted three or four paragraphs to whatever was new before tacking on another 12 or so inches rehashing their old stories. Even we're getting tired of covering this war, Sarah thought, picking up another paper. A wire story on the Columbia riots caught her eye and she sucked in her breath. It was her own story, the one she'd written about the dean being taken hostage. Her heart was pounding wildly, and she glanced around to make sure no one was coming. That no one would have thought twice about what she was looking at had they walked in didn't occur to Sarah as she stared at her byline, feeling suspended in midair, pulled backward just as she'd begun to find her forward stride. She read the story all the way through, and Sarah Adams found herself hoping she could be a fraction of the reporter Sarah Thomas was.

She put the paper aside and rifled through the stack before pulling out another one. This one had what she'd come for – election coverage. Greenview voters had narrowly approved the referendum giving the go-ahead to construction of the new building which, the article said, many were worried could be used to house prisoners from nearby towns that had overcrowding issues. Whether it was actually a valid concern or not the article didn't say, but Sarah knew how rumors ignited and spread, especially in small towns. The fact that it had passed by only a few votes seemed to her to merit more coverage than it had gotten, but probably the lack of staff was to blame.

She put the papers back except for that one and headed back to her desk. She read the article through one more time before picking up the phone and calling the town administrator, the unfortunately named Cletus Coons.

"What can I help you with?" He sounded genial enough, but Sarah thought she could detect a wariness in his voice. Although she could easily have been imagining it – so many years of covering New York City politics made her wont to see deception around every corner. What would politicians in Greenview, Oklahoma possibly have to cover up? But if she believed that, why was she calling?

"I was wondering about the bids for the law enforcement center," Sarah said, keeping her voice casual, conversational.

"The bids? What about the bids?"

"Well, really just who the bidders were," she said. "I'm new in town and I'm trying to familiarize myself with a lot of things that went on here before I came to town."

"I'm really not sure we could provide you with that information," he said. Now there was no mistaking the guardedness in his voice.

It's public record, Sarah thought. *You can and you will*. Aloud, she said, "Oh. Well…shucks. I'm sorry to have bothered you. I'm new on this job – it's funny but between you and me, I just took it because I'm pregnant and bored, waiting for my husband to get home from Vietnam. I was hoping I could impress my new boss with how much I could learn about the town." She sighed delicately. "Oh well. I tried, right?"

"Your husband's in Vietnam?"

"Yeah. I found out I was expecting right after he went back after his last leave. Kind of a kick in the head, right?"

"How'd you end up in Greenview?"

"I have friends, old family friends, who live here and they said I could stay with them until the baby is born. Actually, until my husband comes back for good. It's a nice town. I like it here."

"Tell you what," Cletus said. "Why don't you come by my office this

130

afternoon if you can, and I'll see what background I can give you on that law enforcement center. It's about the biggest project we've done here in awhile."

"Oh!" Sarah's voice was wreathed in smiles. "That would be wonderful. Thank you so much. I'll be by around 2, if that's all right with you."

"Fine. I'll be here."

Sarah hung up and glanced at her watch. It was nearly time for lunch, and Dax was kicking her in the kidneys. She picked up the phone again and called Maggie.

"Mags, want to meet me for lunch?"

"Sure. Ginny's place?"

"Great. See you in a bit."

She grabbed her bag.

"Ellen, I'm going to lunch and then over to town hall for a meeting. I'll be back by 3 or so. Not that there will be any calls for me."

Ellen gave a cracked, smoky laugh and a little wave.

"Already hard at work," she said. "You young people are what keep this paper going."

"Hey! I resemble that remark!" Fred called from his office. Sarah laughed and headed out the door. Seated at Ginny's ten minutes later, she took a sip of grape juice – Ginny had begun keeping it in the refrigerator just for her – and asked Maggie what she knew about the law enforcement center.

"That's a weird question," Maggie answered. "I don't really know too much about it. Why?"

"No reason, really. I was just doing some research on it for a story. Seems like the town was kind of divided over it, from what I read about the referendum results."

"It was, yeah."

"What were the problems? The people who didn't want it, why didn't they? Did you want it?"

131

Maggie shrugged.

"I didn't really care one way or the other," she said. "I knew we'd be getting it no matter what, so I didn't see any point in fighting it. But some people were mighty chapped about it. Said the jail would be full of all sorts of bad eggs that they couldn't fit into other jails."

Bad eggs. Sarah had a mental picture of a prison guard sorting through inmates and stamping every few with a big red REJECT before tossing them down a chute that opened into a cell in Greenview's shiny new law enforcement center.

"I was just curious about it," Sarah said diffidently, slathering bright yellow mustard onto the ham and cheese sandwich Ginny had just set in front of her. "It's rare for a referendum in such a small town to pass by such a narrow margin."

"Is it?"

Sarah had no idea, of course, she'd just pulled that out of thin air because it sounded good. She nodded and took a big bite of her sandwich to avoid answering directly.

"I'll tell you one thing I do know," Maggie said. "Alan submitted a bid to do the roofing work, and he was turned down flat-out for some big city operation out of Oklahoma City. You'd think he'd have had a better shot, being local and all, but I guess those big guys can afford to undercut the little guys just to get the job."

Sarah picked up the second half of her sandwich, keeping her face down so Maggie couldn't see her expression. She felt the familiar stirring in her belly – for once not from Dax, who was apparently passed out on grape juice and ham – the one that told her when she was onto something.

"That's interesting," she said, keeping her tone casual. "Who ended up doing the roof, do you know?"

"Some outfit... let me think. Some kind of bland, boring name. Acme. No, wait. Ace. That's it. Ace Roofing."

"Do you know if anyone else in town had businesses that put in bids on the project and didn't get them?"

132

"Yeah, there was kind of a stink about it for a bit. One of the plumbers in town and a concrete guy both bid and didn't get it either. Same kind of thing. Big city outfits outbid them."

It was all Sarah could do to stay in her chair and finish lunch when she heard that. If there wasn't bid rigging involved here, she'd never trust her instincts again. She forced herself to talk about other things with Maggie – her grandkids, the weather, the church choir director resigning suddenly – and resisted the impulse to look at her watch. Finally, she said she needed to get back to work.

"I'm going to town hall and then over to see this famous law enforcement center," she said, slinging her bag over her shoulder.

"How're you going to get out there?" Maggie asked.

"Out where?"

"The law enforcement center. It's way out on the west edge of town, a good four miles from here."

Sarah hadn't thought of that. She couldn't haul herself four miles, that was for sure. She wondered if she'd ever get used to not being in New York, where she could take a cab or the subway anyplace she needed to go and never think twice about it.

"I don't know," she admitted.

"You ain't in New York anymore, missy!" Maggie teased. "You can take my car. Just drop it off later. I don't need it this afternoon."

They walked back to Maggie's house. By now Sarah could barely conceal her impatience. She kissed Maggie goodbye and drove off in the direction of town hall. She hadn't been this excited about a story since she left New York. The fact that this was the only story she'd done since she left New York may have played a part in that.

"Hi, I'm Sarah Adams, here to see Mr. Coons," she told the woman at the front desk.

"Of course," the woman said, pointing down a short hallway. "First door on the right. He's expecting you."

Chapter 29

Whatever Sarah had expected of Cletus Coons, what she got wasn't it. She'd anticipated an older man, paunchy and bald, with the relaxed attitude and general moseying style she'd come to think of as the Official Greenview Personality. What she got was a tall, well-dressed man not much older than her, with slicked-back dark blonde hair, an angular face, and a deep cleft in his chin. She was so thrown off by his appearance that he asked her if she was all right and motioned for her to sit.

"I'm fine," she said. "I'm sorry, you just…" she faltered. There was no way she could, or should, verbalize any of those thoughts. He leaned back in his chair and smiled.

"Wasn't what you expected?"

"Well, yeah. Sorry."

"No need. I actually get that a lot. Or I did. Now that I've been in town for awhile, I don't hear it quite as much."

"Oh, you're not from here? I thought everyone was born here, raised their kids here, then died here."

"That paints kind of a grim picture, but yeah. Pretty much. I moved here from back east a few years ago. I've gotten used to the Midwestern lifestyle, but I know I still don't really blend in too well."

Sarah laughed.

"No, you don't. Where are you from back east?"

"New York," he said.

Thankfully, he misread Sarah's startled reaction.

"I know, I know. People here recoil when I say that, as if I said I just came from a leper colony. But I was looking to get out of the rat race and settle down someplace quiet. The usual story. Met a nice Midwestern girl and here I am."

"Wow, yeah, funny how life works," she said, trying to keep her composure. Why finding out he was from New York was rattling her so much, she wasn't sure.

"What about you?" he said. "You said you've just moved here. Where do you hail from?"

"Chicago," she said. "Not as glamorous as New York, but still a bigger city than Greenview."

"What did you do before you entered the exciting world of small-town journalism?"

Sarah was starting to get pissed. She wasn't used to being the one answering questions and, as usual when she got agitated, Dax decided to start kicking.

"I was a kindergarten teacher," she invented. "Although I always liked to write, so when I found out about this job, I took it. It's just temporary. I'm filling in for Megan until she gets back from leave."

"Oh yes, I heard about her grandparents," Cletus said. "Nice of her to help out."

"So I do appreciate your willingness to talk with me about the law enforcement center," Sarah said, shifting the subject back to where she could regain her footing. "I really want to do a good job here and impress Fred."

"Fred's a good man," Cletus said comfortably. "So what can I tell you about the law enforcement center? Have you been out there? It's the town's pride and joy."

"I saw it in passing but I haven't been out to really look around."

"Stop by anytime. Chief Weck loves to give tours."

"I'll do that," Sarah said and, after a split second's deliberation, decided not to show her whole hand at once. Something about this guy made her think he wouldn't be easy to fool. "So I understand that a lot of people in town were worried that prisoners from other towns and cities would end up here if their own jails were overcrowded."

"Yes, that was one of the major concerns."

"Is that proving to be the case? I've heard my husband say a thousand times that prison overcrowding is a problem in this country."

"Well, it is a problem in general, but not so much here in the Midwest. We haven't seen any prisoners from other jurisdictions brought in here since we opened, and I don't know that we expect to."

"Why did people think that?"

"Oh, you know how these small towns are. Someone gets an idea in their head and tells a couple of people at choir practice, and they tell someone they bump into at the grocery store and the next thing you know the villagers are out with their pitchforks."

"Mmm." Sarah was thinking.

"But that being said, I'm not saying we'll never have another town ask us to house overflow prisoners," he said. "It could happen, sure. I'm just saying we haven't had any such requests."

"I gotcha," Sarah said. "Now there's one other thing I'm curious about. I mentioned it to you on the phone. About the bids. Was there an RFP?"

"Yes," he said. "It was all routine. We issued a request for bids, got several, and awarded the bid to the one we felt was appropriate."

"The lowest?"

"Not necessarily. It's generally considered the best idea to throw out the highest and lowest, and choose one in the middle."

"Why is that?" Sarah asked, knowing the answer full well.

"Because that's where you'll find the bidders who are actually the most realistic about what a project will cost. Too high and they're usually trying to pad the bill, too low and they're either deliberately trying to undercut everyone else or else they honestly don't know what they're doing. Either way, not someone you want taking on an important project."

"Yes, I get that. So can I see a list of the bidders? You know, because I'm just curious how it works."

"I don't have that here," he said. "You'd have to get that from the clerk's office. They're down the hall."

"Oh, right. Okay. Well, I think those are all my questions. You've been a lot of help. I'll be sure and stop by for a tour from the police chief."

"You do that," he said, offering her his hand.

He watched her go, heard her voice floating up from down the hall as she told the clerk what she wanted. He reached for the phone and dialed the mayor at home.

"Phil, there's a reporter here asking questions about the bids on the law enforcement center," Cletus said.

"A reporter? From where?"

"Local rag."

"Oh. Well, big deal. That crew is the saddest bunch of journalists I've ever seen. Who is it?"

"She said she's new. Temporary. Sarah Adams is her name."

"Never heard of her."

"She's new in town too. But here's the thing, I'm not sure she's legit."

"What do you mean? She's not a real reporter?"

"No, I think she is. But she made it sound like she isn't. She said this is just a temp job, like a hobby. But there's something about her demeanor, the kinds of questions she asked. I've dealt with a lot of media in my day, and no ditzy housewife who wants to play journalist would think to ask about bids, not to mention ask about an RFP."

"She actually said RFP?"

"Yeah."

"Hmm."

"You see my point. And anyway, there's something really familiar about her. I can't put my finger on it."

"Well, let me know if you hear anything else. If we play it cool, maybe the whole thing will die down. There's nothing in those bids that will jump out at her. I'm guessing she'll lose interest and move on to something else."

Down the hall, Sarah found what she was looking for.

Chapter 30

"I'm considering sending a reporter to Vietnam," Zachary told Stan the next morning. When Zachary had buzzed the editor and asked to see him, Stan had run down a mental list of what it might be about. This, however, had not been on the list.

"What? You can't be serious."

"Why can't I be serious?"

"Because it's late in the game," Stan said. "Nixon and Johnson are both saying that if they get elected, they'll pull the troops out."

Zachary impatiently shook a cigarette out of the pack on his desk and lit it.

"We both know that's bullshit, Stan, we're years away from being out of that war."

"And you're sure enough about that to send a Beacon reporter over there?"

"Stan, do me a favor."

"What's that?"

"Remember that you work for me."

Stan took a deep breath.

"Yeah, okay. So you want to send a reporter to Vietnam."

"I do. I am tired of worn-out wire stories that have an inch or two of something new, then repeats of the same old information. I want a reporter on the ground there, I want someone to find an angle that hasn't been told, and I want them to tell it through the Beacon."

"Who do you have in mind?" Stan, finally realizing this wasn't going to be a short visit, sat down in the chair across from Zachary's desk. "It's too bad Sarah's not here."

He's telling me, Zachary thought, rubbing his fingertips across his forehead.

"Yes, that would be great but since she's not, what other suggestions do you have?"

"Rick?"

Zachary considered.

"Maybe," he said. "I would prefer someone with a little more seniority here, though, and then we'd have to put someone new on city hall yet again."

"Denise?"

"Denise can't even get herself to work on time, and you told me yourself you've had some complaints about her work. So no. Not a chance."

"Well," Stan said slowly. "I don't know how you'd feel about this idea, but what about me?"

Zachary looked up sharply.

"You?"

"Yeah," Stan said with spreading certainty. "Why not me? I was a hell of a reporter before I became an editor. And to be honest, I have been itching to get back into it again."

Zachary stared at him. He hadn't considered Stan as a possibility, but the more he thought about it, the surer he was that Stan was the only one he could send.

"Being on the ground in Saigon is a pretty rough way to get back into it, son. Are you sure? Why don't you give it some thought for a few days, talk to your family, then you can let me know if you still think you want to."

"I don't have to give it any thought," Stan said. "I have never been more positive of anything in my life. Send me to Vietnam, Mr. Benton, and I'll bring you home a Pulitzer."

Zachary hesitated, but the look on Stan's face made him smile.

"Shit, kid, you look just like I would have at your age. All right, grab your rucksack. You're going to Vietnam."

At the staff meeting that afternoon, Zachary broke the news to the others. It was, predictably, a mixed bag of reactions.

"If you wanted a senior reporter to cover the war, I'd have thought I'd be the obvious choice," Denise said stiffly.

"Can't spare you, Denise, you're far too valuable," Zachary said smoothly. "Now, we have one related announcement to make, and that is who will be taking over Stan's editor duties. We discussed it at some length, and at Stan's suggestion, we've asked Rick to take over that job, and he has agreed."

"What? Why him?"

"Denise, if you'd like to come to my office after the meeting and explain why you're so unhappy with your job, I'd be interested to hear it," Zachary said mildly. She sank back in her chair with a scowl.

"Now," he went on. "These changes will all go into effect as of Monday. If anyone has any questions in the meantime, feel free to come to me."

Back in his office, he dialed Sarah's number. To his relief, she picked up.

"I wasn't sure you'd be home," he said, letting her voice wash over him.

"I actually just came in," she said. "I was out for lunch."

"Oh? Hot date?"

"Yeah, sort of."

"What? I was just joking!"

Sarah laughed.

"I know, silly, so was I. But I did have lunch with someone. The Presbyterian minister in town."

"That's not exactly what I expected you to say. Who is he?"

"His name is Von Humboldt. He's been very kind to me. I'm starting to kind of consider him a friend."

"I'm glad," Zachary said. "So I don't need to be jealous?"

"If it makes you get on a plane faster and get out here to me, then you should be absolutely insanely jealous."

"Speaking of planes, that's one of the things I wanted to talk to you about," Zachary said. "I'm sending Stan to Vietnam."

"What?"

"I've been giving it a lot of thought, and I have to do something to elevate the Beacon, to really show the Times that we can compete with them, head to head."

"So you decided to send a reporter to Vietnam? God, Zachary, that is a big-balls move."

"You think it was the right decision?"

"Honestly? Yes. My knee-jerk reaction is yes. Probably you should have done it three years ago."

"I thought of that. But better late than never. In fact, I was thinking it could actually give us a chance to really shine, if he can find some angles that haven't been covered yet. I don't know yet what that would be, but I trust Stan."

"I do too," Sarah said. "What made you choose him?"

"He actually volunteered while we were kicking around some names. He first suggested Denise but I shot that one right down."

"Ugh. She'd be a nightmare. She's way too much of a prima donna for an assignment that gritty."

"That's what I thought too. So we bounced around another couple of names, and then Stan said he wanted to go. So that's who I'm sending."

"Vietnam? He's sending Stan to Vietnam?" Hanna stared at Rick through a tendril of smoke. "But darling, that's marvelous!"

"Well, he's got his eye on a Pulitzer for war coverage."

"No no, darling, that's not the marvelous part. I'm talking about you taking over as editor. You'll be in a much better position to see when Zachary may be talking to Sarah on the phone, when letters arrive from her, that sort of thing."

"And of course, doing editor work," Rick said crossly. Hanna waved her hand dismissively.

"Yes, of course. I don't know why you should even sound surprised that Stan named you as his successor. You are miles away the most talented journalist on that staff, including the sainted Sarah. You were the only real choice."

She's finally starting to realize I'm a serious journalist, and not just her toy, Rick thought, taking her hand and pulling her toward his bed.

Men are such simpletons, Hanna thought, allowing herself to be pulled. *He has no idea just how little use he will be to me when this is all over.*

Zachary left the office later than he'd intended, although he was satisfied everything was squared away with Stan's departure for Saigon in the morning. Zachary knew a couple of Associated Press reporters there who had promised to help him get acclimated, but he was also aware that Stan was a seasoned journalist who could handle anything anyone threw at him. Zachary shut his mind to any other dangers he might have placed his employee in. He just had to trust in the gut instinct that had told him to send someone.

The now-familiar click noise sounded from somewhere behind him as Zachary reached for the handle of his car door. His nerves were just about shot. He dropped the bag he was carrying and took off at a run from the direction he'd heard it. He turned one corner, then another, but the parking garage was nearly empty.

"GODDAMMIT!" he suddenly shouted, his voice bouncing off the cement walls. "SHOW YOURSELF, YOU FUCKING COWARD!"

He fell silent except for his ragged breathing. He was shaking in fear and anger. After a few moments, he realized he was completely alone.

"I'm cracking up," he muttered to himself, walking back to his car. "I'm under too much stress. I need a shrink. Or a vacation. Or both."

He got into his car and lit a cigarette, trying to calm down. A pair of headlights came down from the ramp above, making him jump. He had just been up there but there had been no other cars, he was sure of it. He watched in his rear view mirror as the car passed behind him, but it was too dark to see the other driver. The car didn't slow at all as it drove down the next ramp and disappeared from sight.

When his heart rate had returned to what passed for normal these days, Zachary drove to a small post office branch in Queens and mailed Sarah a package of things he'd been collecting for the baby: the books that had started the whole thing, a funky-colored pacifier he knew she'd like, an assortment of tiny New York t-shirts, and the absolute smallest three-piece suit he'd ever seen. He also added a sexy nightie for her, and a box of her favorite doughnuts.

"My sweetest love," he wrote on the note inside. "I have been unable to stop myself from buying things for our little one, and of course for you. It makes me feel closer to you, and closer to our life together. We will have it soon, my love, our life together, our baby, our family, our future, our forever."

He posted the box and drove slowly back to Manhattan, his tumultuous thoughts finally cornering him.

It's time, he thought. *I'm putting the paper on more solid footing now, and it's time for me to cut my ties here and move to Oklahoma with Sarah. We can come back later, when the dust has settled. Our lives are ultimately here, but right now, my life is with Sarah, wherever that may be. I can't stay here. This feeling of being watched, that god-damned clicking noise…I don't know if Hanna is having me followed or if this is a political thing about to blow up in my face, but something is happening. I can't stay here anymore.*

When he got home, he went upstairs and took out the pistol he kept in the bedroom closet. He found the box of bullets behind it, loaded the chamber, put the safety on, and tucked it into his briefcase. Hanna had insisted, years ago, that they have a gun in the house for protection, but never had Zachary carried it. But never had he been this afraid.

Chapter 31

"It's just too much of a coincidence that all of these winning bids are from Oklahoma City," Sarah muttered to herself, flipping through the pages of her notebook for the fifteenth time.

"Uh oh, she's talking to herself again!" Fred said cheerfully, heading to the vending machine in the back for his afternoon can of Pepsi.

"Hey Fred, come look at this," she said. "Does this seem weird to you?"

She showed him the list of winning bidders for the law enforcement center project.

"What's weird about it? A lot of big companies do business here, from Oklahoma City and Tulsa especially."

"I know, but I heard from a pretty reliable source that two local contractors put in bids and didn't get it."

"Well, that's unfortunate as we always like to keep business in town when we can, but it's hardly illegal, now is it?"

"I don't know," Sarah said. "It might be."

"What are you talking about?" He half-sat on her desk, one leg swinging slightly as he looked at her curiously.

"I just wonder if there's a connection between all these bidders," she said.

"You mean like bid rigging?"

"Maybe."

Fred gave a low whistle.

"That's a pretty heavy charge to bring against the town," he said. "Do your homework."

And he was gone, off to get his Pepsi. Sarah knew this was the only nod she was going to get from him to pursue the story, but it was all she needed. She called information and got the number for the tax assessor's office in Oklahoma City. She explained to the woman who answered the phone who she was and what she wanted. Her call was transferred three times, each person less helpful than the last, until she finally landed on the desk of a woman who sounded both young and bored, but assured Sarah she could help.

"Great," Sarah said. "I just need to know the name of the owner of six businesses in Oklahoma City."

"Go ahead."

"The first is Ace Roofing." She read the address and waited. She could hear the woman shuffling papers.

"Here it is, Ace Roofing. The owner is a John C. Drummond."

"Great. The next one is C & S Plumbing."

More paper shuffling.

"That's also John C. Drummond."

I knew it, Sarah thought, her heart beginning to pound.

"How about Reliable Masonry and Concrete?"

"Hang on, I just saw that one… here it is. It says the owner is J.C. Drummond."

"He thinks he's clever, using his initials."

"Beg pardon?"

"Nothing, just thinking out loud."

She read off the rest of the list, and the last two came back with a different name entirely.

"Lisa Dubrowski? Are you sure?"

"Yes, I'm looking right at it."

"Okay," Sarah said. "Okay, thanks. I appreciate your help."

She hung up the phone and read back over what she'd written down. Even if the last two companies were owned by someone else, the fact that this John Drummond person owned the first four was enough to go on. Still, something rankled. She thought for a moment, then got up and grabbed her bag.

"I'm running to the library for a bit," she called to Ellen as she headed out the door.

"I didn't have that much energy when I wasn't pregnant," she heard Ellen remark to Fred as the door closed behind her.

At the library, Sarah easily found the filing cabinet that held hundreds of rolls of microfilm, individually boxed and carefully labeled. And, she was thrilled to see, they had papers from all over Oklahoma. She took out several boxes of The Oklahoman and loaded one onto the reel. She only really wanted the weddings, but as always, she found herself absorbed in the news stories. Dax, unhappy if she sat still for too long, began doing what felt like somersaults.

"Would you be still?" she said. "Mommy's working."

In response, he kicked her bladder.

"What is the matter with you, kid? Knock it off. Oh, you are definitely your father's child."

She went through reel after reel over the past ten years, scanning the marriage announcements. She was just about to give up when she found it.

"Pay dirt," she whispered, staring at the screen. "Lisa Dubrowski Marries Eric Drummond. The bride is a graduate of blah blah blah... uh... here it is. The bridegroom is the son of John and Lillian Drummond of Guthrie. Son of a bitch. He put two of those businesses in her name. Clever, Mr. Drummond, clever. You thought you could pull a fast one on sweet, innocent Greenview. You didn't count on me waddling into town."

Back at the office, she called and introduced herself to Police Chief Weck, who hailed her cheerfully.

"I'm new at the paper, actually just temporary, but Cletus at town hall suggested I come by for a tour of the law enforcement center. He said it's the town's pride and joy."

"That it is," he said. "You're welcome to come by anytime. I'd be glad to give you the nickel tour."

"Well, if you're free later, how about I come by on my way home? Say, around 4?"

"Sure, that actually works well. Looking forward to meeting you."

When she hung up, Sarah sat at her desk, thinking for a long time. Finally she got up and, carrying her notebook, went into Fred's office.

"I just thought I'd tell you what I found out," she said. "Of the six winning bids on that project, four of the companies are owned by a man named John Drummond. Two are owned by a woman I've since found out is his daughter-in-law, using her maiden name."

"Wow," Fred said. "That's big. This could be a big story, Sarah. Are you sure you're up to it? I mean, no offense. But stories like this are usually covered by senior reporters."

"Yeah, I know," Sarah said drily. "But I'm a quick study."

When she pulled up in front of the law enforcement center, she had to admit it was an impressive structure. Two levels tall, it was far more sprawling than she'd realized. In fact, it was huge. No wonder the people in town hadn't been all that thrilled with the idea.

From the outside, it looked more like a large office building, with deep terra cotta colored brick interspersed with bright teal tiles every few feet. The windows still had that shiny, fragile look that new windows have. New buildings always made Sarah feel a little sad. They had no history, no stories to tell.

The police chief, tall and dark impeccably dressed in a navy blue uniform, greeted her warmly.

"Quite a place you've got here," Sarah said, shaking his hand. "It doesn't look like a jail at all from the outside."

"Yeah, I was pushing for barbed wire fences and a guard tower, but the town said no."

Sarah laughed.

"I guess it's a lot more than just a jail, though."

"It is, yeah. On this side is the police department, and on the other side is the fire department. The paramedics are still downtown, in the old building. It's pretty centrally located, and they're happy to have the place to themselves. Anyway, the jail is in the back. It's not huge, but bigger than the four holding cells we had in the old building."

He showed her around, through the police department and back to the jail, then into the fire department, where the stout and jolly fire chief gave her a short tour of the fire department.

Back in Chief Weck's office, Sarah sank gratefully into a proffered chair.

"So how do you like Greenview so far?" the chief asked.

"I like it. Actually, I'd go so far as saying I've started to love it."

"You sound surprised."

"Well, I'm from Chicago," she said, narrowly skidding around the words 'New York.' "So it's been kind of a culture shock for me. But now that I'm used to the, you know, slower pace and the whole small-town scene, I really like it."

"Chicago, yeah, I've been there. It's a great city. But it's funny, people consider Chicago and Detroit the Midwest and they technically are, but they're not like here. This is the rural Midwest at its finest."

"That's what I like about it. It feels almost Mayberry like."

"Mayberry. Yep. That's us all over."

"I guess that makes you Barney Fife?"

"Hey now. I'm Sheriff Taylor and you know it."

Sarah laughed.

"I appreciate the tour, chief, but I need to ask if I can use the ladies room and then I need to get myself back on the road."

"Sure thing," he said, standing up. "You come by anytime, or if you need anything, just give a holler."

As she headed toward Maggie and Alan's to drop off the car, she thought about what she'd seen and heard. She considered herself a pretty good judge of people, and any reporter who'd been in the business as long as

148

she had better have sharp enough instincts to know when someone was hiding something. She was willing to bet everything that the police chief and the fire chief knew nothing about what she was now positive had happened with those bids.

She remembered Zachary saying she could have taken down Tammany Hall if she wanted to and she smiled to herself. Greenview Town Hall was about as far from Tammany Hall as you could get, but she was going to take it down anyway.

Chapter 32

Stan filed his first story from Saigon three days later, and Zachary slammed both his fists down onto his desk in elation. He called Rick into his office.

"Look at this," he said, handing him the story. "The son of a bitch did it. This story is the best one any reporter has done in months."

Rick sat down and read through it. Zachary was right – Stan had apparently befriended two American soldiers and was setting the stage for telling their stories, individually and together. This one was an overview, as deep as he'd been able to go in such a short time, but it was apparent to his editors where he was headed in future articles.

"Put that on the front page," Zachary ordered.

"Yes sir." Rick headed back into the newsroom. For the first time in weeks, something besides stress and fear was making Zachary's blood pound in his ears. This was going to be it. Even if Stan didn't land a Pulitzer from this, it was going to be enough, more than enough, to show the journalism world that Zachary Benton hadn't lost his edge, that he was still a man no one wanted to mess around with. This would be his legacy, his last hurrah before he retired and settled down with Sarah to raise their family.

He was suddenly exhausted. Weeks of not sleeping or sleeping only with the help of his best single-malt scotch, which was morphing disturbingly quickly into an empty bottle, had begun to take its toll on him. He was hearing the clicking noise everywhere now, every time there was even a moment of silence. The night before he was sure he'd seen the same car that had driven past him in the parking garage driving away from an illegal parking spot in front of his brownstone when he'd come home. He wasn't sure if it was the stress affecting his sleep or the lack of sleep making him paranoid.

He picked up the phone and dialed his doctor's office. The receptionist must have been new because she kept insisting Zachary make an appointment.

"Just please ask Dr. Razler to call me," Zachary said. "He can decide if I need an appointment."

Hanging up, Zachary drummed his fingers on his desktop, turning his thoughts back to the paper. He hadn't editorialized on the war in Vietnam – it seemed too easy to take the popular "this is not our war" stance to curry public favor – but maybe now it was time. He turned to his typewriter and, after another moment's thought, began to type. The phone on his desk buzzed, making him jump.

"Zachary Benton."

"Zachary, it's Bob Razler. I got a message you called?"

"Bob, thanks for getting back to me so quickly."

He gave the doctor a brief overview of his insomnia problems.

"Well, you know I'm not going to bother asking if it's stress. You're a journalist in New York. If you weren't stressed I'd be worried about the state of your liver."

"That's why I'm calling you. I need something to help me sleep besides scotch."

"What did we have you on before?" Dr. Razler asked, reaching for Zachary's file.

"Trazodone," Zachary said. "But I'm not sure I wouldn't rather be just be taking good old Valium."

"You shouldn't take either one with scotch," the doctor warned.

"No, I know," Zachary said. "I want something to take the edge off and help me sleep so I can stop the scotch. I hate the way it makes my head feel in the morning."

"Ah, the scotch hangover," Dr. Razler said cheerfully. "Haven't had one of those in years. I'll call in a prescription for Valium, but you first have to promise me you'll stop by for a checkup within the next two weeks, and I am not kidding. I really shouldn't even be writing a prescription based on a phone call, but you've been my patient for years and you are always good about taking care of yourself. So I'll call this in, but you get your ass in here so I can check your vitals."

151

"Yes, boss," Zachary said with a grin.

He stopped at the pharmacy on his way home. By the time he walked in the back door of the brownstone, Hanna knew about the Valium. She jotted it into her tiny red alligator notebook, just beneath "mailed a package from post office in Queens" and slipped it back into her purse before going downstairs to greet her husband.

"Darling, you look exhausted," she purred. "Can I make you a drink?"

"No, but thank you. I've got a whopper of a headache tonight, so I think I'll just stick with coffee."

After dinner, Zachary locked himself in the bathroom where he took a Valium and a hot shower. He didn't even remember getting into bed.

He awoke the next morning feeling like a new man. He picked up the Beacon from his front stoop and opened it over croissants and coffee.

"Look at this," he said to Hanna when she came in. "Stan's first story from Vietnam."

She looked over his shoulder at the front page.

"Hmm, very impressive," she said. "He's interviewing American GIs?"

"Two of them," Zachary said. "One is from New York City, the other is from northern New Jersey. He managed to find a local angle on an international story. That's gold."

"Well, it was a stroke of genius for you to send him in the first place, darling," Hanna said, pouring herself a cup of coffee. Zachary murmured a response before turning to the op-ed page to check his editorial. It looked great. Everything looked great and for the first time in ages, he felt like he was back at the top of his game.

At the office an hour later, he called Sarah.

"Good morning, my love," she said sleepily.

"I always call you too early, don't I? Poor sweet baby."

"No, it's all right. I should have been up ages ago."

Zachary laughed.

"Oh sure," he said. "Today was just a fluke. Ordinarily you'd have been up at the crack of dawn, going out for a jog."

Sarah groaned and rolled onto her side.

"I'm glad you think you're funny," she said. "You're not the one hauling this fat little turd of a kid around in your belly."

"And I'm exceedingly grateful for that. But I am sorry I woke you, my love, I just couldn't wait to tell you all the good news here."

Sarah swung her legs over the edge of the bed and into her slippers.

"So tell me," she said, shuffling into the kitchen and plugging in the coffee pot. "I'm up and I'm all ears."

He told her about Stan's article, about the series it would turn into, and that he'd finally editorialized about the war. When he'd finished, all he could hear on Sarah's end was the faint sound of coffee percolating.

"Are you there, my love?"

"Yes," she said quietly. "I'm here and I'm being ridiculous." He could hear the tears in front of her voice. He immediately understood.

"My Sarah, you know you would have been my first choice to send to Vietnam for this, if you'd been here and if I could have lived with the thought of sending you into a war zone."

"I know," she said, then sniffled loudly. "I know, and I'm just being childish. Dax is wreaking havoc with my hormones."

"Well, but I can understand. You were our star reporter, and the one who covered Vietnam from the local angle. You know I would have sent you. But honestly, the thought of putting you on a plane to Saigon makes me feel ill."

"It's moot anyway," Sarah said. "Greenview, Oklahoma isn't exactly Saigon."

"But the main thing is that if this goes as well as I think it's going to, the paper will be on the best possible footing to compete with the Times, and I'll be able to leave with my head held high."

"Leave?" Sarah's heart was in her throat. "Where are you going?"

Zachary smiled into the phone.

"I'm heading for Greenview, Oklahoma," he said. "I heard it's beautiful this time of year."

Sarah started to cry for real.

"When?" she asked. "When can you get here?"

"Oh my love, you have no idea how much I wish I were stepping off the plane right now," he said. "There is nothing I want more than to touch you again, to feel you in my arms, to hold you close to me at night."

Sarah was sobbing, relief flooding through every cell in her body. Dax stirred crankily. It was still too early for his taste.

"But as it stands, it will be a little while yet. I need to tell Hanna I'm moving out, and I need to tender my resignation with the paper, but most of the legalities I can take care of through the mail and over the phone. I'd say I'll be there within the next six weeks."

"Oh Zachary, oh my love, you'll be here for the birth. I'm getting close to full term and I've been worried you'd miss it."

"I wouldn't miss it for the world."

By the time they hung up, Zachary felt better, stronger, and more focused than he had in months.

He called his attorney.

"Frank, it's Zachary. I'm ready to tell Hanna I'm leaving. Start drawing up the papers."

"Ready to pull the ol' trigger, huh?" Frank lit a cigarette and leaned back in his chair. He was amazed it had taken Zachary this long. Frank had practically been born a hard-boiled attorney, or so his parents always told people, illustrating with the fact that he had once issued his siblings subpoenas to appear in his room and explain the disappearance of a burlap bag of Indian head pennies he'd been collecting. Over the years he'd put people behind bars, he'd argued high-profile cases, he'd been the one phone call of some of New York's most notorious. But even

Frank found Hanna Benton scary as hell.

"It's time," Zachary said. "And I need to get out of New York, at least for awhile. I haven't been sleeping, I'm hearing weird noises, I think I'm being followed."

"Is that for real, or because you're not sleeping? Or are you hitting the hooch?"

"Yes, probably, and yes. Well, I was hitting the single malt pretty hard, but I had to back off now the doc has me on Valium."

"Shit, you are messed up."

"Yeah," Zachary said, taking off his glasses and rubbing his eyes. "But I'm taking my life back. I'm getting away from Hanna once and for all, I'm getting away from the Beacon, and I'm starting a new life with Sarah. No more stress, no more worries, no more of this needless drama."

"Well, good for you, old friend. I'll have the paperwork drawn up by the end of the week. If you want my personal and professional opinion, I'd wait until it's ready to say one word to Hanna. And once you do, Zachary, run like hell. Run like hell and do not look back."

Chapter 33

The problem, Sarah discovered as she delved further into her story, was that she didn't know who she could trust in this town. Ironically, in the deep political sea of New York, she always knew who would give her good information, who was on the take, and who would run her down in a dark alley if she asked the wrong questions. Here, in quiet, pretty little Greenview, she suddenly felt as though there were snipers on every rooftop and eyes in every hedgerow. Fred knew what she was working on, of course, but he was of oddly little help. He seemed to run the paper because he needed a job and not because he particularly cared about journalism. At least not real journalism, with all due respect to county fairs and regional spelling bees.

She finally decided her first stop would have to be Alan. Maggie already had an inkling of what she was working on from all the questions Sarah had asked her over lunch at Ginny's that day. She knew she could trust them. They were the logical place to start. She called Maggie and asked if she could take them out to dinner someplace, preferably in the next town, so they could talk about something she needed to discuss.

"That's real sweet of you, hon, but why don't you come over here instead? I'm making lasagna tonight and Alan always says I make enough to feed 30 people anyway. Besides, if it's something you don't want the gossip mill getting ahold of, even the next town over won't give you enough privacy."

Maggie's suggestion was more than good with Sarah, and she stopped for a bottle of wine on the way over later.

"Now you know you shouldn't be drinking wine, little miss," Maggie said, kissing her.

"Oh, Dr. Weatherby said I can have a little now and then, it doesn't hurt. And it will make a nice change from these damned grape juice cravings. I figure it's only a matter of time until I turn purple, which would only make sense now that I'm grape shaped."

Over a tossed salad, butter-soaked garlic bread, and lasagna filled with more meat and cheese than she'd ever consumed in one sitting, Sarah told Maggie and Alan what she was working on.

"I'll be damned," Alan said. His face was inscrutable. Maggie poured more wine into each of their glasses. No one spoke for a moment.

"You know, that actually makes sense now," Alan said finally. "The whole thing makes sense now. But here's my question: how're you gonna prove any of this?"

"I don't know yet," Sarah admitted. "If there was bid rigging involved, you know there were some hefty kickbacks. I need to first be able to prove that the fix was in for this John Drummond to win all the contracts. Then I need to find out why. There's no question in my mind he was lining someone's pockets. Probably a lot of someones."

"The mayor and his wife got new matching BMWs last year," Maggie chimed in.

Sarah turned to stare at her.

"What?"

"Yeah, last year. One day they both were suddenly just tooling around town in matching dark blue BMWs. She told me they were their anniversary gift to each other. No one in town was impressed. I mean, how ostentatious can you get?"

"You think that might have been a kickback?" Alan said. "Sure sounds like it to me now."

"Yeah," Sarah said, thinking hard. "It sure does. Maggie, anything else like that around town the past year or so that I should know about?"

Maggie considered.

"Well now, I don't think so," she said, but then her face lit up. "Wait, yes there is. Cletus Coons and his wife had a gigantic addition put on their house just before Christmas last year. Remember that, Alan? People thought that was awful uppity of them, especially considering her parents are just poor farmers. They're good people, mind you, but they're a far cry from wealthy. They're just gettin' by. And here these two put on an addition to their house that probably tripled its size.

At first everybody thought maybe her parents were moving in with them, but that never happened. I haven't been inside, but Barb at church told me one room just has a pool table in it. A pool table!" Maggie was sincerely scandalized.

"Oh boy," Sarah breathed. She glanced at Alan. "I think we're definitely onto something here."

"Yeah," Alan said. "Yeah, I think so."

Sarah lay awake for a long time that night, wishing she could talk to Zachary. She knew what she had to do, but she would have loved to talk it over with him, kick around a few ideas. She missed everything about him, not the least of which was the fact that he would get it. He would get why she was chasing this story when the law enforcement center was already finished. He would get why she couldn't just let it go. He would, she thought, closing her eyes and trying to pull him close, just get it.

Chapter 34

"Wait," Sarah shifted the phone to her other ear and instinctively lowered her voice. "Who did you say this is?"

"I didn't," the man's quiet voice said. "I'm a … source. A friend. You can trust me, Sarah."

A journalist has no friends, Sarah thought. Aloud, she said, "Okay, that's good. So what've you got?"

"I've heard about what you're working on. You're right about the law enforcement center," the man said. "The whole thing was rigged. John Drummond is a big time con man. He sets up companies all over the Midwest, and when he gets a whiff of projects like this one, he submits bids by the handful. Sometimes he bids against himself, just to give the illusion that there are lots of bidders."

"Yeah," Sarah said quietly. "That's pretty slick. Especially if you think you're getting one over on a bunch of small town bumpkins."

The man gave a short, dry laugh.

"That's not what this one is," he said. "Not by a long shot. In all your digging you haven't turned up that John Drummond is Phil Conway's uncle?"

"Phil Conway? The mayor of Greenview?"

"That's the one. It's not really common knowledge due to some weird step-parent, adoption thing a long time ago. But yeah. Drummond is Conway's uncle."

"So the fix was in from the beginning."

"Bingo."

Sarah's mind was racing, jumping and stumbling. Dax, who always loved the way her heart raced when she was wound up, gave her an encouraging kick in the bladder.

"Oooof!"

"Beg pardon?"

"Nothing, that wasn't for you. So how do I prove this? It's such a small town and to be honest, I've already raised a lot of eyebrows with the questions I've been asking."

"Well, you're in luck. I have documentation you can use."

"What kind of documentation?"

"Proof, honey. Cold, hard, legal, irrefutable proof of everything that went down."

"And you're giving this to me why?" She was sniffing like mad for a rat.

"I don't know you, but I know Alan, and he's a good man. He didn't deserve to get screwed over like he did. None of the local guys did. And to be honest, I'm one of the people Drummond screwed over a few years back. I did a lot of digging around when it happened, and I found some pretty good information about Drummond and what he's doing. I just couldn't find anyone interested in hearing about it. I went to the paper with it then, but they wouldn't touch it. When I heard about you, I knew you'd be the one to give all this to."

"I appreciate that," Sarah said. "So how can I get this stuff from you?"

"I can't let anyone see me talking to you," he said. "You're too visible now. I'll leave it in the park. You know the statue of the Civil War general on the horse?"

"Yeah."

"There's a hollow place where the stirrup on his right foot doesn't touch the horse. I'll put it in an envelope and I'll hide it there."

"When?"

"This afternoon. Four o'clock. Try to get there as close to that as you can. A lot of times once it gets dark, kids in the park like to prank the statue."

"Prank the statue?"

"Yeah. You know. Put a bra on the general, put real horse shit under the horse's tail."

160

"Oh that's nice."

"Yeah," the man laughed. "Kids. What're you gonna do?"

"Look, I don't know how to thank you," Sarah said.

"Just write the story. Blow the lid off this whole crooked operation. That's all the thanks I need."

Shortly after four, Sarah ambled through the park. It was truly lovely, with well-kept shrubs and flowers and a beautiful white grape arbor. She paused to admire the statue of the general, stern and straight-backed on his horse. She put out her hand and idly touched the general's right foot while looking up at him. Her hand slid forward, into the promised hollow space. Her fingers touched paper. In one swift movement, she had the envelope out and into her bag. She continued her stroll through the park, pausing to take a long, visible sniff of the blossoms on a butterfly bush before walking slowly toward home.

She'd never wanted to run so badly in her life.

Chapter 35

"Mr. Benton, I'm sorry to do this to you, but Stan's story hasn't come in yet and I have to take my mother to the doctor," Rick said, poking his head into Zachary's office door. "Are you going to be around for awhile?"

"That's fine, I'm actually just starting on tomorrow's editorial, so I'll keep an eye out for it," Zachary said. "Is the rest of the paper done?"

"Yep. We're saving Stan's spot and then it's ready to go to bed."

"Great, thanks," Zachary said. He wasn't sorry Rick was leaving early. For some reason the kid really grated on his nerves. If Stan hadn't been so insistent that he take over the editor job, he'd have picked someone else. There was a copy chief at the Times Zachary was pretty sure he could have for the right price.

He turned back to his editorial. He'd been on a roll the past few days, cranking out strong pieces that he knew were not only being read but discussed and, better yet, debated. The Times had written a counter piece to his last missive on Vietnam, insinuating that perhaps the Beacon had been dipping into the liberal well a little too much. That was rich, coming from them.

He wrote late into the evening, unaware of the hour, unaware of anything but his work. A loud click in the darkened newsroom made him leap from his chair and reach for the gun he'd hidden beneath some loose papers on his desk. Just before his fingers found the comfortingly cold metal, the lights came on and he saw the elderly custodian ambling in, pushing his mop bucket in front of him.

"Evenin' Mr. B!" the custodian called cheerfully. "Working hard or hardly working?" Chuckling at his own wit, he began to stab the mop at the black scuff marks left by a week's worth of black-soled shoes. Zachary sat back down at his desk, his hands shaking. He wiped his hand across the sweat on his upper lip and drew a deep, ragged breath. When the custodian had gone, with a boisterous admonition for Zachary to watch his step on the wet floor and have himself a good night, Zachary closed the door of his office and shook out a Valium. Too late he realized his coffee cup was empty, and the pill was beginning its bitter dissolve onto his tongue. He remembered a bottle of bourbon the staff had given him as a Christmas gift the previous year. He'd never been much of a bourbon drinker so he'd stuck it in the bottom drawer of his desk and forgotten about it. Quickly, he broke the seal and took enough of a swallow to get the pill and its nasty little tongue trail down.

"I guess that wasn't the best idea, but what the hell," he said aloud. "One swallow won't hurt me."

He put the top back on the bottle and stashed it in his drawer. Feeling calmer already, he put the paper to bed, another outstanding missive from Stan on the front page, and went back to his editorial.

It was nearly midnight when he finished. He took off his glasses and rubbed his eyes. He supposed he should call Hanna just to let her know where he was, although he doubted she'd care. He picked up the phone and dialed his home number. At least this way he was covering his tracks. In the empty brownstone, the phone rang and rang. Frowning, he poured himself another bourbon.

Even though she was all the way down in SoHo, Hanna couldn't have heard the phone if it had been right next to her, with all the noise she and Rick were making. When they finally fell apart, she lit a cigarette and pushed her sweaty hair back off her face.

"You're wild tonight, baby," Rick said, helping himself to one of her cigarettes.

"I'm always more myself when I'm in a good mood, and nothing puts me in a good mood more than things going my way."

"What's going your way?"

"Everything, darling," Hanna said. "I have enough evidence now that Zachary is still involved with Sarah to hit him with a massive divorce in which I will be the devastated and wronged wife, I will walk away with at least half, although I'm going for everything of course, and I have the sexiest, youngest lover of all my friends." She gave her silky laugh. Rick shifted uncomfortably.

"You and your friends all have younger lovers? That seems kind of weird."

"Does it?" she looked at him in genuine surprise. "Why?"

"Well it might not be weird that you have them, but it does seem weird that you all talk about it."

"Oh my poor sheltered darling, you have no idea that women are worse about locker room talk than men are. Yes, my lover, we talk about it. But don't worry. None of my friends know who you are. I don't name names."

"But if they find out, won't it hurt your divorce case?"

"Trust me, darling, no one is going to betray me. They can't. I would destroy them and they know it."

For the first time, it occurred to Rick to wonder what he'd gotten himself into.

Chapter 36

When Sarah's story hit the paper, the town exploded. Angry residents crowded into the council chambers at town hall so tightly they had to move the meeting to the auditorium at the high school. They screamed for Phil Conway's resignation or, if he wouldn't tender that, public execution. They demanded restitution for the local contractors who were wronged. They wanted Cletus Coons tarred and feathered and run back to New York on a rail.

Sarah sat in the back row with her notebook. Fred had been against her covering the meeting, afraid she'd be a target, but she pointed out that in Greenview, she could just as easily be a target at the grocery store or the library, if someone really wanted a piece of her that badly. Besides, she said, the residents were ready to canonize her.

"It's not the residents I'm worried about," Fred said. He'd been uncharacteristically grim since the moment the story went to press. "We've made a mighty enemy of Phil Conway."

"What's he going to do to me? Come on, Fred, this is journalism. Real journalism. We live in a country where people fought and died to protect freedom of the press. The fact that we don't have militants telling us what we can and can't publish is something we need to grab hold of. Do you know what we did here, Fred? We stuck it to the bad guys. That's damned good journalism, my friend. And you should be proud of it. I know I am."

As Fred watched her Joan of Arc her way out the door to cover the meeting, he was no longer sure that Sarah Adams was who she said she was.

By the following day, Cletus Coons had come to the same conclusion. He was pacing around his office, chain smoking, thinking hard. He'd had the strong feeling from the beginning that Sarah Adams was no housewife with Lois Lane fantasies. He'd said as much to Conway. If the stubborn ass hadn't been so cocksure, they wouldn't be in this mess.

"Let her look at the bids, Cletus. She won't find anything, Cletus. She's a hack like the rest of them, Cletus." Coons crushed out his cigarette into the already overflowing ashtray. He sat down and thought for a moment. Then he reached for his Rolodex and flipped through the cards before pulling one out. Picking up the phone, he dialed the New York Press Association's office.

"George Gray, please," he said. "It's Cletus Coons calling."

A moment later, his old college roommate had picked up the phone.

"Cleats?"

"Hey, Georgie. How's everything?"

"Oh, you know. Same shit, different day. What's new with you?"

"I wondered if you could do me a favor."

"I could almost say that right along with you, Cleats. I should say no. No more favors until you just call me to shoot the bull once in awhile."

"I know, I'm a prick like that. We'll catch up for real soon, I promise. But in the meantime, I'm a bind. There's a new reporter here in town, and I think I know her from back in New York but I'm too embarrassed to ask."

"You? Embarrassed? Give me a break. I've seen you naked and drunk out of your mind with a girl on either side of you and one on your lap."

"Oh God. That was college. You can't hold that against me. Anyway, this is professional. I know it's probably a long shot that this is the same woman, but I'd like to find out if you know before I make an ass of myself."

"What's her name?"

"Well, she says it's Sarah Adams. She says she's from Chicago. But I really think I know her from New York."

Cletus waited to see what George would say. He had never met Sarah Thomas in person back in New York but had seen her picture in the paper when she won the Pulitzer. His memory of her was fuzzy and distant, but he had the feeling he'd stumbled onto her truth. He knew he was asking his old friend to give him information that should probably be held in professional confidence, but George had never been the sharpest blade on the plow. He prayed he wouldn't question him too much.

"Sarah Adams? I don't know any reporters in New York named Sarah Adams. And I've been with the press association for a hundred years. What does she look like?"

"Tall, kind of a big nose, long red hair, she would be thin except she's pregnant."

"Holy shit."

"What?"

"That sounds like Sarah Thomas. Except the pregnant part, but I guess ... Hmm…"

"Sarah Thomas?" Cletus tried to keep his voice neutral.

"Yeah. I had heard she left the Beacon and moved away, but we don't keep track of our members like that. If they're here and they pay their dues, they're in. If they leave, they leave. But her I know, of course, because she's Sarah Thomas."

"But why would she turn up here, pregnant and using a fake name?"

"This is more than I should really discuss with you, because I have no proof of anything, just gossip from the grapevine."

"Who am I going to tell in Greenview Fucking Oklahoma, George?"

"Yeah, well… okay. Word was going around for awhile that she was sleeping with Zachary Benton. Then one day she disappeared. There was some story that she'd gone to visit relatives who needed her help so she was taking a leave of absence, but I don't know that anybody ever really believed that. Some people thought Zachary had dumped her which is why she split. Some others said she might be pregnant so he sent her away. But they always say that about women when they leave town suddenly, don't they? So I never put a lot of stock into it, but I gotta tell you, a woman who looks like you just described turns up in Oklahoma, pregnant and claiming to be a reporter? What are the odds of that?"

Good old George. He never could keep a secret.

"The odds are not good, my friend," Cletus said, leaning back in his chair. "Not good at all. Don't worry, I won't repeat any of what you told me. But you've given me enough to go ahead and approach her."

"Why are you interested in blowing her cover, anyway?"

"Wait… sorry, George, hang on a second." Cletus moved the receiver down by his chest and covered it loosely with his hand.

"What?" he said to the empty room. "The mayor? Now? God. Okay, fine. Tell him I'll be right there."

Back into the phone, he said "Sorry, George, I have to run. Duty calls. I'll give you a shout later and we can finish this."

He hung up.

Glancing at his watch, he picked up the phone again, dialed the newspaper office, and asked for Sarah. He could hear the wariness in her voice when she answered.

"I just wanted to congratulate you, Sarah. That was a mighty fine bit of investigative journalism."

"You didn't call to congratulate me. What do you want, Mr. Coons?"

"Hey, no need for the attitude. I was caught red-handed. I screwed up and you busted me. Even I'm smart enough to stand back and appreciate the made-for-TV-movie quality of that. It almost sounds like something too big to happen in Greenview, Oklahoma, doesn't it? Seems more like something that would happen in New York."

Sarah gripped the receiver. He couldn't possibly know. But her silence seemed to confirm everything for him.

"Yeah, New York politics are full of scandals like this. But you already know that, don't you, Sarah Thomas?"

Her head was screaming silently through clenched teeth.

"I don't know what you're talking about," she said, hoping her voice was steady. Coons laughed.

"Yeah, you do," he said. "I know who you are. And misrepresenting

168

yourself professionally may not be a crime like you busted me for, but it won't be looked at favorably by many people, will it?"

Sarah didn't respond.

"It's not likely anyone in Greenview will care all that much, but I know some people in New York who would be very interested in knowing where you are and what you're up to. Speaking of what you're up to, looks to be about, what, for you and Baby Benton? Eight months or so?"

Sarah slammed the phone down, her whole body shaking violently. She tried to think but was overcome with dizziness and nausea. She took several deep breaths and reached for the phone again. With trembling fingers, she placed a collect call to Zachary at the paper, but the phone on his desk rang unanswered.

At that point, Sarah was left with one choice. She knew Coons would make some calls to New York – he was probably making them already. She couldn't call Zachary at home. Even if he happened to be the one to answer, which he rarely was, she couldn't be sure Hanna wouldn't have the call traced or be recording it somehow. There was no time.

Within an hour, she was packed and in the backseat of what passed as a taxi in Greenview, an enormous and ancient Lincoln Town Car driven by Link Stratton, a retired school bus driver. He hadn't been too thrilled at the prospect of taking her all the way to the airport, but in desperation, Sarah had promised him double the usual fare. She bought a ticket on the first flight back to New York. Whatever Zachary was about to face because of her, she'd be damned if she was going to let him face it alone.

Back in his office, Cletus Coons had just successfully tracked down Zachary Benton's home number. And that, he thought, is why you always keep your contacts.

Hanna answered the phone. By the time Coons had told her his whole story, nearly half an hour had passed with Hanna scarcely saying a word.

Sarah Thomas is going to get what's coming to her, Hanna thought, her hands in fists so tight her knuckles were white.

Sarah Thomas is going to get what's coming to her, Coons thought, smiling to himself.

Chapter 37

Stan's stories kept coming in with a regularity Zachary found both impressive and alarming. He continued to follow the two American soldiers he'd been interviewing, but his stories were becoming darker and more frightening. The day he called Zachary to say he was going to try to get into North Vietnam to see what was going on there was the day Zachary's frayed nerves finally snapped.

"You cannot go into North Vietnam, Stan. Absolutely not. It's far too dangerous."

"You sent me all the way to Vietnam to cover the war and now you're worried about what's too dangerous? Are you kidding me, Zachary?"

"Salisbury from the Times has been slaughtered by every publication out there and the Pentagon for reporting on the bombing there. There's a reason not too many correspondents are going north, Stan. I'm sorry, but the answer is no."

"I think you misunderstood me, Zachary." Stan's voice had an edge Zachary had never heard before. "I'm not asking you. I'm telling you."

The line went dead. Zachary stared at the phone in his hand, his mind struggling to process what had just happened. Mild-mannered Stan had basically told him to go fuck himself, and while Zachary wanted to punch something, part of him knew that if anyone could find something staggering to report on in North Vietnam, it would be Stan. He hung up the phone, anger and excitement jockeying for space inside him.

Click

Zachary leaped to his feet, his heart nearly pounding out of his chest. There was no mistaking it that time – it was the same click that had been haunting him for weeks, but this time it was louder, and right outside his office. He quietly picked up his gun, took the safety off, and slipped to the door of his office. The newsroom was dark, but New York's night lights provided enough illumination for him to see a little. He stood in his office doorway for what seemed like hours, but he could hear nothing except his own pulse roaring in his ears.

Eventually he went back to his desk and sat down, gently putting the gun down and reaching for his bottle of Valium. Looking at the bottle, he suddenly couldn't remember when he'd taken the last one. It hadn't been for awhile, he was pretty sure. He shook one into his hand and chased it down with bourbon. Leaning back in his chair, he tried to will his heart to stop racing. The newsroom was quiet now but for sounds of the streets far below. He was so tired. He could never make anyone understand just how completely exhausted he was. He'd just close his eyes for a minute and then he'd head home. As he nodded off, he remembered thinking he'd better call a cab. He was far too tired to drive.

A sound in the newsroom jerked him awake. This time it was a quiet rustling sound, and the unmistakable sound of someone walking towards his office. In a fog of Valium, alcohol, terror and rage, he grabbed his gun, aimed for the newsroom, and fired.

A moment later, Sarah was in his office doorway, one hand on the door frame, the other over a ragged, bloody gap in her chest.

"My love," she whispered, her face ashen. She leaned against the doorway for a moment before sliding slowly to the floor.

Zachary couldn't move. He couldn't feel his legs, couldn't breathe, couldn't think. From somewhere in the distance, a voice started to scream, a high animal keening of pure pain. As he dropped to his knees beside her, he realized it was coming from him.

"Oh Sarah, my Sarah, my love, what have I done? I didn't know. I didn't know, my Sarah, my Sarah." He rocked her, crooning a crazy lullaby fractured by gasping sobs. "I'm sorry, I'm sorry, I'm sorry. Please, my love. Please, my love. Please, my love." He turned her face toward his and kissed her mouth, his tears running down her face. She gave a shudder and then went still in his arms.

"No," Zachary whispered. "No." He stared down into her sightless eyes, touching her face, tracing her lips with his fingers. "No. No. No."

Somewhere in the depths of his grief he remembered the baby. He jumped to his feet and grabbed the phone on his desk. Then he held her in his arms, breathing into her mouth, telling her about their new life in Oklahoma, the little house he was going to build for them, with a backyard for Dax to play in, how he'd buy the paper for her and she could turn it into the best paper in the whole Midwest, how they'd go to church on Sundays and have cookouts with friends and make love in their own bed and never, ever have to say goodbye again. Her hair was soaked with his tears by the time the ambulance arrived to take her away.

Chapter 38

Zachary paced, no longer trying to stop the tears that he'd been unable to stem for the past two hours. He'd lost Sarah and the baby. He'd killed Sarah and he'd killed their baby. He kept seeing her white face in the doorway of his office as she slid slowly to the floor. It was more than he could live with, he realized. He reached in his pocket for change for the pay phone down the hall. He'd call a cab to take him back to the newspaper and he'd turn the gun on himself. There was no recovering from this. He'd lost everything.

He found a dime and walked, like a man already dead, to the phone. He had just lifted the receiver when a doctor came out of the doorway where they'd taken Sarah.

"Mr. Benton?" The doctor looked around before spotting Zachary. He put the receiver down and hurried back to where the doctor waited, with the slightest trace of a smile on his face.

"Doctor! Oh my God! Sarah? Is she…"

The doctor shook his head and led Zachary to a row of chairs.

"No, Mr. Benton, I'm sorry but I thought you knew – she was gone before we even got her to the hospital."

"Yes," Zachary said, his mind not able to close over any one thought. "Yes. But I thought…your face…"

"Mr. Benton, the baby is alive."

Zachary lifted his haggard, salty face to look the doctor directly in the eye.

"What?" His voice was barely a croak.

"The baby is alive, and what's more, he seems fine. I've never seen anything like it in all my years of practice. The child should not have survived for more than a minute or so after his mother died. When I say it's a miracle, I mean there is literally no other explanation for it."

"He's alive? He's alive! Oh my God, thank you!" Fresh tears began to flow, and the doctor patted Zachary on the knee.

"Would you like to see him?"

"Yes! Oh God, yes! Please, I want to see him."

He followed the doctor through the doorway, down a short hallway, and into a room where a young nurse held a small bundle wrapped in a blue blanket. Behind her, a curtain had been pulled around a single bed. Zachary swallowed hard, knowing who was in that bed, but he kept his eyes on the bundle.

"Mr. Benton, this is your son," the nurse said, putting the warm little bundle in Zachary's arms. He looked down at the pink, cranky little face in awe.

"My son," he whispered. "Our son. Oh, Sarah."

A tear splashed onto the baby's forehead and he opened one tiny eye and gave his father a look. Zachary's laugh mixed with his tears.

"He opened his eye," Zachary said to the doctor. "Isn't that odd for a newborn? I think he looked right at me."

"I'm not surprised," the doctor said. "Nothing about this baby surprises me now."

Zachary looked back down at his son, who had gone back to sleep.

"We'll take the baby into the nursery if you'd like to..." the nurse motioned toward the closed curtain.

"Yes," Zachary said, wiping the back of his hand across his face. "Yes, thank you."

They went out and he stood for a moment, his trembling hand on the curtain. He took a deep breath and stepped inside, pulling it closed behind him. Sarah looked beautiful, her eyes closed as though she were merely asleep. A sheet and blanket pulled up to just below her chin shielded from Zachary all that her body had been through.

"Sarah," he whispered. "My love. My sweet, sweet, forever love. Our son is here. Dax is here, my love, and he's fine."

He touched her cold cheek with his finger, and the reality of the whole situation crashed over him like a tidal wave. He was suddenly furious at the blanket covering her. He should see what had happened to her, what he had done to her. Anguished and angry, he pulled the blanket back. She was naked, and what Zachary saw knocked the breath out of his body like a sucker punch. Between the emergency C-section and the ragged hole above her left breast, her body was a mess of gaping wounds through which the life had been ripped from her. He had done this to her. He had sent her away to protect her from Hanna and in the end, it had been Zachary who had killed her. He pulled her into his arms, sobbing, his face buried in her hair which still smelled faintly of her jungle gardenia perfume.

"Mr. Benton." The doctor's quiet voice came from the other side of the curtain.

"No!" Zachary shouted. The anger in his voice startled and frightened him. "You can't take her! I can't leave her! I won't leave her!"

The doctor slipped in to stand beside Zachary. He put his hand on his shoulder, gently but firmly.

"Mr. Benton, who can we call to come for you?"

The doctor knew from the paramedics what had happened. They told him they'd pieced the story together from Zachary's grief and panic-stricken ramblings in the back of the ambulance. He knew there would be an investigation, and the police would have already been notified. He also knew who Zachary Benton was, and had connected enough dots to have a pretty good idea of the whole picture. In his years of medical practice, he'd seen more grief than he wanted to think about but this – this was beyond grief. This was a man who had lost his very soul.

"Mr. Benton," he said, leaning down and looking into Zachary's face. "I can't tell you what to do, but I would like to suggest we contact your attorney to come for you."

Zachary nodded numbly.

"Yes," he whispered. "Yes, please." He gave the doctor Frank's number. When he came back, the doctor gently suggested a shot of something that would let Zachary sleep and regain his strength for all that was to come.

"No," Zachary said, suddenly finding his real voice. "It was drugs and alcohol that did this to me, to Sarah. I'm not taking any more. I need to feel this pain. I have to feel it, for both of us. For all of us."

"I understand," the doctor said. But it turned out he didn't need to worry – by the time Frank strode in, Zachary was barely conscious.

"So now what?" Frank asked. Zachary had spent a feverishly restless two nights with him, but by the third night he must have slept because he emerged from the guest room looking halfway human again. They sat on the sun porch where Frank's wife had put out coffee and croissants before discreetly disappearing. Zachary refused food but lit a cigarette and nursed a cup of coffee.

"I don't know," Zachary admitted. "I literally have no idea what to do now."

"The hospital called me this morning," Frank said, reaching for Zachary's cigarette and using it to light his own. "The baby is ready to go home."

For the first time, a hint of a smile hit Zachary's face.

"Did you see him? He's a great looking kid. Looks like his mother." Then the smile slid away and Zachary's face took on a shuttered look. Frank had never seen him like this. Something in him had died with Sarah, it was clear.

"Zachary, before we go to the hospital, before we do anything else, I want you to tell me everything. It was more than the Valium and booze that made you shoot Sarah. I know you better than that. You mentioned once that you thought you were being followed. Now I'm your friend, but I'm also your lawyer and if you want me to get you out of this, you have to tell me everything. And I mean every last fucking detail, Zachary, and I'm not kidding. I can't hold the police off any longer. I'm not sure how I've been able to do it this long, to be honest. You've got some weird kind of clout in this town."

"Not enough," Zachary said. "Has it been in the paper?"

"No. Without a police report or any real facts, the Times isn't going to touch it. Not when it's about you. But I repeat, Zachary, you have to tell me what happened. And eat a croissant or I'll force feed you."

Zachary stared down into his coffee cup, unsure of where to even begin. Finally he drew a choppy breath and told Frank the whole story, from the time Sarah left for Oklahoma through the eerie clicking sound he'd been hearing, the cars he suspected were following him, Hanna's disconcertingly normal behavior, the sleeplessness, the Valium, the increasing feelings of uneasiness as he worked late at night at the paper. Finally, he recounted that fatal night, the click, the footsteps in the darkened newsroom.

"They were so heavy, like a man's," Zachary said. His voice was hoarse. He took another sip of coffee. "And I'd been asleep in my chair, so when I heard them, it woke me. Scared me, you know? And I jumped up and grabbed the gun and just fired. I was such a mess, it was all a blur. Seems like a dream now. But I remember shooting out into the newsroom. And then Sarah was … there… in the doorway," he faltered, then stopped, no more words able to struggle up through his thick throat. His eyes felt dry and sandy, all of him wrung out, empty.

"Wait, the footsteps were heavy?"

"Yes," Zachary said. "They sounded heavy to me. But remember, I was basically passed out."

"No, I get that," Frank interrupted. "But I've seen Sarah. Even pregnant she couldn't have weighed more than 130 pounds."

"So?"

"This is going to sound like a non sequitur, but indulge me. What kind of shoes was she wearing?"

"I don't remember seeing her shoes, but she would have been wearing sandals. She always wore sandals, literally right up until the first snow."

"Zachary, listen to me. I can find out from the hospital for sure what she was had on her feet, but I'm positive you're right. So if skinny Sarah was wearing sandals when she walked across the newsroom toward your office, the chances of her footsteps being heavy enough to sound like a man…"

"She wouldn't sound like a man," Zachary said. "No, you're right. She always had a very light step. That's how she managed to overhear me saying I'd put her at city hall because of her hot body."

"Okay, there's more to that story that I'd no doubt love to hear, but I can't let us get derailed here. I understand that you were pretty much passed out, but do you think maybe her footsteps just sounded louder because the newsroom was empty? Kind of an echo effect?"

Zachary ground out his cigarette and lit another. Frank could see his jaw clenching and unclenching. When he spoke, it was the only word Frank needed to hear.

"No."

Chapter 39

Zachary sat on the edge of the bed, smoking a cigarette, his other hand on the phone, thinking. Rick had been running the Beacon since the night Sarah died and although he had been told there'd been an accident, he didn't know too many details and was under the strictest of orders not to talk about anything to anyone. Zachary had had been staying at Frank's since that night, and had not spoken so much as one word to Hanna. He didn't know if she knew what had happened, he didn't know if she wondered where he was. Frank strenuously objected to him having more than minimal contact with her, and he'd have preferred none. But Frank's assistant was going over there to collect some of Zachary's things, and he knew he'd better warn her or it might not go well for the young man.

Her voice had been cool and unruffled as always when she picked up the phone.

"I'm sending someone over to collect some of my things," Zachary said quietly.

"I heard what happened," Hanna said. She didn't say how she knew, and Zachary didn't ask.

"I'm sure you did."

"I suppose I should say I'm sorry, but it would be a lie. You two were deceitful and disgraceful. You were making a mockery of me all over New York."

"Don't flatter yourself. And if I were you, I'd keep my mouth shut."

"And what is that supposed to mean?"

"Just what I said. And you will let my messenger in to get my things and you will not give him any sort of difficulty or he will be back with the police. And with me. And believe me, Hanna, you do not want to see me right now."

He hung up. Fury pounded in his ears. He ground out his cigarette.

"Zachary?" Frank stuck his head in the door.

"Don't knock or anything. I could have been jerking off in here."

"I thought Hanna kept your cock and balls in a jar on her mantle."

"Did you come in here for something specific, or just to practice being an asshole? Because you're doing great. Bravo."

Frank grinned.

"Are you ready to go pick up the heir apparent? I'll drive you."

"Thanks, that would be much appreciated. I was dreading taking him in a cab. Is there going to be a diaper bag and all that stuff?"

"Judy said they'll give you stuff for him, but in the meantime she's got you covered. She pulled out a mountain of stuff from the attic that she kept from when our kids were babies, and anything else she's been out buying."

"What? I didn't know that. God, Frank, she didn't have to do that."

"I told her that, but she wanted to. She is over the moon that you're bringing a baby into the house. She figures since Liza is crazy and Brent is gay, the chance of her having grandkids is pretty damned slim. So let her do this. It makes her happy."

In the car, Zachary lit another cigarette and stared pensively out the window.

"Before we get busy with the kid in the car, there are a couple of things I should tell you," Frank said. "I asked a private investigator I know to start looking into what actually happened that night in the newsroom. I can't say for sure because I wasn't there, but every instinct I have tells me you and Sarah weren't the only two people in the newsroom that night."

Zachary turned to look at him.

"You think someone else shot Sarah?"

"No," Frank said. "Sorry, old man, but the police have already said it was a bullet from your gun."

Zachary swallowed down the lump in his throat that never quite went away. He cleared his throat.

"So what are you saying?"

"Again, this is just a hunch, but I think someone else was there. But I don't think he was there to kill Sarah. My guess is he was there to kill you."

"Holy shit. So I was right. All my paranoid delusions were right. I was being followed."

"I can't say for sure. We'll see what he comes back with, but that's what I'm suspecting."

"Hanna."

"Is there someone else you think might have wanted you dead?"

"No," Zachary said, gripping his cigarette so hard it snapped in two, raining ashes and sparks onto his leg. He cursed and brushed them away, stepping on the tiny bits of orange that fell onto the floor mat.

"Don't mind my car. It's only a brand new Cadillac."

"Sorry," Zachary said. "I'll have it cleaned. But to answer your question, I don't have any enemies like that, at least not that I know of. A lot of people don't like me, but that's to be expected in my line of work, especially as long as I've been doing it. But none of them hate me enough to want me dead."

"It is pretty extreme, even for Hanna," Frank admitted. "But she's the only one who has enough of a motive, at least in her mind."

He pulled the car to a stop in front of the hospital. "I'll wait here," he said. "Go get your boy."

The reality of just how much his life was about to change hit Zachary with the force of a full-body blow as he stepped into the elevator. The life he'd planned with Sarah had died with her, and now he had a child to take care of. He thought of Hanna and wondered what was going to happen. He wasn't sure he could even face her now, and he sure as hell didn't trust her. He wanted to blame her for the fact that his life had been turned upside down and kicked in the ass, but he knew that he really had no one to blame but himself. His head ached and reaching for the elevator button took all his strength. He still wasn't really sleeping.

When the nurse put the warm baby, wrapped in a blanket and wearing a light blue knit hat, into his arms, Zachary felt a momentary panic. He'd never carried a baby before, and he was suddenly aware of how many things could go wrong. The nurse, long accustomed to this reaction, gave Zachary a few pointers which left him feeling exactly no better.

"Well, let's see the little slugger," Frank said when they got back into the car. Zachary pulled the blanket back from Dax's wrinkled, slightly yellow face. He looked like an old pear in a hat. He made a low grumbling sound and turned his face into the blanket. Frank laughed.

"The nurses said it's already clear he's not a morning person," Zachary said. "It's the funniest thing. They said all babies sleep a lot but this guy does not appreciate being bothered before about eleven."

"I'm with him on that," Frank said, merging into Lexington Avenue traffic. "He's a good looking kid, Zachary. Congratulations."

"He's kind of jaundiced. The nurse said that's normal, though."

"Our kids were too," Frank said. "We'll put his crib by the window. He'll be pink and fat before you know it."

When they got back to Frank's, Zachary took the baby into the room where he was staying. He put the small bag the hospital had given him down on the floor, and sat down in the arm chair by the window. Crossing his long right leg over his left knee, he made a little square and nestled the blanketed bundle in securely. Gently pulling the blanket back, he looked down at his sleeping son.

"Dax," Zachary said, trying out the name. "Dax Benton."

As if on cue, the baby opened his eyes and looked at his father. The nurse had told him that babies don't see well at first, that Dax may open his eyes but wouldn't focus clearly for awhile. Looking down at him, Zachary wasn't sure. It looked to him like Dax was looking right at him, laser focused.

"Hello, son," Zachary said quietly. "I'm, well… I'm, uh, your father. I'm your dad. You can call me Dad."

Dax blinked and stuck one tiny fist up out of the blanket. It looked like some kind of salute, or maybe a declaration of power. That's probably what it was – he was Sarah's kid, after all. By tomorrow he'd probably be reading the newspaper, and by next week writing it.

Zachary touched Dax's fist with one finger. The skin was so soft he almost couldn't feel it at all. The tiny fingers were deeply creased and topped with miniscule flecks of fingernails. Zachary gently pulled off the little hat, static cling making the baby's pale copper fuzz crackle. He was definitely Sarah's son. Zachary smiled as he lightly smoothed a hand over the perfectly round head. Every detail of Dax was a miracle to Zachary. All else was forgotten as he marveled at the beautiful life before him. Everything on this tiny person was new, at its beginning. Eventually his hair and nails would grow and be cut, his skin would toughen in the sunshine, he would get dust in his eyes and bruises on his arms, at some point he'd suffer through broken bones and a broken heart, but right now, he was perfect.

Whatever he and Sarah had done that brought them to this moment could not have been all wrong, not when this beautiful miracle had been the result. Looking at Dax made Zachary miss Sarah anew. She should be here for this, she should be sitting beside him, cradling her child. But he had taken that from her. Zachary wasn't sure he could survive.

Dax opened his fist and closed it again around his father's index finger, and through his tears, Zachary felt a rush of love and protectiveness that brought with it a dawning sense of strength. He was going to be fine, everything was going to be all right. It had to be: he was a father now.

Chapter 40

"I know this is a difficult time for you, Mr. Benton, but we need to ask you some questions," the police detective said. Zachary, not wanting to appear to be squirming, forced himself not to shift in the hard metal chair. Frank, sitting next to him, apparently had no such compunction and was trying in obvious vain to find a comfortable position.

"Of course, detective. I understand. Please go ahead."

"At the request of your legal counsel, we waited for as long as we could until you were able to recover from your shock."

"I appreciate that."

"Now can you tell us exactly what happened the night Miss Thomas was killed?"

"Yes. I was working late. I was the only one still left at the paper, so the newsroom was dark. My office is at one corner of the newsroom," he explained. "I'd been feeling very jittery lately, between insomnia and the strong suspicion that I was being followed."

"You were being followed?" the police detective interrupted. "Did you file a police report?"

"I wasn't sure I was being followed, it was just a suspicion, so no, I didn't notify the police. At any rate, I had been feeling very jumpy lately from a combination of those suspicions, and as I said, not sleeping well. My doctor prescribed Valium to calm my nerves and to help me sleep. He had told me not to mix it with alcohol, but I did."

"How much alcohol?"

"That's not really relevant," Frank said.

"Frank, please," Zachary said. "I've nothing to hide. Bearing in mind that 'much' is a subjective term, detective, I would say that no, I didn't have much alcohol. I had a bottle of bourbon in my desk drawer, a gift from my staff a couple of Christmases ago, and I drank some of that – to swallow the pill with, in fact. I know it was stupid, but it was all I had on hand, and I was so tired and already pretty out of it. I guess I just wasn't thinking straight. Anyway, not long after that I dozed off in my chair. And I woke when I heard footsteps in the newsroom."

The detective was making notes.

"Go on."

"They were heavy footsteps, like a man. And in my fog of fatigue and Valium and booze, I was sure I was about to be killed. So I grabbed my gun and I fired out into the newsroom."

Zachary paused and swallowed hard. He would not cry in front of these hard-boiled New York cops.

"Mr. Benton, did it not occur to you that it could have been any member of your staff? Or the custodian, maybe?"

Zachary decided against telling them he'd almost shot the custodian a few hours prior.

"No, my staff never comes back at night unless there's a breaking news story, and the custodian had already been and gone. There should have been no one in the newsroom that late at night."

"You said they were heavy footsteps. But they could have been Miss Thomas' and in your altered state, you only thought it was a man."

"Excuse me, detective, but I have evidence that there was in fact a man in the newsroom who had been sent to kill Mr. Benton."

The detective turned to Frank.

"You what?"

"I have a private investigator working on it," Frank said smoothly. "He has discovered that Mrs. Benton hired a hitman to kill Mr. Benton. She had someone else following him, tracking his every move. And she had yet a third person working to find out where Miss Thomas had gone. When she had compiled all the information she needed, she ordered the hit. Trouble was, she didn't know that Miss Thomas had chosen the same night to fly back to New York from where she'd been staying. She also didn't know that Mr. Benton had begun to suspect he was being followed and had taken a handgun from their home to the office. It was basically a perfect storm. As the hitman was walking through the newsroom to kill Mr. Benton, Miss Thomas stepped in the way, and Mr. Benton shot her. It was, if you look at it logically, self-defense."

"It was an accident," Zachary said quietly.

"I'm not sure how the self-defense argument would hold up in court, but I understand the situation now," the detective said. "We will need documentation from your private investigator."

Back in Frank's car, Zachary sagged against the upholstered seat. For the first time in his life, he felt defeated.

"What happens now?" he asked as Frank eased the huge car into midtown traffic.

"When they get the report from the private investigator, you won't be charged," Frank said. "I'm positive of it. Then what it will come down to is you and Hanna."

"What do you mean, me and Hanna?" Zachary lit a cigarette.

"Whether you want to press charges against her for attempted murder. If you really wanted to push it, you could probably charge her with murder, since she indirectly caused Sarah's death."

Zachary exhaled. He hadn't considered any of that. His grief over Sarah and worries about bringing Dax home had left his usually sharp mind muddled.

"I don't know," he said. "I don't know what to do. I can't understand how any of this hasn't been in the papers."

"The police aren't going to release anything until you're charged, and you haven't even been arrested," Frank pointed out. "And like I told you before, nobody at the Times is stupid enough to run gossip."

"The Post would."

"The Post," Frank snorted. "If it comes down to that, you leave The Post to me. And anyway, I'd rather you were thinking about what we're going to do about Hanna and less about the publicity."

"Sorry." Zachary rubbed his eyes. "Occupational hazard."

"I can advise you, as your legal counsel, but as your friend I don't want to tell you what to do."

"Hanna could destroy me."

"You could destroy her."

"I stand to lose a lot more than she does."

He ground his cigarette out in Frank's already overflowing ashtray and leaned back, closing his eyes. If he had Hanna charged with attempting to have him killed, there would be no way to keep it quiet. If Hanna decided to go public with the whole story – and he had no doubt she'd take it right to the New York Times – it would destroy his reputation and Sarah's. And now he had Dax to consider. He didn't want the boy to know all the ugly details, at least not until he was much older, but he also didn't want him to grow up knowing nothing about his talented, beautiful mother. Zachary's head ached.

"I think," he said, opening his eyes and turning to look at Frank, "We need to drop the whole thing."

Frank didn't respond.

"And I want you to make it go away," Zachary added.

Frank nodded.

"Consider it done."

Chapter 41

"So you got away with murder," Hanna said quietly. She refused to turn and look at Zachary, who was holding Dax. "Naturally you did. It's the oldest story in the book, isn't it? Affluent, influential, white male gets away with murder."

"May I remind you, my darling wife, you have also gotten away with something," Zachary said, his voice full of steel. "You could be behind bars right now on charges of attempted murder."

"And the only reason I'm not is because of the magnanimity of the great Zachary Benton," Hanna said acidly.

"Frankly, yes. I should think you'd be grateful."

"You may get more gratitude out of me if you weren't standing their holding your bastard child."

"Let's get one thing crystal clear," Zachary said. "I declined to press charges against you for hiring a hit man to kill me. All I'm asking from you in return is to keep everything else that happened quiet. If you don't care about protecting me, and to be honest I don't blame you at all, you must know this isn't Dax's fault. He's an innocent child. Come on, Hanna, there's a shred of compassion in you, I know there is."

Hanna kept her cold gaze fixed on her husband's face, refusing to look down at the child. She was angry, but deeper than that, she was terrified. Her plan had not only failed, it had failed spectacularly. Now Zachary was calling the shots. If he wanted to, he could send her to prison for the rest of her life. Hanna had married Zachary because she'd wanted access to his power. Now that power would make the rest of her life a living nightmare.

Book Three
Dax

Chapter 42

"Why can't I go to the paper with you?" Dax asked his father as Zachary stood in front of the broad expanse of mirror, the razor chewing clean rows through the shaving cream on his cheeks and chin. Dax was perched on the closed toilet seat, aching with the desire to have whiskers he could shave off, to have after-shave he could slap on, to have expensive clothes and shiny shoes and a newsroom full of people waiting for him to come striding in and, with just a few words, set the tone for the entire day.

Zachary smiled down at his son, only six but already showing signs of real physical beauty, peach-toned skin, slate blue eyes and deep auburn hair, like his mother. This was one of those moments when Zachary felt Sarah's absence so sharply it was a physical pain. He turned back to the mirror.

"When you're a little older you can. Right now you have school, and that's your job. Just like when I was your age, that was my job. Now this is my job."

"And someday that will be my job," Dax finished for him.

"Maybe," Zachary said, rinsing the razor. "If that's what you want. You might not want to be a newspaper publisher. You might want to be a scientist, or an astronaut, or a novelist."

"I want to be a publisher like you," he said. "Or maybe a reporter, like my mother was."

Zachary's hand stopped in mid-air, reflexively squeezing the bottle of cologne hard. He set it down carefully and avoided his son's eyes.

"Your mother was a tremendous journalist. She was respected in her field."

"Hanna says she was common and a homeraker."

Zachary laid his hand on Dax's head. The boy could smell soap, shaving cream, and his father's own scent, a bit like black pepper, that always smelled to Dax like safety and success.

"Hanna didn't know your mother very well," Zachary said. "All you need to know is that your mother was a wonderful woman and she loved you very much."

Zachary had never tried to hide Dax's heritage from him. He didn't see that such an omission would serve any real purpose, and the child's naturally inquisitive nature meant sooner or later he'd find out anyway. He was careful to only tell the boy as much as his mind could process, but tried to answer his questions as honestly as he could. Dax knew his mother's name, her history, and her reputation as a journalist. He also knew she'd died when he was born, but Zachary had never told him what had actually happened. He wanted to wait until the boy was older, and until he could figure out how to tell him.

Zachary knew most marriages would not have survived what he and Hanna had done to each other, and he now sometimes wondered if she stayed only to bask in the obvious delight she took in tormenting her husband. Zachary was aware that she hated Dax, hated the child in a way that was almost too disturbed to understand, but she was shrewd enough not to abuse the child physically. Zachary would have quickly and quietly killed her, and they both knew it. Sarah's death was a shadowy secret that bound them together in a hell from which they would never escape. For Zachary, the hell was Hanna. For Hanna, it was Dax.

Sometimes when Zachary looked at Dax, a tight fist of agony slammed into his throat and he couldn't breathe at all. The boy had Sarah's features and her quick wit. Unfortunately, Zachary thought, he also had his father's ambition and drive. He often heard the boy in his room, pretending to bark out orders to his reporters and hammer out deals on the comb he pretended was a telephone. The first time Zachary had overheard Dax growl, "That story will not go to press or I swear to God I will shut down every newspaper in this town and half the country!" was the first time Zachary wondered if the boy knew too much.

He longed to be able to tell his son that journalism was no place to make a real life, that he should move to some quiet place upstate and marry a nice girl and get a job as an accountant, have cookouts with the neighbors on Saturdays, go to church on Sunday mornings. But every time the boy looked at him with those big eyes, raw adoration for his father and his father's world seeping out of every pore, Zachary knew he would never be able to do it. Zachary loved the newspaper world. It was the very fire in his veins and he knew that to tell the boy otherwise would be a shallow, awkward lie and one that Dax would see right through. The kid's sharp mind made him a real pain in the ass sometimes.

"Dax, do you feel all right?"

"I feel fine, Daddy, why?"

Zachary crouched down on the floor so his face was level with the little boy's. His eyes sent a twinkling, unspoken message to his son.

"Are you sure? If you're not feeling up to going to school today, well… Hanna is going to be out all day and I can't leave you home alone."

Dax's face lit up like a flashbulb.

"Oh yes, Daddy, I think I'm sick today. I'm very sick. I can't go to school, I'm too sick."

He fell off the toilet lid and rolled around on the floor, clutching his stomach and groaning. Zachary laughed and nudged him with his foot.

"Get dressed or we'll be late," he said. Dax scrambled to his feet and ran out of the room, whooping. Zachary smiled and shook his head as he shut off the bathroom light. He was worrying for nothing – the kid was obviously destined for Hollywood.

Zachary's Mercedes pulled into the private parking garage and the guard, glancing up, smiled and waved as the arm went up.

"He knows you," Dax said reverently. "Everyone knows you."

The cigarette lighter popped out of the dashboard with a loud click that still made Zachary jump every time he heard it. He really needed to remember to bring a lighter. Zachary lit his cigarette and pushed the lighter back in.

"Not everyone," he exhaled. "But when you work with the same people every day, they do get to know you."

He was playing down his own importance, and he knew Dax knew it. They pulled into Zachary's reserved space, and Dax was out of the car before his father had even cut the engine. They crossed the parking garage and got into the elevator, Dax holding Zachary's hand tightly. When the paneled doors slid open and decanted them into the Beacon newsroom, Dax's breath caught in his throat. He'd been here with Zachary before, but it never failed to make his pulse race. Reporters pounded away on typewriters, editors shouted for copy boys, telephones rang... it was the sound of the city's news, pulled from every borough, organized, smoothed out onto smudgy pages and sent back out so the city could read about what it had done. Dax felt like he was in the middle of a tiny Mardi Gras, only more important. This one felt like success. The very air he was breathing buzzed with it.

"Morning, Zachary," Dax heard a male voice say.

"Morning, Abe," Zachary answered. The two men shook hands and chatted briefly.

"Daddy," Dax whispered as they continued toward his office. "Was that the mayor?"

"Yes." Zachary glanced curiously down at his son. "You may be the only five-year-old in New York who knows Mayor Beame on sight."

"I'm learning the news business," Dax said importantly. "I have to pay attention to stuff."

Zachary smiled but would not laugh. His son's dreams were as important to the boy as Zachary's were to himself, and he would never belittle them. Dax, meanwhile, kept glancing over his shoulder as the mayor made his way through the newsroom toward the elevator.

They went into Zachary's expansive, oak-paneled office, with windows overlooking Manhattan. His Manhattan. Beame might have been the mayor, but Zachary knew that New York was his, to control, to possess, to wrap around himself, to own. It was a troubled but faithful partner to Zachary, feeding him continual news stories, showing him its roughness, its darkness, the side of the city that mocked the gleaming, beautiful New York that flirted with tourists from postcard racks in Chinatown. Zachary understood New York, his restless lover, always giving her enough space to do her own thing, knowing that in the end, she'd come back to him with her confessions, her secrets, her endless stories.

The only one who had come close to understanding Zachary's fanatical devotion to his work had been Sarah. It had been years since her death, but he still expected to look out into the newsroom and see her sitting at her desk, her long red hair pulled back from her face in a messy bun, usually secured with a pencil, while her fingers flew over her typewriter. There were times, alone in his car, when he swore he could smell her Jungle Gardenia perfume. She infiltrated his dreams, and her spirit shone, beautifully and continuously, through Dax.

Zachary glanced over at his son, who was standing in the doorway, his hands clasped behind his back, looking out over the newsroom. It was the same way Zachary always stood.

Chapter 43

Dax yanked open the back door and jumped into the kitchen. He could never decide if it was better to put his left foot in first or his right, so he'd long ago just started jumping into any room he was entering so both feet landed at the same time and the problem was eliminated. It also made the room give a satisfying shudder and made Hanna shout "DAX!" from whatever room she was in. He shouted it along with her now, his spirits too high to care. He had just slung his backpack onto the kitchen table when a voice from the doorway made him spin around.

"Hello, Dax."

"What the hell are you doing here, Philip?"

His cousin shrugged his bony shoulders.

"I'm family. I can be here whenever I want."

"Can not. It's my house."

"It's Uncle Zachary and Aunt Hanna's house."

"And my house. I live here, dingus, so it's *my house.*"

Philip helped himself to an apple from the bowl on the table.

"You didn't pay for this house so it's actually not yours. And Aunt Hanna said I could stay here after school today and spend the night because my mom and dad are out of town."

"Probably ran away to get away from you," Dax said.

"Nuh-uh. They went to find a lawyer to sue you for having such an ugly face."

It was a good insult. Dax wished he'd thought of it. Philip wasn't usually that quick.

"Gimme that apple. It's mine."

"Is not."

Dax jumped on Philip and they fell to the floor, screaming and punching.

"Boys!" Hanna's voice sent anger spraying through the kitchen. She strode in and yanked Dax to his feet. "I know what you're thinking, Dax, and I'm too smart for you. You think if you fight with Philip I'll send you to your room and you won't have to play with him. Well think again, little boy. Now go play outside, both of you."

She put her hand on Dax's shoulder to steer him toward the door. He twisted away from her touch, grabbed an apple, and stormed out the door, followed by Philip who was at least smart enough not to gloat.

They sat down on the back steps. The worst part, Dax thought, deliberately eating the apple as noisily as possible, was that sometimes he actually liked Philip. He was pretty smart, and in his own way really loyal to Dax. Since he had no siblings, Dax took a comfort he would never admit aloud in knowing that Philip shared his blood; Philip's mother was Sarah's sister. But most of the time he just kind of wanted to punch him in the face. He tattled too much and was such a huge nerd.

"What should we do now?" Philip asked.

"Dunno." Dax raised his arm and threw his apple core as hard and far as he could. It bounced lightly off a parked car and rolled down the storm drain. "Let's go over to the park."

Philip deposited his own apple core into the trash can next to the back steps, the perfect example of something Dax found just so punch-worthy, and they shuffled toward the park where Dax could hear older boys playing basketball. The tenor thumping of the ball against pavement was punctuated with shouts and laughter. Philip heard it too and slowed his shuffle.

"Those sound like big kids," he said doubtfully.

"So what?" Dax said. "We're not babies. We're in the third grade. Besides, they don't own the park."

As they rounded the gate, Dax could see them, just another random group of guys that seemed to crop up like weeds through the cement in the city's numerous parks. When there was just a basketball court, there was nothing else to do but watch them play and Philip somehow always got hit with the ball. At this park, though, there was some playground stuff on the other side of the court. Dax and Philip scuffed along the fence, heading for the gate on the other side.

"Hey, I'm open, dude! Here! Pass it!" Dax heard laughter and suddenly the basketball flew in their direction. Philip, conditioned, ducked but Dax grabbed the ball, dribbled it a couple of times to show off, then threw it toward the boy closest to him.

"Thanks!" the boy called.

"Hey, c'mere kid," Dax heard another voice shout.

"Me?" Dax wasn't sure but something made him think it was him they were talking to.

"Yeah, you. You shoot hoops?"

"A little."

"Dax!" Philip whispered, stricken. "No you don't!"

"Shut up," Dax whispered back furiously.

"So come over here and shoot some with us," the bigger boy said.

Without hesitation, Dax jogged over, motioning for Philip to follow. He could see his cousin holding back, unsure, and Dax turned around.

"Come on, Philip," he said loudly, partly to embarrass his cousin into it, and partly to cover his own nervousness. Dax was worlds braver than most kids his age, but he wasn't sure he was brave enough to play basketball with these peach-fuzzed giants. They had to be at least 16.

The boy holding the ball bounced it to Dax and he caught it, dribbled it, then shot wildly at the basket, missing by a good two feet. The bigger boys roared.

"He shoots like you, Rabbit!" one of them howled. Rabbit laughed and punched him. One of the others had caught the ball and was dribbling it intently, then suddenly shot around the others before leaping into the air and slamming the ball through the net. His friends cheered.

"I could do that too if I was nine feet tall," Dax yelled, his face flaming at his own boldness. Laughing, one of the boys passed him the ball and Dax dribbled and ran, dodging big hands and arms that tried to guard him. Spotting a perfect V between a nearby pair of long legs, Dax ducked and ran through them, still dribbling. The boys hooted with laughter and Rabbit grabbed Dax from behind and lifted him up. Dax threw the ball with all his might. It arched through the air and sailed neatly through the net.

"SWISH!" The bigger boys shouted in unison. They were all laughing, slapping Dax high-fives. He had never felt more alive.

"I didn't know you could play basketball," Philip said later as they walked home.

"I can," Dax answered. "I can do anything."

Chapter 44

It was hot, as only New York in summer can be, the kind of slow, pressing heat that made everyone feel as though they were being cooked from the inside.

Dax and Philip were hanging around outside Dax's brownstone, drinking tepid cans of soda they'd bought from the bodega a few blocks away. It was that interminable time when summer had stopped being fun but no one was ready for school to start either, and Hanna seemed to always make things worse by telling Dax he had to play with Philip. Dax still didn't like his cousin most of the time. Increasingly effeminate and well-behaved, Philip's very existence insulted Dax, who considered anything besides drive and ambition an unforgivable weakness. Philip was as weak as they came.

As they grew, Dax found his cousin hard to tolerate for a million reasons, not the least of which was a tiny bit of unadmitted jealousy. Being good came easy to Philip. It didn't to Dax. There was too much he wanted to find out, and you couldn't find stuff out while you were stuck inside practicing the violin and being good. Unfortunately, Dax couldn't figure out how to find stuff out without getting into trouble at the same time.

Still, Dax preferred Philip's company over Hanna's, although that was a pretty shallow pool. If he'd stayed in the house with her, Dax knew he'd have been sent to his room to "read or do something quiet, for God's sake, you're just hell on wheels." Sitting still wasn't one of Dax's strengths, and he considered any time in his room not spent sleeping as wasted, time that could have been better used finding out what was going on in the world.

Dax carefully put his empty soda can on the sidewalk, then stomped his foot down on top of it as hard as he could, the tin crumpling satisfyingly under his sneaker. He stomped it a few more times for good measure, then picked it up and tried to throw it like a Frisbee toward the nearest garbage can. It missed by several feet and clattered to a stop on the sidewalk. Dax, bored, suggested they take the train down to Chelsea Piers.

"No, Dax. You know Mother doesn't let me leave the neighborhood," Philip said resolutely. Dax exaggeratedly looked around.

"Your mother? I don't see your mother. Where is she?"

"You know what I mean, Dax."

"When are you going to stop being such a baby? We're ten now. Double digits, Phil."

He knew his cousin hated being called Phil.

"No, Dax. I said no. You're always trying to get me in trouble."

"Fine, suit yourself. I'm going down to the piers."

He started off down the street. Behind him, he heard Philip get up and start after him, stopping to pick up the crushed soda can and put it into the trash can. Dax smiled to himself. His weakness also made Philip malleable, which generally worked in Dax's favor.

Chelsea Piers' heyday as a busy port had long ended and it was in ruin, slated for demolition. Dax had heard that gangs of older kids hung out there, smoking cigarettes and drinking beer, sometimes with their girlfriends, and he wanted to see them, hear what they talked about, smell their badness. Philip, predictably, had completely freaked out at the thought of older kids and especially girls, but Dax finally badgered him into it. The subway ride, old hat for any native New York kid, was uneventful except for a grubby man in a filthy knit cap who wore battered Kleenex boxes for shoes, called Philip "pretty" and asked them for a dollar. But when they got to Chelsea Piers, Dax knew immediately the cure for their summer boredom was right beneath his feet. He'd been a city kid long enough to know what pot smelled like, and he could smell it now, twining around teenaged voices from beneath the broken pier and slithering through cracks in the wood up to where Dax crouched, rapt, listening. Their language was coarse, guttural, peppered with pubescent laughter and the occasional girlish giggle. To Dax, who had grown up on Central Park West and heard language only as strong as what passing cabbies shouted below his window, this was life. This was the real New York, the one he had always known existed beyond his own cocoon of privilege.

"I can't believe you stole that car, man." One male voice came up clearly from below.

"I can't believe you fucking got away with it," another voice added.

"No one would ever suspect me," a newly deepened voice boasted, cracking a bit at the end. "My old man's a big shot downtown."

So is mine, Dax thought, *and I'd never think to steal a car. Even if I could reach the pedals.*

"Hey! Hey kid! What the fuck?" Another voice, much louder because it was pants-wettingly close, smashed through Dax's reverie. A boy of about seventeen was coming towards them.

"Quick!" Dax said to Philip. "Run!"

They turned and fled, sneakers pounding on the pier, nearly drowning out the older boy's angry shouts to his friends that two punk kids had been spying on them. By the time they ran back onto the subway, the doors closing protectively behind them, Dax was laughing and exhilarated. Philip was crying and wheezing.

"It's not funny, Dax!" Philip shrilled when he could speak again. "We could have gotten killed!"

Dax scoffed. "He couldn't kill us, none of them could. They'd go to jail for, like, forever. They're just showing off because they're teenagers and think they're so cool. There is one thing, though…"

His voice trailed off and he sat on the lurching, swaying subway car, thinking hard.

"What?" Philip asked. His scrawny body was hot and his damp knee touched Dax's, instinctively making Dax slide away a little.

"That one kid said he stole a car and got away with it."

"Yeah? So? I've heard my dad say cars get stolen all the time."

"If I could catch him talking about it again, and find out who he is…"

"How're you gonna do that?" Philip's voice always registered somewhere between a whine and an accusation.

"Sneak back down there, maybe, with one of Dad's little tape recorders."

"Then tell the police?"

"No, stupid, write a story for the paper. I'd be a hero, a real reporter. Maybe get the Pulitzer!"

"I don't think you can get the Pulitzer until you're older. Like maybe 13."

"Any reporter can get the Pulitzer if they're awesome enough," Dax informed him, irritated. This kid had absolutely zero understanding of journalism.

Philip was dubious, but he knew better than to argue with Dax when he had that look on his face. Still, he didn't like the idea of Dax going back down to the piers, and even less did he like knowing, and he knew, that Dax would drag him along. It worried him so much, all that evening, all during dinner and his bath, that he blurted the story out to his mother as she was tucking him into bed.

"What?" she said, her hands pausing mid-tuck while she stared at her son. "You and Dax went to Chelsea Piers? Alone? And now he wants to... oh no. Oh hell no. Ethan! Get up here!"

Philip's father appeared in the doorway, and Aggie repeated for him what her harebrained sister's idiot kid was up to now, and before Dax even had time to figure out how to get one of the mini tape recorders out of Zachary's home office, he was grounded and the Pulitzer Prize went up in smoke.

Chapter 45

"I'm bored," Philip said. "Let's do something."

"We are doing something."

"No, we're not. We're just hanging out in your room."

"That's still doing something."

"No it isn't, it's just stupid and boring."

"Then you should love it since it's just like you."

"Shut up, Dax."

"Why don't you make me?"

"I don't make monkeys, I train them."

"Oh, that's so funny. It's so funny I forgot to laugh."

Philip, in an uncharacteristically aggressive move, took a flying leap and landed on top of Dax, already punching when he got there.

"HEY!" Dax, surprised and angry, started punching back. In no time they were rolling around on the floor, punching and shouting and swearing.

"What is going on in here?" Hanna's voice thundered from the doorway. "Dax! Get off him this instant!"

"He started it," Dax panted, rubbing his upper arm where Philip had landed a lucky punch.

"Did not," Philip said, putting a finger to his split lip and drawing back blood. He stared at his hand and started to hyperventilate.

"Oh for God's sake," Hanna snapped. She grabbed Philip's hand and yanked him to his feet, then dragged him down the hallway to the bathroom. Dax stood up and checked himself for any serious damage. He had to admit there was a tiny part of him that was impressed with Philip for starting a fight like that. Dax never would have guessed he had it in him. A few moments later, Hanna marched Philip back through the door. He was holding a wet washcloth against his mouth and glowering at Dax.

"Now listen to me, both of you. I don't like having you underfoot and if I had any choice in the matter, I'd never look at either of you again. But as I don't have that option, I'd suggest you behave yourselves from this moment on as I will not have you fighting and destroying things in my house. You are both 13 years old. It's time you stopped acting like babies. There will be no more warnings."

She turned on her heel and strode out, closing the door hard behind her.

"What does that mean?" Philip asked. "What's she going to do?"

"Nothing," Dax said, flopping back onto his bed. "She always says stuff like that to me, but she can't do anything. She's not my real mom."

"I know," Philip said. "Your real mom was my mom's sister, remember?"

"Yeah, I know. I just like saying that Hanna's not my real mom. It makes me feel better when I think about what a bitch she is."

"Dax!" Philip was scandalized, but laughed in spite of himself.

"Well, she is. She's mean to me all the time, but especially when my Dad's not around."

"You should tell him how mean she is."

A quiet camaraderie was building between them, united against Hanna.

"He knows," Dax said. "She's pretty mean to him too. That's why he's gone so much. He's almost always at the paper."

"You could run away," Philip suggested. His own mother drank a lot, but he never told anyone. He wasn't even sure his father knew. "I'll go with you."

"I'm going to, someday," Dax said, silently adding that there was no way in hell he'd take Philip with him when he did.

"Where're you going?" Philip asked.

"I don't know yet," Dax said. "Maybe Hollywood. Or Hawaii. Or maybe I'll travel all around the world and go on safaris and junk."

"I thought you were going to be a newspaper reporter."

"I am," Dax said. "How do you think I'm going to afford to pay for all that stuff?"

Chapter 46

Dax knew he was not good looking, at least not in the traditional sense. He spent many pre-pubescent hours in front of his bathroom mirror, not preening, just taking stock. His hair was an interesting blend of his father's thick, dark mop and his mother's coppery brown resulting in a deep rust color that everyone, when they glanced at him a second time, were sure they'd never seen before. His features were thin and fine, although his large, oddly round eyes were such a striking slate blue that no one really ever noticed the rest of his face – his wide, flat nose like his mother's, the feminine bow of his upper lip, his slightly crooked teeth. He'd overheard Hanna telling Zachary repeatedly that his smile was an ugly reflection on her and that he really must see an orthodontist. Dax didn't care one way or the other what his teeth looked like, but once he knew they bothered Hanna he staunchly refused any suggestion that he get braces and made sure to give her a big toothy grin whenever the situation warranted, and often when it didn't.

As he entered his teens Dax discovered, entirely by accident, two important things: first, that sex appeal really had nothing to do with looks, and second, if a girl felt respected and appreciated, she was putty in your hands.

"Hey, are you all right?" Dax said to the weeping girl behind the high school gym. She was sitting on the ground, her head on her knees. The basketball game had just ended and people were streaming out of the gymnasium and into the parking lot. Dax knew the girl from a couple of his classes, but wasn't sure she knew him. He had overheard her arguing with her steady boyfriend in the stands shortly before the last quarter. She had told him she couldn't go with him down to the piers. Dax didn't need to hear what the boyfriend, a meatheaded senior who was the school's star wrestler, wanted to do down at the piers. Everyone went there to drink or screw, usually both. With a predictability that made Dax roll his eyes as loudly as he dared, the meathead began to apply the "Aww, c'mon baby, I thought you loved me" logic of the horny high school boy. Her continued refusal, weakened by her visible upset, only served to build the meathead's self-righteous anger. He had no way of knowing his parting shot before leaving her crying in the bleachers would hand Dax the keys.

"Don't blame me if you die a fuckin' virgin."

She looked up now, her mascara traitorously defecting to her cheeks and her argyle sweater.

"Oh, hi… uh…"

"Dax," he supplied, offering her his handkerchief.

"Amanda. Thanks." She dabbed at her face as Dax sat down on the ground beside her.

"You know you're the only guy under thirty to carry a handkerchief, right?" she said, handing it back to him. Dax stuffed it into his pocket and smiled.

"I'm not like most guys, I guess."

She looked at him warily.

"That's the oldest line in the book," she said, then lifted her left hand to display a class ring the size of a Buick. "And besides, I have a boyfriend, so whatever you're thinking, you can forget it."

Dax held up his hands.

"Hey, I come in peace," he said. "I was just leaving when I heard you sniffling so I thought I'd see if you were okay."

Amanda stretched out her jean-clad legs, her penny loafers shiny under the diffused light from the ancient streetlamp nearby. From inside the gym, Dax could hear the pep band laughing and clunking as they loaded their instruments back into their cases after a long night of keeping the crowd energized with "Smoke on the Water" and "The Horse." The last time he'd wished they'd play something else they so badly massacred "Billie Jean" that he considered sending a letter of apology to Michael Jackson.

Amanda was staring out across the parking lot, adrift in a sea of hormones, teenage angst, and Love's Baby Soft.

"Yeah," she said finally. "I'm okay."

"If you want to talk about it, my ex-girlfriend always said I'm a good listener."

"How come she's not your girlfriend anymore then?" she asked, right on cue.

Dax shrugged and looked away.

"It's kind of embarrassing."

"You can tell me," Amanda said. "You have my makeup all over your nice hanky now. I think that qualifies us as friends."

Dax smiled but didn't meet her eyes.

"She wanted us to go all the way, and I didn't think we were ready. Well, maybe she was ready. I don't know. She said she was. But I wasn't."

Amanda was looking at him intently.

"That's the embarrassing part. I mean, I'm a guy. I should have been the one pushing her for sex." He deliberately still didn't look at her.

"What do you mean you weren't ready?"

"I cared about her a lot," he said quietly. "But I didn't love her. I guess it's like the handkerchief – I'm just old-fashioned. But she didn't see it that way. She said I was uptight, a square, and probably gay. Then she broke up with me. A few weeks later, her family moved to Arizona. I haven't seen her since."

Amanda got to her feet and held out her hand. Dax took it and let her pull him up.

"Let's go for a walk," she said. "I think we could both use some fresh air."

A month later, she and Dax took each other's virginity, in Dax's bed, by candlelight and The Police's "Every Breath You Take," on a night when Zachary and Hanna were attending a political event downtown.

"Isn't this better than in the cramped backseat of a Camaro down at the pier, kicking the headrest and hiding from the cops?"

Amanda laughed and kissed the side of his neck.

"Totally." She nuzzled up behind his ear. "Oh, and by the way, I need your ex's number."

"What for?"

"I want to let her know you're definitely not gay."

The other thing Dax discovered about girls was that if you treated them with respect even after you broke up, they would remain fiercely loyal to you. When Amanda had told him her father was being transferred to California, he had held her hands and tearfully told her it just wasn't fair for a girl as beautiful as her to be tied down to him from such a long distance. He wanted her to be free, to be happy, to have all she ever wanted. In his heart of hearts, he told her, he would always believe there was the chance they'd be together again someday, a little older, a little wiser, ready to settle down and raise a family. She wrote him a letter every week for years afterward.

Chapter 47

Dax was a junior in high school when he was elected president of the Drama Club. He'd acted in all of the school's productions and after his first performance as a non-speaking street thug in "Oliver Twist" –in which he'd pulled so many hilarious faces and exaggerated gestures that the audience roared, Oliver got pissed, and he was mentioned in the local paper's review of the play – it was generally accepted that besides his obvious talent for journalism, he was also a great actor.

"He certainly does have a flare for the dramatic," Hanna commented sourly to Zachary later, when Dax had jubilantly showed them the review. "I suppose it's refreshing to see him using it for something other than trying to drive me mad."

For Dax, being editor of the school paper and president of the Drama Club gave him a rush like he'd never known. He realized he was born to lead and loved the feeling he got when a group of his underlings carried out one of his ideas. Of course, he didn't call them "underlings" to their faces. Underlings never appreciated that. But he was constantly coming up with ideas and he needed help making them happen. He was focused and driven but naturally charismatic, so no one ever seemed to question him, at least not to his face.

One afternoon in mid-autumn, after the untrodden feel of the new school year had begun to fade but before the inevitable lethargy had descended on the school, Dax rapped on the door of Mrs. Branford, the Drama Club advisor.

"Hello, Dax, what's new?" Mrs. Branford was an affable, slightly over-weight woman of about 40 who loved teaching and the theater in equal measure. She delighted in Dax, who was a good student and showed tremendous aptitude for the theater arts.

"Mrs. Branford, I wonder if I could run an idea past you," he said, pulling up one of the hard plastic chairs from under her window.

"Of course, my dear, what's on your mind?"

"I have been thinking about the long stretch of time between the school's fall play and the spring musical, and it seems to me like there's an opportunity there we're missing."

"What sort of opportunity?"

"Well, I'm thinking it would be fun and a good way to get more of the student body involved in theater if the Drama Club put on a student playwriting competition. The winning play could be produced sometime over the winter. I'm thinking one-act plays, of course, as we don't want to get into anything too huge that would start to overlap with the play or the musical."

"I have to tell you, Dax, I think that's the most amazing idea I've heard out of a student in ages. In fact, make that the best idea I've heard out of anyone in ages."

"Great! In that case, I'm going to start putting up flyers about it so we can get the ball rolling. You'll help me, I hope?"

Mrs. Branford smiled into his excited blue-gray eyes. Students like Dax were a rare gift.

"Of course," she said. "Anything you need."

Dax was in the hallway outside the auditorium the next day posting a flyer he'd made when two girls he knew only on sight approached him.

"Hi Dax," they said in sing-song unison. "What are you doing?"

"Posting some information about a playwriting competition we're having this winter. Either of you foxes a playwright?"

They folded toward each other and giggled.

"No," one of them said. "But for you I might give it a try."

They sauntered off, still giggling, a synchronized duo of swinging hair and swaying denim hips. Dax smiled and shook his head, moving off down the hall to finish putting up the flyers.

They got more entries than Dax expected, and certainly more than

Mrs. Branford ever thought they would.

"Who knew we had so many young Neil Simons in our school?" she mused as she and Dax pored over the entries one afternoon in her office. "I am starting to worry about hard feelings among those who aren't chosen."

"That's a good point," Dax said thoughtfully. "Well, what about this? We give everyone whose wasn't chosen a part in the play that was."

"What if there aren't enough parts?"

"Then they'll be stage crew or tech crew or something. We can make everyone feel important and involved."

Mrs. Branford glanced up at Dax, who was still looking down at the scripts in his hand. She'd never known a student with a mind as sharp as his, and she'd seen her share of gifted kids. She liked Dax, but the longer they worked together, the more she began to notice there was something odd about him. She couldn't quite put her finger on it, and didn't spend too much time thinking about it. He was a teenager, after all, and teenagers were always weird.

Chapter 48

"No," Dax said loudly. Everyone else on stage turned to look at him. "That's not how that line should be said. In fact, this isn't how this scene should even be blocked."

"Dax," Mrs. Branford said wearily from her seat on the front row of the auditorium. "It's not customary for an actor to also direct. That's why I'm here."

"With all due respect, Mrs. Branford, this is my project and I think I should have some say in how it's done."

"Actually, Dax, it's MY play," Bonnie Cavoto said, stepping out from the side of the stage where she'd been watching the rehearsal, script in hand. "I'm the one who wrote it, and the way it's blocked is exactly what I had in mind."

Dax stared at her for a moment as though he were seeing her for the first time. Except for adults, no one ever challenged him. He sized her up and his expression slowly changed, softened.

"You're right, of course," he said. "I should never have criticized your art. My apologies."

He winked at her. She scowled and retreated to her stool offstage.

"Okay, everyone, let's get on with it," Mrs. Branford called. "Let's take it again from the top of page five."

After rehearsal, Dax found Bonnie.

"Again, I'm sorry about that. I get very wrapped up in acting sometimes, and wanting everything to be perfect."

"If you don't think my play is perfect, why did you choose it to win the competition?"

"Because it's an outstanding play," Dax said. "I think you have real talent."

Bonnie studied him. Her dark hair was piled loosely on top of her head in a messy bun, and her oversized tortoise shell glasses gave her a kind of sexy librarian look.

"If you think I have talent, leave my play the hell alone or I'll tell Mrs. Branford I don't think you're right for the male lead." She picked up her bag and went out, leaving Dax gaping. And a little turned on.

He left the auditorium and headed for the journalism room. He needed to finish laying out the paper before the morning as they had to get it on the press before the end of first period. The room was dark and he fumbled for the light, then stopped for a moment to appreciate the familiar smell of paper and ink and hot wax. It was a bit like the smell of the Beacon news-room, but with the added aroma of sweaty teenager wafting up from the gym below.

He went over to the table where the large sheets of lined paper waited, a few things already held in place with wax. Dax studied the pages, then the dummy sheets, for a long time. Suddenly he tore all the dummy sheets in half and threw them into the waste basket. Taking out a stack of fresh sheets, he picked up a pica pole and a blue felt-tipped pen and sat down at the drafting table. Two hours later, he had not only laid out the entire paper again, he had changed it completely. Photos were larger, text wrapped artfully around graphics, headlines were bigger, and he'd added a whole column down the entire left side of the front page for news briefs. It was a radical departure from the way the school paper had always looked.

"What the hell is this?" the student teacher asked the following morning when he came into the room and saw the pages waiting to go to press. "Who did this?" He asked the journalism teacher. She shook her head.

"It was like that when I got here this morning," she said. "But it could only have been Dax."

"I know he's the editor and all, but he changed the whole format? Without talking to anyone?"

"It wouldn't occur to Dax to talk about it with anyone first," the teacher said. "As far as he's concerned, it's his paper. I learned from the first day I had him in class that his mind doesn't work like other students'. He doesn't mean any malice, I know. He just wants things the way he wants them. He's just… Dax."

Chapter 49

The play was a huge success, and Dax and Bonnie were asked to make a presentation about it at the monthly board of education meeting.

"Why?" Bonnie asked, when Mrs. Branford gave them the news.

"What do you mean why?" The teacher was flabbergasted. "Because what we did here is an excellent model of getting students involved in extra-curricular activities in a new way."

"I appreciate that, Mrs. Branford, but I'm not really comfortable talking in front of people."

"That's okay, I am," Dax said.

"Oh, big surprise," Bonnie muttered.

"Thank you for that vote of confidence. I believe Mrs. Branford is saying they'd like us both there, but I'm willing to do that talking if you'll go along for moral support."

Bonnie looked like she was about to say something else, but Mrs. Branford interrupted.

"I think that's a fine idea," she said. "I'll be there as well. And honestly, great job, you two. You've made the whole school proud."

Dax and Bonnie walked to the parking lot together, more because they were both headed that way than because she particularly wanted to walk with him.

"So," Dax said. "Feels weird to not have rehearsal anymore, doesn't it?"

"I guess," Bonnie said. "Kind of. Yeah. But you've got a lot of other stuff going on, so it's not like you'll miss it too much."

"I'm busy with the paper, and studying and stuff, but still. I've always wanted to be a journalist, and I know my old man loves it that I'm following in his footsteps, but sometimes I think maybe I was meant for the theater."

"Really? Are you thinking of studying theater in college?"

"I don't know," Dax admitted. "I've been so busy just trying to survive high school that I haven't thought all that much about college."

"But you are going to college?" Bonnie put her bag on the hood of her car and bent to tie her shoe.

"Yeah, of course. I'm thinking about leaving New York for it, though."

"Well if you're thinking of studying theater seriously, that would be a mistake."

"No, I know that. I'm still going to study journalism, as that's really what I want to do, but I will probably still stay involved in theater as much as I can, wherever I go."

"I'm glad," Bonnie said. "Because I might think you're a giant pain in the ass, and don't get me wrong as I totally do think you are, but you're also pretty talented on stage."

Dax's smile was sudden and huge.

"Don't go getting all big-headed now. God, I knew I shouldn't have said anything." Bonnie laughed and looked away.

"Will you go to the winter dance with me?"

"What?"

"You heard me."

"I heard you, I just don't believe you actually asked me that."

"Why not? Do you already have a date?"

"Well, no. But it's still like six weeks away. Probably nobody has a date yet."

"You will, and I will, if you say yes."

She looked at him then, in the broken sunlight of late afternoon, and suddenly couldn't see Dax Benton, the ego maniac she'd always detested in class and avoided in the hallway, the spoiled rich kid who always got everything he wanted because his father was a big shot newspaperman. At that moment, in the parking lot of their high school, standing beside her battered Chevrolet, he was just Dax, a sweet boy from school.

"Yeah," she said. "Yeah, okay. I'd love to go to the dance with you."

The night of the winter dance was cold but so clear the stars looked like diamonds strewn across black velvet. Dax arrived at Bonnie's in a taxi, and chatted with her dark, stern-looking father and attractive mother while he waited for Bonnie to appear. This was a rite of passage for a teenaged boy, Dax knew, making feeble stabs at small talk with the parents in a stuffy living room that reeked of rules and convention until the pretty girl appeared on the staircase and made his jaw drop. The only thing that could have made the moment any more of a TV movie would be if Bonnie had braces that had been removed just that afternoon.

His jaw did drop a bit, without his permission, when she came into the living room in a red satin dress, her hair swept to the side in a low ponytail. He wondered if she had put in contacts – her glasses were nowhere in sight.

"Wow," he said. "You look amazing."

"Thanks. So do you."

They bid her parents goodnight and got into the back of the waiting taxi.

"Sorry I don't have a car, but I never learned to drive, so it seemed like a waste of money."

Bonnie laughed. Smiling, Dax studied her face. He had literally never heard her laugh before. She was always so serious, so studious, as though she had a lot on her mind or a dark history. It seemed unlikely an upper-middle-class kid would have a dark history, but Dax liked thinking she did. It made him feel as though he were rescuing her, albeit New York-style, which was basically just whisking her away in a taxi.

"It's okay," Bonnie said. "I almost never take cabs, so it's still kind of exciting to me. My parents got me that crummy old car because they wanted me to learn how to drive in the city. This is much more glamorous."

"Do you ever wonder if we're missing out on some important part of our youth by going to a school that has its dances at a catering hall instead of their own gym?"

Bonnie laughed again and wrinkled her nose.

"I think you've been watching too many John Hughes movies. Don't tell me: what you really wanted tonight was for me to have been transformed from a skirt-and-sweater-wearing mousy little bookworm to a total babe with an hourglass figure in a skin tight dress, and when we walked into the dance – for which our crappy, smelly gym would have magically become a streamer-festooned wonderland of revolving lights and rose petals and lots of glitter – and the crowd of kids would part so you could lead me to the center of the floor and everyone would gather around us in a circle and clap and cheer while we show them all just how to Wang Chung tonight?"

Dax was laughing. They both were. The streetlights showed him quick glimpses of how pretty she looked, with tears of laughter making her eyes shine. He leaned over and kissed her. He felt her stiffen in surprise, but then she leaned into him and kissed him back. The taxi pulled up outside the catering hall, and Dax led Bonnie inside, his hand on the small of her back. Both were smiling, but neither said a word.

Chapter 50

Dax really liked Bonnie. The realization hit him like a sock full of nickels two days after the dance, when he found that part of his mind kept sneaking back to her when the rest of it wasn't pay attention. He'd never felt this way about a girl before, and it threw him. Always before, girls had been a learning tool, a soft and fragranced experiment in seeing how far he could go, how much he could get away with, what he could get them to do. But with Bonnie, he never even thought to try any of that. She was so real, so solid, so unblinkingly in his face that it made him feel exposed. Vulnerable. He wasn't entirely sure he liked it. He wasn't entirely sure he didn't.

When Mrs. Branford called the two of them into her office and told them she'd like them to do a spring version of the student playwriting competition, Dax didn't even hesitate.

"I think that's an awesome idea," he enthused. "I know a lot of the kids who submitted scripts for the fall contest will submit again." He turned to Bonnie. She shrugged.

"I'm game, I guess," she said. "I wasn't going to get involved with anything else because I've got so much going on to get ready for graduation, but I do think it's a great program."

"Great!" Dax said, swinging back to face Mrs. Branford. "So we'll start right away."

Mrs. Branford laughed. Dax's almost drunken enthusiasm for everything he did was what she'd be counting on to really get this off the ground.

"Get to it, you two," she said.

Dax and Bonnie spent the better part of a week making and putting up flyers announcing the spring version of the wildly successful fall student playwriting competition, and the response was overwhelming. It wasn't long before the drop box they'd set up outside Mrs. Branford's office for submissions was bulging.

"How are we going to get through all of these?" Bonnie asked, unloading another stack into Dax's arms. "I have other school stuff to do, you know."

"Hey, so do I," Dax said. "You don't think the school paper puts itself out, do you?"

"You're the one who practically drooled when Mrs. Branford asked us to do this again. You don't get to whine."

"I'm not whining."

"Not much you aren't."

Bonnie snapped the box shut again and put the tiny padlock into place. She glanced at her watch.

"I was going to suggest we go to the library to start reading through these, but it's later than I realized. They'll be kicking us out of here soon."

"We can take them to my place," Dax suggested. "No one will bother us. My father won't get home until late and his wife doesn't talk to me unless she has to."

"His wife? Isn't she your step-mother then?"

"She's not MY anything, except pain in the ass."

"Oh, I see."

Dax had expected her to act shocked, as anyone did when he spoke his true feelings about Hanna, but Bonnie was genuinely unflappable. It was one of the things Dax liked most about her. She absorbed whatever she heard and saw, and he could almost see her mentally rubber stamping everything as either important or unimportant, and the unimportant she shrugged off and never thought about again. The important he wasn't sure what she did with, but he knew it was all in there, somewhere.

"So are you good with that? Going to my place?"

"Sure, why not? Let me just run to my locker and get my books and my coat. I'll meet you at the side entrance in about five minutes?"

"Great." Dax shifted the stack of papers in his arms a bit so they didn't slip away and headed for his own locker.

"I have to admit, now I'm curious to meet your father's wife," Bonnie said a few minutes later, as she merged onto the West Side Highway.

"Why? She's God-awful."

"I think that's why. Everyone else I know has such traditional mothers. This one sounds like a handful."

"She's a handful of something."

"Can I ask what happened to your real mom?"

"She died when I was born," Dax said. "My father doesn't like to talk about it very much, and Hanna won't talk about it at all. But I know she was a reporter at the Beacon. Dad always says she was the best reporter he ever knew, before or since."

"Wow," Bonnie said quietly. "You don't know how she died?"

"Dad always said he'd tell me the whole story when I was old enough to hear it. I guess he hasn't decided yet when that will be. I've always kind of figured she might have died in childbirth and he doesn't want me to feel I was responsible. I don't know, though. And in some ways, I kind of don't want to know. If that makes any sense."

Bonnie nodded.

"It's more romantic that way."

"I guess so. I hadn't thought of it like that, but yeah. I just like thinking of her as he knew her, Sarah the reporter, Sarah the kickass journalist, Sarah the fiery redhead who swept my father off his otherwise sensible and unsweep-offable feet."

"That's what I meant," Bonnie said as she pulled into a parking spot near Dax's brownstone and cut the engine. She took his hand, lacing her soft white fingers around his. "Romantic."

He smiled into her eyes and felt something squeeze inside him.

"Yes," he said. "Very."

Hanna wasn't home when they went inside, much to Dax's relief.

They spread out the pile of scripts on the kitchen table and Dax got them sodas from the refrigerator.

"You can tell which ones came in first," Bonnie remarked awhile later.

"Yeah," Dax said, turning a page. "They're crap."

She laughed.

"They are! It's like people thought if they rushed, they'd win for sure. I don't get it."

"Me either," Dax said. "I'm putting those into a pile over there. You can just put yours with mine."

"I'll bet you say that to all the girls," she teased, dropping the script she'd been reading onto the pile.

"Yeah, that's me. I'm a regular Don Juan."

Bonnie's smile evaporated and she fiddled with the paper clip on the next script in front of her.

"I actually had heard that about you," she said. "It's why I wasn't sure I wanted to go out with you."

"Heard what?" Dax was genuinely confused.

"That you're a ladies' man."

"I am? Nobody told me."

"Well, I hear the girls in school talking about you sometimes. This one thinks you're sexy, that one thinks you've got a cute butt, this one thinks you're charming, that one has the hots for your smile."

Dax was dumbfounded. He'd never considered himself any more of a ladies' man than any other teenaged boy, although he had been pretty proud of the way he'd stolen Amanda right out from under that idiot wrestler's nose.

"I've only had one girlfriend since I started high school, and we broke up when she moved away last year," he said.

"Yes, I know. Amanda."

"So whatever these girls are saying about me is all news to me. So, just curious – if you thought I was so into playing the field, why did you agree to go to the dance with me?"

"I don't know," Bonnie admitted. "I wasn't going to say yes, when you first asked me, and then you just suddenly seemed so normal, standing there in the parking lot."

"I am normal."

"No, actually, I don't think you are." She was studying his face. "I think you believe you are, but you aren't."

"I'm not sure if I'm supposed to feel insulted or not."

"No." She took his hand. "I'm not being insulting. Normal is something kids always think they need to be for some reason, but I came to the conclusion ages ago that normal is overrated. Being an oddball is way better."

"Oh, an oddball. Okay, now I feel better."

She laughed again.

"Listen to me," she said, squeezing his hand hard. "I'm saying the less you care about fitting in, the more interesting you are. Who wants to be like everyone else? And you, Dax, are not like everyone else."

"What am I like?"

"Damn, I was afraid you were going to ask me that. I'm not sure I can answer that very well. I've never known anyone who colors just outside the lines like you do. Teachers love you because you're a good student and you always do what you're supposed to do, but then you do a little bit that you're not supposed to do, and they all just kind of shake their heads and let it go. Because it's you. Do you see what I mean? You're able to push the envelope because you're smart and charming and most of all, I think, because it always seems like you know exactly what you're doing. You said to me the other day that no one ever seems to question you, and I think that's why. You're a born leader. People follow you because they trust you. Sometimes it almost seems to me like you could get anyone to do anything you wanted."

"Including you?"

"Of course not. I'm a billion times smarter than you, and you know it."

Dax laughed and shook his head. They went back to reading scripts, but he kept rewinding her words in his head and playing them again.

He had always done his own thing, she was right, but within the confines of what was expected of him. Being Zachary Benton's son wasn't the free ride the other kids always seemed to think it was. They were all under the impression that Dax was born with pockets full of privilege and a get-out-of-jail free card in each hand, but they had no idea what it was like to live under the cloud of realization that everyone in the city knew how to reach your father if they saw you screw up, and everyone's tolerance for Dax's screw ups was considerably less than for other kids. There was no writ of "boys will be boys" applied to Dax's misdeeds, not when people couldn't wait to crow about what the Benton kid did now. And while pissing Hanna off gave Dax a tremendous amount of enjoyment, even now, he never wanted to feel he let Zachary down. His father never struck him, he rarely even raised his voice, but when Dax felt he'd disappointed his father, it was more than he could take.

Still, Bonnie was right, and he was a little amazed she'd seen it: he did do his own thing, and without thinking about it. He was never trying to deliberately rock the boat, he was just doing what he believed needed to be done. There were always things that needed doing, needed trying, needed fixing, and someone had to do them. Dax just always believed he was that someone.

Chapter 51

"Chicago?" Zachary didn't know why he was surprised. He may have wanted his son to attend Columbia University as his mother had, but because he was also his mother's son, Zachary should have been ready for the boy to completely run off in another direction with both guns blazing. "What made you decide on Chicago?"

"They have a good journalism program, and to be honest, I need to get away from New York for awhile," Dax responded. "I want to be a journalist, Dad, a great journalist like you are, and like Mom was. But I feel like in order to do that, and to find out who I really am in the process, I need to be where people don't know me, and if I'm being honest, don't know you and don't remember Mom."

Zachary understood. He didn't necessarily like it, but he understood the boy's need for independence. It didn't seem that long ago that Zachary had told his own father, respectfully but firmly, that he wasn't going to study law. He remember the ensuing arguments, his father's stony silences when Zachary talked about what they were doing in his journalism classes, the palpable friction between them that only got worse the deeper Zachary got into his studies until finally he stopped telling his father anything and created a chasm between them that was wider than ever when Cornelius died. Zachary refused to let his relationship with Dax suffer the same fate.

"I think Chicago is a great idea," he told his son, clapping him on the knee. "I've heard good things about their program. And I really do understand your need to get away, to be your own person. I've been there myself. To be honest, I can't imagine that it's easy to be my son."

Dax smiled. He adored Zachary.

"I wouldn't say it's not easy being your son, but if I stay in New York to study and then come to work at the Beacon right away, I'll always only ever be Zachary Junior. I want to make my own way out there, find out who I am, what I'm capable of. Then if I decide to come back, I'll have more to offer. New eyes, new ideas."

"Do you think you'll want to come back after graduation?"

"Sure I do. New York is my home. You're here, this is where Mom was from, this is where my whole life has always been."

"Your mother actually was from Connecticut."

"Eh," Dax waved his hand. "From everything you've told me, she was as much a New Yorker as you or me. Being from Connecticut was just an accident of birth."

He looked and sounded so much like Sarah in that moment that Zachary had to turn away and light a cigarette before the boy saw the tears in his eyes and thought his old man weak.

"So tell me more about Chicago. What does your girlfriend say?"

Dax averted his eyes and swallowed hard. He longed to tell his father that Bonnie had suggested they date other people while they were at college, that she'd said she loved him but she didn't want to be tied down and didn't think he should be either. He ached to crawl onto Zachary's lap like he'd done as a little boy and lean his head on his father's chest and sob out his heartbreak, and above all to have Zachary tell him everything was going to be okay. He cleared his throat.

"Bonnie's cool. We've talked about it and neither of us thinks we should be tied down during college. She got a full ride to Brown, by the way."

"Impressive."

"Yeah. Anyway, we talked about it and we're still going to be friends and stay in touch and all that, but not be any kind of committed to each other."

"I think that's sensible. And you're good with this?"

Good with it? It feels like she pulled out my heart and lit it on fire and then stomped it out.

"Actually, it was my idea," Dax said. "I think she was coming around to the same thought, but I'm the one who brought it up."

Zachary was relieved. He'd met Bonnie and liked her, but he was afraid Dax may have inherited some of his father's tendencies to throw caution to the wind in matters of the heart. He was glad to hear the boy was being level-headed about it. In fact, he seemed to be well in control of everything. Zachary felt a bubble of pride.

"I know it's too soon to talk about what you'll do after college, but I want you to know that if you decide you want to come back and eventually take over the Beacon, I'd be honored to hand you the reigns."

Dax felt a lump rise unexpectedly in his throat.

"I'd be honored too, Dad, but I could never be more than a pale imitation of you."

"Nonsense. You are born to be a newspaperman, Dax. I've never tried to steer you in that direction but when I could see you were headed in that direction of your own volition, I can't say I wasn't pleased. Your mother would have been too."

"Dad, speaking of Mom…" Dax faltered and Zachary felt himself stiffen reflexively.

"Yes?"

"Well, you always said you'd tell me the whole story about how she died when you thought I was able to handle it. Don't you think I can handle it now?"

"You probably can," Zachary said quietly. "I just don't think I can."

Chapter 52

The Chicago streets were dark when Dax ventured out that first night. He always felt safer after dark, even in New York. Friends constantly admonished him, telling him how crazy it was to be out at night, but Dax knew that daylight only shows you what a city wants you to see. Wide-eyed tourists, window boxes full of flowers, quality stores and clean sidewalks, laughing children with brightly colored backpacks swarming to school like happy little turtles. At night, the sleeping city can't hide its soul. Like a post-coital lover, it's defenseless, stripped of its makeup, drowsy and vulnerable. It's then you can see a city for what it truly is. Dark, dripping alleyways, neon signs, cracked, flickering, struggling to stay awake, shadows and secrets slipping quietly out after the sun goes down.

Dax had arrived in Chicago on a sunny September morning, the taxi driver at O'Hare wordlessly loading his two huge suitcases into the trunk of the cab before whipping Dax out of the airport and into his new life. Chicago seemed so different from New York, but then every place did. Dax felt a surprising twinge of homesickness that he quickly pushed away. He wasn't gone from New York forever, not by a long shot. But this was something he had to do. If he didn't find out now who Dax Benton really was, he'd spend the rest of his life being Zachary Benton Junior.

The taxi rolled onto the campus of the University of Chicago. Dax stared out the window at the sprawling, beautiful campus. He was here. He was home. He was majoring in journalism and minoring in business. His future was clearly mapped out in his mind, and this is where his life would begin, this is where he'd finally stretch his wings and learn to soar. The cab pulled up in front of Vincent House, and the driver got Dax's bags out of the trunk. Dax was too excited to even look at the meter, he just pushed a twenty into the man's hand, his eyes on the building's Gothic architecture. He went inside and found his room, clean and sparse. He'd chosen Vincent House because it was made up almost entirely of single rooms. He didn't want a roommate. He had far too many nighttime plans already to have to bother with putting a necktie on the doorknob.

Dax loved Chicago from his first day, almost as much as he loved New York. There was a coarseness to Chicago, under the refined exterior it had cultivated since its wild heyday. Even walking down glittering Michigan Avenue, you still could sense the ghosts of its past, lingering, remembering. Dax knew how they felt.

"I'm considering not using my last name while I'm here," he told his advisor during their first meeting. "Just my middle name as my last name."

"And why is that?" Dr. Marie Fredericks tried to hide her amusement. She knew Zachary Benton by reputation, of course, but this boy, this shiny kid with big eyes and a bigger ego, this kid was a little too impressed by his own surname. He wanted to be incognito, she knew, so the masses wouldn't bother him, wouldn't get him dirty as they strained to touch the hem of his robes.

Dax leaned forward earnestly.

"I don't want any special treatment," he said. "I don't want people to think that I believe I'm any better in any way than they are. I'm here to learn, Dr. Fredericks, the same as any other student. My father wanted me to go to Columbia, then work my way through the ranks at the Beacon, but I just couldn't do it."

There was an innocence in his eyes, a sweetness that betrayed the searching little boy within. Dr. Fredericks felt her first impression slipping away.

"I don't want to be just another trust-fund kid," Dax went on. "That's why I came to Chicago. I want to study and learn with kids who don't have publisher fathers. I just want to be…" He paused, visibly feeling around for the right word. "Normal."

Normal is overrated. Being an oddball is way better. Bonnie's voice echoed through his mind. *Sorry, Bon, I have to pretend to be normal first. I'm saving oddball for later.*

Dr. Fredericks sat back in her chair. Whatever she had expected to come out of Dax Benton's mouth, that hadn't been it. Before she could respond, the boy was leaning forward again.

"Can I admit something else to you, Dr. Fredericks?"

"Go ahead." She found her voice.

"Well, my father... he's a good man. Don't get me wrong, he's a very good man, but he's a little, uh, outdated, with some of his views."

"How so?"

Dax cleared his throat and shuffled his feet, looking uncomfortable.

"I would appreciate you keeping this just between us."

"Yes, of course."

"Well, my father is a bit sexist. He tends to view and treat women as second-class citizens, especially professionally. I've watched too many talented female reporters not get the work or the recognition they deserve simply because they were born with a vagina. Pardon my bluntness."

Dr. Frederick nodded but didn't speak, completely unsure of what she'd have said if she could.

"I saw it at home too, sad to say. My mother died when I was born, but I was raised by my stepmother. She is a warm, kind, intelligent, talented woman, but my father has always treated her like she's just some fluffy, brainless bimbo who shares his bed."

"You're close with your stepmother then."

I hate the bitch. I'd kill her without a second thought if I could get away with it.

"Very close," Dax responded. "As far as I'm concerned, she is my mother and I do everything I can to build her up after he tears her down."

"It was brave of you to move away from her," Dr. Fredericks said.

"I had to," Dax answered. "For myself and for her. He is not physically abusive so she isn't in any danger of that type. She just needs to stand on her own two feet more. We are in touch all the time. She'll be fine. But what all this has taught me, Dr. Fredericks, is that I want to help empower women to reach their potential at every stage. Women's potential, well this is true for everyone really, changes at different stages of their lives. Like you, for example. The potential you had in college was different from what you could have achieved in high school. Then in graduate school – very impressive, by the way – you were capable of more, but not nearly as much as you're capable of now, or will be in the future. One of the reasons I chose this university is because of Dr. Gray. She's the first woman president of a major university. Not only is that huge, but look at the example she's setting for young women everywhere. It just seems to me that women too often lose sight of their own potential while struggling to make half the salary of a man and doing the same job. It just makes me so angry."

"I can see that." Dr. Fredericks was already blown clean away by this young man's wisdom and passion.

"I don't know, I guess you could say I'm a feminist." Dax dropped back in his chair and sighed, spent. "But I believe that the new generation of female journalists is in a great position to affect change, both for themselves and for all women. And if I can be a part of that, well then I'll consider myself a success."

Near tears, he took a moment to compose himself before continuing.

"So you see, Dr. Fredericks, that's why I needed to get away from New York for awhile. To step out of the shadow of the great Zachary Benton and help bring about the kind of change I think the world needs most."

That young man is the most enlightened, promising student I've ever had, Dr. Fredericks thought as Dax left her office.

One bottle of wine and she'll be in my bed and begging for it, Dax thought, closing her office door behind him. *One down, two thousand to go.*

Chapter 53

Dax adapted to university life faster than even he expected. On campus, he was Dax Thomas, good student, aspiring journalist, popular, heavily involved in campus activities. He good-naturedly declined to pledge a fraternity, claiming he had no love for anything Greek. To the women, though, countless pretty and ambitious co-eds, Dax would emotionally declare that he could never be part of an organization that persisted in segregating the genders and glorifying idiotic male behavior. He was perfectly happy to belong to the many campus organizations that involved men and women equally and promoted the things that enrich and unite, rather than divide: literature, art, and music.

He dated plenty, but never took any of the relationships to the sexual level. He didn't want to destroy his painstakingly crafted reputation on campus as a gentleman and, more importantly, a feminist. The girls, for the most part, didn't seem to mind that Dax never made any blatant moves on them. A couple of the more brazen ones would drop subtle, and sometimes nowhere near as subtle, hints at the end of a date, whispering against his mouth that their roommate was out of town for the weekend. Dax always declined, but with carefully rehearsed regret.

"I respect you too much to let this get physical before we're ready," he'd say softly, touching her face. "We could be so much more."

After a formal dance sophomore year, a particularly eager tennis player had pulled away from him in a fit of the kind of hazy anger that drifts up from a mixture of lust, frustration, and cheap booze.

"You're gay, aren't you?" she demanded, completely and immediately sold on the idea that any man who didn't want her must be an MVP for the other team. Dax, unsmilingly, had pulled her tight against him so she could feel his hardness pressing against the front of her satin dress. He looked wordlessly and directly into her eyes. Word got around campus pretty fast after that that Dax Thomas wasn't gay, he just wasn't a player.

His popularity grew on campus, the women loving him for his relentless defense of feminism and proven respect for them as people, and the men liked him because he was affable, could hold his liquor, and posed no threat.

Off campus, he was free to be Dax Benton, because no one knew or cared who he really was. He became a regular at Chicago's best and most exclusive nightclubs, where he was always in the company of the city's richest and loneliest wives. Many a bartender and maître d' turned a blind eye to Dax, who was neither of legal drinking age nor the husband. The women tipped them generously into silence. Dax took his pent-up sexual frustration out on woman after woman, leaving stains on $400 Egyptian cotton sheets he knew would be slept on the following night by the fat, rich bastard of a husband who was either too stupid to know what his wife did when he was out of town or else chose to ignore it.

These women were a much better match for Dax than the girls on campus. He knew that any love affairs he had at school would lead to broken hearts, recriminations, sobbing late-night phone calls, tear-stained letters shoved under dorm room doors. If he ever thought he was overestimating himself, he had only to look around at what happened to other guys on campus. The whole place was a hormone-driven soap opera, so Dax made sure to find release only with women who could not make any demands on him, women who willingly bought him drinks in return for what his young body would do to them in bed later. He'd walked out of many an expensively decorated Lake Forest bedroom exhausted, satisfied, and smelling of Chanel No. 5.

It was his nights out in Chicago that taught Dax about wine. He'd had beer, or an occasional wine cooler to put girls at ease, but he'd never had wine. For the rest of his life, he remembered that first sip of a fat, flirty red, the vapors hitting his nose before the grapes found his tongue, and the slow spreading warmth that accompanied a feeling of wellbeing stronger than Dax had ever known. He had smiled at the voluptuous brunette across from him.

"I have found my drink of choice," he said, raising his glass. "To wonderful wine and the most beautiful woman in the room." They finished two bottles that night, and Dax noticed that he had some trouble in her bed later. His penis flopped to the side, uncooperative and unenthusiastic. *No more wine for you*, he cursed it silently. Fortunately, his playmate was too drunk to notice, and his hands and mouth picked up the slack.

Over the next several months, Dax learned exactly how much wine he could drink and still perform in bed, and was always careful to make sure his companion drank more. The heady feeling of being in control over the women was powerful, and he noticed that when they were drunk enough but not to the point of passing out, he could convince them to do anything.

Far from having a negative effect on his academic life, Dax found he'd struck the perfect balance and was able to shut off everything but school when he was in class or studying. His grades improved steadily and by his junior year, he was president of three academic clubs and editor of the campus newspaper. He'd even started doing some community theater in Chicago, he reported to Bonnie during one of their Sunday night phone calls.

"Aren't you getting in over your head?" Bonnie asked. "I know you like being busy, but that schedule sounds insane even for you."

"I know it does. The logical part of my brain knows it does. But for whatever reason, the busier I am, the more energy I have."

"I wish you'd send some of that to me. I'm exhausted. Between classes, the theater, and my part-time job, I sometimes have to stop and remember where I am and what I'm supposed to be doing."

"Come to Chicago," Dax said, lowering his voice. "I'll give you something to do."

"Aaaand there's the old Dax," Bonnie said. "Some things about you will never change."

"I'm thinking of starting a wine appreciation club," Dax said one afternoon to Heather, a pretty senior who lived down the hall from him.

They were in Dax's room, ostensibly studying like they did many Saturday afternoons, but this particular day was unseasonably warm and Heather was lazily unbuttoning her blouse, transparently blaming the heat. Dax watched her appreciatively, leaning over to slide one hand under her lacy bra. She moaned softly and pulled him closer. Dax kissed her, long and deep, and she wriggled impatiently beneath him.

"Come on, Dax, you know I want it. Why won't you give it to me? I know you want it too. Come on, baby."

He smiled down into her eyes.

"You know, I'm trying to tell you about my idea for a new club that could bring some culture and refinement to this school, and all you can think about is sex. I feel like a piece of meat now."

Heather sighed gustily and rolled her eyes. Then she laughed and pushed Dax off her, sitting up and rebuttoning her blouse.

"Okay, okay," she said. "Tell me about your idea. You have my undivided attention."

"I was really just thinking that there are so many students here who are a little too refined for the keg parties and puking in the bushes scene," Dax said, leaning back against the wall and crossing his long legs. "A lot of girls don't feel comfortable at those parties, or maybe it's more accurate to say they don't feel safe, and I also know a lot of guys who aren't into that whole scene either. I was thinking a wine appreciation group would give people like us a chance to socialize and enjoy an adult beverage without it going all frat boy."

"I think that's a great idea," Heather responded. "I love wine. And it's more refined, you're right. No one has wine keggers."

"That's just what I mean. We're talking about a high-minded group of civilized people with common interests and respect for each other."

By now, Heather was really excited.

"Dax, you've got to get this going. Do you need to get the school's approval?"

"No, it's not going to be a school-affiliated club, just an informal group that meets… I don't know. Someplace. Maybe here or the common area of one of the houses, or maybe someplace off campus. I'll figure that out. Now…" he leaned over and kissed her, long and deep. "As our first charter member, will you tell your friends? The right friends. You know."

Heather's eyes were wide and shining.

"Yes, yes of course! I'm going to go call a couple of them right now!" She kissed Dax again and jumped up, grabbing her shoes and hurrying out the door. Dax leaned back and smiled to himself. Everything was coming together beautifully.

"Ladies and gentlemen, if you would please," Dax called, tapping his wine glass lightly with a dessert fork. "Thank you all for coming to the first gathering of the Wine Enthusiasts Club. All of you have expressed an interest in being a part of an organization that doesn't have to teetotal in order to keep it classy, but doesn't have to funnel beer through a tube to have fun."

Everyone applauded, and Dax smiled around at the group, ensconced in the back room of a local restaurant that had agreed, reluctantly, to host them. The manager hadn't been willing to risk serving wine to college kids, not when the state of Illinois had raised the drinking age to 21, but the wad of cash Dax pulled out mid-way into their conversation had changed its course. It always did.

He had considered quietly telling the manager who he was and who his father was as a kind of added insurance, but something he couldn't pinpoint held him back. He never used Zachary's name to wield influence, and he wasn't going to start now. This was his project and his life. Not his father's.

The room they were in was beautiful, all dark red velvet draperies and furnishings, highlighted with dark wood and wrought iron. It had a deeply medieval feel, with just the right amount of Chicago swank.

"Before we begin, I want you to know that this is not a wine tasting club," Dax went on. "I know we all understand why people swirl and spit, but first of all it is my opinion that is a grievous waste of good wine and second of all, we can handle our booze a hell of a lot better than those old people." Laughter and applause rippled over Dax. He was beginning to feel intoxicated without taking a single sip.

"Our first wine tonight is a 1974 Brunello di Montalcino. It's strong, so be warned, with a huge spicy bouquet. Tastes a bit like meat to me, and dried fruit."

Glasses were raised and the general consensus was one of vast appreciation for this, their first bottle of wine as a group. By the end of the meeting, they had each consumed a full bottle and had a vast appreciation for everything.

Chapter 54

Dax tapped lightly on the open door to his advisor's office.

"You wanted to see me, Dr. Fredericks?"

"Hello, Dax. Yes, please sit down."

He smiled easily at her as he leaned back in the now-familiar leather chairs across from her desk. He was a junior now and had never been in trouble. It never occurred to him that he could be. Dax's brain just didn't work that way.

"Dax, I've received some information on an internship available at the Chicago Tribune this summer. They are only looking for one student, and I immediately thought of you. So it's yours if you want it."

"Yes."

Dr. Fredericks, long accustomed to Dax's cocky directness, merely smiled.

"You might want to take a few days and think about it, decide if that's definitely how you want to spend your summer, maybe talk to your father and see..."

"Dr. Fredericks, I've known all my life I am meant to be a journalist. You know me well enough by now to believe me when I say it isn't even about following in my father's footsteps. In fact, it's about leaving my own footprints. If I can get in the door of the Tribune, it would push me leaps and bounds ahead in my education and career plans. I don't need to talk to my father first – he'll be thrilled when he finds out what I'm doing. You asked me if I want this internship, and now you have my answer. Yes. An unequivocal, unhesitating yes."

Dr. Fredericks handed him a file folder.

"Here's the application. It's just a formality, I'm told, since you will have the school's endorsement. There's some other information in there about everything the job entails. For the school, you'll need to keep an internship journal, and submit a paper on your experience. All that information is in there too."

By the end of his first week on the job, Dax had already made his mark at the Chicago Tribune. He followed a lead he'd overheard one night at a nightclub downtown, a very drunken and very loud revelation from a man at the next table about some insider trading going on at his company. Dax had gone back to his dorm that night, made some phone calls, and worked feverishly until the early hours of the morning.
He took a fast shower and stopped at the student union for a cup of coffee before heading to the Trib. He had to skip two classes to do it, but he didn't care. He handed it to the editor, Wilson, with hands he could barely keep from shaking with excitement.

"Where did you get this?" Wilson asked after he'd read it.

"I wrote it," Dax said impatiently.

"This is a big story, if it's true," Wilson said, looking at Dax steadily.

"What do you mean, 'if it's true'?" Dax demanded. "I quote credible sources. I did the goddamned work. Of course it's true."

Wilson shrugged. It wasn't the first time he'd had an intern so full of himself he could barely get his head in the newsroom door, and it wouldn't be the last.

"I'll just verify a couple of facts before we run it," he said, turning back to his typewriter.

Dax was furious. He turned on his heel and strode out of the newsroom. He took a cab back to campus and made it to his next class with two minutes to spare, but his thoughts were loud he couldn't hear a word the professor was saying. He kept replaying the scene in the newsroom in his head. Wilson had been so smug, so condescending. He should have been slapping Dax on the back and thanking him profusely for breaking such a huge story. Dax seethed all through the rest of his morning classes. The next day, on his way to his internship, he stopped at a newsstand downtown and asked for a copy of the Trib.

His story was the banner headline on the front page.

Dax gave a whoop so loud the man at the newsstand jumped.

"Sorry," Dax said, handing him a five-dollar bill. "Thanks. Keep the change."

When he walked into the newsroom and approached Wilson's desk, he pretended to be absorbed in reading the front page.

"Oh look, someone broke a story on insider trading at one of Chicago's biggest financial firms," Dax said. "Isn't that interesting? I wonder who that ace reporter could be?"

"All right, all right," Wilson said. "You made your point. It was a good piece, all right? But next time let me know what you're working on before you finish it."

"Why?"

"Because we might have somebody else already working on the same story."

Dax gave a derisive laugh.

"Not likely," he said.

He was at his desk typing up the police blotter – Wilson's idea of a punishment – when Mr. Neely, the executive editor, came out of his office and asked Dax if he could speak with him. He sauntered in and sat down in the chair across from the editor's desk in an office that was Spartan and cold, completely unlike Zachary's lair at the Beacon.

"Dax, you did a great job on that story this morning," Mr. Neely began. Although he allowed Dax to use the name Dax Thomas in his bylines, he knew who the boy was, more specifically who his father was. He chose his words now carefully. "I'm not sure where you got your information and I don't need to know, but you did a hell of a good job. If you keep your ear to the ground like that, I can see a position here for you after graduation. If you want it, of course."

"Thank you, sir," Dax said, smiling broadly. "I'm honored to even be considered."

"I know you may want to go back to New York after you're done with school, to work at the Beacon-"

Dax cut him off.

"I don't think I'll be doing that, sir. Chicago is my home now."

"Well, you have a little time to think about it, so you do that, and keep your cranking out stories like that in the meantime. You could go far here, Dax."

"Thank you, sir," Dax repeated. "Actually, I'm glad you brought this up because I've been wanting to ask you if I can spend part of my internship learning all the functions of the paper."

"You don't know them all already? I figured you grew up at the Beacon."

"I did, yes, and I have a basic knowledge of everything, but I'd like to really learn. I'd like to spend some time in production, the press room, all of that."

Mr. Neely was watching Dax intently. A lot of interns had come in and out of the Tribune, but he'd never had one so eager to soak up every bit of it. He couldn't say he was surprised – it was obviously in Dax's blood – but he was impressed that the boy didn't seem to take anything for granted, to assume that any particular privileges would be coming his way just because he was a Benton.

"Would you like to go out with one of the paper carriers on his route?"

Mr. Neely was teasing him now, and Dax knew he'd be getting what he wanted.

"I think I'll skip that part," he said. "I'm not sure I'm qualified."

He walked back into the newsroom, still smiling to himself. Wilson glanced up and Dax gave an exaggerated point and wink. Wilson turned away in disgust.

Back in his dorm room later, Dax finished a paper due the next day and the reading for two other classes. By the time he was finished, it was nearly 9 p.m. He took a shower and changed into a pair of charcoal Italian silk trousers and a white dress shirt with the first three buttons open. He was standing outside his door trying to close the clasp on his watch when he saw Heather heading toward him.

"Hey," she said. "You're all dressed up. And you smell good. Where are you going?"

"Dinner with a friend," Dax said, checking his pockets to make sure he had his keys.

"A friend?" A shadow crossed Heather's face. Dax knew from past experience she had an irritating tendency to be jealous. He put his hand on her hip and pulled her up against him, kissing her long and deep. His trusty erection jumped to attention, reassuring Heather of all she needed to know.

"Yeah," Dax said, resting his forehead on hers and looking into her eyes. "And old family friend. He's in town on business and he asked to see me. But you don't have to worry, he's thoroughly and completely gay, and I'm not his type anyway."

Heather laughed, visibly relieved. Dax kissed her again.

"Don't forget we have the Wine Enthusiasts' gathering tomorrow night. Can you help me make sure everyone knows?"

"Sure, baby," Heather said, kissing him again. "I'll see you later?"

"You bet." He gave her juicy little ass a squeeze before extricating himself from her arms and heading down the stairs. On the cab ride to Judith's, he mentally went over everything he had to take care of that week. Judith tonight, Wine Enthusiasts tomorrow night, exams the rest of the week, three day's work at the Tribune. Most people would have passed out at the very thought of a schedule like Dax's, but the more he had going on, the better he functioned. And when he got tired, he could always count on a beautiful cocaine buffet like the one Judith had laid out for him on her antique coffee table. After they'd inhaled most of it through the rolled up ten dollar bill she kept just for snorting purposes, Dax leaned back, sinking into her buttery leather sofa.

"Come here, you sexy thing," he said, holding out his hand. "It's been a long day and it does me a world of good just to look at you, so I can only imagine what touching you will do for me."

Judith was a svelte, smoldering brunette of about fifty. She had recently separated from her husband, a cosmetic surgeon who was constantly away attending conferences, although she told Dax she didn't believe he was attending anything except private parties in the beds of certain sluts scattered conveniently across the country. The night he'd met her at a nightclub uptown, Dax had told her he was 35 and a graduate student at the university. Dressed up, he knew he could easily pass for 35, and that age appealed to Judith. Any younger and she'd have felt like a predator. Much older and there wouldn't have been the same level of satisfaction at getting into his pants.

"I saw someone in the Tribune today with the same name as you," she said, kissing the side of his neck and unbuttoning his shirt.

"The same name as me?"

"Yes. Different last name, but his name was Dax. It was right there on the front page. I thought that was funny. You don't see that name very often."

"No, you don't, although it isn't as uncommon as you'd think," he said, running his hands up and down her firm back. "It means 'leader.'"

"Mmmm," she said, slithering out of her dress. "You can lead me anywhere you want."

He was back in his dorm in enough time for a two-hour nap and a shower before his first class. He felt like a million bucks.

"I'm not sure I'm going to make it, Dax." Even through the phone, he could hear the fatigue in Bonnie's voice. "I've just got too much going on."

"So throw something back," he said. He was a little tired himself, actually. He tucked the phone between his shoulder and his ear and took a bottle of wine out from the cabinet and poured some into a long stemmed glass. Absently, he held it up to the light and gave it a slight twirl, appreciating the color without really seeing it.

"Physician, heal thyself."

"You can't compare us, Bon. I'm made for this kind of crazy pace. You aren't. Neither of us is right or wrong, that's just how we're wired."

"I know, but I want to do all this stuff. That's why I said yes to everything in the first place."

"That's the curse of being like us. It's hard to say no. I don't remember the last time I said no to anything. Or wanted to."

"That sounds like you."

"Like us," he corrected. "Are you sure you can't come to Chicago for a visit?"

"I'm sure. At least not right now. Maybe for spring break."

When they hung up, Dax sat for a long time, sipping wine and wondering what would happen if Bonnie actually did come for a visit. He'd either have to hide all that he'd been doing, or let her in on it and hope she'd understand.

Chapter 55

Dr. Fredericks hung up the phone in her office and sat for a moment, deep in thought. Finally, she got up and pulled Dax Benton's student file from her cabinet. Sitting down again, she rifled through it. He had top grades, was involved in several academic clubs, was well-liked among his classmates and, she'd just been informed, was performing spectacularly at his internship.

Still, she was sure she'd seen him the previous evening at a nightclub on the other side of the city. She couldn't be sure. She'd been out with a group of her friends celebrating two of them receiving their PhDs and she thought she'd seen him dancing with a woman considerably older than him. Actually, she was playing fast and loose with the word "dancing," given what she'd actually seen on the dance floor. It was more like sex standing up and set to music. But Dr. Fredericks had been around long enough to know that a student who partied like that off campus never lasted very long as a student, and Dax seemed to be excelling. Maybe it was an isolated incident. Or maybe it wasn't Dax. She put a note in his mailbox and asked him to stop by her office at his earliest convenience for a chat.

Standing in the student union the next day, flipping through the stuff he'd pulled out of his mailbox, Dax unfolded Dr. Fredericks' note. He smiled to himself and shook his head. He knew what she wanted. He'd seen her two nights ago at the club, but had pretended he hadn't noticed her. No doubt she wanted to find out as many of the lascivious details as she could without being too obvious about it. Dax couldn't wait to see how she'd pull that off.

"You wanted to see me, Dr. Fredericks?" He tapped lightly on her door and stuck his head in.

"Yes, Dax, please come in."

He sat down and leaned back, smiling easily at her. He still kept his school demeanor in place when he was talking with her, but he started to carefully let a bit of his off-campus persona show. She was slightly aware now of the other side of Dax, and he wanted to bring her over slowly.

"Dax," Dr. Fredericks said, then paused. What was she doing? Why had she called him in here? His off-campus life was none of her concern as long as his academic performance wasn't suffering, and it wasn't. He was waiting, watching her, his faint smile oddly disarming. She finally made herself speak again.

"How is everything going?"

"Fine, Dr. Fredericks, just fine. My classes are going well, and my internship is really turning into a great experience. I don't know if you've seen it, but some of my work has made the Tribune front page."

"Yes, I've seen that. You're doing a great job."

"Thank you. Actually, I should thank you for helping me get the internship in the first place. With all the good students on this campus, I still can't believe I'm the one you asked."

Dr. Fredericks looked at Dax steadily. He was flattering her. They both knew she had nothing more to do with him getting that internship than handing him the paperwork. He'd gotten it because he was Zachary Benton's son and a great student. She realized she'd been holding his gaze for too long, and looked down at his file, clearing her throat and needlessly rearranging some papers.

"I'm glad it's going well," she said. "I just like to check in with my students now and then to make sure they're not having any problems and see if there's anything they'd like to discuss."

Dax averted his eyes, crossing and uncrossing his legs and looking uncomfortable.

"Dax? Is something wrong?"

"No, Dr. Fredericks, nothing. It's nothing."

"You can talk to me, you know. I'm your advisor."

Dax smiled at the floor, looking suddenly childlike, almost shy. He glanced up at her, the back down at the floor.

"Well, it's funny you mention being my advisor. Because I've been thinking that maybe I should…" he faltered and stopped.

"Should what?" Dr. Fredericks prompted.

"Well, that I should ask the university to switch my advisor to Dr. Cunningham."

"You want to change advisors? What brought this on?"

"I don't want to," Dax said quietly. "I just think maybe it would be better if I did."

"But why? Have I done something you disagree with? Something that you didn't like?"

"No," Dax said quietly. "It's nothing like that. I'm just not sure it's appropriate for a student to have feelings like this for his advisor."

Marie Fredericks felt her breath catch in her throat but not, she was pretty sure, audibly. Now what was she supposed to do with that? Not only was she his advisor and a faculty member at his university, she was a good 20 years his senior. What she had felt stirring in her southern states watching him on the dance floor that night had been nothing more than pure animal instinct helped along by one too many grasshoppers. She had a PhD and tenure. She wasn't about to throw it all away on a student.

"That's flattering, Dax, but I think we both know it's completely inappropriate."

"I know," Dax said softly. When he finally forced himself to look up at her, his eyes were shimmering with tears. "But a woman as amazing as you deserves to at least know someone feels this way about her."

He reached across the desk and took her hand. Before she could react, he had given it a warm, firm squeeze. Then he got up and walked out of her office without another word, closing the door quietly behind him.

Dr. Fredericks leaned back in her chair, her hands shaking, unsure of what had just happened. In all her years at the university, she'd never found herself attracted to a student. And she wasn't even entirely sure she was attracted to Dax – it was different than mere sexual chemistry.

There was something about him that had, from the moment she'd met him, soaked into her slowly, and before she even realized what was happening, it was too late and she was wringing wet. She made up her mind right then to put in the request herself for Dax to be transferred to a different advisor. Then she made up her mind that she wasn't going to do anything of the sort.

Dax, walking back to his dorm, jingled the coins in his pocket in a rhythm with his whistling. She was his now.

The following night, Dax went back to the same club by himself. He sat at the far end the bar, sipping a glass of wine and smoking a cigarette. He nodded occasionally when someone he knew came up to the bar for a drink, but he spoke to no one and he didn't get up. He'd been there nearly an hour when she came in. He saw her pause, just inside the door, and look around. He made no move, nothing that would tell her he was there, he just watched her. He saw her see him, and hesitate only a moment before walking toward him with a forced casualness. Wordlessly, she slid onto the chair next to his and ordered a mai tai. He lit another cigarette.

"Hello, Marie," he said softly.

"Shut up, Dax. I shouldn't even be here."

His laugh was short, gravelly, lusty.

"And yet here you are."

He motioned for another glass of wine and they drank without speaking. Dax deliberately didn't touch her, didn't pay for her drink, didn't even look directly at her. When she put her empty glass on the bar, he crushed out his cigarette, stood up, and without looking at her headed toward the back, skirting the crush of dancing couples. There was a small, dark, empty room he frequently made use of, down a dimly lit hallway behind the dance floor. He could hear her footsteps behind him and as he opened the door to his private room, he reached for her hand, pulling her inside and up against him in one fluid motion.

"I shouldn't be here," she repeated, her voice scarcely a whisper.

"Then why are you here?" Dax whispered, brushing his face through her hair, breathing against her neck.

"I don't know," she answered, melting against him. "But I'm here."

He pushed her tight skirt up and pinned her against the wall with his torso, her legs wrapping around his waist. He took her unceremoniously, without a sound, without another word. Everything she was risking no longer mattered. She would have risked it all again and more for him.

Chapter 56

Marie stood at her campus mailbox shifting through a mountainous and largely nonsensical pile of faculty memos and flyers for campus activities, dropping them one by one into the garbage can near her feet. A long, white envelope fluttered thinly to the floor and she picked it up. Inside was a handwritten note on plain white paper.

"Dear Dr. Fredericks,

Please consider this your invitation to become an official member of the Wine Enthusiasts Club. We are not a sanctioned campus club, but in every other respect, we are as official as it gets. We meet every other week. Meeting dates and directions to the restaurant are below. Our club officers have discussed inviting select university faculty members to join us to add another dimension to our membership and to further round out what our members bring, if you will, to the table.

We would be most honored to have you join us at our meeting this evening. No need to RSVP, we will simply await the pleasure of seeing you.

Yours sincerely,

Dax Thomas
President"

Marie smiled to herself and tucked the letter into her bag. She hadn't seen or spoken to Dax since their encounter at the bar nearly a week ago. During that time she'd done a lot of thinking about the situation, but try though she might, she couldn't bring herself to be sorry for what they'd done. It had been a natural, biological urge and they'd given in to it, just as animals have been doing since time began. To deny their natural instincts would have been like turning away a glass of water to slake a parching thirst. If word got out and it meant losing her job, then so be it. Dax was of legal age so nothing else could come of it, and deep inside she knew she didn't care if it did. This invitation was Dax's way of not only asking to see her again, but beginning to publicly acknowledge their relationship.

She arrived at the restaurant that night carefully dressed in a business suit and low-heeled pumps, pearls around her neck, glasses primly settled on her face. She wanted the other students to see her as they always did. Only Dax knew what lay beneath.

A girl named Heather whom Marie only vaguely knew by sight greeted her when she walked in.

"Dr. Fredericks! What a nice surprise. Dax will be so pleased you've joined us."

"Thank you. Is he here? Dax?"

"He is running a bit late but he should be on his way," Heather responded. There was a familiarity, an intimacy in the way she spoke of Dax that made Marie's skin feel prickly. "Please help yourself to refreshments while we're waiting. Dax doesn't bring out the wine until he has called the meeting to order."

All around the room, students were leaning against cocktail tables, eating cheese and prosciutto on thinly sliced French bread. Fat grapes and red strawberries were piled in the middle of each table and long stemmed wine glasses glittered eagerly about the room, waiting. But even without the wine, there was an oddly sensual feel in the air, even odder when Marie noticed with a start that nearly all of the people in the room were female. In fact, she thought as her eyes ran through the room, with the exception of a couple of male students, they were all female. The prickling crawled across her skin again. What had she gotten herself into?

"Hello, Dr. Fredericks, so nice to see you here."

Marie turned to see a student in one of her classes smiling glassily at her over a plate full of bread and cheese.

"Hello, Serena," she responded, trying to hide her distaste at seeing the girl in a social setting. She could barely tolerate her smarmy phoniness in class. She was wearing a cocktail dress so tight Marie wondered briefly how she could walk. "I didn't know you belonged to this group."

"Yes, I was one of the first people Dax asked to join," Serena responded silkily. "You may not know it, but I'm very knowledgeable about wine.

I was so pleased when Dax decided to form this club. We are all in such desperate need of a little class and good taste, don't you agree?"

"Oh my, yes. I couldn't agree more," Marie said. "Please excuse me, Serena, I see someone I must say hello to or there will be some very hurt feelings."

She moved to the other side of the room, looking around desperately for someone – anyone – to talk to, but at that moment, Dax walked in and a chorus of happy sounds rippled across the room. He hadn't seen her yet as he clapped his hands and smiled.

"Everyone, thank you for being here, and my deepest apologies for being late." He winked at Heather who blushed deeply and smiled back at him. Marie felt the sudden urge to turn and run. What was she doing here? She was the oldest person in the room by a good 20 years, and what's more, she was their professor. Dax, in a collegiate sweater, was her student. She felt sick and leaned back against the wall to steady herself.

"I would also like to welcome our newest member, Marie. Most of you know her, at least by sight, as Dr. Fredericks, math professor and academic advisor. She is the first faculty member to join us, but as she was hand selected by me, I know you will all welcome her with open arms. I have not discussed this with her, but I believe she will agree with me that as we are in a different atmosphere here, off campus and in a social setting, a very social setting, you should address her as Marie. On campus, however, please continue to call her Dr. Fredericks and show her the respect due her as a distinguished member of our university faculty."

This time his wink was aimed at her, and Marie shifted uncomfortably from one foot to the other, the urge to run still coursing through her.

"Now," Dax said. "Let's talk about wine. I think you'll all like what I've chosen for tonight." He leaned out the door and motioned down the hall and in a moment, two waiters came in bearing multiple bottles of a dark red wine. "This is a 1967 Borgogno Barolo. I think you'll find it has an interesting and complex aroma. I always pick up a bit of licorice and roses in this, but see what you think."

Marie watched as the waiters poured wine into each long-stemmed glass and the students all sniffed and swirled expertly before sipping.

"We don't spit," Heather said to Marie, noticing her confused look. "Dax feels you can't truly appreciate all the gifts of a good wine if you don't actually take it into your body."

"Oh, yes I see," Marie murmured, taking a sip from her glass. It was a bit bland, she thought, but after a few more sips she began to detect the licorice Dax had mentioned, and felt a slow spreading heat in her body. She looked up to see Dax watching her and, to her chagrin, felt color rising up from her chest. She lifted her glass and drained it, more to hide her face than anything, and the moment she set it down, someone filled it again.

The room was warm from all the bodies and wine, and Marie began to notice an odd feeling flowing. No one was doing anything unusual, but the atmosphere had a palpable and growing orgiastic feel about it. She glanced around. It wasn't in anything anyone was doing, or even saying. It must just be her own middle-age sexual peak crowding in on her, as it did lately at more and more inconvenient times. Feeling this way around Dax was one thing – the kid radiated sex – but to feel it around all these other students was something else entirely. The knowledge that she shouldn't be here was losing the battle with the feeling that she really couldn't be anywhere else.

More people had arrived and more bottles of wine appeared. Finishing her second glass, Marie went in search of some bread to slow the wine's mad course through her system. Edging her way toward a cocktail table where she'd just seen a waiter put a basket, she heard Dax's voice coming from somewhere nearby, although she couldn't see him.

"I'm starting to think we should move our meetings to someplace more comfortable," he said, his voice the same velvet hue it had been the night he'd pressed her up against the wall.

"Like where?" came the female response.

"A hotel suite, maybe, or an apartment that's big enough for everyone. This place is nice, but it's very … restauranty. We need a place where we can stretch out if we want to."

"Stretch out. Listen to you, Dax, you filthy boy." The girl's laugh was low in her throat.

Two people moved from Marie's line of vision and she had a clear view of Dax, leaning over a petite blonde girl who was gazing up at him in worshipful rapture.

"You told me yourself you'd like to do it with Heather," Dax said. "If we were someplace like that, you could."

Marie felt like she'd been hit with a cattle prod. He was planning an orgy. This whole wine appreciation club was nothing but a cover for his plans to get everyone comfortable with each other and plied with enough wine to drown any inhibitions they had, although she was beginning to doubt there had been many to start with. She thought she and Dax had a deep connection, but it was sharply and painfully clear she was just another woman for his collection. Why her? All these girls were co-eds his own age with tight bodies and breasts like desk bells. Marie was 45, wore a panty girdle and had to use reading glasses to see anything more than five inches from her face. She was obviously just a challenge to Dax – or she should have been. Marie put her glass on the table and headed for the door, slipping between people, ducking and weaving until she was out in the hallway. Taking a deep breath, she tried to stop shaking. She had to get out of here. A relationship with Dax was risky enough, but this was more than she'd bargained for. She would transfer Dax to another advisor first thing tomorrow morning, and she would get her head on straight and stop this. All of it. She was done. She was out.

Chapter 57

Dax expected the notice that turned up in his campus mailbox two days later notifying him that he had been transferred to a different advisor. He had watched Marie leave the wine club meeting and had deliberately not gone after her. He found women to be blissfully uncomplicated creatures, despite what he'd always heard other men say. They're driven by conflicting needs for acceptance and independence, they're territorial and competitive and all of them, regardless of what they show the world, have a soft underbelly where their weaknesses and insecurities live. A smart man knows how to access that spot and use it to his advantage.

He didn't have to talk to Marie to know why she'd run out of the restaurant. She'd had an attack of conscience or jealousy or both. He knew she would wrestle with it for awhile, then she'd be back. He wasn't going to chase her, he wasn't going to stop by her office or send her a note. She would come back of her own accord. Dax had chosen the members of his wine enthusiasts club carefully, and only after spending time alone with each of them, allowing himself time to get a sense of their appetites, their passions, their lusts and loves. And only when he could tell that the woman was becoming devoted to him would he invite her to join the group. By that point, each besotted woman took it as not only a compliment but a sign of Dax's feelings for her that she be allowed into his inner sanctum, to spend time enjoying his favorite pastimes with him.

The group was now exactly 32 members strong, and as it had grown, Dax had carefully added four males, all known on campus to be homosexual. Their presence made the women feel more at ease, and they posed no threat to Dax. He actually found them appealing in that smooth, fresh way that young gay men have about them. He had never had sex with a man, but having them around would increase his range of choice, should he ever decide to try expanding his horizons.

The time had come, Dax knew, to take the club to the next level. He'd mentioned changing their meeting to a more "comfortable" location to Debbie, knowing the little motormouth would have told the vast majority of the others by now. He had told her he was thinking of a hotel suite, but he knew just the place he had in mind. He headed back to his dorm to shower and change, and in under half an hour was in a cab on his way downtown.

"Dax, darling! Where have you been, you naughty boy?"

He stepped through the front door and swept Judith into a deep kiss.

"Lost in dreams about you, baby, where else would I be?"

She led him by the hand to the sofa.

"It's like you knew I had champagne chilling," she purred, handing him a glass. They settled onto her Corinthian leather sofa and she leaned back against him with a contented sigh. He put his arm around her.

"You always have champagne chilling," Dax said, rubbing a thumb lightly back and forth across her nipple. "Which reminds me of something I've been meaning to ask you. Do you like wine?"

"Wine? Yes, of course. Why?"

"Well, I have wanted to ask you this for awhile now but I wasn't sure how you'd feel about it. I started a wine appreciation club on campus, and it's doing really well. We call ourselves the Wine Enthusiasts. It's popular, but I've had to limit the membership, as you can imagine."

"Of course," she murmured.

"I know it may sound like a bunch of wine-swilling co-eds to you, but it's actually a pretty sophisticated bunch."

"Go on."

"Well, I was wondering if you would be interested in joining us."

Judith sat up and faced him.

"Me? Oh Dax, darling, you're very sweet, but what you and I have is just for fun, and private. You wouldn't be any more comfortable with me hanging about your college friends than I would be feeling like the baby sitter in the room."

Dax smiled and pulled her toward him, kissing her long and deep.

"That's for distracting me from what you were saying by how sexy you look. But anyway, I should add that we've had faculty members from the university join our ranks, so you wouldn't be the baby sitter, as you say. And you could even invite a couple of your more open-minded girlfriends along."

Judith still looked doubtful, but Dax could feel her starting to weaken.

"I don't know, it still sounds like it would feel rather awkward."

Dax thought for a moment.

"Well, how about this? Since not everyone shows up at every meeting so it's never a huge group, we could have our next gathering here."

"Here? At my place?"

"Sure, why not?" He kissed her again. "I've always rather wished you and I could give a party together so I could show you off."

"Oh darling, what a sweet thing to say. When is your next meeting?"

"Next week."

Judith poured more champagne into both of their glasses.

"You know what? Sure. What the hell. Since Andrew left I've been telling myself I need to broaden my social circles. Let's do it."

"Brilliant," Dax said. "Now, my love, come to me."

Chapter 58

Marie Fredericks had gone to work the day after Dax's wine club meeting and, before she even took off her coat, submitted the paperwork to transfer Dax to another advisor, followed by a request for a week's vacation. Then she called a friend who had a small cabin on Druce Lake she rarely used and was always offering use of to Marie.

With that arranged, she spent the rest of the day locked in her office, rescheduling appointments, arranging for coverage of her classes, clearing up paperwork, and hiding. She didn't want to admit she was hiding from Dax, but she was. Whenever she thought about him, which was basically every other thought, she cursed herself for her weakness. He wasn't the first attractive, virile student to strut across the university campus over the years, but he was the first one who had ever made her step outside herself so completely that when she looked back on it, felt as though she were watching a movie she wasn't enjoying.

That was the problem with Dax, she thought over the next few days as she took stock of herself in the solitude of the cabin. He was more than the sum of any of the characteristics that usually made men appealing. He was charming, but it felt coincidental, as though he'd just accidentally stepped in some charm and didn't get it all wiped off. He was magnetic, hypnotic. He pulled people in so slowly and steadily that they didn't even realize what was happening. Most charismatic people started on the surface and gradually got under your skin and into your mind. Dax started on the inside, so that by the time you realized you were fully involved, there was nothing left to do but give him the outside as well. She had no doubt that was the reason behind the sexual energy alive in the room the night of the wine club meeting. Dax had taken over the soul of every person in that room, connecting them to him and, without them knowing it, to each other. The orgy had already begun without a single piece of clothing hitting the floor.

Marie spent the week sleeping, reading, writing in her journal, thinking, meditating, clearing her system of the spell she'd been under, preparing herself to go back to work and move on with her life. She hadn't survived a tumultuous childhood, a nasty divorce, and a five-year PhD program to throw it all away on a meaningless fling with a student.

By the time she went back to the university, Marie felt renewed, reborn, able to face the world again. She stopped in the university commons for a coffee and a small mountain of mail before retreating to her office. She was sorting through the usual morass of memos and flyers when a familiar long white envelope slipped from the stack and landed on her blotter. She picked it up as though a corner were on fire and leaned over to drop it in to the wastebasket but stopped. Almost against her will, she loosened the flap with her finger and pulled out a single sheet of white paper. It was dated that day.

"Dear Wine Enthusiasts,

It is with great pleasure that I announce a new home for our meetings. Beginning tonight, we will gather at a private residence in downtown Chicago. The address is below. Please meet us at 9:00. As always, I will bring the wine. You supply the enthusiasm.

Dax"

Marie crumpled the letter and dropped it into the wastebasket.

"I don't think putting out cocaine is a good idea, Dax darling," Judith said, setting out rows of wine glasses on the kitchen island.

"I'm not saying to put it out in bowls with little spoons like cocktail peanuts, I just mean when things loosen up a little, people may want some. Some of them might even have brought their own and will just be looking for someone to get it started."

"If they bring their own, that's fine, but the last thing I need is word to get out that I'm supplying cocaine to half the student body at the University of Chicago."

Dax laughed and squeezed her appealingly tight ass.

"I already told you, this is an elite group. I hand selected them."

"I'll bet you did. I know what those hands are capable of."

He winked at her.

"Let's have a drink of our own and maybe do a couple of lines before people start arriving," Dax said. "Enjoy a little time to ourselves."

She obligingly got out the mirror they always used, and shook out small piles of the white powder. Dax cut it with a razor blade and they took turns sucking it up their noses. Wiping his nostrils, Dax reached for his wine.

"Who did you invite?"

"A few of my girlfriends I go to the club with most weekends. Let's see, there's Angela, Mandy, Suzanne, Carol, and Tiddly."

"Tiddly?"

"Tiddly Towson. Her name is actually Matilda, but we've always just called her Tiddly."

Dax hadn't been asking who she was – he already knew her quite well. This should be interesting.

The buzzer on the wall signaled the first arrivals, and within 20 minutes, Judith's apartment was comfortably full. All the students from the campus group had come, and Judith had chosen her friends well – they were right in there mingling with the students as though they had all known each other forever.

Dax had just introduced the evening's wine selection when the buzzer sounded. He crossed the room and pressed the button. A moment later, there was a knock.

"Hello, Dax."

"Hello, Marie. So glad you could make it."

Chapter 59

The moment Marie opened her eyes, she stared straight up at the ceiling and prayed that when she looked around, she wouldn't see what the bruised and foggy memories of the night before were warning her she'd see. She closed her eyes again. Surely she hadn't snorted cocaine with her students. Surely she hadn't had sex with some of them. The cotton in her head and mouth must be because she was coming down with the flu, that's all.

She felt someone stirring beside her and opened her eyes again, turning her head gingerly to look around. Heavy drapes blessedly kept the room dark, but enough daylight was seeping in that she was able to see naked and half-dressed bodies strewn about the living room that Marie last remembered seeing clearly about half an hour after she'd arrived. Dusty mirrors and stained wine glasses were everywhere. She raised her head and surveyed the room. Dax, who she didn't see anywhere, had clearly gotten the orgy he wanted. Marie felt sick. She got to her feet as quietly as she could and moved gently about the room until she'd gathered all of her clothes, which were disturbingly all over the place. She found the bathroom, got dressed, then tiptoed to the front door. She had just managed to get the chain off and reached for the knob when a hand came from behind her and landed palm-first against the door. She didn't even turn her head.

"Dax, please. I'm leaving."

In one fluid movement, he had opened the door and pulled her into the hallway with him.

"Why?" he asked, pulling her up against him. "Didn't you enjoy yourself last night?"

"I have no idea," she said, trying to push him away. "I remember very little about last night. All I know is that it was a huge mistake. I never should have come here."

"But you did." Dax's face was very close to hers. His mouth was smiling but his eyes weren't. "And everything you said you can't remember, you actually do. Don't you, Marie?"

"Please." She was suddenly close to tears. "Please, I have to go."

"You'll be back." It wasn't a question.

"No, Dax, I won't. I don't know why I came last night and I won't be coming again."

"I think you will. And do you know why?"

Marie didn't answer, turning her face away, willing him to go back inside so she could go home and shower and try to feel clean again.

"Because you showed up last night of your own volition. You want to be a part of this group. You feel at home with us, Marie, you feel like true self, finally. The rest of the world might only see the buttoned-down college professor you show them, in your prim little suits, but I know who you really are. And now everyone in there does to. You can only be yourself with us, Marie, as no one else would understand."

She was crying now, her face still turned away. Dax cupped her chin and forced her to look at him.

"You're one of us now, my love. You know you won't get this kind of uninhibited freedom to be yourself anywhere else. And you know what else, Marie? You can't tell anyone. Who would believe you? And if you did happen to find someone who believed you, your secret would be out. Your secret cocaine-snorting, student-fucking life would be exposed. And then your life would be ruined. Do you see what has happened here, Marie? You're bound to us now. This is where you belong."

He bent his head and kissed her, and she felt herself surrendering. He was right. She'd never felt more alive, more herself, than she had last night. Or at that moment.

Chapter 60

The phone on Dax's desk rang, bringing a blessed reprieve from the obituaries Wilson was making him type up.

"Dax Thomas," he said.

"Mr. Thomas..." It was a man's voice, halting, hesitant.

"Yes?"

"You don't know me, and I'd prefer to remain anonymous, but..."

Dax rolled his eyes and leaned back in his chair. He knew what was coming next. Somebody had a grudge against his neighbors for their barking dogs or loud mufflers and he wanted Dax to do a big expose on the direction in which Chicago's neighborhoods were going in a handbasket.

"I saw your piece a few months back on that insider trading situation, and I thought you might like to know that there's some of that happening here on a much bigger scale."

Dax sat up and reached for his notebook.

"Go on."

"I work for one of the big savings and loans, downtown, and I know for a fact they're heading for a world of trouble."

The man clearly wanted to unload his mind, and possibly his conscience, but Dax could tell he was nervous. Whistleblowing, he knew from conversations with his father, was one of the hardest things to do, as much as everyone wanted to believe they could do it if they had to.

"Would you rather meet somewhere, to talk in person?" Dax asked.

"No," the man said quickly. "Well, I don't know. Maybe. The phone makes me nervous."

"Why don't you come here?" Dax said. "There's a back entrance where you could park and come inside without being seen."

He could hear the man's uncertainty.

"Look, I need to know you're a legitimate source, and you need to feel you can talk to me without being overheard. I promise you right now I'll keep your name out of the story."

"Okay," the caller said. "Okay, I'll come to your office. I'll be there within the hour."

Dax hung up and glanced around. The newsroom was fairly deserted. Wilson wasn't at his desk, and the reporter at the next desk was on the phone. Turning back to his typewriter, Dax finished the obituaries and another story he'd been working on and had just dropped them on Wilson's desk when his phone buzzed again and the security guard told him he had a visitor.

The man waiting for him was in his mid 50s, with a dark moustache and wearing a suit, tie, and uneasy expression.

"Dax Thomas," Dax said, extending his hand. The man just nodded, and Dax led him upstairs and into a small, seldom-used conference room. He closed the door.

"Thank you for meeting with me," the man said.

"Thank you for coming to me, Mr..." Dax let the question trail off.

"Barber. Curtis Barber." He handed Dax a business card. Dax glanced at it. He worked for the biggest savings and loan in Chicago. This was for real. He felt his pulse shiver as it always did when he was on the verge of something big.

"First of all, I appreciate you giving me your identity," Dax said. "I know it's nerve-wracking, but it's important that I be able to tell my editors I got the information from a legitimate source. No one will know who you are but me."

As Curtis Barber gradually relaxed, the details began to flow and Dax realized he was now sitting on one of the biggest stories to hit in a long time.

"So you're telling me the savings and loans, not just in Chicago but all over the country, are in danger of collapse."

"Actually, Chicago is probably in better shape than some other areas, but yes. That's what's going to happen. I don't think there is anything that could even be done now to fix it. The damage was done from the moment President Carter deregulated the industry, but of course none of us really knew that then. It was just another attempt by the feds to put a Band Aid on something that needed a tourniquet."

"So you really trace all this back to deregulation."

"Well, yes. I mean, the government thought that by deregulating, they'd be able to stop excessive lending and minimize failure. They had no idea just how lazy and corrupt the savings and loan industry already was, and that it was getting worse. They basically unlocked the door and looked the other way."

"You said something on the phone about insider trading?"

"Yes. That's part of it. That I've seen with my own eyes. Insider trading, fraud... it just gets easier and easier with no real oversight. And there are so many more investment options now. The muddier the water gets, the harder it is to see what's really going on."

By the time Barber left, Dax had the names of three other savings and loan employees in the greater Chicago area that Barber said would talk to the paper.

"Thank you again for your trust in me," Dax said, walking Barber to the elevator. The man shook his hand.

"I don't mind telling you now that I wasn't sure I'd done the right thing when I first saw you," he said. "I had no idea you were just a kid."

Dax smiled.

"I'm on the young side, but I'm a newspaper veteran," he said. "You did the right thing, Mr. Barber, I can promise you. I'm going to blow the lid off this story."

"Well?" Mr. Neely was looking directly at Wilson, who looked as though he were four seconds away from having a stroke.

"I don't know, Mr. Neely. I told Dax to let me know whenever he was working on a big story."

"That's not what I asked you," the publisher said quietly. "I want to know why the goddamned intern broke one of the biggest news stories in the country. Where were you, Wilson? You're the managing editor. Why is a source calling Dax with a story like this?"

"I don't know." Wilson was getting angry. "I have no idea who his source even was. Probably one of his drinking buddies. I'm pretty sure that's how he got the last one."

"I'm sure Dax doesn't go out drinking with senior officers from savings and loans, Wilson," Mr. Neely said. "But the point is that this intern – this kid – is out there, with his nose and his ear to the ground, and people are starting to think he's the person in charge around here."

Wilson ground his teeth and said nothing.

"You've been here a long time, Wilson, and I'm starting to think you're burned out. This isn't our first conversation about it. You've been putting less and less in around here, but to have an intern break a story like this, without you even knowing it, that really tells me something about your commitment to this paper."

Twenty minutes later, when Dax showed up for work, Wilson was putting the last of his things into a box on top of his desk.

"Mr. Neely would like to see you in his office," Wilson said tightly. It was all he could do not to jump over the desk and beat the shit out of Dax.

"Where are you going?" Dax asked, suppressing a smile. He'd realized what was happening the moment he walked in.

"None of your fucking business."

"You wanted to see me, Mr. Neely?" Dax asked, tapping lightly on the publisher's door frame.

"Yes, please come in. Have a seat. And close the door behind you."

Dax did as he was asked.

"Dax, you did a hell of a job on that savings and loan story," Mr. Neely said. "I know I don't even have to tell you how huge this is. The Associated Press and UPI have already been ringing our phone off the wall. This is a national story, Dax."

"Yes sir, I figured it would be."

"I'm curious why you didn't tell Wilson what you were working on. He said he specifically told you that you should tell him anytime you were working on anything, but particularly something big."

"I know he did, and I apologize for what must have looked like me doing an end run around him. But honestly, sir, I was so caught up in the story and when I gave it to the night desk, they must have just assumed I had his approval."

His hesitated.

"Go on," Mr. Neely prodded.

"Well, sir, Wilson had a tendency to try and keep me working on things like obituaries and news briefs, and I don't really feel that's what I am meant to be doing here."

"You don't feel an intern should be doing whatever his supervisor asks him to do?"

It was a weighted question and Dax knew it.

"I feel an intern who has been given the opportunity to work in his chosen field should be asked to do things that help him find his footing and launch his career."

"And before you filed this story, and for that matter any of the other major stories you've broken, did it occur to you to check with Wilson?"

"No, sir." Dax was being honest. "I know I should have, but I have a good sense of what's news and I have a tendency to forge ahead when I know I'm right about something. I kind of always have. Drives my teachers crazy."

"Yes, I can understand that. Dax, we've never made a point of talking around here about who your father is. I'm not sure that anyone has really connected the dots since you use a pen name, and I'm also not sure it matters. But to be completely honest with you, that's part of the reason you were offered this internship. I don't know Zachary person-ally, but his reputation is huge. And when I found out you were in Chicago studying journalism, well… you can understand my curiosity."

Dax shrugged.

"Of course."

"I said all that to say that you've impressed me, Dax. You may be Zachary Benton's son, but you're a hell of a journalist in your own right. You've proven that you have the skill to go far in this field, and also the instincts. Some people are natural born journalists – they just have the feel for it. Some people can be taught what to do, but it's not the same."

"No," Dax agreed. "It isn't. I knew from the time I was very young that I wanted to follow alongside my father's footsteps, but not directly in them. I also know I wanted to make tracks of my own. That's why I came to Chicago."

Mr. Neely nodded.

"I thought as much. So here's my point in all of this. I know you're going to be graduating soon, and I don't know what your plans are, but I'd like to offer you a job."

Dax's face split into a huge grin.

"Really? That would be great, Mr. Neely, thank you. Is it a reporter job?"

"Well, actually, it's the managing editor position. But of course you'd be doing some reporting as well."

"The managing editor? But that's Wilson."

"Wilson has left the Tribune to pursue other opportunities."

"Oh, I see," Dax said, trying not to smile.

"If you'd like to take some time to think about it, that's fine."

"No need," Dax said, standing up. "I'll take the job. And thank you, sir, for your faith in me."

Back in his dorm that night, Dax called Zachary with the news. Zachary felt an odd mix of pride and disappointment. He'd hoped the boy would come back to New York and work at the Beacon, but he knew at least part of that was just selfishness. To have Dax in the newsroom would be as close as Zachary would ever be to having Sarah back. But his rational mind knew that it wasn't fair to put that on Dax. The boy was absolutely right to forge his own path. And to be offered the job of managing editor of the Chicago Tribune before he'd even graduated from college? It was unheard of.

"My Sarah, look at our boy go," Zachary said quietly, his hand still resting on the phone he'd just hung up. "He is making you proud, my love."

Back in Chicago, Dax hung up the phone and poured himself a glass of wine. He sat for a moment, thinking, perched on the arm of the sofa, swirling the wine and watching its legs streak up the side of the glass. Then he got up and went to look at himself in the mirror. He lifted his glass in a silent toast.

Now to show the world what Dax Benton could really do.

Chapter 61

Dax graduated from the university with honors, stepped into his new job, and proceeded to tear through the Tribune's newsroom like Sherman on his march to the sea. Reporters who complained to Mr. Neely about how hard Dax was working them found themselves presented with two options: work harder, or get out.

"He's a kid. He's nothing but a punk-ass kid. I'd love to know why Neely is giving him free reign to do whatever the hell he wants," Bob Connors grumbled to three of his colleagues over drinks one night after work. "He's still wet behind the ears. He doesn't know shit about the newspaper business."

"I agree he's an asshole," agreed Brett, the sports editor. "But I don't think you can say he doesn't know shit about the newspaper business. I think he does."

"Oh, get your nose out of his ass already. He isn't here. He can't hear you."

Brett shrugged.

"It's just my opinion, but have you looked at our circulation numbers in the past six months? They're up. They're way the hell up."

Bob wasn't willing to hand this victory to Dax.

"Circulation numbers go up and down all the time. Doesn't mean anything."

Everyone laughed.

"Bob, you're a crotchety old-school reporter all the way," said Ray Fortner, the municipal reporter. "You fart dried ink."

"Oh fuck you." Bob motioned for another drink.

"I know you don't like Dax, dude, none of us do," Ray said. "But if he can get our circulation up like that in six months, who knows? In the next year or two, we might all be making a real living."

"If that happens," Bob said, glaring around the table over the rim of his glass as though getting them all in his sights. "Drinks are on me. Drinks are on me for the rest of my life."

The newsroom grew dark around Dax without him even realizing it. He was bent over his desk, copies of the Los Angeles Times, the Washington Post, the New York Times and the Seattle Post-Intelligencer spread out everywhere. Blue pen in hand, Dax circled things he liked, and drew hard, derisive Xs through things he didn't. The papers that were making no attempt to change with the times Dax had no use for. But those in front of him knew what they were doing. These were the papers he had to watch. If he was going to take the Chicago Tribune to the front of the pack, he had to keep an eye on what everyone else was doing.

"You're working late." Mr. Neely's voice made Dax jump. "Sorry, didn't mean to scare you."

"I didn't hear you come in." Dax bent back over his work.

"What's that you're doing?" Mr. Neely, as Dax had been fervently hoping he wouldn't, came over to look.

"I just like to keep an eye on what the other metro papers in the country are doing."

"Good idea." He surveyed the papers Dax had spread out. "Where's the New York Beacon?"

Dax kept working, not bothering to even look up.

"I'm not worried about the Beacon," he said, turning a page. "I know my father's thought processes better than he does. I know exactly where the Beacon's at, and where it's going as long as he's in charge."

Chapter 62

Dax glanced at his watch. He'd intended to get out of the office much earlier than this. The Enthusiasts were having their holiday party tonight and he'd promised Judith he'd be over early to help her finish setting up. She'd be livid if he wasn't there soon, even though he knew she didn't need his help. She never did. Still, he couldn't afford to piss her off, as hers was the only apartment big enough for their gatherings, and over the past year everyone had gotten comfortable there. The last couple of times they'd all gotten together, the orgy had already been underway when Dax got there. He hated being late for orgies.

It pleased and amazed Dax how well they all fit together. There was never any fighting, any jealousy, any recriminations or problems between them. In the years since they'd been gathering, a community-like spirit had taken them over. They genuinely loved each other. Dax thought of the Enthusiasts as his relationship. He wasn't in love with any one person, he was in love with all of them, as one entity. When he was naked on a mountain of cushions on Judith's living room floor, wine and cocaine flowing freely through his system, it didn't matter who was pressed against him or whose mouth was sliding against his skin – they were all one.

The Enthusiasts' devotion to Dax was deep and intense. They all knew him outside their gatherings in different ways, but that Dax didn't matter to them. Their Dax was the one who brought them all together, who taught them to love with no inhibitions, to not only admit their own darkest carnal desires but to act on them, celebrate them, use them to connect with themselves and each other. After all, everyone has their dirty little thoughts, intense moments of animal urges that they hide from the rest of the world. In each other, the Enthusiasts were allowed to bring those urges out, to find them and feed them, to revel in them.

Dax knew they worshipped him, and that was its own aphrodisiac. The power he wielded during their gatherings brought with it the same heady rush he got when he ordered a reporter to delve deeper into a story, to work over a weekend, to follow up on a lead he'd gotten from one of the hundreds of sources that seemed to creep out of the shadows to spill their bags of secrets at Dax's feet. He knew his staff hated him, and the thrill he got from forcing them to bend to his will was very similar to the excitement he felt when one of the Enthusiasts acted out one of his perverse fantasies, down to the last sticky detail. Dax's life was one long shuddering orgasm, regardless of where he was or what he was doing.

The private phone he'd had installed at Judith's apartment jangled. Not one limb in the pile of bodies stirred. It jangled again, and this time an arm rose like dawn over the landscape of flesh and picked up the receiver. One hand passed it to another, then another, then another, until the last one handed it to Dax.

"What?" He sat up, disentangling himself from the others. "Say that again."

He tucked the phone under his ear and began pulling on his pants while the paper's night desk editor filled him in. The pressmen were on strike. The paper was at a standstill.

"I'm sorry to call you, Dax, but with Mr. Neely on his cruise... I didn't see this coming. I'm sorry."

"You were right to call me," Dax said. "I'm the next in command after Mr. Neely. I'll be right down."

He put the phone down and finished dressing in a fury. He'd warned Mr. Neely over and over again that this could happen. The pressmen wanted a better raise than they'd been getting, and Dax thought they deserved it. What they didn't deserve was the inflated benefits package their union rep, Harry Sanders, had been demanding. It was far more than anyone else at the paper had, and Mr. Neely had told them no. Then he went on this goddamned month-long cruise, and now Dax had to deal with the fallout.

"Everything's going to be fine," Mr. Neely had assured Dax. "I have a good relationship with the unions. They're just trying to get as much out of me as they can, just to see how far they can push me. I am giving them their salary increase, but they know they're not getting that benefits package.

They're testing me, Dax, they've done it before. We have nothing to worry about."

Except now they clearly did. Without the pressmen, everything was at a standstill. And Dax wasn't sure there was anything he could do about it.

When he arrived at the Tribune, the pressmen were lined up outside, some sitting on the curb, others pacing around, many of them smoking, all of them angry. A chorus of shouts greeted Dax when he stepped out of the backseat of the cab. Most of them liked Dax. They knew he was tough, but they respected tough. They also knew from Harry that Dax had been pushing for their pay raise. Still, they hadn't gotten what they wanted, and right now Dax was management. Sanders pushed through a small knot of men and strode toward him.

"I'm sorry it's come to this, Dax, especially with Neely out of town and unreachable, but we have to do what we have to do," the union rep said. Dax squinted at him through his mirrored aviators. He was aware that Sanders couldn't see his eyes, and he was glad. It gave him more of the upper hand.

"What is it you want, Harry? The benefits package is the holdup?"

"Yeah. That's the rub here. These men have families, Dax. They have wives and kids and the package they've got costs a lot out of pocket when they need to go to the doctor. It's not right, Dax, and it's not competitive with what the other metro papers offer."

"I understand your point," Dax said. "You do know that I'm not in a position to meet your demands."

"You're the honcho under Neely," Sanders said, lighting a cigarette. He picked a bit of fresh tobacco off his tongue and flicked it away. "So it seems to me you are."

"You son of a bitch." Dax dropped his voice so only Sanders could hear him. "You deliberately waited until Neely was gone because you thought you could strong arm me into giving you what you want. You son of a fucking bitch."

Sanders grinned.

"You kiss your mama with that mouth, kid?"

Without another word, Dax pushed passed Sanders and went inside. The newsroom was overflowing with what sounded like a hundred voices at once. Naturally every person on staff was in today. Their voices rose to a fever pitch when they saw Dax.

"Listen! Everyone, please listen!" He had to shout to be heard. "I know what's going on. I've been talking to the union rep outside. I'm going to figure this out. Okay? Everybody just stay calm."

"Dax, if there are no pressmen, there's no paper."

"Thank you, Bob. When this all blows over I'm going to make you Editor in Charge of Stating the Obvious."

"What are we supposed to do now?" the lifestyles editor asked. "If there's no paper, it seems stupid for us to be here."

"Stupid? If you think it's stupid to be here, Linda, feel free to go home. But don't bother coming back. That goes for all of you. Your jobs are not to run the press, and they are certainly not to tell me how to manage this paper. Your jobs are to give me content to put in the paper. That's it. Now you can either get back to doing that, or you can get the hell out."

The sudden and violent silence that filled the newsroom told Dax all he needed to know. He turned on his heel and went into his office, slamming the door behind him. He was furious. Furious at Mr. Neely for not having seen this coming, furious at Sanders for thinking he could take advantage of Dax's youth and inexperience to get what he wanted, furious that his paper was at a standstill. He paced around his office, thinking hard. Finally he opened the door and strode through the newsroom, ignoring all the eyes that followed him. He went into the production department and found Bernie Williams, the production supervisors.

"Is the paper ready to go to press?" Dax asked.

"Yes, but Dax -"

"I know about the strike, Bernie, I had to walk through a wall of it to even get into the building. I'm asking you if the paper was ready to go when they walked out."

"Yes, it's completely pasted up, the plates are made, and as far as I know it's ready to go on the press. I figured they chose that moment to walk out so it made a better impact."

"Yeah, well, they fucked with the wrong guy," Dax said. "Come with me."

Dax and Bernie headed down a corridor and a short flight of steps into the press room.

"Dax, are you doing what I think you're doing?"

"Yeah," Dax grunted, finding a toe hold and swinging himself up to where he could see into the press's huge, greasy innards. "We're getting this paper out."

His brain feverishly going back over all he'd learned about running the press during his internship, Dax put the plates onto the press and checked the paper and the ink. He couldn't afford any mistakes. He worked feverishly until he was sure everything was ready.

"All right," he said to Bernie. "Let's print this thing."

The press rumbled to life. Dax held his breath, waiting, and fully exhaled only when the papers started to emerge. He grabbed the first one and quickly thumbed through it.

"It looks good," he said to Bernie, who nodded, still unsure of what exactly he was witnessing. Dax started to laugh. "It looks great! It looks amazing!" He gave a whoop and ran around the press, watching it work, marveling at every beautiful moment of the offset process he'd never fully appreciated before.

When the print run was finished, Bernie clapped Dax on the back.

"Now what, chief?"

"What do you mean, now what? Now the trucks pick them up and deliver them like usual."

"Uh, Dax…"

"Aww shit. What?"

"The truck drivers aren't coming in. They're siding with the pressmen on this. Sorry, Dax, I thought you knew."

Dax was ready to cry with frustration, but he wouldn't let Bernie see him crack. He wouldn't let anyone see him crack. Dax Benton did not crack.

"I'll take care of it," Dax said. "What's the name of their union rep?"

"Sean Myers. Good luck with him. He's a real asshole."

"Yeah? Good. So am I."

Dax went back into his office and closed the door. He found a number for Sean Myers in the Rolodex he'd inherited from the remnants of Wilson's desk and dialed. He left a message with the woman who answered the phone and sat, drumming his fingers on his desk impatiently. Part of him wanted desperately to call Zachary, to beg his father to tell him what to do, to bail him out, to please have favors owed somewhere in Chicago that he could call in right now. But the strong arm of pride held him back. To go running back to Daddy now would be to admit failure, to concede defeat, and Dax was far from defeated.

The phone rang.

"What can I do for you, Mr. Benton?" Sean Myers' voice was like old asphalt.

"I want to make sure your guys are coming to pick up the paper for delivery."

"No, we won't be doing that. We discussed it as a group, and the truck drivers feel that when even the most basic human rights are denied to one group, it won't be long before they're denied to all of us. I don't expect you to understand that, since from what I'm told you're just punk-ass spoiled rich kid who only works for shits and giggles."

Dax felt the blood drain from his face. His hand gripped the receiver so hard he couldn't feel his fingers.

"You listen to me, Sean. I work because I'm a newspaper man, and a damned good one. If you and your union, and the pressmen and their union, think they can take advantage of me because I'm young, you can all go fuck yourselves. I'll tell you something else, Sean, health care is a basic human right, but no one in this country has the right to have an employer pay for their medical treatments and vacation days.

278

You might need to check with your legal representative, or even just a fucking dictionary, on the difference between a privilege and a right, you condescending asshole. Tell your men they've got the day off, and not to worry about a thing. I don't need them to put the Tribune out."

"If you're talking about scabs-"

Dax cut him off.

"Here's an interesting fact about rights. You have the right to strike. And I have the right to get my paper out by any means necessary. If you're smart, you'll go put your feet up and watch your soap operas and stay the hell out of my way."

He slammed the phone down. He was in over his head and he knew it, but Dax had spent his entire life biting off far more than he could chew, and he hadn't choked yet. Picking up the phone again, he dialed Judith's apartment.

"Dax, darling, where are you? We were about to make breakfast and open the champagne."

"I had to slip out early because of a crisis at the paper."

"What's going on?"

Judith and Marie were the only ones who knew he worked for the Tribune, although after today, they'd all know. He filled her in quickly on what was happening, and instructed her to rent ten trucks and meet him at the Tribune's loading dock in an hour.

"Is everyone sober enough to do this?" he asked. "You know what, don't answer that. It doesn't matter. I just need you all right now."

"The Enthusiasts would kill for you, Dax," Judith said. "You should know that by now."

Chapter 63

Mr. Neely came back from his cruise to so many headaches, he was tempted to turn around and head back out to sea. And hopefully sink.

"Of course I'm glad you got the paper out, Dax, and that whoever the helpers were you brought in to do it were willing and able to lend a hand, but now I've got a load of trouble with the pressmens' union and now the truckers' union."

"With all due respect, Mr. Neely, you shouldn't have gone on vacation without addressing the issue. I warned you it would blow up in your face."

"First of all, please remember that I'm your boss. I know you think this is your paper, and I appreciate your commitment, but I'm still in charge. I made what I believed was the right decision. Second of all, you don't just cancel a cruise. We planned that vacation for months. I'd be divorced right now if I'd bailed out on it."

"I get that, Mr. Neely, and please know I meant no disrespect to your authority here. But I need you to understand the position I was in. These men waited until you were unreachable, out in the middle of the ocean, to pull their little power play. They thought they could take advantage of the fact that I'm young, and get out of me what they couldn't get out of you. As I am not in the position here to grant them what they were asking, I did the only other thing I could do. I got the paper out."

"Yes, I understand, and you honestly did do a hell of a job. Everyone tells me there wasn't even a blip in the process."

"Thank you, sir."

"Well, I'll tell you what," Mr. Neely said, taking off his glasses and rubbing his hands vigorously over his eyes. "I think you need to take a short vacation and let me get things sorted out here."

"A vacation? I can't go on vacation."

"You can and you will. I will tell everyone you're away but leave it vague enough so that no one really knows where you are."

"So … what? You're sending me into hiding?"

"Not hiding. I don't care where you go, or if you just stay home for a week in your pajamas. I just need you out of the view of these union guys so I can finish negotiating all this bullshit with them and get everything back to normal. We have a tentative agreement and they're getting back to work, but I have to get it all finalized before it blows up in my face. Again."

Dax was furious. He had poured every ounce of his soul into the Tribune, and had single-handedly kept the presses running and the paper in the subscribers' hands. And to show his deep appreciation, Mr. Neely was kicking him out of his own newsroom.

He was so angry he canceled the Enthusiasts meeting for that night, throwing Judith completely off balance. When he said he just needed to be alone, she assumed he was sick. Dax never wanted to be alone. He thought about calling Bonnie, but he didn't want to admit to her that he'd failed. Besides, since she'd gotten engaged to some hot shot actor everyone said was the second coming of Michael Crawford, she hadn't been returning his calls as often.

Obviously the only solution was to get shit-faced drunk. He thought better when he was buzzed, and when he was really drunk he was a certifiable genius. This he was sure of.

"Take me to a bar where I don't know anyone," he said to the driver as he climbed into the back of a cab.

"What're you, some kind of smartass?" the driver asked.

"As a matter of fact, I am. Thanks for noticing."

"How the hell am I supposed to know who knows you where?"

"Okay then, think of a bar where you personally would want to go to knock back a few drinks and not be bothered. Then take me there."

The driver shook his head and mumbled as he pulled into Chicago's gathering nighttime traffic. Dax leaned back and watched the familiar pieces of the city fly past the cab window like slides stuck on fast-forward. He couldn't get his head around why Mr. Neely wanted him out of the way while he finalized his negotiations. Dax hadn't even attempted to negoti-

281

ate, he'd just done his job. The more he thought about it, the angrier he got. No one would ever have dared to try and push Zachary around that way, not even in his younger years. But Zachary had always had an authority about him that Dax had never managed, at least not in the newsroom. People on all levels of the newspaper industry automatically respected Zachary. Even moving to Chicago hadn't gotten Dax out from under Zachary's giant shadow, and it had never pissed him off more than it did right now. Someone had once told Dax that the reason Zachary commanded such respect was that he'd started at the bottom and come up through the ranks, working hard and earning his stripes before taking over as the boss. Well what the hell did they think Dax had done? He'd been an unpaid intern, for crying out loud, and he had deliberately not done it at the Beacon, so no one could accuse him of taking advantage of his father's position to get in the door. Dax had worked his ass off, at college, during his internship, and in the years he'd been managing editor of the Tribune, and it still made no difference. He was still seen as an also-ran, a watered down version of his father.

When he got home that night, solidly and bracingly drunk, he dialed Zachary in New York. Hanna answered the phone.

"I want to talk to my father," Dax said, impressed with how strong and not-drunk his voice sounded.

"It's Dax," he heard her say as she passed the phone to Zachary. "He sounds drunk out of his mind."

"Dax, are you all right?" Zachary's voice came over the line.

"I'm fine, I'm just pissed at you."

"Pissed at me? What on earth for?"

"For being so goddamned perfect that I will never be able to measure up."

"Son, what is this about?"

"It's about everything, Dad, don't you see? I've done everything I can to be my own man, to be a journalist in my own right, and no matter what I do, I'm still nothing more than little Dax, son of the great Zachary Benton."

"Son, are you having trouble at the…" Zachary's voice trailed off and into such a long stretch of silence that Dax was confused.

"The Tribune?"

"Right. The… Chicago Tribune."

"Yes I'm having trouble at the Tribune. It's nothing I can't handle but I'm so incredibly pissed off right now."

"I'm… did you tell me this already?"

"What? Dad, are you all right? Did I wake you?"

"No, you didn't wake me. I'm just tired. It's been a long day."

"Yeah, for me too. And Hanna was right. I'm a little drunk. Let's talk later, when you're not tired and I'm not drunk."

"All right, son." For the first time Dax could remember, Zachary sounded old. "But one thing you should know, Dax. I'm proud of you."

After they hung up, Dax sat for a long time, fists screwed into his eyes, trying not to cry.

A few days later, Zachary called Dax.

"Son, do you want to talk about what's bothering you?"

"I don't know, Dad. Maybe. I know it's not your fault, none of this. You've just spent your life doing what you're good at. I'm starting to think maybe I'm not that good at it."

"What is that, self-pity? That's not really your style, Dax."

"I know it's not. And I'm not really feeling sorry for myself anyway, I'm just being realistic."

Zachary had heard about the strike at the Tribune, and about how Dax had handled it, but he didn't want to be the first one to bring it up.

"I think it's a little too early in the game for you to decide whether you're cut out for this or not. Stick with it awhile longer, son. I'll let you in on a little secret – I had plenty of problems along the way, but I got past them."

"But how? It's hard when it feels like the world is just kicking the shit out of you."

"I know it is, son. And the way I got through it is just by telling myself that I was destined for greatness. It sounds egotistical, and I'd never say that to anyone else, but that's the bare bones of it. I knew I had what it took, and I knew I could make it. So I just kept at it until I made it. The Bentons are nothing if not stubborn."

Dax didn't answer.

"Let me ask you something. And I want your knee-jerk response, don't take time to think about it. Do you love being a journalist?"

"Yes." Dax's response was immediate and vehement.

"Then I think you have your answer."

"I do see myself succeeding, Dad. That's the funny thing. I see myself as a leader, as someone people follow, and respect. Maybe even love."

"And besides journalism? What fuels your fire?"

"Wine, women and song."

He's his father's son all right, Zachary thought. *For once I'm glad Sarah's not here to hear this.*

When Dax spoke to Zachary again a week later, his father had no memory of the conversation at all.

Chapter 64

Dax stretched his arms and yawned, reaching around Judith, Tiddly and two women whose faces he couldn't see to get to his watch. He was late for work, and he didn't even really care. Last night had really taken it out of him. He couldn't even pretend to remember how much cocaine and wine he'd put into his system, but judging by how he felt, it was at least enough to kill a medium-sized elephant. And probably half of the safari.

As he showered in Judith's obscenely elaborate and enormous shower they'd had installed, he wondered what to do about the Enthusiasts. The group had grown too large for Judith's apartment. Fortunately, they often slept stacked on top of each other anyway, but still, he knew they needed a bigger place. He wasn't entirely sure how new women managed to get in, but they seemed to find a way, and each one was more succulent and tempting than the last. Dax didn't see how he could be expected to turn them away. It was actually quite charitable of him, he thought, to be so open to new members.

In the nearly two years since his phone conversation with Zachary about his future as a journalist, Dax had redoubled his efforts to make a name for himself in Chicago, and it was beginning to pay off in spades. He worked hard at the Tribune, so much that Mr. Neely often left him in charge when he went on what seemed to Dax an endless parade of vacations with his spoiled wife. Still, her constant need for expensive coddling meant Dax's power over Chicago's biggest source of news was growing, and every day he felt his footing was a little more solid. He spent his days in the newsroom, and his nights in the arms of the Enthusiasts. His only real worry at the moment was Zachary. Whenever they spoke, his father seems more and more forgetful. It was hard for Dax to picture the powerful Zachary Benton as a doddering old man, so he avoided going back to New York to see him. He wanted to keep Zachary in his mind just as he'd always been, sealed in emotional amber, perfect and strong and running New York.

*

"Dax is starting to catch on that Zachary's mind is failing," Hanna said, mixing two strong martinis.

"Really?" Philip asked, accepting one. "I didn't know they spoke that often."

"They never used to, but lately they're developing this buddy-buddy relationship. Dax calls him for advice about the paper, and Zachary loves to talk about his glory days at the Beacon."

"So you think Dax is going to come back here and take it over?"

"Don't you?"

"I don't know," Philip admitted. "Any normal person would, but Dax wouldn't know normal if it bit him on the ass."

"I think we can agree that we don't want Dax taking over the Beacon."

"I agree. In fact, I don't want him back in New York at all."

"Nor do I. Now you know I've always thought of you as family, Philip, which is why I always did my best to protect you from Dax when you were children."

"I always appreciated that," Philip said. "Dax used to say the most horrible things about you. I never understood it. Most women in your position wouldn't have wanted me around at all, much less Dax."

Hanna gave a hard little laugh.

"Dax never wanted to share Zachary with anyone, and since my darling husband was always very open with him about who his mother was, Dax had me cast as the wicked stepmother in his little mental play from day one."

"I know Sarah was my aunt, but still, I can honestly tell you that I've always admired the way you stepped in and raised another woman's child."

Hanna smiled demurely into her drink. She'd been grooming Philip for this moment for years, taking him under her wing when Dax had gone

286

off to university, subtly melding his mind with hers – the fact that he was such a simpleton made it easy – until he was such a staunch ally it surprised even her. Although she wasn't sure why it would, as his own mother had become such a drunk over the years she barely showed any interest in Philip. The boy was crying out for a mother figure.

"Philip, how would you feel about taking over as publisher of the Beacon?"

He stopped twirling the cocktail onion in his glass and looked up at her blankly.

"What are you talking about? I don't know anything about the newspaper business. And Zachary still runs the Beacon."

"Philip, we both know Zachary is months away from a full descent into dementia. He can't work there anymore. Stan and Rick cover up a lot of his mistakes and handle the extra work so Zachary can maintain some dignity, but we all know he'll be in a nursing home within the year. He'd want the paper to stay in the family, and if we don't want Dax coming back and taking it over, we need to do something now."

Philip stared at her.

"And the fact that I know nothing about the newspaper business?"

"First of all, darling, I think you know more than you realize. You've grown up around it. And secondly, the same staff that is keeping Zachary from spectacular failure would be there to help you. And I would as well. By now, I know the industry almost as well as Zachary does."

"I don't know..." Overwhelmed, Philip left the sentence swinging. Hanna patted his hand.

"I'll tell you what, you think it over for a few days. And if you decide you don't want to do it, that's fine. We'll let Dax take over the Beacon. As long as it stays in the family, that's all that matters."

"Philip?" Zachary said. "Philip wants to take over the Beacon?" Something didn't sound right, but he couldn't put his finger on what it was.

"Yes, my darling, don't you remember? We talked about this a few days ago," Hanna purred. "I told you that Dax phoned and said he was going to stay in Chicago indefinitely. And since we've talked about you retiring soon so we can travel and spend more time together, it seems the only way to keep the paper in the family is to let Philip run it."

"Philip? Philip doesn't know how to run a newspaper. All Philip knows how to run is his mouth." Zachary laughed at his own joke. Hanna smiled thinly.

"It sounds as though you've changed your mind from our earlier conversation, darling. If you don't want Philip to run the Beacon, we can sell it."

Zachary's mind fought itself, trying to remember having the conversation with Hanna she was claiming they'd had. He didn't recall telling her he thought Philip should take over the paper, but she said Dax had phoned, and he did think Dax had phoned, a few days ago maybe. They'd talked about the paper he managed in Chicago. It wasn't right. Something wasn't right. His brain writhed.

"I don't know," Zachary told Hanna. He was suddenly exhausted. "I'll decide tomorrow."

When Zachary was asleep, Hanna called Philip.

"Come over tomorrow, around 6:30. He said he's ready to talk to you about taking over the paper. He thinks it's a great idea."

It still didn't sound right to Zachary, to have Philip take over as publisher of the Beacon, but Hanna kept insisting that Zachary had already agreed to it. She knew he was having trouble with his memory, and he suspected she was taking advantage of it, but he had no proof. He couldn't even remember what he'd had for breakfast, let alone a conversation she said took place weeks ago.

It was beginning to make Zachary angry, this business of losing his memory. All that he was, everything he'd known, every bit his brain had collected over the years was stored carefully in the only safe place he knew, and now it was betraying him. He knew who he was, he knew those around him, but he was beginning to lose details, facts, memories. There were days he would look around his office at the Beacon, unable to remember coming in that morning. He was losing himself, and he was afraid he was going to lose his memories of Sarah.

"Philip, tell Zachary what you told me, about your plans for the Beacon." Hanna poured wine and smiled abstractedly at Ilsa, who was so startled by it she nearly dropped the soup tureen she'd just carried in.

"Well, Uncle Zachary, I was thinking that I would work very closely with Stan and Rick to oversee the day to day operations of the paper, and I was also thinking it would be a good idea to keep you on in an advisory capacity. Sort of a publisher emeritus."

Zachary lifted his head, the first spark of light in his eyes Hanna had seen in three years.

"Advisory capacity?"

"Yes, of course," Philip said. "The Beacon is your paper, Uncle Zachary, you've made it what it is. To carry on without your input at all would be not only ridiculous, it would be unthinkably bad for the Beacon. I don't think the paper could survive without you being there in some way."

Hanna smiled at Philip. He was staying beautifully on script. Zachary looked thoughtful.

"So I'd come into the office every day?"

"Not every day, darling," Hanna interjected, taking his hand. "I want you to spend some time with me. Remember how you always promised me we could travel? See the world?"

No, Zachary thought, as he studied his wife's face.

"You could come in as you need to, and of course I'll keep in touch by phone when I have questions or need advice," Philip said. "You'd be doing me a tremendous honor, Uncle Zachary, to let me take over the Beacon."

"Dax might want to."

"No, darling, remember? We talked about this. Dax phoned weeks ago and said he will be staying in Chicago. He's doing very well there. He told you. You talked to him. Remember?"

A memory fluttered in Zachary's mind, of talking with Dax about the Tribune, about his life in Chicago. He always dreamed his son would come back to the Beacon, to step into the place where his parents had found each other, to represent both their spirits there, to be the physical manifestation of their love for the Beacon and each other. Dax was all they had left, now that Zachary's memories were slipping away.

Later that night, as Hanna slept, Zachary crept downstairs to his office and called Dax.

"Dad? Are you all right?" Zachary could hear female voices in the background.

"I'm fine. Did I interrupt you at a party?"

"Well, in a manner of speaking, but it's okay. It's good to hear from you."

"Son, did we talk lately about your job in Chicago? And did you tell me you're happy there?"

"Yes and yes," Dax said. "We did talk about it, and I told you how your encouragement over the last few years pulled me out of a bad spot and got me to work harder. I'm at the top of my game now, Dad, and the Tribune is the best paper it's ever been."

Zachary felt as though he were standing at the edge of dark chasm, looking down into the vortex of nothingness. Everything was gone. He'd lost Sarah, he'd lost Dax, now he was losing the Beacon. He had nothing left.

The next morning, he signed the papers turning over the Beacon to Philip.

Chapter 65

Dax became more involved in Chicago's day to day life, finding it a great way to keep in touch with what was going on around him while gaining people's trust. And once they trusted Dax, they automatically trusted the Tribune. He was appointed to the board of directors of Children's Memorial Hospital and the Art Institute of Chicago. He became a familiar face at major events but made sure to never show favoritism in the paper. He'd learned years ago from Zachary that a good newspaperman could be as involved in his community as he wanted to be, as long as those around him understood that at the end of the day, his duty was to journalism and the truth.

The night of the institute's annual gala, he was sipping a bitter and bitterly disappointing red wine, Marie beside him and resplendent in a white silk wrap dress, when he saw the governor winding through the crowd in his direction. Dax had no idea the governor even knew who he was, but there was no mistaking the broad political smile on his face that was aimed directly at him.

"Mr. Benton, it's a pleasure to finally meet you. I've heard all good things about the Tribune since you took over, and I have to say I'm glad to finally have a good working relationship between Chicago and its paper."

"Thank you, Governor, that's nice to hear. But I can't take all the credit. City hall has been keeping its promise of more transparency, and it makes our job easier when we don't have to wonder what's going on behind closed doors."

Dax studied the governor's face for a reaction, wondering if he had any clue the Tribune was about to blow city hall wide open in the biggest corruption scandal the city had ever seen. The governor, though, seemed to genuinely have no idea. He beamed at Dax over his cocktail.

"To even see a journalist of your stature out at a cocktail party like this is a nice change of pace," the governor said. "We don't usually see much press at these events unless they're covering it."

"Actually, I'm on the institute's board of directors," Dax said. He introduced Marie, then turned back to the governor.

"So what brings you out this evening?"

"Oh, I just like to get out to events whenever I can. That's not as often as I'd like, of course, but my schedule was a little lighter than usual this week."

"I can certainly understand that," Dax said. "I've been so busy lately I wasn't sure I was going to make it myself."

"I was sorry to hear your father stepped down from the New York Beacon," the governor said. "I met him a couple of times a few years back. Fine man. Hell of a journalist. It's easy to see where you get it."

Dax had stopped listening after the governor's first sentence.

"I'm sorry, someone misinformed you," he said. "My father hasn't stepped down from the Beacon."

The governor looked confused.

"Oh. Well, my apologies. I must have gotten bad information somewhere. Or I misunderstood. That's probably what it was. Old age is hell, you know!" The governor's laugh was forced. "Well, I'd better go mingle. It was a pleasure to meet you."

He couldn't get away fast enough. Dax tuned to Marie.

"Would you excuse me for a moment?"

"What was he talking about?" she asked.

"That's what I intend to find out. I'll be right back."

Dax took the elevator upstairs to the board room and closed the door. He reached for the phone with shaking hands and dialed Zachary's house in New York. Hanna answered the phone.

"What the fuck is going on?" he growled into the phone, not entirely trusting his voice.

"Well hello, Dax, how nice to hear from you. I'm fine, thank you for asking. And you?"

292

"Cut the bullshit, Hanna. I just heard from the governor of Illinois that my father has stepped down from the Beacon. Is this true?"

"Why yes, darling, it is. If you came around more often, you'd have known. But of course, you're so busy running Chicago now that we didn't want to bother you."

"Let me talk to my father."

"He's not here, darling."

"Don't call me darling, you fucking bitch. Where is he?"

"He's in a nursing home, Dax. His mind is almost entirely gone."

Her voice was as light as if she were talking about a sunny forecast for the Fourth of July. Dax felt the room begin to sway.

"What are you talking about? What are you saying to me?" His voice rose fast into a scream.

"Dax, calm down. You getting upset won't change anything."

"He is my father, goddammit. If you don't tell me what's going on, Hanna, I swear to God I will have you killed before the day is over."

"I could promise the same to you," she purred into the phone. "But I'll play nice with you, Dax. Zachary has been having memory problems for awhile. He went downhill very fast, and I was unable to care for him at home any longer. He was a danger to himself and to me."

Dax couldn't breathe.

"He's in a nursing home?" None of it was making any sense. He'd just spoken to Zachary…when was it? He fumbled with a mental calculation and realized it had been several months. He'd noticed his father was having trouble remembering some things, but he'd put it down to age, and possibly stress. He was furious with himself. Hanna was right: he hadn't stayed in touch with his father as much as he should have lately. But Zachary understood how hard it was to run a metropolitan paper, how many demands on his time there were. He had understood. Hadn't he? Dax suddenly felt as though a hole had opened somewhere deep inside him and everything rushed out, down a drain, into an ever-widening pool of darkness.

"Who is running the Beacon?" He could barely speak.

"Philip."

"I beg your pardon?"

"Philip is running the Beacon. When you told your father you were doing so well in Chicago and didn't want to come back and take over as publisher, he signed everything over to Philip.

"He never asked me if I wanted to come back and take over," Dax said, trying to remember their last call. "We hadn't even talked about it in ages. The last time I talked to him, he asked how things were going at the Trib and if I was happy." In that moment, Dax realized what had happened. "When I told him yes, he didn't ask me anything else," he whispered. He was talking to himself now. "He didn't ask me anything else. He thought he knew the answer so he never even asked."

Chapter 66

Dax called in sick to work for a week. He'd never taken so much as one sick day, and Mr. Neely was concerned, but he had heard what happened and knew the best thing he could do would be to give his volatile managing editor all the space he needed to come to terms with what was going on, and decide what to do next.

For Dax, it wasn't that simple. For the first three days, he didn't even get out of bed except to open another bottle of wine and take whatever pills he could get his hands on. He didn't know if he'd come out of this, and he didn't care. It was as though his present and his future had been erased with the same swipe that had eradicated his past. He felt as though his spirit was hovering, stuck, not alive and not dead, just waiting for something to swoop in and tell him it had all been a mistake and he would be free from this purgatory of disbelief. In his groggy waking moments, he tried to sort through his feelings and stack them up neatly into two piles: the ones that mattered and the ones that didn't. But then the stacks would get too high and collapse onto each other and everything mattered or everything didn't.

It wasn't that Dax thought he failed Zachary, a typical adult child's mantra at his dying father's bedside. He knew he hadn't failed him at all, in fact he'd done everything he could to make Zachary proud, and to keep the Benton tradition of good journalism alive. It was, he finally realized, that he'd lost his identity, the very identity he'd gone to Chicago to find. Without Zachary, Dax was completely and bottomlessly alone.

When Dax walked into the newsroom the following week, everyone immediately stopped what they were doing and turned to look at him. He looked the same, but they instinctively felt he wasn't.

"Get back to work," he said shortly, and went into his office, closing the door behind him. He sat down at his desk, dialed the Beacon, and asked for Philip.

"Who may I say is calling?" the receptionist asked in a perky, plastic voice.

"Dax Benton."

He could hear the look on her face.

"Just a moment please. I'll see if he's in."

Oh he's in, Dax thought. *He's in so far he'll never get out.*

"Hello, Dax." Philip's voice came over the line, sounding stronger than Dax remembered.

"Philip, would you like to tell me what the hell you think you're doing?"

"I think I'm running the Beacon. Because, newsflash, I'm running the Beacon."

"How did you get Zachary to hand it over to you, Philip? Come on, we both know you're not smart enough to come up with this on your own. Who's the puppet master?"

"I don't know what you're talking about. I'm family. You were gone, so Zachary left it to me. Surely even your booze and drug-clogged brain can figure that much out."

"You son of a bitch. You don't even have the balls to tell me the truth. You think I haven't figured out that Hanna put you up to this? You're pathetic, Philip. You've always been nothing but a groveling little worm who would pledge your allegiance to anyone who would pay attention to you. You make me sick. You think you're running the Beacon? You're not running the Beacon, Philip, Hanna is."

"I haven't even seen Hanna in days."

Dax laughed.

"You're an idiot. You don't have to see her for her to be controlling everything. Does the staff come to you for decisions? When was the last time you approved a bill? Before I called, when was the last time your phone even rang?"

Philip was getting angry.

"Fuck off, Dax, you're just mad that for once you can't get what you want. I'm running the Beacon. Not Hanna. And sure as hell not you."

"I'm not," Dax said. "But I'm about to be."

"You'll never get in the front door," Philip said. "All you know about me is the pale and sickly kid you used to push around. Well guess what, buddy boy? I'm not that kid anymore. I'm running the most influential newspaper in New York. People respect me. People listen to me. And if you think you can just come shoving your way back in here in a sad little attempt to take over, you'll find out just how connected I really am."

"Are you threatening me?"

"Are *you* threatening *me*?"

They were getting nowhere, and the vein in Dax's temple was about to burst from the pressure of his grinding teeth.

"This isn't over, Philip."

His cousin laughed.

"Oh Dax, you always did talk like a bad film noir. Quite a flair for the dramatic. Now fuck off. I'm busy."

Philip hung up. Dax slammed the receiver down.

He had to go home to New York, and soon.

Chapter 67

Two days later, Dax was working on some spectacularly bad copy that had come across his desk from a new reporter when his phone rang. He picked it up distractedly.

"Mr. Benton, this is Alex Ames from the New York Beacon."

"From the Beacon?"

"Yes, I'm a reporter."

"Okay, what can I do for you?"

"My boss has asked me to do a story on you."

"On me? What? Your boss?"

He certainly sounded eloquent. He hoped the kid was getting all these pithy quotes down.

"Yes. We've gotten some documentation at the paper that basically says you're, well, a fraud."

"What the hell are you even talking about? Back up here and tell me what's going on, please."

"We received some documentation, some legal paperwork, that says you're not Zachary Benton's son. It says your mother, Sarah Thomas, who was a reporter here back in the 60s, got pregnant and claimed Zachary Benton was the father, but new evidence has surfaced saying that Zachary isn't your father at all."

Dax felt his head begin to pound.

"I can assure you that's not true."

"Do you have anything to back you up on that?"

"Who put you up to this story, Alex?"

The reporter hesitated.

"I told you. My boss."

"What does that mean? Which boss? Your managing editor?"

"No, actually it was the publisher. Philip James."

"Let me tell you something, kid. Philip James is the fraud. I'm Zachary Benton's son. Just because my scumbag cousin said otherwise-"

"It wasn't him," the reporter insisted. "I have documentation."

"Fax me a copy of that documentation, please."

"I'm not sure I can do that."

"You listen to me, cubby, if you are claiming to have legal paperwork that says Zachary Benton is not my father, I have every right to see it. Now are you going to fax it to me or am I going to have to slap you with legal papers of my own?"

"Fine, I'll fax them over. But you should also know that other family members have come forward and said you're not Zachary Benton's son."

"What other family? Hanna Benton?"

"No." He could hear the kid flipping through papers. "Aggie James, for one."

Aunt Aggie. His mother's sister. Philip's mother. Dax felt as though he'd been punched.

"She said I'm not Zachary's son?"

"Yes, she said it on the record."

"She has no proof of that."

"She says she does."

"What proof is that?"

"I don't know. I haven't seen it yet."

"Alex, where did you go to journalism school?"

"NYU."

"And in your journalism classes at NYU, did they teach you to write news articles based on rumors, innuendo, and questionable sources?"

"No, but this…"

"This is bullshit, that's what this is. Look, kid, I know this isn't your fault. I put the blame squarely on your publisher. So I need you to tell him something for me. Tell him if he publishes even one word about me, I don't care how good he thinks his sources are, I will destroy him and my father's paper with him."

That night, Dax took out more anger than he even knew he felt on the Enthusiasts. He slammed himself into woman after woman, cocaine and alcohol burning through his veins with a white hot intensity that kept crossing into pain. He wondered dimly if he was hurting them, but they crawled around him worshipfully, eager for anything he gave them and begging for more. And when there wasn't enough of him to go around, they helped themselves to each other.

Later, as they lay in a tangled pile, Dax breathed into the sticky, dark air, bringing the essence of all of them and their love for him into his soul. He was going to need it.

Chapter 68

Philip was far more worried than he'd let on to Dax on the phone. If Dax came back to New York, Philip would have nothing but problems. He knew his ownership of the Beacon was legally binding, even Zachary couldn't take it away from him now, but if Dax made enough noise, he could ruin Philip and the Beacon. And if there's one thing Dax was good at, it was making noise.

He thought about telling Hanna his concerns, but Dax's comment that Philip was nothing more than Hanna's puppet still rankled. Philip knew Hanna thought he was in her hip pocket but she, like the rest of the family, had always underestimated him. He had long known Hanna was only nice to him to irritate Dax. He was only nice to her for the same reason. But it wasn't until Dax left for university that Philip realized he could use the dysfunction in the Benton family to his advantage. During the four years Dax had been in school, Philip had worked hard at not only his own schooling but getting close to Hanna, casting himself in the role of the son she never had, and taking full advantage of the fact that although Philip was a blood relative of Zachary's mistress, he and Hanna were actually on the same side, a united front against the Benton empire. And in a way, they did understand and appreciate each other. They were outsiders. And no matter what, they always would be. Their only way to beat the system was to rewrite the rules.

"Mr. James?" Alex tapped on his door.

"Hello, Alex. Come in."

The young reporter sat uneasily down in the chair across from Philip.

"Something on your mind?" Philip prompted.

"It's about this story you asked me to write on Dax Benton not really being Zachary Benton's son."

"What about it?"

Hesitatingly, Alex told Philip of his conversation with Dax.

"He said if we run the story, he'll destroy you. And the Beacon."

Philip clenched and unclenched his teeth, thinking. He had only planned to have the reporter ask Dax a few questions, shake him up a little, let him know that Philip was in charge now. He'd never really planned to run the story, but Dax's response felt like a line in the sand. He had no legal rights to the Beacon, and the more Philip talked to people who knew the Benton family, the more convinced he was that Dax really wasn't Zachary's son. Enough people had been willing to say so on the record that Philip knew he had a story if he wanted it. Looking at his young reporter's stricken face, his decision was absolute.

"We're running the story," he said. "If Dax wants to tangle with someone, it'll be me, Alex, not you."

"But with my byline on the story…"

"I'll be honest with you, Alex, this is a big story. The Bentons have a long history and deep roots in New York. This story is going to change what a lot of people have accepted as the truth for years. But this is the truth. Now if you don't want your byline on it, I'll put the generic staff byline on it. But if you want it, you've done all the work on it and by all rights, it's yours."

Alex cleared his throat.

In your journalism classes at NYU, did they teach you to write news articles based on rumors, innuendo, and questionable sources?

"With all due respect, Mr. James, I don' want my name on this story. In fact, I wish I'd never had anything to do with it."

Philip watched Alex walk back into the newsroom, his head held high. He knew what the boy was feeling: fear, pride, the swell of ethics every reporter gets when they first take a stand on a story they don't think should see print. Part of Philip was proud of Alex for making such a gutsy decision. The rest of him was past that and firmly sinking into the realization that Philip had no choice now. He had to run the story. He'd managed to wrest the Beacon away from Dax. Now all he had to do was strip him of the Benton name and all Dax's power in New York would be gone. He wouldn't dare show his face in the city ever again.

The story went to print the next morning.

At his desk in Chicago, Dax finished reading the article and slowly lowered the paper to his desk. His hands were clenched in such rage he couldn't feel his fingers. A faint veil of red mist had descended over his consciousness and all he could think of was killing Philip. Of literally choking the life out of the miserable little bastard, then every person who had lent their name to that pile of garbage article. Forget slander and defamation, to Dax this was far worse than either of those pitiful terms that amounted to nothing more than someone tattling to the legal system that they'd been picked on. This was Philip taking away Dax's very birthright.

As long as he could remember, Dax had clung to Zachary, and to the stories about his mother that Zachary shared in the quiet moments alone with his son. Other kids at school always had funny stories about their embarrassing parents or riotous family gatherings. Dax was only an observer in those stories about his own parents, never a participant. After Zachary would tell the boy a story about Sarah, something that had happened at the paper, or a sweet moment they'd shared, Dax would lie awake for hours, embroidering the story further, filling in the details, seeing it play out in his imagination until he felt like he'd been there too, like his friends at school with their stories. Dax had never met his mother, but in his mind, he and Zachary and Sarah had been as much of a family as any other kid had, maybe more.

And now Philip was trying to take that away from him.

As Dax's first rush of anger began to ebb, he realized Philip was as weak and powerless now as he'd ever been. There was no question in Dax's mind that the article was a complete fabrication, but more than that, it was a snapshot of Philip's fear. He was terrified that Dax would come back to New York and claim his rightful place as the head of the Beacon. Even though Philip and Hanna had tricked Zachary into signing the paper over to Philip, Dax knew he could contest it in court. Zachary had clearly not been in his right mind when he signed the papers. This little power play of Philip's was nothing but smoke and mirrors, trying to break Dax's will by taking away what he knew was really all that Dax had left. Maybe in his own little flea-brained way, Philip was even trying to punish Dax for going away, for leaving him behind in New York.

Dax had been away, sure, but he'd been away becoming. People who left their hometowns always went away to become something better, to step away from the shadows they had always cast and find the center of their souls, the trueness that radiates out and make their skin finally fit. What would be the point of trying to realize your potential in the town you'd grown up in? Dax was convinced it couldn't be done. No one who had stayed where they started had ever really come to fruition. No matter what you did or how you matured, it was impossible to be taken seriously by people who saw you vomit on the risers during the second grade spring concert or crash your bike into a light pole or sprout magnificent acne right after you turned 15.

That was Philip's problem, Dax knew. He'd stayed behind and even a city the size of New York was still just your hometown if you never ventured further than your old neighborhood. And Philip hadn't. He'd stayed where he'd grown up, apparently focused on someday taking what rightfully belonged to Dax. Dax hadn't realized it, but even if he had, he wouldn't have known to feel threated. Philip was just his putzy cousin, a hanger-on, a wannabe. That's all he'd ever been.

Dax wondered now if his constant underestimation of Philip hadn't been his mistake all along, even when they were kids. When Dax remembered how Philip had told his mother about their adventure at the piers, it was easy to see Philip's deception. He wanted to get Dax into trouble so he could get the scoop himself. How he thought he'd manage that when he was such a big weenie about everything Dax never had sussed out, but since they'd both gotten grounded it didn't matter anyway. Now it all made sense. Even as a child, a pale little weakling, Philip was planning to overthrow Dax one day. He'd studied Dax, studied Zachary, learning all he could without actually getting his hands dirty, so he could beat Dax at his own game. Well, he'd tried. But Dax wasn't about to concede defeat. Not now. Not ever.

Chapter 69

"Dax Benton?"

"Yes?"

"We've never met, Mr. Benton, but my name is Alan Bernhardt. I'm an old friend of your father's. And your mother's."

Dax's heart stopped for a moment, then began to race.

"I know who you are, Mr. Bernhardt. My father always spoke very highly of you. He told me you and your wife helped my mother when she was pregnant with me."

"Yes, that's right," Alan said, relieved. He'd been hesitant to call – the very idea of talking to the bump that he'd seen Sarah hauling around for so many months was just too odd. But he had seen the article in the Beacon and realized he had to tell Dax what he knew. He had no idea if Dax really believed what the article said about him, but he wouldn't be able to look at himself in the mirror ever again if he didn't speak up now.

"Mr. Benton-"

"Please call me Dax."

"All right, Dax, and please call me Alan. Now I'll get to the point of my call."

"By all means."

"As you said you know, your mother came here not too long after she found out she was expecting you. Your father wanted her someplace safe."

"Safe from Hanna."

"Well, yes. I wasn't sure how much you knew already, but yes. He wasn't sure what Hanna might do, and he was afraid for your mother and for you. So she came here to Greenview to live. My wife Maggie and I got real close with your mom. She was a fine woman, Dax. I hope you know that. To this day, Maggie misses her. We all do, actually."

Dax swallowed hard, not trusting his voice to respond.

"At any rate, I saw the article in the Beacon about you – I get it in the mail – and that's why I'm calling. For them to say you're not Zachary's son is absolute horseshit. You are Zachary's son, Dax. Your mother was far too in love with him to have even looked at another man. If you could have seen what we saw, you'd know why I say that."

"I appreciate that, Alan. For the record, I don't believe for a second that I'm not Zachary's son. The article in the Beacon was, well, it's a long and complicated family thing, but it's an attempt by my cousin to discredit me in New York and keep me from coming back and, well…"

"Kicking his ass?" Alan supplied. Dax laughed.

"Yeah. Yeah, that's it exactly. Kicking his ass. But what I don't like is that he's not only trying to ruin my name, he is dragging my mother's name through the mud. She's not here to defend herself, and my father can't speak up for her anymore, so my cousin and Hanna are taking advantage of that situation and trying to paint my mother as some kind of whore who slept her way around New York, got pregnant, and tried to pin the paternity on Zachary Benton to take advantage of his name and wealth and position. I'm furious, but frankly I'm not sure at this moment how I'm going to prove them wrong. It's the only reason I haven't gone back to New York yet."

"Well, that's the other reason I'm calling," Alan said "I think I can help you there. When Maggie and I were cleaning out the house your mother stayed in while she was here, we found a shoebox full of letters she wrote to your father. She never sent them. As far as we can tell, she wrote them because she wasn't able to call him whenever she wanted, but she wanted to share every detail of her days with him. Of course, she obviously couldn't risk mailing them either, so she'd write them, then put them in this box. Maggie opened the first one to see what it was, and when she realized, she put it back. She didn't read any of the others, and she wouldn't let me read any of them. We weren't sure what to do with them. I didn't want to send them to Zachary and cause him any more headaches with Hanna, but we just couldn't throw them out. Now I know why we found them, and why we kept them. I'd like to send you these letters, Dax. If you want to read them, I'm sure you'll know all you need to about your parents."

Chapter 70

"My darling love,

I just came back from an appointment with Dr. Weatherby, and want so much to be able to tell you all that he said. I will be able to tell you when you next call me, of course, but our conversations tend to be so rushed and furtive, and it makes me feel like we're discussing the heist we're planning, instead of our baby. But in a nutshell, he said the baby is healthy and fine and growing normally. I am positive it's a boy, but of course I have no way of knowing for sure. Dr. Weatherby agrees with me. When he was listening to the heartbeat with his stethoscope, he said the heartbeat sounded to him like a boy. He said girls' heartbeats tend to be a little faster. The reporter in me wanted to get up and write that down – sounds important.

I really have to tell you that as much as I used to always say I was "married to journalism" and never wanted to be tied down with a husband and a bunch of rug rats, I lately find myself dreaming, day and night, about having a family with you. A rambling old farmhouse upstate, maybe, full of kids and dogs and laughter and love. I always liked that I grew up in a big family. Having two brothers and two sisters always seemed just right to me. My friends who were only children or had just one sibling always seemed strangely out of balance to me, although sometimes I wondered if we were the ones who were out of balance. My family always seemed to me to be exaggeratedly uncool, sore thumbs, some kind of societal outcasts. I imagined myself as the Marilyn character in a house full of Munsters, the only one who could relate to both the world within and the world without, apologizing to everyone without in hushed tones before stepped back into the madness within and closing the door.

Looking back now, of course, I don't think we were particularly odd, and from conversations I've had with old friends in recent years, I'm pretty sure no one else thought so either. We were just regular people, you know? It was probably just my angsty teenage outlook that had me convinced we were the town laughingstock. No one could possibly understand that we all took baths on Saturday night so we'd be clean for church on Sunday morning. I was sure none of my friends' families laughed so uproariously at each other's farts, that no one else's father complained quite so loudly about the government, no one else's mother slept in curlers, no other families out there considered Jiffy Pop and the Disney Sunday Movie the highlight of the week.

But somehow I knew, even then, that I embraced my family because I thought they were different. They were nuts, but they were my nuts, and what I saw as our excruciating uncoolness was actually what made me feel closest to them.

My love, I want our family to be big, happy, close, and nuts.

I love you,

Sarah"

"Dear Zachary,

Today is one of those days when it is probably for the best that we are not physically together. I am in a vile mood, and by vile I mean Vile. I am exhausted, fat, and irrationally angry that I'm here and you're there. And I know if you were talking to me right now, you'd be sooth-ingly telling me all the reasons we have to postpone our future, all the ways this wait is making us stronger as a couple, how even in our few and whispered phone calls we are connecting on a spiritual level and growing together, just as our child is growing inside me. And I'd wonder how a newspaperman got to be so hippie dippy and I'd want to punch you in the head. I don't care about all the practical, noble, and safety reasons we're waiting. All I want is for Dax to stop kicking me in the kidneys, Hanna to stop being a psycho, and for you to either take me out of Oklahoma, or put on your cowboy boots and come make it feel like home.

I love you. You big huge bastard.

Sarah"

"My sweetest love,

It was a good day today, apart from the missing you. Greenview is starting to feel, if not quite like home, then at least comfortingly familiar. People call me by name on the street, ask me how I'm feeling, or bring me muffins and Bundt cake at oddly random intervals. I'm getting to be as big as a barn door. There, you see that? I never would have compared something big to a barn door back in New York. Ye cats, Zachary, I think I have Stockholm Syndrome.

At first I felt silly, writing these letters that I can't send, but when I'm faced with the other options, like calling you, or actually putting a stamp on these and dropping them into the blue box on the corner, my rational mind reminds me that I can't, and why. Every road that could lead to Hanna is, for me, a dead end. Today is one of those days when I don't want to understand why you can't just divorce her and be done with it.

I love you endlessly.

Sarah"

"Dearest love,

Another hot summer day on the prairie. I found out from my neighbor today that if I want to, I could raise chickens in the backyard. I might talk to Alan about it. I don't think he'd mind, and it would be nice to have fresh eggs. I just re-read what I wrote and now I can't decide whether to laugh or cry. Come get me and take me to Zabar's, pronto.

You know, lately I'm finding myself feeling bad for Hanna. Or maybe it's more accurate to say I'm feeling bad about her. I never intended to steal you away from her. In fact, I know it sounds terrible to admit this, but I never really thought of her at all. I knew that you had a wife, of course, but she never came to our office picnics, you don't talk about her, there are no pictures of her on your desk … if it hadn't been for that time she stopped by the office to pick up your car because hers had broken down, I'd have just figured you were one of those men who bought a cheap wedding ring and wears it to try and pick up women.

I like to think that line just made you laugh. God, I miss your laugh. I miss everything connected with your face. And don't even get me started on how much I miss the rest of you.

But back to my point. I knew of Hanna's existence but she was always in the distance. Indistinct. I could never see her clearly, so it was easy to pretend she didn't exist. I'm not a homewrecker. Oh man, now I sound like some DC hooker who got busted with her hand down Congressional pants. But in my case, I'm really not a homewrecker. I didn't intend to fall in love with you, but, well, you try being around Zachary Benton for awhile. He's impossible to resist. Trust me, I'm with the press.

I love you,

Sarah"

"My sweetest love,

Dr. Weatherby said Dax is growing beautifully and his heartbeat is strong and perfect. I could have told him that without any of his medical equipment. Our son is perfect, my love. I'm feeling pretty good. The heat here has finally broken, which helps. I have a weird amount of energy during the day – I've been wondering if it could be from all the grape juice. I crave it constantly. I was worried about how much sugar is in it, but Dr. Weatherby said he's seen pregnant women put a lot worse than that into their mouths. I'd better not tell him that lately I'm craving wine even more. I've no idea what that's about. You know me – I don't even like wine.

I'll write more later. I may have more energy during the day, but at night I'm flat-out exhausted. I wish you were here to cuddle up with.

I love you,

Sarah"

"My darling,

I am the lowest I've ever been tonight, my love. After supper I sat on the porch, in the little swing that Alan hung up for me, sipping a glass of peppermint iced tea and watching the fireflies do their summer dance across the yard. They are silent, beautiful. Their soft yellow lights have for centuries given children something to chase and adults the melancholy feeling of waning summer, inspired artists and songwriters to try and capture the simple beauty that to us is a summer night's mystery but is, to the firefly, nothing more than the seeking of a mate. So many millions of fireflies all over the world, each one sending out a tiny pulse of light. What are the chances that their true mate will see their light, among so many others? Oh my love, this missing you is more than I can bear. My light is shining in the darkness, my darling, can you see it?

Sarah"

Twilight had overtaken Dax's apartment as he read his mother's letters. He slowly put the last one down and sat for a long time, comforted by the dark that protected him and his knotted thoughts. There had never been a doubt in his mind that Zachary was his father, but his mother's letters showed him far more than he'd ever known about her, about her relationship with Zachary and, Dax realized, about himself. A sense of himself he'd never felt before was stirring somewhere deep inside. He felt as if the smoke and mirrors that had made up his whole life were suddenly shattered and swept away, leaving him staring down a clear, straight road in both directions. He knew now where Dax Benton had come from, and he knew where he was going.

After a long time, he got up, turned on a single lamp, and poured himself a glass of wine. He sat down again and looked at the pile of letters strewn across the coffee table. Carefully he folded each one without reading them again, tucked them back into the box, and reached for the phone to call Judith.

"Darling, get the Enthusiasts together. We're going to New York."

Chapter 71

Stepping out of La Guardia, Dax knew, immediately and soul-soakingly, that he was home to stay. People bumped into him without a word as they hurried off to wherever they needed to be that was more important than where they were, yellow cabs moved past in a haltingly fluid stream, the air tinged with the warm, tinny, slightly sour smell that was unique to New York. Dax filled his lungs with it as gratefully as if he'd been holding his breath for the past ten years. Beside him, Marie and Judith were looking around, wide-eyed.

"You look like tourists," he said. "You're both big-city girls."

"I've never been to New York before," Marie said.

"Neither have I," Judith echoed. "But I've always wanted to see it."

Dax grinned.

"Then let's see it," he said. "This is just the airport. This is nothing."

The other Enthusiasts were on the next two flights, and Dax had arranged for them all to meet at the Plaza. He'd booked the Royal Plaza Suite for their gatherings, and a few extra rooms in case they needed them. He pointed out various sights to Marie and Judith as their cab sped uptown. Tiffany's made them swoon and required several bad attempts to imitate Audrey Hepburn. FAO Schwartz made them laugh and Central Park made them positively giddy, especially when they caught sight of a horse-drawn carriage. Dax smiled indulgently. Although his demeanor would never give it away, he could feel his own heart pounding with excitement at being home again.

That night, he ordered a lavish room-service dinner and dozens of bottles of wine. How Judith had managed to get her usual obscene stash of cocaine, plus acid and ecstasy on the plane was unclear, but it didn't really matter. Their sexual adventurousness grew even bigger wings now that they were in a new city. The pulse of New York at night pounded through all of them, throughout the endlessly long night. When Dax woke the next morning, early as always, he quietly showered and slipped out, leaving everyone sleeping just where they'd dropped and making sure there was enough coke and chilled champagne for when they awoke. He needed them to stay in a constant state of drunken, aroused euphoria for what he would soon be asking of them.

On the corner, he bought a bagel with cream cheese and a cup of coffee in a paper cup. Sitting on a low wall, he ate and watched people heading to work, each one surrounded by that peculiar intensity New Yorkers have when they're on the street. He'd been gone for nearly a decade, but everything felt comfortingly familiar to Dax, as though the city had been treading water, waiting for his return. Brushing off crumbs, he dropped his empty cup and bit of waxed paper into the garbage can on the corner and started walking, past stores whose names had changed but facades had not, some already doing a brisk business, others with their heavy roll-down gates still in place. Without thinking about it, he crossed Broadway and walked uptown, and as the pedestrian and car traffic thinned simultaneously, he glanced to his left and realized he was at the gates of Columbia. He paused, looking up at the statue of a tall, thin woman holding a book, open towards him. He had seen her a million times in his life, her impassive face, the hem of her skirt just out of reach, and as a child he'd believed she was a statue of his mother, one the university had made to honor her, and whenever he'd see her, he'd give a little half-wave, making sure she saw him, letting her know he was doing all right, and feeling somehow relieved to see her still standing there, keeping an eye on things.

He walked through the gates and onto the campus, trailing his fingers along every railing and wall, wondering if he was touching anywhere his mother had touched, if any stray bit of her DNA might still be lingering, worked loose from the cement's grip at just the right time to grab his finger as he passed. He'd read somewhere that all the air everyone breathed had already been breathed by someone else, over and over again, centuries of recycled air, so it was possible the air he was breathing right now had been exhaled by his mother, or even by Joseph Pulitzer.

For all the times Dax had passed Columbia's campus, on foot or on his bicycle or in the back of a cab, it had never occurred to him to actually go onto the grounds. Part of him had always staunchly rejected the idea

314

of attending Columbia, mostly because he knew Zachary wanted him to and Dax felt that if he did, he'd be stepping into a scripted role, with every expectation set out for him like yellow painted footprints on the floor showing you the way in, the way around, and eventually, the way out. The whole concept seemed Orwellian to Dax, and although he had always known he wanted to be a journalist, it had seemed important to him to do it in his own way, and on his own path. Sitting on a bench on the Columbia campus now, he suddenly felt like crying. Running from his destiny had almost cost him everything. But he was home now, and everything was falling back into its rightful place.

"Dad?"

Zachary turned away from the window, which he'd been gazing out of when Dax walked in. Dax sucked in his breath when he saw how old his father looked, how shriveled and empty, as though his very soul had evaporated and left only bones and skin. He was dwarfed by the armchair he was sitting in. If it weren't for that relentless explosion of dark hair now streaked with silver, Dax would have thought he'd walked into the wrong room.

"Hello." Zachary was polite but there was no recognition on his face.

"Dad, it's me. Dax."

"Dax?"

"Yes. Dax. Your son. You remember me, right?"

Please say you remember me, Dad. I'm sorry. I'm so sorry.

Zachary didn't respond. Dax knelt beside the chair and took his father's cool, soft hands in his own.

"Dad, I'm back. I'm back from Chicago. I'm living in New York again and I'm going to take over the Beacon. Just like you wanted."

"Who are you?"

"It's me, Dad. It's Dax. Please Dad, I'm sorry. I'm sorry I didn't stay in New York. I'm sorry I didn't go to Columbia like you wanted me to. I'm not sorry for the reasons you might think, Dad, because I had an awesome ten years in Chicago. I got a great education, and I turned the Tribune around so completely you wouldn't believe it. And I met some amazing people and built a truly great life for myself. I'm not sorry for any of that, Dad. But what I am sorry for is for letting you think I didn't want to follow in your footsteps. Yours and Mom's. I did. I always did, but I just wanted to do it in my own way. Never knowing her at all, and always having to share you with the paper and with... Hanna... it just seemed to me like I'd never really find out who I was and what I could do if I just did it all the easy way, riding on the coattails of the great Zachary Benton. But somewhere in all of that, I lost sight of what matters most – that I'm your son."

Zachary's eyes were fixed out the window again. Dax couldn't even tell if his father had heard anything he said. His face was as cold and impassive as the stone statue outside the gates of Columbia. It was too late. He'd lost everything. The tears he'd been holding back for so long began to slide down his face, hot and thick, and he leaned forward, his forehead on Zachary's thigh. The familiar, faint scent of soap and black pepper enveloped him, and he began to sob. Zachary turned his head, not sure what was going on. Looking down, he saw his son. He placed his hand on the boy's head, his familiar hair still smooth and shiny, the same soft coppery brown as Sarah's.

"Dax," Zachary said quietly. "My son."

Chapter 72

Dax breathed in the familiar smell of the theater while he waited in the empty lobby. All theaters had the same smell – old, still, dusty, faintly waxy. The young woman he'd asked to please let Bonnie know he was here had not been happy to be bothered, but Dax reassured her Bonnie would want to see him, would in fact be livid if she found out that Dax had been in town and this young woman, clearly named Tiffani or Bambi or something, had not let her know.

Dax actually wasn't at all sure Bonnie would be happy to see him. They hadn't spoken in years, not due to any sort of fight or other falling out, but rather the far more deadly slow erosion suffered by a relationship that is unable to overcome time and distance. Still, when he'd bumped into Mrs. Branford at the Strand bookstore and she'd mentioned that Bonnie had moved back to the city and was currently directing a play off Broadway, Dax had gone straight over to the theater without the slightest hesitation, the same way Dax did everything.

"Dax!"

He turned to see Bonnie coming through the ornate double doors. Her face answered all of his questions, and he swept her into his arms.

"What on earth are you doing here? How did you find me?"

"I ran into Mrs. Branford and she told me you're back and what you're doing. Good for you, Bon. Off-Broadway, wow."

"Yeah, well, I kind of stepped into it. You know how it goes. Right place, right time."

"Are you working with… sorry, I can't remember your husband's name. Roger?"

Her face went the wrong sort of shape.

"No, we split up. He's gone." She forced a laugh. "Fin. Curtain."

"I'm sorry," Dax said. "His loss."

"Yeah, well. Anyway, what are you doing in town?"

"I'm back."

"Back to stay?"

"Looks that way. I got in a few days ago. I've been kind of getting reacquainted with everything. Can I buy you a coffee?"

"Sure, that would be great," she said. "Hang on just one second, let me tell them in the back that I'm going out for awhile."

Twenty minutes later they were seated in a tiny coffee shop, and Dax felt as though no time had passed at all and they were still kids, hanging out after school. Bonnie's face was thinner, her hair shorter, her eyes a bit weary, but she was still so beautiful. Dax impulsively took her hand and she smiled.

"I can't believe you're here. You know, this is going to sound weird, but do you still do any acting?"

"A little, yeah. I did some community theater in Chicago."

"That's right, I remember you telling me that. Well, the reason I'm asking, and this is totally random, but my lead actor called me right before you showed up and said he has bronchitis. And then you walked in, and I've gotta tell you, you'd be perfect for the part."

"Me go on stage? Don't you have an understudy?"

"Yeah, but he won't care. He hates everything about this play. He's only here because his uncle is the producer. Something about the guy's mom. I don't know, I try not to pay attention when they start up with the family drama. Trust me, he'd be thrilled to not have to go on."

"When?"

"Day after tomorrow. Two nights from now."

"Holy shit, Bon, that's fast. You think I can learn all the lines by then?"

"Frankly, yes. I know you, Dax. Theater was your second greatest love after journalism." Her face was so alive, so familiar, that Dax smiled and instinctively touched her hair.

"Third greatest," he said softly. Bonnie flushed and looked away. Dax cleared his throat.

"Okay, what the hell," he said. "Give me the script."

He got back to the Plaza at dusk. Up in the suite, the Enthusiasts were getting cranky.

"Where have you been all day?" Judith said in the petulant voice he hated.

"Out," he said, taking off his jacket. "I'm an important man in this city, you know. I figured you all would have started without me."

"We're out of champagne," came a voice from across the room. Dax couldn't even remember how many people he'd brought with him. It seemed an eternity since he'd arrived.

"Not for long," he said grandly, reaching for the phone. "I will get another case of it from room service right now. We are going to celebrate!"

"Celebrate what?" Marie slipped up behind him and ran her slim white hands over his shoulders.

"I am going onstage, in two nights, in a stellar off-Broadway play, and you all are going to help me rehearse."

A rumble went around the room as those who had heard what Dax said processed it, then passed it on to those who had just come to.

When the champagne arrived and the room service waiter had been tipped into discretion, Dax poured glittering glasses full for everyone.

"Who has the ecstasy?" he called. Someone put a pill into his hand and he swallowed it with a long pull of champagne.

"Now," he said. "Let's do this."

The Enthusiasts, long unused to doing much but drinking and sleeping, were a bit like herding cats at first, but Dax explained what they needed to do, where they needed to stand, and what each of their roles were. Even after he'd gone over everything, he still wasn't sure they got it.

"Now here's the best part," he announced. "I'm playing a cross-dresser."

319

The room dissolved into whoops of laughter. Dax, wiping his eyes, got up and picked up someone's discarded bustier and satin hot pants.

"I need to borrow these, so thank you to whomever they belong."
No one seemed to know, or care, and the laughter got more and more raucous as Dax stripped down and redressed himself in the new outfit. Someone passed him a pair of stilettos and he somehow managed to get them onto his feet.

"Presenting the new Dax Benton!" he announced. The Enthusiasts applauded and shrieked as he paraded around the room, reading from the script. He was amazed how easily it all came back to him, how well he was able to remember his lines, and how surprisingly at home he felt in drag. The Enthusiasts were basically useless as extras, but they cheered Dax on enthusiastically, getting higher and drunker with every passing hour. This was an orgy unlike any they'd ever had, and Dax was glad to watch them reach the necessary fever pitch.

Chapter 73

Dax's debut performance off-Broadway was heralded as a triumph by the small number of people in the audience, and by one critic in the Village Voice, although no one actually knew it as he'd insisted that Bonnie bill him as Thomas Thebes.

"Why? Are you embarrassed to be in my play?" She had been irritated, and slightly insulted, when he'd asked her.

"Not at all," he assured her. "It's nothing to do with you or your play at all. It's a family issue. There are certain people I'm not ready to have find out yet that I'm in town. And since this was just for fun anyway, I figure I'll just use a stage name. What the hell."

Bonnie wasn't happy about it – she'd half hoped that Dax's name would bring some of the city's more influential theater people out to see what he could do – but she knew him well enough to know when to choose her battles. She was able to convince him to go on for two extra nights, however, when her lead actor remained resolutely ill.

"Whoa," she said to Ron, the stage manager, as she peeked out from behind the curtain on the third night. "Full house!"

"I was just wondering what was going on," Ron answered. "We've had decent attendance all along, but it looks like we're sold out tonight."

"It's Dax," Bonnie said, her eyes still on the people pushing past each other in search of their seats.

"It's what?" Ron asked absently, looking for his clipboard.

"It's Thomas," she amended hastily. "He's really good. I guess word is getting out."

"He is good. He's great. Where did you find him again?"

"He's just an old friend," she answered. "He's in town for awhile and we just got lucky he said he'd do it."

When the curtain came down on that night's performance, Dax grabbed Bonnie and kissed her, making the cast and crew cheer and laugh.

"I want to invite everyone back to my suite at the Plaza for a celebration," he said. "The cast, the crew, anyone you want to invite. Everything's on me!"

The phone on Philip's desk rang, startling him. Everyone had gone home hours earlier and the only sound in the darkened newsroom was the persistent crackling buzz of the police scanners.

"Is this Mr. James?" The female voice was raspy, and Philip could hear what sounded like street noise in the background.

"Yes. Who's this?"

"You don't know me, but I'm a friend of Hanna's. And I hope of yours too. I just wanted to let you know your cousin Dax is in town. Hanna has told me the whole story, so I knew you'd want to know. I tried to reach Hanna but I couldn't."

"How do you know he's in town?"

"I know everyone, Mr. James. I heard it from a few of my more reliable sources, and since then I've seen him with my own eyes. For the past few nights he's been on stage in an off-Broadway play directed by a friend of his."

"How is that possible? Our arts editor would have heard something, and his name would have set off some alarm bells around here."

The woman sighed, as though Philip were a colossal disappointment.

"He's been using a stage name. Very few people knew who it really was, but I have a friend whose sister works at that theater. Trust me, it's Dax Benton."

"I see."

"I don't presume to tell you what to do as it's your family and your business, Mr. James, but he is having a party at his suite at the Plaza tonight. As I said, Hanna has told me what's going on, and if you want to get him out of New York and out of your life, I'd pop in there tonight.

This was his last night in the play, so I can only imagine you're his next stop. I'm sorry to have to dump all this on you, but as I said, I haven't been able to reach Hanna, and I'm really getting worried."

Philip's brain was spinning.

"You said the party is at the Plaza? But wait, it doesn't matter. He'll never let me in."

"Oh, I wouldn't worry about that," the woman said with a laugh. "He was playing a drag queen, along with just about everybody in the cast, and I heard him say he wanted everyone to stay in costume for the party. All you have to do is get yourself into drag and you're in. He won't know who you are. From what I've heard, Mr. James, your cousin is into some freaky-ass shit. I wouldn't be surprised if he has no idea who he is half the time."

"Yes, I know," Philip said drily. "I appreciate the information."

He hung up and sat at his desk, thinking hard. On the other end, Marie replaced the pay phone receiver.

"All set," she said, smiling at Dax. "He'll be there."

Chapter 74

The night's revelry tore up the dictionary definition of both "party" and "orgy" and entered into the realm of the surreal. After making a few phone calls, Dax had fresh supplies of cocaine, acid, and the purest ecstasy he could find delivered surreptitiously to his suite, along with hundreds of bottles of wine. The Enthusiasts had been perfect hosts for the first couple of hours, making sure the wine flowed with just the right amount of decadence demanded by the New York theater crowd. When the first wave of actors and crew had departed, including Bonnie, some of the remaining actors fired up joints and passed them around. Dax, who hadn't smoked weed in years, took a couple of tokes and, as he nearly coughed himself to death, remembered why he'd never really liked it. Wine was still his drug of choice, he thought, soothing his smoke-seared throat with a long, leggy swallow.

He watched from his usual perch at the head of the bed as the party grew more frenzied around him and noticed that, as seemed to be the way of all his parties these days, the revelers were almost all women – although since some of the men were in some damned impressive drag, it was hard to tell for sure.

Dressed in his costume, Dax felt himself still in his character of Lydia, who in the play was a cross-dressing man but in Dax's mind was actually a lovely, ethereal blonde woman. Feeling as though Lydia had taken over his spirit, he perched on the bed he'd had moved to the center of the room and watched the party unfolding around him as though he were watching a bawdy movie. "The Filthy Life and Dirty Good Times of Dax Benton." The title needed work, but it pleased him anyway and he laughed aloud. The combination of ecstasy and wine were just sweeping beautifully through his system when the suite door opened and he saw his aunt Aggie come in with two other women.

Holy shit, he thought, how did she get here? He hadn't seen her in years, but there was no mistaking the red hair, the long thin face, like photos he'd seen of his mother but with a harder edge. She was clearly pretty tipsy already. Dax poured a fresh glass of wine and made his way over to her.

"May I offer you a drink?" he said with a serene smile. Lydia was a gracious and graceful hostess.

"Oh my God, it's you! It's Thomas Thebes! You were amazing tonight, Mr. Thebes, really amazing. I'm Aggie James. These are my friends, Linda and Melanie."

"Charmed." Dax took each woman's hand, turned it palm up, and placed a warm, wet kiss in the center, lingeringly, with a light tickle of his tongue. He was Thomas, he was Lydia, he was Dax. He was aroused beyond reason, and higher than he'd ever been. "I will be direct with you ladies, this party is about to get very intense. If at any point it's more than you can handle, please feel free to go. I only ask that you respect me by not telling anyone outside this room what is going on here."

Aggie swayed against him, spilling a little of her wine.

"That's the only kind of party we like," she said, as though letting him in on a great confidence.

"Then by all means, make yourself comfortable," he said. "Please excuse me for a moment."

He moved away from her and her friends and glanced the clock, wondering if Philip would actually show up. Just the thought of what the smug little prick had tried to do made Dax angry all over again. New York was his home, he belonged here. How Philip thought he could not only take away Dax's home but his very identity was more than Dax dared think about right now. He put more ecstasy into the candy dishes and signaled Judith to cut more lines of coke. The room was warm and pieces of clothing were beginning to drop to the floor like leaves in an autumn breeze. Dax had just pulled Marie onto his lap and slipped his hand beneath her skirt when he glanced up and saw Philip coming through the suite's ornate double doors. He was in drag – terrible and unconvincing drag – but there was no doubt in Dax's mind it was Philip. He'd know that dim-bulb look anywhere. He glanced around to see where his aunt was, but she was laughing in the corner, still spilling wine.

"Excuse me, darling," Dax said, depositing Marie onto the sofa and standing up. He moved through the crowd, keeping one eye on Philip. He could tell his cousin was looking for him, but he kept moving, making sure to keep his face averted as much as possible.

"Darling, the man in the horrible blonde wig and wrap dress who just came in – please offer him a drink and make him feel welcome," Dax said to Judith, who immediately slithered over to where Philip stood. Dax resumed his spot on the bed, watching. An hour passed and still Philip made no move to talk to Dax, if in fact he'd seen him at all. The women were getting louder and sloppier, and Dax started to worry they'd be passing out soon. It was time.

"May I have everyone's attention, please!" he called, straining to be heard above the din. "Ladies, please! I have something I need to say to all of you."

Gradually the noise ebbed, and dozens of wine-flushed faces and glassy eyes turned in his direction. The level of drugs and wine flowing through these women was insane. He could only hope they'd be able to understand him

"I would like to thank you all for coming out this evening, not only to my party, but to my play. It has been an honor for me to perform for all of you, and to spend the rest of this evening basking in your beautiful company, so beautiful that it makes me want to make love to each and every one of you. Feel free to enjoy each other until it's your turn. My darlings, my angels..." he raised his hands in a kind of blessing, feeling the surge of power he always had when he addressed the Enthusiasts. "To love!"

The room erupted. Dax glanced up and deliberately caught Philip's eye. His cousin's glare narrowed and he began to work his way toward Dax, who watched with a slow, lazy smile.

"Hello, Philip," he said quietly. "How nice of you to come. And you look quite lovely, by the way. Like Phyllis Diller after a bender."

"Don't fuck with me, Dax. What are you doing in town? What are you doing here, with ..." he waved his arm around the orgiastic scene playing out in every square inch of the suite. "...them? This isn't even legal,

Dax. You think you're so important in this town, you think you can just waltz back into New York and get away with whatever you want. Well you can't. This is my town now, Dax. I got rid of Zachary, now I'm going to get rid of you. Fortunately, Zachary made my job that much easier by killing your worthless slut of a mother for me."

Dax froze, his face absolutely expressionless, his eyes locked with Philip's. He stood for a long moment, motionless, suspended in time by Philip's words.

"Oh, wait, you didn't know that, did you? Yeah, Dax. He shot her. Right in the Beacon newsroom. It's only a shame the doctors were able to save you or we'd have all been better off."

A slow red film was descending over Dax's eyes.

The Enthusiasts would kill for you, Dax. You should know that by now.

He wasn't even sure at first that the voice he heard shouting was his.

"Help! Help! This person is trying to kill me! HE'S GOING TO KILL ME! HELP ME, PLEASE!"

In a matter of moments, it was over.

Chapter 75

"Thank you for taking the time to talk with me, Mr. Benton."

"Please, Alex, call me Dax. After all, I feel like I know you already."

"I wish we'd met under better circumstances," Alex Ames said. "When I called you at the Tribune that day, I knew the story I was doing was bogus, but I was just a kid, you know? Doing what my editor told me I had to do."

"I remember those days myself," Dax said. He leaned back in his chair, obviously comfortable from his smile to his feet. "I seem to recall hearing you left the Beacon shortly after that."

"Very shortly, actually. I was constantly at odds with Mr. James after I told him I didn't want my byline on that story, and it didn't take me long to wise up to the fact that it wasn't going to get any better as long as he was in charge."

"Well…" Dax splayed his hands and gestured around his office and out into the Beacon's newsroom. Alex smiled.

"Nice segue," he said. "Yes, let's get to the point. As I mentioned on the phone, I'm a feature writer for Time magazine now, and my editor assigned me a story on Bentongate, ten years later."

"Bentongate?" Dax laughed. "That's a new one on me."

"I made it up," Alex admitted. "Just trying to jazz it up a little."

"I don't think the truth could get any jazzier."

"That's what I want to hear from you," Alex said, pulling out a tiny tape recorder and holding it up. Dax nodded and he put it on a corner of the desk. "I'm going to ask you some questions that I already know the answer to, either from my own research or from my previous conversations with you. They're going to sound leading, but I need to do it that way to get the answers in your own words."

"Yeah, I'm familiar with how it works."

Alex laughed.

"You would be, wouldn't you? Okay, so let's get started. Dax, the whole world, or at least all of New York, was completely floored by what happened ten years ago when you came back to town. Time magazine did a story on all that went down at the time, from your cousin taking over the Beacon under what you later said were false pretenses, to the Beacon's slanderous story about your parentage, to Zachary's succumbing to dementia, to you coming back here to clear your mother's name, to your cousin being killed at the Plaza by a horde of angry women, including his own mother, bent on protecting you."

Dax nodded, his face impassive.

"So now, fast forward ten years. Tell me what has happened to Dax Benton since that infamous night at the Plaza."

"Well, as you know, the women involved were charged with murder but were acquitted when the jury decided – in a matter of hours, mind you – that they'd acted in my defense. Every eyewitness in that room testified that Philip had been about to kill me. Even the hotel manager, who happened to be just down the hall, testified that he heard me shout for help."

"So while they were acquitted of murder, you were never charged."

"I didn't kill him," Dax said. "I was charged with drug possession, however, and rightfully so. I did have drugs in the room. I admitted it then, and I admit it now. But I think we've all made mistakes in our lives we wish we could forget, right?"

"Sure. I know I have."

"And not to make excuses, but that was an incredibly difficult time in my life, Alex. In the space of a few short weeks, I'd been informed that my father had completely succumbed to dementia, my cousin and his family were attempting to slander my name and my parents' names, I'd lost the newspaper I'd hoped to take over from my father someday, and my cousin had launched an all-out war to keep me from ever coming back to New York. To my home. I dulled the pain with drugs and alcohol. If society had wanted to hang me for that, they would have. But they didn't."

Alex nodded.

"Now I know this part is probably difficult to discuss, but one of those women who killed your cousin Philip was his mother, Aggie James. What happened there?"

"My Aunt Aggie was a widow, a lonely woman, with a years-long drinking problem. To be honest, there were so many people at that party I didn't even know she was there at first, or that she was coming at all. She didn't know who I was either. It was just a fluke that we ended up at the same party that night. Anyway, all I can assume is that she got caught up in the same drug-and-booze fueled frenzy that everyone else did. And remember, most of us were in costume as we'd just come from the theater, and others showed up in costume."

"Including Philip."

"Including Philip. So when he advanced on me and I shouted for help, my friends reacted instinctively. All I can figure is that my Aunt Aggie followed the crowd and attacked Philip. Since he was in costume, she never even realized it was her son."

"She realized it later."

"Well yes, of course. She had to be told when she'd sobered up. She didn't believe it at first, but when she found out it was true, she kind of…" Dax faltered.

"Go on," Alex prodded gently.

"Well, she just went completely insane, for lack of more tactful way to put it. She had a complete mental breakdown. She never did recover. She's been in a hospital upstate ever since."

"That's too bad."

"Yeah, a real shame," Dax said. "So that's what happened in the days and weeks following, what did you call it? Bentongate?"

"Tell me about your father now. I've heard he is still living."

"My father is well taken care of in the nursing facility that's been his home for awhile now," Dax said. "I visit him most days."

"Does he remember you?"

Dax shook his head.

"No," he said. "He doesn't remember anything anymore. Although there is one thing."

"Go on."

"I don't know if I want to say it in a national magazine."

Alex waited, instinctively knowing Dax would continue. He did.

"Every time I walk in the door to his room, he looks up and says 'Sarah?' Every single time."

"And Sarah was…"

"My mother."

"He thinks it's her walking into the room?"

"I don't know what he thinks. But she is the one person he remembers. As far as I can tell, the only person. His wife, Hanna Whitcomb-Benton, as you probably know, disappeared a few years ago."

"Disappeared?"

"Just like that. No one knows where she went."

"That wasn't investigated as a mysterious disappearance?"

"No. She has no family but me, and I made the decision not to pursue it. Hanna was always very odd and secretive. I don't think she wants to be found."

"I hadn't heard about that. Okay, so let's end this by talking about today," Alex said. "What are you doing now?"

"You're looking at it," Dax said. "I've been publisher of the Beacon for nearly ten years. I live on the Lower East Side, not far from where my father used to live when he was a young reporter here. I do some charitable work here and there in the city."

"And Wild Man Dax?"

Dax shrugged.

"I have some friends, but overall, my life is quiet and simple. I like it that way."

"Hard to believe."

"It is, isn't it?"

Alex shut off the tape recorder and smiled at Dax.

"Perfect ending," he said. "Thank you so much for your time. I'll be in touch if I have any more questions, and I'll make sure you get some complimentary copies of the magazine when it comes out."

They shook hands. After Alex left, Dax sat at his desk for a long time, lost in thought. It all seemed so recent, yet so long ago. In some ways, everything had changed. In other ways, nothing ever would. He glanced at his watch, reached for the phone and dialed Judith.

"Hello, darling. Tell the Enthusiasts I'm on my way."

www.ingramcontent.com/pod-product-compliance
Lightning Source LLC
Chambersburg PA
CBHW050921250626
47155CB00001B/329